Guardians of Allon
Book Two

Reprieve

Christine,

Enjoy!

SKL

Shawn Lamb

GUARDIANS OF ALLON – BOOK TWO
REPRIEVE by Shawn Lamb

Published by Allon Books
209 Hickory Way Court
Antioch, Tennessee 37013
www.allonbooks.com

Cover illustration by Robert Lamb

International Standard Book Number: 978-0-9964381-0-0

Other Books by Shawn Lamb

Young Adult Fantasy Fiction
ALLON ~ BOOK 1
Published by Creation House, a division of Charisma Media

Published by Allon Books

ALLON ~ BOOK 2 ~ INSURRECTION
ALLON ~ BOOK 3 ~ HEIR APPARENT
ALLON ~ BOOK 4 ~ A QUESTION OF SOVEREIGNTY
ALLON ~ BOOK 5 ~ GAUNTLET
ALLON ~ BOOK 6 ~ DILEMMA
ALLON ~ BOOK 7 ~ DANGEROUS DECEPTION
ALLON ~ BOOK 8 ~ DIVIDED
ALLON ~ BOOK 9 ~ IN PLAIN SIGHT

GUARDIANS OF ALLON – BOOK ONE – THE GREAT BATTLE

PARENT STUDY GUIDE FOR ALLON ~ BOOKS 1-9
THE ACTIVITY BOOK OF ALLON

For Young Readers – ages 8-10
Allon ~ The King's Children series
NECIE AND THE APPLES
TRISTINE'S DORGIRITH ADVENTURE
NIGEL'S BROKEN PROMISE

Historical Fiction
GLENCOE
THE HUGUENOT SWORD

Mortals

Sir Dunham of Garwood, Lord of the Southern Forest
Madelyn "Maddy"– age 17, daughter of Dunham
Garrick – age 12, son of Dunham
Elias, Vicar of Jor'el
Tristan – age 20
Ethan – age 27
Baron Renfrow, Lord of the North Plains
Karryn – age 23, daughter of Renfrow
King Ram
Grand Master Magelen
Prince Ramsey
Lord Razi
Hadwin, Master-of-Arms at Garwood

IMMORTALS

Captain Kell, Commander of the Guardians of Jor'el
Armus, 1st Lieutenant
Avatar, 2nd Lieutenant
Eldric, physician
Mahon, warrior
Wren, huntress
Gresham, vassal
Jedrek, warrior
Valmar, warrior
Barnum, warrior

SHADOW WARRIORS

Dagar
Tor
Commander Altari
Commander Witter
Nari
Shaka
Roane
Indigo
Cletus
Bern
Cassius

Chapter 1

ATOP A GENTLY RISING PLATEAU SURROUNDED BY FOUR MAJESTIC hills stood the Temple of Providence. Each province in Allon contributed to the Temple. The pillars of marble were quarried in the far range of the Northern Forest where it bordered the foothills of the Highlands. Carved on the pillars were images of Verse and Allon's history. The pillars guarded massive wooden doors hewn and gilded by the craftsmen of the Southern Forest. Twin bell spires of gleaming white marble topped with golden steeples rose to the heavens. The bells came from the sister provinces of the North and South Plains. The entire facade of the Temple consisted of white marble with gold accents. The arch shaped windows of colored glass were assembled in Midessex. At certain times of day, the Temple reflected the sun's rays in a brilliance of white with a kaleidoscope of gold and rainbow effects dazzling the eyes.

Gold, white and crimson were the colors of the interior décor. Metal workers of the Highlands forged the golden lamp stands. Tapestries from the Lowlands hung on the walls. The crimson carpet leading to The High Altar came from the weavers in the Meadowlands. Sun cascading through the windows made a bright mosaic of color on the white marble floor. Each window represented a province with six on each side of the Temple. The incense was supplied by the West Coast, exclusive importers of such finery. Not to be outdone, leading merchant families of the East Coast donated exquisite Altar furnishings. Wood for the High Altar came from the oldest tree in Allon harvested in the Delta.

Late into the night, Vicar Elias sat at the desk in his study. The amount of candles told the importance of his task. Two spent candles lay on one side of the single candlestick providing him light for writing. Three unused candles lay on the other side. The candle in the stand grew dim. He took a new candle and lit it with the flame of the dying candle. He blew out the old candle, removed the nub from the stand to place it beside the spent ones. He put the new candle in the stand then went back to work.

At one hundred forty-nine years old no one would have guessed his age past eighty. Having some Guardian blood inherited from his father, helped him to stay in good health. There remained patches of golden hair among predominately white strands. His handsome mature features showed the resemblance to his father, which made King Ram and Magelen suspicious. Fortunately, no open confrontation happened since his position as Vicar of Jor'el shielded him from reprisal. Thus under divine protection and mandate, he diligently rewrote the holy books to replace all the manuscripts destroyed during the Great Battle. Now that Magelen had Ram's permission to act against the local Fortresses, Elias felt hard pressed to finish the Book of Prophecy and have copies secretly distributed to the faithful.

With a deep sigh of fatigue, he placed down the pen. He rubbed his aching right hand. He might have appeared eighty, but his joints betrayed his full age.

"You really need to get some rest."

Startled, Elias pulled out a dagger hidden under his robes. Once on his feet, his unusual height of six and half feet became visible.

"Easy, Father. It's just me." A tall man in a black hooded cloak stepped into the light. He pushed back the hood to reveal a golden-haired young man of twenty. His winning smile stretched from ear to ear.

"Tristan! What are you doing here?" Elias tossed the dagger onto the desk.

"Visiting you." He approached the desk. The lamplight revealed bright blue eyes as merry as his smile. Standing beside Elias showed he stood the same height as his father.

"You shouldn't be here. It's dangerous."

"No one followed me. I know how to move silent and unseen." Using a black-gloved hand, he pushed the cloak over one shoulder to show his complete black attire. Tristan took a closer look at the writing. "What's this?"

> *Those after his own heart shall he seek and find. From the fowls of the air, to the beasts of prey and the faithful shall he gather to himself the hope of Allon.*
>
> *Among them shall be one whose birth shall be linked to his by a season. Whose soul shall mirror his own and the twain shall become one in desire and purpose."*

"Prophecy concerning Jor'el's promise of a son to restore the truth." Elias picked up another piece of paper and read.

> *"And by her shall the path be made straight for the strength of Jor'el's host to return. And he shall give the Guardians charge over Allon."*

"The Guardians will return? When?" Tristan asked with excitement.

"When the prophecy is fulfilled by the birth of the Daughter of Allon." Elias sat and took up his quill pen.

"Daughter of Allon," repeated Tristan. "When will she be born?"

"I don't know." Elias absentmindedly twirled the quill in his fingers as he spoke in remembrance. "Before she died, my mother told me how the blessing of my birth was just the beginning of Jor'el's promise. From their descendants will come a son to take back what Dagar usurped, and a daughter to restore the Guardians. I'm simply making the promise known."

Tristan sat on the desk to eagerly listen. "How did she know? Did Jor'el tell her directly?"

"No, Kell did."

"As in *Captain* Kell? She saw the captain?"

Elias chuckled. "You're forgetting Guardians were in charge of Allon at the time. They interacted with mortals on a daily basis. That was one hundred and fifty years ago. Oh, and in that time, how we mortals have suffered."

"Ay," Tristan heartily agreed. "It's not enough taking action against the Fortresses; he has summoned the lords to Ravendale to once more swear allegiance."

Moved by urgent concern, Elias seized Tristan's arm. "You're not going with Dunham, are you?"

"I'm his squire, of course I am."

"You must not! One look at you and Ram, if not Magelen, will know who you are. Except for the height, you look more like him than I do."

"They haven't moved against you."

"They dare not because I am the Vicar. You have no such shield."

"I can't refuse to go."

Elias stood, and drew Tristan to his feet with a strong grip on his son's shoulders. "Don't you understand? You are my only surviving child. For this prophecy to come to pass *you* can't go to Ravendale."

"If it is Jor'el's promise, then nothing will happen to me."

Elias groaned in vexed frustration. "You are more taxing in your stubbornness than any of your brothers! You are also the most faithful and trusting. Still, I'm too old to father more children. As the last one, you must carry on the line!"

"I will. Yet I can't shrink from my duty; not only to Sir Dunham, but more so to Jor'el. You are not the only one who hears things." Tristan motioned toward the writing.

"Meaning?" asked Elias in guarded apprehension.

"I am compelled to go to Ravendale. I believe my future; *our* future depends upon it. Besides, we know his time is short. This may be the only opportunity to save him."

Overcome, Elias sat. Tristan knelt beside the chair and took hold of Elias' hand. "Father, this is what I came to tell you. The plan is in place. Sir Dunham is awaiting my return. Don't be afraid for me. With Jor'el's help, I will not fail you or Grandfather."

Elias stared at Tristan, words difficult. "I don't know what to say."

"Your blessing would be nice." Tristan smiled like when he first arrived.

Elias embraced Tristan to hold him close. He then took Tristan's face in his hands. "Go with my blessing and Jor'el's strength, my dear son." He kissed his son's forehead.

Tristan's smile grew. "Armed with that I know I will return, and with Grandfather."

"Oh, you are too taxing on old nerves!" said Elias with exasperation. "I've heard nothing to say he is still alive after five years."

"There is rumor of a prisoner the King can't kill for with it comes his own death."

"You know I hold no stock in rumors." He reached for his pen to continue writing, dismissive in attitude.

"The only person the King would think twice about killing is his twin."

Frustrated beyond measure, the quill snapped in Elias' hand. "Now look what you made me do?" He tossed it aside. When Tristan chuckled he added, "This is no laughing matter. It was my last quill. How will I finish tonight?"

Tristan mischievously grinned. "You won't. This means you can rest and harass your clerk in the morning about new quills." He drew Elias to his feet. Holding his father by the arm, he picked up the lantern. "I will see you to bed. Once you are asleep I will leave."

"So you make me responsible for your departure?"

"If it's the only to way to make you stop and rest."

<hr>

He sat on the log waiting at the rendezvous with seeming indifference. Two saddled and tethered horses grazed beside the log. He lowered the hood of his black cloak for better visibility. He had dark hair with youthful clean-shaven features that hid his true age of twenty-seven. Along with wearing a sword, a bow and quiver were slung across his back over the cloak. His indifference vanished upon hearing the sounds of approach. His sword was instantly in hand.

"It's me, Ethan." Tristan appeared with his hands up.

Ethan sheathed his sword. He stood four inches shorter than Tristan "Took you longer than I thought."

Tristan chuckled. "I had to make certain he really fell asleep and not just pretending. I love my father, but he is stubborn and crafty."

"Not unlike his son," said Ethan with the easy smile of one accustomed to mirth. "At least you know your father. All I remember of mine is his beard was scratchy and he had huge hands." He made a gesture to indicate size.

Tristan cocked a contrary, teasing grin. "Hands that large?"

"To a four-year-old boy anyway." Ethan looked at his gloved hands. "Even as a grown man, my hands aren't nearly as large."

Tristan mounted and headed east, further into the woods.

Ethan grabbed the reins and leapt into the saddle to follow. "Did you learn anything?"

"No."

"No? Then why did we come all this way from the Southern Forest? Just to say 'Hello, Father, how are you?'"

"Something like that."

"You dragged me all this way just to say *hello*? I should have stayed in bed."

"Ethan."

"Ay?"

"Shut up."

"Are you saying I talk too much?"

Tristan snorted an ironic chuckle. "Not for the night animals. But for those of the day, who wish to sleep, you are disturbing them. Not to mention giving away our position."

"That wasn't what the Fortress Guard said. He actually appreciated my talking since it alerted him to trouble. He took charge of the man."

Tristan drew rein, which allowed Ethan to pull alongside. "What guard? What man?"

"A brigand who stumbled upon me."

"Did he follow us?"

13

"I don't believe so. He acted surprised to see me. I was about to dispatch him when the guard showed up and took him into custody."

"You believed this guard?"

"Why shouldn't I? He wore the uniform. However, when I looked at him, I felt I could trust him without question," he spoke the last sentence with thoughtful unction.

"You feel you can trust anybody!" Tristan lashed out in frustration.

"That's not fair. Just because I like to jest, you know I take your safety seriously."

Tristan took a moment to calm his temper. "Did you get a good look at this brigand? Any identification?"

"No. He dressed for night travel, like us, without badge or crest."

"So he could have followed us."

"No. I believe him a thief or woodsman, who innocently ran afoul of me. I was grateful the guard came. I didn't want to kill him, though I would have to prevent discovery."

Tristan sarcastically scowled. "Anything else happen that I should know about?"

"No. We have a long way to the border." Ethan kicked his horse to take the lead.

In another part of the woods, the Fortress Guard held the struggling man, who insisted on being let go. The guard swung the man around by the shoulders, looked directly at him and said, *"A steach do cadal rach agus cuimhne no."* Immediately the man fell asleep.

The guard lowered him to the ground. The guard exhaled with fatigue as he sat back against the trunk of a tree. The façade faded from the image of a Fortress Guard into the form of an unusually tall and brawny being. He wore a muted tan and gold-trimmed uniform complete with an impressive sword and dagger. He was thick-necked with massive chest, broad shoulders and bright chestnut eyes set in a handsome clean-shaven face.

Hearing footsteps, he pushed himself to his feet. He stood seven and half feet tall. Before he drew his sword, someone grabbed his arm in support not aggression.

"Armus. I think you need to rest."

"Kell! Don't sneak up on me like that."

The Captain of the Guardians chuckled. He stood the same height with black hair; linked with strong good-looking features, made an impressive setting for golden eyes. "You are tired if you didn't sense me before hearing me."

"Being at half strength is taxing when forced to use our power." Armus rubbed a weary hand over his face.

Kell motioned to the unconscious mortal. "I hope they don't suspect who you are or that they're being watched."

Fatigue made Armus glared crossly at Kell. "No. I took him from Ethan while in the uniform of a Fortress Guard. It drained me of energy, but needed to be done to keep them from being discovered. Taking on the appearance of a mortal used to be so easy."

"Did Tristan meet with Elias?"

"Ay. Now I must go."

"Wren is waiting at the border."

Armus again became cross. "Are you changing my orders of protecting them?"

"No, simply informing you in case you need help."

Armus' frustration came forth. "When will this punishment end? When we will be restored to our full strength and walk among the mortals again?"

Kell shook his head. "I don't know. Jor'el told me a change is coming. What form it will take or how it will affect us and the mortals, he didn't say."

"Will the mortals be ready when it does? And will they be grateful? Over the last century and a half, most have forgotten the old days."

Kell clapped Armus' shoulder as a gesture of encouragement. "We'll know when it happens, old friend. Until then we remain legends, yet ever watchful for their welfare."

"Speaking of them, I better be going, so they don't get too far ahead."

Kell released him and watched Armus run off in an easterly direction.

Chapter 2

ONE HUNDRED FIFTY YEARS AGO, THE GREAT BATTLE AMONG the immortal Guardians of Jor'el ended in their banishment from Allon. This left the mortals defenseless against the Dark Way. Dagar, Guardian of Jor'el's Temple, held deep-seated jealousy along with an unquenchable desire for dominance. His rebellion tore through the ranks of the Guardians, leading to the unexpected defeat of those loyal to Jor'el.

With Dagar's success also came his punishment in the Nether Dimension. His last act before being restricted was to place his son, Ram, upon the throne. By various means of communication and conduits to the mortal realm, Dagar used Ram and others to unleash his supernatural power. For his part, Ram ruled with a heavy hand. He ruthlessly employed the feared Shadow Warriors to silence critics. He issued edicts against further promulgating of the Old Faith.

For the mortals, the change brought more terrible consequences than ever anticipated. Their relatively easy and abundant life under the Guardians dramatically changed. Living to the ripe old age of two hundred fifty to three hundred years became shortened by half. Unity of the twelve provinces descended into a feudal society. Each province looked to their local lords or prominent merchants for direction and protection. Trade between the provinces grew minimal, due to unregulated competition, corruption and thievery. The peaceful and prosperous country turned into one of oppressive resentment.

As time passed, the general population drifted from Jor'el, feeling it more advantageous to live peaceably with the king than fear reprisal. Memories of the Guardians faded into legend. Still, a remnant of faithful mortals remained. No matter the effort, Ram and Dagar could not destroy the Temple of Jor'el or provincial Fortresses. These stood as bastions against the evil.

Then, slowly, almost unnoticed, a coming change gave rise to a seed of hope for those who had not embraced the Dark Way. The sense of change intensified to the point of unsettling Ram. For this reason, he took bold action against the priests and faithful remnant. The buildings might stand, but mortals were flesh and blood.

King Ram's Castle of Ravendale stood in the province of Midessex. The grounds and walls covered twenty acres, taking thousands of men and twenty years to build. Every turret, gate, window, rampart and battlement heralded the strength of Ravendale. Large stone ravens and two legged dragons called wyverns guarded the massive front gate and four smaller side gates.

Now one hundred sixty-eight years old, Ram looked his age. For decades his Guardian side retarded the mortal aging process, giving him longer life than the new normal lifespan. Lately, he suffered cruelly from illness. The years took a toll on his mind, or so people told him. His white hair grew brittle while his goatee unkempt. The once bright blue eyes appeared dull and his cheeks hollow. Swathed in royal robes for warmth, he sat slumped in the chair at a desk listening to his son, Ramsey.

Conceived late in life by Ram's second wife, the sixty-year-old Ramsey appeared the picture of health and vitality. His face and unusual height of six feet seven inches reminded people of Ram in his youth. Ramsey had the light brown hair and hazel eyes of his deceased mother. He wore his royal station as fashionably arrogant as his elegant regal clothes.

Also in attendance was Grand Master Magelen. Even at age eighty, he cut a fine figure of a man, tall and straight in back with broad shoulders. His keen light blue eyes observed everything. He kept most of his short blond hair hidden under the skullcap. He wore robes of deep blue over his long matching jacket, with both highlighted in black and silver.

Draped from his shoulders across his chest, hung a large heavy silver chain holding a raven-crested talisman.

"Enough!" snapped Ram. "I know what it is you both want me to do, but I cannot!"

"Sire, it is the only way," began Magelen. "Without the information he can provide our attempts to discover the source of this unrest is fruitless."

"Rumors." Ram made a feeble, dismissive wave.

"You know it is not."

Ram glared at Magelen. When their eyes met, Magelen carefully reached for the talisman. Anger brought the aged King to his feet. "Do not try your Dark Way wiles on me! Or have you forgotten who I am?"

In a casual gesture, Magelen let his hand fall from the talisman. "I have not forgotten, Sire. However, I think you forget who *he* is and the threat he poses."

"My brother! The man who was supposed to be your king!"

"I'm aware of that."

"Father, we know the history of his betrayal, of how you became king because of it. But you must face reality. Razi knows more than he is saying."

"Razi only knows as much about Prophecy as we do."

"Because his son, Vicar Elias, writes it," said Magelen with scorn.

"What proof have you brought me to confirm your conclusion?"

"Sire, you have only to look at Elias to see the strong family resemblance. Nor is my conclusion solely based upon my own observation. You voiced the same belief. Why else order me to take action against the Fortress save to thwart him?"

Frustrated, Ram lashed back. "You know I cannot mar a single stone of the Temple! By Jor'el's will it survived the Great Battle, and by divine power it is sustained. Being Vicar, Elias is off limits to us."

"Which is why the Prince captured your brother." Magelen indicated Ramsey, who stood smug with pride.

"Against my wishes!" Suddenly overcome with weakness, Ram sat. Neither Ramsey nor Magelen appeared concerned. This did not escape notice. "You wait like vultures for my death."

"Sire, Allon will grieve your death," Magelen spoke with indifference.

For a moment Ram stared at Magelen. Whereas Ramsey was a product of his upbringing and possessed the natural vanity of his station, there was much more to Magelen. More than Ramsey knew, and more than Ram had the ability to deal with at present. After a resigned sigh, he stood. "I'll speak to him again." In slow, deliberate steps, Ram left the study.

Ever since Razi's capture five years ago, Ram experienced many fitful nights of dreams filled with painful memories. Every incident from early childhood until the horrible day of Razi's betrayal replayed in his mind. Ram knew that with the help of a disowned young mortal woman, Dagar put his plan into action. He hoped for one son. Having twins was welcomed news, at least at the time.

Ram and Razi were close as children, doing everything together. In the original plan, the shrewd Razi would be King with the stronger Ram serving as his general. They felt no jealousy concerning the arrangement. However, when Razi fell in love with a mortal female named Janel, their world changed.

After the discovery of a clandestine marriage, Ram and Dagar learned that one of Dagar's Guardian Trio Mates had secretly tutored Razi in the ways of Jor'el. The girl merely became the final catalyst for Razi to break free and betray them to Kell. To Dagar's delight, Razi's defection did not prevent victory.

Ram spoke to Razi on several occasions, but his brother remained stubborn. Now time was of the essence. Of that single fact, he must convince Razi.

In the dungeon, Captain Murdock made his rounds. A fifty-five-year-old grizzled war veteran, his wounds kept him from the battlefield. Being assigned to the royal prison provided a relatively easy task that fluctuated from boredom to demanding, depending upon the number of prisoners. Few stayed longer than several months since being here usually meant death. Other veterans considered it a demotion to serve as a jailer, not Murdock. He witnessed enough battle to last a lifetime. Being a childless widower, he didn't mind the peace and quiet that came with the job. Everything about his duties changed with Lord Razi's capture.

The daily routine consisted of guard changes ever two hours. Grand Master Magelen wanted to curb Razi's contact with anyone to lessen his attempts of swaying a weak-minded soldier. Being made personally responsible by the King for Razi's welfare, Murdock had the most interaction with him. Whereas his subordinates weren't aware of Razi's relationship to the king, he knew; not by way of Magelen or Ram, rather Razi. The longer Razi remained a prisoner, the finer line Murdock walked in taking care of him.

Murdock just finished changing the guard when Ram reached the bottom of the steps out of breath. "Sire?"

"I'll be fine in a moment. I want to speak to him." He motioned Murdock to the door.

Although a dungeon, a high window opened to the outside world for light, thus the cell wasn't as dark, damp and dingy as expected. Razi lay on a cot made from leather straps with a thin mattress. The similarity was striking; only Razi appeared in better health. His white hair was dirty and an unkempt from being in the dungeon, yet full and supple compared to Ram's thin, brittle strands. Razi's clean-shaven features showed age and fatigue but nowhere near the decline displayed on Ram's face. With gritted teeth of pain, Razi carefully sat up on the cot.

"Something wrong?" asked Ram. "Captain, have his needs been neglected?"

"No, Sire."

Razi flashed a rueful smile. "Murdock is not to blame. You haven't noticed my new adornment?" He indicated the ankle fetters.

Ram swore at seeing the dark metal iron. "Who ordered the stygian chains?" he demanded of Murdock.

"Grand Master Magelen, Sire."

"Take them off!"

Murdock promptly complied. He tossed a compassionate smile to Razi before backing away with the chains.

Razi rubbed his ankles. His words to Ram came laced with heavy sarcasm. "Thanks, but they had their intended purpose. I don't have the strength to do anything even if I wanted to. You're in no danger."

Ram ordered Murdock out then sat in the cell's only chair. "How long have they been on?"

Razi stared at Ram, skeptical. "Six months. Since the last time you came to visit me."

The answer annoyed Ram. "He didn't tell me."

"You expect me to believe that?"

"I would never order stygian chains to be used. Just like I didn't order your capture." When Razi continued to stare at him, Ram became frustrated. "I swear I didn't!"

Razi heaved a careless shrug. "If you say so."

"By the heavenlies, Razi, what will it take for you to believe me?"

Razi's attitude changed to hot annoyance. "I once asked you the same question when I tried to explain why I married Janel. You were too angry to hear what I had to say. A bit of an ironic reversal, don't you think?"

Ram moved to sit on the cot beside Razi. He spoke low and urgent. "Those memories have haunted me since your capture."

Razi surveyed Ram's deteriorated appearance. "I can see that."

"What you see isn't a result of memories. Like ordering the chains to weaken and break you, Magelen has been slowly poisoning me this last year. When I think I figured out how he's doing it, he finds another way." He winced with great lament. "The worst part is I believe Ramsey is involved. My own son." When Razi didn't speak, Ram asked, "Don't you understand what I'm trying to tell you?"

"You're being poisoned, and the only way to stop it is for me to betray my family."

"No!" Ram seized Razi's arm. "I'm the only one keeping you alive. Once I'm dead, they will kill you whether you tell them what they want or not! Yet if you tell me, I can protect them."

Razi laughed in disbelief. He knocked away Ram's hold. "I'm not so foolish as to believe you. My life is near its end, same as you. I won't help *him* to keep hold over Allon any longer."

"Magelen will stop at nothing to make you talk."

Razi's eyes narrowed in deadly earnest. "I don't mean Magelen, I mean our father! I know Dagar works through the talisman Magelen wields to keep his influence strong."

Ram returned Razi stare and said, "Magelen is our brother."

"What?"

"You forgot the arrangement. The bride of the king is brought to the Cave for Dagar's use. The first-born male is made Grand Master when he comes of age. How else can Magelen use the Dark Way if he weren't part Guardian like we are? No mortal can control it." His tone turned regretful. "Sadly, it cost my first wife her life in giving birth to him."

Razi let the news sink it. "I had forgotten."

Ram shook off the remorse to continue. "Dagar hates you as deeply as he hates Kell. He will spare no one to destroy you and your family. He knows you had at least one son with the female."

"Janel!" snapped Razi with great offense.

Ram ignored the objection. "Magelen suspects Elias is *that* son." He saw Razi's unguarded fretful reaction. "I see you don't deny it."

Razi turned away to cover his indiscreet reaction.

Ram again took hold of his brother's arm. "Elias is safe in his position. *But,* if you have other children or they have children-none will be safe from Dagar and Magelen. Tell me and I swear to protect them."

Razi's voice grew harsh with intense personal pain. "A little late for that promise don't you think, *brother*? You can't bring back the dead!"

"What are you talking about?"

Outrage brought Razi to his feet. "Don't pretend ignorance. The blood of thirty-three of my family, children, their wives, husbands, grandchildren and great-grandchildren already stain Magelen's hands! Now you tell me he wants more. Well, I won't give him any more!" Impassioned, he bolted to his feet to cross the cell with his back to Ram.

Astonished, Ram remained momentarily silent. "I didn't know. I swear, Razi, I didn't know! It would account for my haunting dreams, sometimes accompanied by prophetic warnings." In urgency, he said, "If I'm to stop the bloodshed between our houses, I must protect what remains of your family."

Razi's tone matched his very sarcastic expression. "If you die from this poisoning then how will you protect them? *If* any more exist."

"I'll find a way, I swear!"

For a moment, Razi studied Ram then shook his head. "No. Jor'el is the only real protection. You don't have the power to withstand our father. That's already been proven. You came here for nothing." He again turned his back to Ram.

Deeply pricked by the refusal, Ram lashed out. "You don't know what you're doing. The consequences your refusal will have on all of us." Razi remained silent. Ram shouted, "Murdock!" He headed for the door.

After Murdock closed and locked the cell, Ram drew him across the corridor to speak privately. "See he receives extra portions of food to recover his strength. Next time Magelen orders chains or anything suggesting punishment, tell me immediately."

"Ay. I'm sorry, Sire. I tried not to comply. However, if I didn't, someone else would. Maybe even my replacement."

"We can't have that. Find a way to get word to me next time."

"Ay, Sire. Shall I escort you upstairs?"

"Ay. My legs aren't working so well today." Ram held onto Murdock's arm.

Chapter 3

THE BUILDING SITE FOR THE CASTLE AT GARWOOD SAT UPON the highest peak in the Southern Forest, overlooking the town from which it took the name. When completed, the castle would act as a sentinel protecting the town and the road leading to Jor'el's Fortress. The ramparts offered a commanding view of the countryside. Although rich in timber and the craftsmanship such resource offers, the Southern Forest was the least wealthy of Allon's twelve provinces.

Sir Dunham, lord of the province, oversaw every detail of construction. The fortified manor house his great-grandfather built at Dunlap served the family well for over one hundred years. However, the house needed many repairs. The time was right to construct a new castle rather than spend the time, money and effort to reconstruct the old castle. Garwood's size doubled Dunlap by enclosing four acres.

The living quarters, stables, barracks, carriage house and servants quarters were complete. Even though the defenses remained unfinished, the family moved in two months ago. Dunham considered it a gesture of goodwill for the people in area. However, his seventeen-year-old daughter Madelyn expressed displeasure about having to establish the household in a half completed castle. His son, twelve-year-old Garrick, had great fun scampering among the timbers and stones of construction while harassing the workers.

As if "Maddy" didn't have enough to contend with, keeping track of Garrick and his nonsense proved irritating. She complained to her father. He stood at a table in the courtyard barely listening. Construction went on all around them. Behind Maddy waited a comely young lady of twenty-three, with auburn hair and hazel eyes.

25

"It's all Tristan and Ethan's fault! If you had more responsible squires, Garrick wouldn't be taxing on me. They are supposed help tutor him." Exasperated, Maddy sat on a crate beside the table.

Dunham chuckled. At age forty-two, he was a strong man standing six feet tall with neatly trimmed brown hair, beard and light hazel eyes. His voice matched his size. "I thought you liked Tristan?"

Maddy flushed. She averted her brown eyes while brushing away a wisp of brown hair the wind blew onto her face. "He's tolerable," she said with embarrassment. At his amusement, she spoke in dispute. "That's not the point. Garrick needs a firm hand, and you made them responsible. I have enough to contend with trying to keep the kitchen maids from making googly eyes at the workers."

Her description only increased his mirth. "What do you expect me to do about that?"

"I expect more help in establishing my place as lady of the manor! Since mother died, I'm laughed at."

His humor faded at her distress. "I can command them to listen to you, but only you can earn their respect."

"I'm trying! Mother was so good at organization. I'm beginning to think I'm not cut out to run a household."

He sat on the crate beside her. "You didn't pay attention when she tried to teach you. Too busy with your nose in books."

She looked stricken. "I thought you encouraged learning?"

"I do. Yet there are other methods of learning than from books. You chide me about my squires tutoring Garrick. Can you not accept the same criticism when it comes to your lack of interest?" When Maddy frowned at his rebuff, he said, "I brought Karryn here to help you," he spoke of the other woman.

"I have tried, my lord," said Karryn with a hint of exasperation.

"I know," he said in wry agreement before returning to Maddy. "That is why I haven't interfered. You wouldn't learn from your mother so I gave you a companion to help. If you spurn Karryn's influence, you'll have to learn on your own."

Their attention became drawn to the main gate upon hearing shouting along with the sounds of a horse. A royal rider arrived. Hadwin, Dunham's master-at-arms, greeted the man. A fifty-year old veteran of surprisingly meek countenance, Hadwin took his duty seriously. He seemed to argue with the rider.

"I wonder what he wants?" asked Maddy.

Dunham sent Karryn a sharp warning glance. He gave a firm pat on Maddy's shoulder before moving off to greet the rider. "How is the King this fine day?"

The man smiled, humorless and formal. "He sends you this, my lord." He pulled a letter out from a saddlebag to give Dunham.

Dunham signaled to a nearby servant, and indicated the rider. "Water." The servant responded by bringing a bucket with a ladle to the messenger. While the man drank, Dunham read.

"I'm to await a reply, my lord," he said after swallowing.

"Tell His Majesty, I will make haste as soon as I can get away from construction."

"If you please, my lord, *that* was your answer last week."

Dunham made no polite pretense in his response. "It is the same answer now! I cannot leave with my defenses incomplete. His Majesty will understand that even if you do not."

The messenger tossed a hasty bow as far as the saddle permitted. "My apologies, my lord. It's been a long a difficult journey to the provinces."

"Are you making the journey to all twelve by yourself?" asked Maddy.

Dunham frowned at her arrival. Karryn followed Maddy, and didn't look pleased.

"Ay, my lady."

"Perhaps I can offer you more than a drink. Food—"

"We are not set up yet for guests," said Dunham, much to Maddy's surprise and the messenger's chagrin.

The man again bowed at the waist. He flashed a kind smile. "Thank you for the offer, my lady." His smile faded when speaking to Dunham.

"I will convey your excuse to the King, my lord." He jerked the reins and left Garwood.

"Father, why—" His rebuking snarl stopped her question. She obeyed when he bade her to follow him back to the table.

Dunham carefully looked around. Workers and servants paid attention to their task. Still, he kept his scolding voice low. "I've been trying to avoid this summons. Your offer was ill-timed and inappropriate to that avoidance."

"I don't understand."

"Of course not, because you don't pay attention to what is happening around you! Did you not understand my gesture to stay put?" He placed a hand on her shoulder and forced her to sit on the crate.

She became abashed. "I guess I'm not keen in the ways of subtlety."

"I tried to stop you," said Karryn.

"To understand the ways of the world you must study people, how they move, speak, act, react and interact. You can't get that from a book," he rebuffed.

Maddy unsuccessfully fought back tears. "I'm sorry I disappoint you."

Dunham sat beside her. His tone softened now that he made his point. "It's not disappointment, rather concern. Just like your mother, I won't always be around. You must learn to handle yourself."

She wiped away the tears. "I'll do better, I promise."

"You can start by taking command of the household. Don't compromise or reach a consensus. You are the lady and they are the servants."

"The Book of Verse says to treat everyone with equal respect."

"That doesn't mean letting them take advantage of you for their own purposes or tolerating ridicule. There is an order to life. An order of submission to each other and Jor'el."

"I think I understand. In order for them to respect me enough to obey, I must show I have respect for my position and myself. Not in a haughty way, rather with firm resolve."

He smiled. "Ay. It doesn't mean it'll be easy," he added in warning.

"*That* I already know," she groused.

He gave her a quick kiss on the cheek. "Now off with you. I have a lot of work to do."

"What about the summons?"

He scowled in displeasure. "I can't do anything until Tristan and Ethan return."

"Where have they gone anyway?"

"On an errand."

"They left nearly a week ago."

"And should be back any day. Enough talk. It's time you should be overseeing dinner preparations." Dunham made a shooing gesture.

Returning to the house, Maddy thought about what her father said. Indeed, she spent long hours reading or studying to avoid life lessons and chores her mother insisted upon. When her mother unexpectedly died six months ago, Maddy became thrust into a position she felt woefully unprepared to handle. All those books proved to be of little practical use in dealing with rowdy, unruly servants; most of whom she had known all her life. They treated her kindly when a child since they considered her the cute girl with a penchant for books. Upon becoming lady of the manor, the relationships changed. Karryn, the butler, Hadwin and a few others tried to help. Some took advantage of her soft nature and inexperience. These were the same ones her mother often scolded and kept in a tight line.

Karryn's strong self-possessed character bolstered Maddy's timidity. Karryn also knew the inner workings of a manor. However, she wasn't mistress of Garwood. Any authority was Maddy's responsibility. This is where the difficulty occurred.

"Will you finally heed your father?" asked Karryn.

"I must. I just don't know if can."

Karryn stopped Maddy at the kitchen door. "You have only to act with the confidence instilled by your position, and the instruction your father referred to in Verse."

"It's so hard."

"You make it hard because you fear people thinking ill of you. This allows others to dominate. Even those heroes in your books stood up to opposition, regardless of criticism."

From the kitchen, they heard female giggling along with a male speaking in teasing tones. Inside, they spied a maid and a worker at the exterior threshold wrapped in each other's arms. Five other kitchen maids continued working yet cautiously watched the couple.

Fire rose in Karryn's eyes, yet she waited for Maddy to act.

"What is going on here, Edith?" demanded Maddy.

Edith flashed a wry smile. "We were just talking."

Continuing her staunch manner, Maddy said, "Is this how you spoke to my mother; with an insolent tone and sarcastic smile?"

"That was different."

"No difference. She was the lady of manor then and I am the lady of the manor now. I will not tolerate what she did not tolerate. Get back to work," she ordered Edith then spoke to the man. "Don't show your face in the kitchen again or I'll have my father discharge you."

"Ay, my lady." The man tossed her a hasty bow and left.

"We are engaged," insisted Edith.

"Only after her father found them together and forced the engagement," one of the maids said to Maddy.

"You mean … together?" stammered Maddy with embarrassment.

Edith scornfully spoke, "Being with a man might do you some good."

"Mind your tongue!" Karryn jerked Edith away from Maddy.

Maddy fought to cover her discomposure. "This is your last warning, Edith. One more act of insolence and you are discharged. Do I make myself clear?"

Edith flashed a toothy smile. "Very clear, my lady."

Maddy left the kitchen. In the corridor she leaned against the wall in an effort to regain her composure. She knew it would be difficult, but not ridiculed to her face in such a base manner. She shied away when Karryn arrived and made as if to speak. Karryn complied and fell silent.

Beatrice the cook approached. "Miss—I mean—my lady, I must apologize."

Maddy looked curiously at Beatrice. "Why? You did nothing wrong."

"Oh, I have. Your mother—may she rest in Jor'el's peace—was a good woman. She too had difficulty when she first arrived. I took it upon myself to help her. Alas, I failed to do the same with you. For that I apologize. As head of the kitchen, Edith is my responsibility. If she acts up again, I will resign so you may appoint one of your choosing to run the kitchen."

Maddy softly smiled. "I appreciate the offer. Where you may bear some blame, more falls to me in not following my mother's lead in dealing with such matters."

"If I might say, that was a good start, taking charge like you did. I will see Edith doesn't accost you with such contempt again."

Maddy's smile was a bit shaky, as she still battled for control.

Karryn dismissed Beatrice then once again tried to speak.

"No! Leave me to prepare the dining room. I must deal with this myself." Maddy rushed down the hall to the private family salon. Her knees grew weak, which made her collapse into a chair. Her hands trembled. "Why am I so frightened?"

"Because you are tenderhearted. Being tough goes against your nature."

"Karryn, I said—" began Maddy before looking up. The speaker wasn't Karryn, rather a beautiful woman with long auburn hair and bright green eyes. Tall, perhaps her father's height and dressed in a clothes of a forester. She wore a crossbow and quiver across her back. It took her a moment to recognize her. "I've seen you before."

"Ay, my lady. I live in the forest."

"Indeed. You helped me when I got lost."

"On several occasions," she said, widely smiling.

Maddy chuckled with embarrassment. "Thank my brother for that. He's always wandering off. What are you doing here?"

"I brought meat. With such a large crew of workers I thought venison would serve nicely."

"That was kind of you. What can I offer in return?"

"Nothing. Consider it a neighborly gesture. If I may continue, don't be troubled by having to deal sternly with others. When done in a right manner it gains respect."

"How do you know what is right?"

"Let knowledge and truth guide your actions. You know Edith's behavior was wrong so confronting it was right. Such unchecked behavior can have a bad influence on others."

"Others I'm responsible for."

"Ay." She smiled, her bright green eyes direct upon Maddy.

Maddy shifted at bit uncomfortable in her seat. "Your counsel and meat are appreciated."

"Then I will leave you to enjoy the one and consider the other."

"Stop by the kitchen and help yourself to whatever you need before leaving."

She just smiled and withdrew.

For a moment Maddy remained in the salon, considering what the woman said. True, she had a soft nature, and not good at confrontation. Responsibility to deal with unpleasant situations came with being in charge. She returned to the kitchen. To her surprise, she didn't see the woman while kitchen maids busily portioned out the venison.

"Did she get what she needed so quickly?"

"Who?" Beatrice asked.

"The woman who brought the venison."

Beatrice appeared perplexed. "We found it outside the door. We don't know who brought it, and it is almost completely dressed."

Maddy stared at Beatrice trying to comprehend the answer. The woman existed, as the venison proved she was not a figment of imagination. Why hadn't the kitchen servants seen her? And how did she know she scolded Edith if not a witness?

"My lady!" A male servant rushed in from the exterior kitchen door.

The shout startled Maddy from her pondering. "What is it?"

"Master Garrick took his pony and headed northwest. He mentioned something about exploring unknown territory. We tried to stop him. "

"Unknown territory?" she repeated then grew concerned at what he meant. She hastily asked, "Have you told my father?"

"He left with Hadwin for the quarry. Word came of trouble with the shipment."

"Have the squires returned?"

"No, my lady."

She snarled in anger. This was so like Garret to cause trouble while others were away. He wouldn't get away with it this time. "Saddle my horse!" She ran from the kitchen up the back stairs to her chamber.

Maddy rushed to change from a day dress into breeches and tunic. If Garrick headed where she feared, a riding habit would be of little use. She quickly tied back her hair, took a sheathed dagger from a vanity drawer and placed it on her belt. She ran from the house to the stables.

The man held the reins of her horse. He took note of her change in clothes. "Should I send men with you, my lady?"

"No. Just tell Karryn, my father or the squires when they return." She mounted.

"Where shall I say you went?"

"To tan my brother's hide!" She kicked her horse.

"But where?" he insisted, running after her.

"Dorgirith!" she shouted over her shoulder.

"My lady, it is forbidden!"

Chapter 4

GARRICK PRESSED HIS PONY HARD. THE BORDER OF DORGIRITH lay five miles from Garwood. He had an opportunity and intended to make the most of it. After all, exploring the forbidden held a sense of danger no adventurous twelve-year-old boy could resist. Not that he wanted to come into conflict with this father, but being so occupied with construction, Garrick believed he wouldn't notice. He wanted to go with Tristan and Ethan on their errand. His father denied permission, once more citing his young age. Actually he was closer to thirteen since his birthday was in three months. He knew how to defend himself. He began instruction with a sword at age five with other weapons added along the way. He couldn't wait to get off his pony and onto a real soldier's horse. Unfortunately, that wouldn't happen until he turned thirteen, the age signaling the beginning of adulthood. Maddy on the other hand, would notice. The thought made him scoff. His sister tried to coddle him since their mother died. Naturally he missed their mother only Maddy's sensitive nature irritated him.

Seeing the destination on the horizon, he snapped the reins for more speed. The pony protested. It already ran at top speed. Within fifty yards of Dorgirith, the pony suddenly stopped and became greatly agitated. Garrick fought to bring the animal under control.

"Colter, calm down!"

The animal threw him. He landed hard on his buttocks and back. The pony ran off.

"Colter! Come back here!" He gingerly stood. "Cowardly beast. I'll sell you for another!" he shouted, though the pony was nowhere in sight.

For a moment he stared at the forest, wondering what made Colter act so bizarre. The pony was usually docile. Too gentle for a soldier's horse yet fine for a boy, at least according to his father. Another reason he wanted a new horse. Then again, falling from a larger horse would have hurt more. He stretched then massaged his lower back and buttocks. He flinched in fear at hearing an eerie moaning coming from the forest.

"Get a hold of yourself, it's just the wind. You came here to explore." Garrick gripped the hilt of his sheathed sword and entered Dorgirith.

Maddy rode a tall, lean hunter. The horse's long strides were easily capable of covering the five miles faster than Garrick's pony. The same reaction happened with her horse when nearing the boundaries of Dorgirith. Agitated, it refused to go any further. Being a superior horsewoman, she brought the gelding under control.

"What is it, Merin?"

The horse snorted and angrily pawed the ground.

"I won't let anything hurt you." She tried to get Merin to move forward. He became excited and even bucked. She turned him around before dismounting. She stroked the horse's face. "Calm down. I won't make you go further, though I must find Garrick." Merin pushed against her to which she said, "I can't go back without him." Merin whinnied. To her surprise, a whinny came in reply. The pony appeared. "Colter. Come here, boy."

The pony did as instructed. It gratefully nibbled at her hand.

"Something frightened you too, didn't it?"

Colter rubbed against her hand with a whinny, as if in affirmation.

"At least I know I came the right way." After a brief look around, she noticed a fallen log. She tethered the horses to it. "Hopefully I won't be long."

She walked toward Dorgirith. Near the line of trees, a moaning noise stopped her. Perhaps Garrick was hurt. "Garrick?" she called. The moaning again. Listening more carefully, it didn't sound human. She took out her dagger, muttered a prayer and entered Dorgirith.

The sound stopped, yet with every step into the forbidden forest her nervousness grew. The words caught in her throat each time she tried to call for Garrick. Her mind raced back to the tales she read of haunted woods, people in danger and gallant knights rescuing them from certain doom. One of those tales could become reality, and she didn't like it!

"Garrick!" she finally forced the name from her throat.

She heard the eerie unnatural moaning, only louder, as if right on top of her. She screamed and backed into a tree. Something dangled overhead. It took a moment to register the object as a wind-chime. When caught in the breeze made an eerie moaning sound. She sagged in relief.

"Ingenious, isn't it? Scared me too at first."

Startled, she pushed herself off the tree and held her dagger ready. "Garrick! I'm going to box your ears for this."

"You'll have to catch me first." He ran further into the woods.

"Come back here!" She ran after him.

In trying to keep him in view, she lost her footing. She tumbled down a long steep incline. She didn't stop until she slammed her back against a tree trunk at the bottom. She lay winded and in pain, not wanting to move. Someone called her name. She didn't dare turn her head to see the person. Garrick slid to his knees beside her. He looked anxious.

"Are you hurt? Can I help you sit up?"

Maddy held her breath against the pain as Garrick helped her to sit up. When finished, she closed her eyes with an exhale of relief.

"I didn't mean for you to get hurt."

She opened her eyes. "Why?"

"For adventure, why else go exploring?"

"No, why here? The horses are afraid."

"You got thrown too?"

"No. I left them tethered to a log. We need to get back."

"I'm not going back."

"Don't argue with me. You're coming home."

"I'm here now and I will explore. You can go back."

She seized him when he began to rise. "You'll leave me alone when I'm hurt? Some brother you are!"

"Some sister you are trying to be my mother! Well, you're not!" He shook off her hold to follow the ravine deeper into Dorgirith.

"Garrick!" Gritting her teeth in determination, she got to her feet. Once standing, she saw him disappear beyond a crop of rock. Biting back the pain of movement, she followed.

<hr>

The sun sank low on the western horizon. Tristan and Ethan crossed the river plain from the Region of Sanctuary into the Southern Forest. Tristan drew his horse to a halt. He stared north toward the border of Dorgirith.

Ethan pulled his horse alongside. "If we tarry, we won't reach Garwood before dark." Tristan didn't answer so Ethan asked, "Why do stare at that cursed place every time we ride this way?"

"For that reason. It *is* cursed. I shudder at the evil Magelen inflicts upon the poor creatures inhabiting the forest."

"Agreed. Sad to say, there is nothing that can be done about it at the moment."

Tristan sneered in painful anger. "Many times I've prayed to have a hand in ending the reign of the Dark Way. It destroyed my family." A lump caught in his throat.

Ethan clapped Tristan's shoulder. "I share your prayers. We must hold that thought, and hope Jor'el fulfills his promises during our lifetime." He kicked his horse to continue.

Tristan followed. "Do you really mean that?"

"About Jor'el? Or course I do. I may not speak often about my faith but you know I believe in the Almighty, and share your abhorrence of the Dark Way."

"No, I mean doing something about it."

Curious, Ethan pulled to a stop, this time allowing Tristan to come alongside him. Only it wasn't Tristan's question stopping him.

Tristan noticed what caught Ethan's interest. "I wonder who would leave their horses in the open?"

Ethan shook his head. "Those aren't just anyone's horses, it's Merin and Colter."

Tristan stood in the stirrups when a cloaked and hooded individual came from around the pony. The person stooped to inspect the animal's hooves. Tristan snapped the reins to send his horse into a gallop. "Stop! You there! Stop!"

The individual stood just as Tristan sprung from the saddle. Tristan reached for his sword. The hood was thrown back to reveal the person's face.

"Karryn?" Tristan stuttered in utter surprise. She wore men's clothes, armed with two daggers and her hair pulled back.

Karryn's attention became diverted at Ethan's arrival. He too exhibited curiosity at her appearance. "About time you two showed up," she said.

"What are you doing? And why are you dressed like a man?" asked Tristan.

"I came to find Maddy and Garrick."

"Why? What happened?" asked Ethan.

"A groom said Maddy left to *'tan Garrick's hide'* and pursued him to Dorgirith. I just arrived. I wanted to learn if some mishap occurred with the animals before proceeding."

"Again, why dressed like a man?" Tristan repeated his question.

"I can't make a proper search in a skirt." She returned to her investigation of the horses.

Ethan chuckled at her retort. His keen eyes scanned the ground for signs of disturbance.

Tristan watched with intense interest, aware of Ethan's expertise. "Anything?"

"I believe Garrick arrived first, since the pony's tracks go further toward the forest, then run off that way," said Ethan.

"Colter is tethered," said Tristan.

Ethan continued to investigate the area. "Because Lady Madelyn arrived. Merin stopped shorter, only not as violent in refusal."

With narrow eyes of contemplation, Tristan stared at the forest. "Maddy wouldn't go willingly into Dorgirith, meaning she arrived after and followed Garrick into the forest."

Merin nudged Karryn in a demand to be petted. She ran a soothing hand along the horse's neck. "The animals are nervous. That may be why she tethered them before leaving."

"Ay," agreed Ethan. "Garrick has been anxious to explore Dorgirith since Sir Dunham chose the new building site. Our absence gave him the opportunity to sneak away. Which begs the question, how did Maddy slip past your watchful eye?" he asked Karryn, a wry smile on his lips.

"We were tending to separate duties. Tristan is not always within your bow sight." Her retort made his smile widen.

Deep in thought, Tristan ignored the humor. "Maddy coming alone shows Sir Dunham wasn't at Garwood either."

"He went with Hadwin to the quarry. Garrick took advantage of everyone," she groused.

Now serious, Ethan said, "This is one time I don't think he will excuse his son's behavior." He whistled for his horse. When it obeyed, he took the reins to tether it beside Merin.

Tristan called his horse by name, which also came when summoned. After he tethered the animal, he drew his sword. "Let's hope we can find them before they come to harm. Arm your bow. It has a longer reach."

"We'll find them," said Ethan to Karryn.

"Ay, *we* will."

"You're not coming."

"Who is going to stop me, you?" She tossed the cloak back over her shoulder to draw one of her daggers, though not holding it in threatening manner.

"Let's not argue, we've wasted enough time," said Tristan.

They entered Dorgirith, Ethan armed to shoot, Tristan and Karryn with blades at the ready. In cautious steps, they traveled deeper into the forest.

"Maddy! Garrick," called Tristan. He and Karryn stopped when Ethan knelt to examine the ground. "Do you see any more tracks?"

"A disturbance goes this way."

Tristan hurried in the direction Ethan indicated. They traveled about a hundred yards when Ethan shouted in warning.

"Tristan! Down!"

Tristan squatted. An arrow whizzed over his head along with a flying dagger. Ethan reloaded for another shot while Karryn readied her second dagger. A rattling sound along with a strange moaning came from the direction Ethan fired. He again took aim. Tristan moved to investigate, obscuring Ethan's line of fire.

"Tristan!" Ethan hissed when forced to lower his bow. By the time he and Karryn joined Tristan, the source of the noise lie on the ground at the base of a tree with the arrow lodged in it.

Tristan picked it up. A mischievous grin appeared. "You shot a wind chime. Shall we have it stuffed to hang in the new hall?"

Karryn coughed aside a laugh at Ethan's embarrassment.

"Well, it moved. Besides, you have to admit to a superior shot of small moving target at such a distance. She missed and hit the tree."

"Check the rope." Karryn held up the end of the rope on the wind-chime to the portion dangling from the tree. The cut ends came together directly where her dagger impaled the tree.

"Lucky," groused Ethan.

She pulled the dagger out the trunk. "As lucky as your shot in killing a wind chime."

A distant growling caught their attention. Tristan dropped the wounded wind chime. "Sounds like real prey for you to shoot."

They moved in the direction of the growling.

Two snarling beasts shadowed Maddy and Garrick. The beasts used the trees to screen their movements and obscure identification. Maddy experienced difficulty running due to the pain in her back. Finally, out of breath, she fell to all fours. In nervous fear, Garrick held his sword ready to defend Maddy.

The stalking beasts moved closer, which gave a clearer view. Two unusually large, fanged mountain lions with exaggerated haunches, tail and large heads made the beasts half the size of Garrick's pony. The fangs measured six inches long while the eyes an unusual blood red with black slits for irises.

"This is not the kind of adventure I meant!" His voice trembled.

"What does it matter now?" she scolded.

"Quick! In here." Garrick pulled Maddy into what appeared to be a protected hollow. In reality, it proved to be a rocky outcropping forming three quarters of a circle. The only way out was the way they entered. The lions blocked the path.

"We're trapped!" she scolded him.

"I'll protect you." Garrick's hand shook so fiercely that he gripped the sword with both hands to hold the blade steady.

One lion roared making Maddy scream. She seized Garrick to draw him back. The lions came no further.

"Maddy!"

She heard her name, yet with some confusion since it wasn't Garrick. At the second call she recognized the voice. "Tristan!" she cried out.

A lion leapt at them. *Whiz! Thud!* An arrow from overhead pierced its neck. It fell hard to one side, wounded. When it rose, another arrow struck it in the head, killing it.

The second lion roared at the attacker. On the ridge overlooking the hollow, Ethan aimed for a third shot. The lion began to climb toward him. A dagger struck between its haunches. The lion slipped off the rock. It turned toward Karryn. She took out her second dagger to make for another throw. She recoiled a step when it roared.

"Stay still!" Ethan shouted a warning. He aimed, only the lion backed out of his line of fire.

Tristan took up position in front of Maddy and Garrick with his sword ready. He moved to keep himself between the wounded lion and them. When it leapt, he moved aside and slashed at it in passing. His blade sliced through its side. The lion stumbled upon landing within two feet of Garrick. It snapped and caught the hem of Garrick's tunic. Maddy tried to draw him away from the lion. A swiping paw knocked her aside.

Garrick clouted the lion in the head with the hilt of his sword. It released him. Tristan's sword plunged through the lion's neck then mercilessly ripped out. An arrow pierced the lion's head behind the eyes, finishing it.

"Are you all right?" asked Tristan. Garrick nodded since fear made him mute. Hearing Maddy groan, Tristan knelt beside her. She flung her arms about his neck and wept. "*Shhh*, it's all right. Are you hurt?"

"My back and hip."

Tristan examined where the lion clipped her. Claws ripped the breeches and grazed the skin. "Small scratches. Doesn't look too serious. How did you hurt your back?"

"I fell down a ravine and struck a tree at the bottom."

"I said I was sorry," Garrick spoke in a quaking voice.

"Sorry may not get us out of here before sundown, young master." Ethan had climbed down the rocks to join them.

Garrick adamantly shook his head. "We can't spend the night here!"

"It would be safer than not being able to see where we're going."

"Wh—what about them?" The boy motioned to the dead lions.

"We can use their hides for warmth and carcasses for meat."

Garrick paled terror. Tristan stood and gave Ethan an admonishing nudge.

The silent rebuked didn't sway Ethan. "He needs to learn to make do with what's available in the wilderness."

"Those are not natural beasts. I wouldn't use any part of them," chided Tristan.

Ethan easily shrugged. "Very well. We can trap rabbits."

Tristan expression told he did not approve of Ethan's ill-time humor.

"It's not sundown yet, so we can make it back," insisted Garrick.

Ethan gazed with skepticism at Garrick. "Do you remember which way you came, young master?"

The boy began to answer, but paused with confusion. To his shame, he admitted, "No."

"Then how do you know we can make it out before dark?"

"I suppose I don't."

"You thought this was a game and dared me to catch you," complained Maddy.

"How many times must I apologize?"

"Until you understand what your foolishness has caused!" She flinched in pain, both from her back and hip.

Tristan again knelt beside Maddy. "I didn't come prepared for the outdoors so I don't have my medical kit to give you something for the pain."

"I'll survive. I think." She glared again at Garrick.

The boy rolled his eyes in exasperation. He moved to leave the hollow. Sight of the dead lions stopped him. Garrick looked bashfully to Ethan. "What do you suggest we do?"

"Take advantage of the remaining light to make camp."

"With the lions still here?"

"Under normal circumstances this place is sheltered and relatively safe."

"How do you figure that? The lions trapped us here."

"I said under *normal* circumstances. If the carcasses aren't used they will attract night scavengers, so no, we won't make camp here. We'll find a similar place, and quickly."

Karryn carefully approached the lion to retrieve her dagger. To make certain it was dead, she kicked the hindquarters. To her relief it didn't move.

At her caution, Ethan withdrew the dagger. He wiped the bloody blade on the lion's hide to clean it. He smiled when he handed it to her hilt first. "Nice throw."

"Good shooting." She returned his smile.

"Karryn? I almost didn't recognize you," said Maddy.

"That's the idea. I'm glad you're both safe."

"Not until we get out of here." Ethan took the lead. Garrick and Karryn followed him with Tristan aiding Maddy.

Being an experienced woodsman, Ethan quickly found a suitable place not far from the hollow. Along the way, he managed to kill a small feral pig that wandered across their path. Tristan built the fire while Ethan prepared the pig. He cut it into smaller pieces then placed them on his and Tristan's sword for cooking.

"I understand Tristan and Ethan coming to find us, but why you?" Maddy asked Karryn.

"You are my charge."

"Not to mention her throwing skill surprised all of us," said Tristan.

"Tell me, are you as lethal with knitting needles?" asked Ethan with merry smile.

Karryn flashed a modest smile at Ethan's teasing.

"I still don't understand why? Especially if no one knew of your *other* skills," said Maddy.

Karryn heaved a shrug and avoided eye contact.

A howling gust of wind whipped through the trees making Maddy move closer to the fire. Tristan handed the hilt of his sword to Karryn to continue cooking. He removed his cloak to drape over Maddy's shoulders.

"Won't you be cold?" she asked.

"No, I'll be fine." He took the sword back from Karryn.

"I suppose I'll be giving you my cloak," said Ethan to Garrick.

The boy squared his shoulders in a smug manner. "No, I'm fine."

Ethan and Tristan exchanged private smiles at the boy's bravado.

Garrick slumped to warm his hands over the fire. "You acted as if you knew where to go in bringing us here. How? Have you been to Dorgirith before?" he asked Ethan.

"No, I listen when told a place is forbidden. That aside, I pay attention to the surroundings. I took note of this place in the fading light."

"Why did you do it? Run off and come here?" Tristan asked Garrick in a harsh tone.

"To spite me," chided Maddy. She drew the cloak closer about her in a huff.

"No! Why must it always be about you?" said Garrick.

"You left after Father went with Hadwin to the quarry and they weren't back yet." She motioned to the squires. "Why else do it if you didn't think I would stop you?"

"Because I wanted to! And no, I didn't think you would come after me."

"No one thinks I'm capable of anything." She sniffled back rising emotion.

"That's not true. Everyone is still adjusting to the change, that's all," said Tristan.

Maddy barely looked at him. "You're being kind, but I know the truth. I kept myself occupied with books for so long I didn't pay much attention to anything. Then when I became lady of the manor, I was ill prepared. Father even employed Karryn, whose known and *unknown* skills are beyond anything I possess."

Tristan laid a gentle hand on Maddy's shoulder. "So you try to prove yourself by coming after Garrick and not waiting for your father or us?"

She made a shy nod. She gathered the cloak tighter for comfort rather than warmth.

Tristan sent an admonishing eye to Garrick while tilting his head toward Maddy.

"I've already apologized numerous times," the boy disputed.

"About coming here. Not for failing to support your sister in a difficult time."

"She was my mother too!"

"The responsibility of running the manor didn't fall to you. By coming here, you not only defied your father, you also abused your sister's authority."

Garrick grew offended. "You're just a squire! Who are you to scold me?"

Ethan made a loud contrary snort. Tristan pretended his foot slipped when in actuality he kicked Ethan.

Curious about Tristan's reaction, Maddy sat up. "What was that about?"

"Nothing. My leg cramped so I stretched it out." Tristan pretended to rub his leg.

The answer didn't satisfy her. "No, you meant something by that."

Tristan affected a smile. "To keep Ethan from burning dinner."

"As if I, an experienced woodsman, would do that," said Ethan in his usual humor. He tested the meat by pulling off a piece. "Perfect." He held out a portion to Maddy. "Careful, my lady, it's hot."

She took it, though her focus remained on Tristan. "You're mocking me. He coughed like this," she mimicked Ethan, "and you kicked him because you didn't like it. I can read people as well as books. You're doing it again," she added when Tristan sent a cautious look to Ethan.

Tristan replied in a not too pleasant tone. "You picked a bad time to employ your newfound powers of observation."

"So, I'm right," she said with triumph.

"This is not the time to discuss it."

Despite Tristan's displeasure, Maddy grinned with satisfaction and began eating.

Ethan took the sword from Tristan after giving the rest of meat from his sword to Garrick. He removed portions for him and Karryn, leaving some on the sword for Tristan.

Garrick screwed his face after taking a bite. "Why does it taste different?"

Tristan stopped Maddy from taking another bite. Ethan snatched the meat from Karryn to sniff it. He took a tentative bite then sent a sarcastic scowl to Tristan.

"It's fine. Just not your fat, lazy domestic pig so it tastes slightly tougher." Ethan gave the meat back to Karryn. "Eat, then try to rest. We'll keep watch."

"I don't think I can sleep," groused Garrick.

"Ay, it is unusually cold," said Karryn.

"And in a terrifying way," added Maddy.

Tristan softly smiled at Maddy. "We'll keep watch."

Armus raced across the river plain to where all five horses stood tethered. Normally he took greater care not to be seen. However sensing where Tristan and Ethan headed, he abandoned caution. He drew his sword with the intent to enter Dorgirith when someone called to him. The woman who spoke to Maddy about the venison arrived. She stood to her full height of seven feet.

"Wren. Did you see them go in?"

"No, I returned to Garwood when I sensed trouble."

Again Armus headed for the forest only this time Wren physically detained him.

"You know we can't go in there! Even if we were allowed, with our diminished strength we would be of little use against the Dark Way."

"Magelen and Dagar could be laying a trap for them," he argued.

"No, this is the boy's doing. His sister and Karryn followed to stop him. As good squires, Tristan and Ethan are doing their duty."

He looked askew at her. "You said you didn't see them go in."

"I didn't. I told you I returned to Garwood where I learned Maddy left to stop Garrick. Karryn pursued her. I recognized Tristan and

Ethan's mounts, so I assumed the rest since they wouldn't let them venture into the forbidden forest."

A menacing growl came from the forest. Armus stiffened with ire. "How can we simply stand by?" he lashed out in frustration.

Though apprehensive, she tried to ease his vexation. "You know we must! Pray Jor'el protects them since we cannot."

He slammed the sword back in his scabbard and sat on the log.

"We can't wait here and risk being seen."

The glare of chestnut eyes conveyed his unwillingness to move.

Alert, Wren looked southeast. With nothing immediately visible, she announced, "Someone's coming."

Armus stood to draw his sword at seeing movement on the horizon. "At least we can keep more trouble from harassing them."

"Sir Dunham and his men." Wren nudged Armus to move. "We must leave." She grew more forceful in her attempt to make the large warrior budge "Hurry! I know a place to watch." Wren spoke the Ancient to move unseen by the mortals.

They had no sooner left then Dunham and his men arrived. Dunham wore part of his armor over his brown leather tunic. His men wore the brown and gold livery of his house, and all armed to the teeth.

"Here's proof, my lord," said Hadwin about the horses. "Tristan and Ethan are with them."

"No, in pursuit since they hadn't returned when Garrick, Maddy and Karryn left."

Dunham kicked his horse intent on entering Dorgirith. The horse refused. In no mood to accept the animal's contrariness, he tried to force the horse. It became agitated until finally he lost his balance. He managed a controlled fall. One of his men snatched the horse's bridle before it bolted off.

"In this case, I think the horse is wiser than you, my lord," said Hadwin.

"Meaning what?"

"Meaning going into Dorgirith is foolish anytime, doubly so at night. Take comfort in the fact the squires are in pursuit. At first light, we'll follow, only on foot."

With great irritation, Dunham bellowed, "Make camp!" While his men obeyed, he stood in front of the log to stare at the forest. "Jor'el, guide Tristan, Ethan and Karryn in their search. May they find my children alive and unharmed."

Chapter 5

A CIRCULAR TOWER ROOM AT RAVENDALE SERVED AS MAGELEN'S study. The shelves and tables contained assorted books and parchments. A portion of the room served as a laboratory with glass beakers and jars of crockery. The countryside surrounding the castle could be seen from each of the directional windows. The north window faced toward the Region of Sanctuary. Underneath the sill stood an ornate wrought iron basin. It contained sod and water from the Region of Sanctuary. The basin water began to boil, producing stream.

Magelen sat at an impressive oak desk covered with papers. Hearing his name, he moved from the desk to the basin. He watched Dagar's image appear in the steam. The Master of the Dark Way was an impressive figure of noble and awesome perfection, tall and muscular wearing a scarlet suit trimmed in gold. The white undershirt showed through slits in the doublet. His boots and belt were of finely crafted black leather. A jewel encrusted dagger hung from the belt. His sun-yellow hair, matching small beard and flawless complexion stood in marked contrast to the suit. Bright mahogany eyes shone forth with pure authority. He wore an identical talisman to Magelen.

"My lord. This is an honor," said Magelen in cordial greeting.

Dagar made gesture of impatience. "You don't appear upset, so what are you doing about it?"

"Lord Razi is stubborn. He refuses to reveal any members of his family. Although after Elias' wife twenty years ago, he has not remarried. His last son, Lord Mather, died by my hand, along with his family. There may not be any more offspring."

Dagar's brows leveled in concentration. "Something stirs. I believe it has to do with Razi. Keep applying pressure."

"How far shall I go?"

Dagar spoke mercilessly. "To his death if necessary."

Magelen fought displaying fear. "Taking such action will cause more unrest among the people, perhaps revolt. He is very popular. Much has already been made of his imprisonment. Ram summoned the lords to swear allegiance in hopes of quelling the protests. I fear Lord Razi's death will undermine his effort."

Dagar didn't argue, instead he said, "Razi's popularity was designed for when he became king. Alas, plans had to be altered since Ram lacks Razi's intelligence and natural charisma. But I meant what are you doing about the disturbance in Dorgirith?"

"What disturbance?"

"You mean Witter hasn't told you?"

"I've not seen Commander Witter in several days."

"Fool!" swore Dagar. "There are intruders in the forest."

"I didn't know," Magelen said with restrained anger. "If I had I would not be here. Come!" he snapped at hearing a knock at the door.

Two Shadow Warriors entered. They wore similar black uniforms with traces of scarlet. Both had black hair. The bulkier Warrior had hands capable of crushing anything. A vicious cut ran from above the right eye across the bridge of his nose to his left cheek. Unusually cold and bright hazel eyes looked at everything with marked scorn. The slender one had light gray eyes, a color not seen among mortals.

Magelen sent them a sneer of great indignation before returning to the image. "Commanders Witter and Altari have arrived, my lord Dagar."

Hearing whom he addressed, Witter and Altari rushed from the threshold to where they could see the basin and be seen. Witter wore the scar with Altari being the thinner of the two. They bowed to Dagar, who appeared very put out.

Remaining bowed at the waist, Witter spoke. "My lord, we came as fast as we could to inform Grand Master Magelen—"

"Liar!"

Witter looked up in guarded anticipation of the rebuff. Altari's jowls flexed with nervousness when Dagar continued.

"You have other means by which to travel than on horseback."

"Your orders are to refrain from using our power in the presence of mortals. Our appearance already make many suspicious of our true identities as Guardians," said Witter.

"Ay," agreed Altari. "With only a thousand of us remaining, we need more if we are to maintain this level of intensity against the Fortresses and remnant."

"Has there been any success in the reconditioning process?" asked Witter.

Dagar's irritation only slightly moderated at the argument. "Not yet, though Griswold assures me some are on the verge of breaking. I'm working on methods to increase your powers. Full strength is not totally possible, yet enough to cause more intimidation. Now, what about these intruders?"

"A boy and girl. We set the lions on them," replied Witter.

"No! There are others. I sense something unsettling among them."

"Then we will return to deal with them."

"*I* will deal with them," declared Magelen. Seeing the Warriors' skepticism, he demanded, "Do you doubt my powers?"

"They would be advised not to," warned Dagar.

"Not doubt. Simply faster if we dealt with them," said Witter.

Dagar became irate. "If those intruders discover our experiments, I will personally take my displeasure out on the two of you!"

Altari's hard grip stopped Witter from answering. Instead, Altari spoke to Dagar. "It will be as you command, my lord."

"No delays! For this task you are exempt from your orders."

"Ay, my lord." Altari nudged Witter to approach Magelen. Each placed a hand on the mortal's shoulders. "*Siuthad!*" said the Warriors together. Immediately, all three vanished in a white flash of light.

The Nether Dimension to which Jor'el banished Dagar was a cavernous domain. He conducted business from what he termed his main audience chamber. An identical basin to that in Magelen's chambers stood in one part of the cavern. A stone altar with emblems of ravens and lizards stood beside the basin. By way of these stations, Dagar communicated with the outside world. The basin served as his direct link to Magelen while the talisman a conduit of power. The stone altar served for receiving the worship of lay people who dabbled in the Dark Way. The influx from the outer world served both to inspire and infuriate Dagar. Since being imprisoned, he had time to think, to plan, to brood and to hate. That hatred inspired him towards his goal yet infuriated him at the slow pace by which everything proceeded.

"That went well."

Dagar whirled about at hearing the sarcastic voice. He came face-to-face with Tor, a redheaded, bright blue-eyed fellow Guardian warrior. Tor served as a member of Dagar's Trio in the Region of Sanctuary, and joined the rebellion.

"What do you want?" demanded Dagar.

"Time for the daily report," said Tor, casually smiling. "We have recruits."

Dagar's demeanor changed to pleased. "Who?

"Nari, Shaka, Bern, Roane, Indigo, Cletus and Carvel. "

"Carvel? Armus' former archer commander? I thought he would offer more resistance to the reconditioning," mused Dagar with a small satisfied smile.

"It's been a hundred and fifty years. I suspect many more will break now that a breech has occurred. The other recruits are all warriors. Griswold thinks Nari and Shaka will make good Enforcers."

"Excellent. What about certain others? Vidar, Mahon and Gulliver?"

"Not yet. Gulliver has always been stubborn, probably due to all the saltwater in his veins. Mahon's been spared too much discomfort by the actions of a fellow warrior named Cyril. Vidar seems to have taken personal interest in the welfare of a vassal named Elgin, even to the point of distress when Elgin is receiving his reconditioning treatment."

"Fascinating. Where are the new recruits?"

"In the chamber awaiting your inspection. I thought it would be fitting for such a ceremony to take place where all could see and hear." Tor grinned with satisfaction.

Dagar chuckled in wicked delight. He took Tor's shoulder to steer him from the chamber into a connecting tunnel.

The reconditioning chamber measured one hundred feet in diameter by fifty feet high with various implements of *instruction*. Cages surrounded a central floor at different levels reached by stone stairways. Narrow walkways circled the chamber on each level. The cages held several thousand Guardians of different stations and genders, all in various stages of suffering. Two hundred warriors tended to the prisoners.

The seven recruits assembled in the middle of the chamber. Before them stood a Guardian whose bulk, massive arms and chest no tunic or double could hide, so he wore none. He had on leather breeches and boots. Yellow eyes watched Tor and Dagar approach.

"Griswold. Tor tells me your methods have finally yielded results."

"The fruits of my labor." Griswold's voice matched his size. His smile conveyed warped enjoyment of his task.

Dagar surveyed the recruits, paying particular attention to the females. Both wore fixed, stoic expressions. "Which is Shaka and which is Nari?"

"This is Shaka, my lord." Griswold indicated a female with dark violet eyes and medium length dark brown hair. "She is already proficient in lethal hand-to-hand combat."

Dagar addressed Shaka. "Who was your mentor?"

"Jayden."

Dagar grinned at hearing the name of the former Trio Leader of the Delta yet quickly covered his reaction. "It is my sad task to inform you Jayden perished in the battle."

Shaka didn't flinch or change her expression. "So I've been told."

Dagar's regard passed to Nari. She had close cropped black hair and nearly colorless eyes with only a trace of blue. "Same question."

Nari boldly answered. "I'm an Original, same as you, so I had no tutor. Roane was my apprentice." She indicated the male standing beside her.

Again Dagar quelled a smile when shifting his gaze from Roane back to Nari. "Are you acquainted with any of the others?"

"Shaka and the archer are the only ones I didn't know. The rest of us served together over the centuries."

"And will do so again. After further training as an Enforcer, you shall form your own unit. Carvel will be given command of the Shadow Archers."

"Shadow Archers? I've not been told of any other archers," said Carvel.

"That's because you will pick from among the recruits as they become available. Shaka," continued Dagar with consideration, "Well, I can find various uses for a silent assassin. Welcome to the ranks."

"My lord," they said in unison and bowed.

This time Dagar didn't hide his proud smile. He looked around the chamber and raised his voice in address. "All of you will someday realize the benefits of changing your allegiance." He heard a loud jeering *'Hah!'* coming from his right. He turned to see who dared to interrupt him. However, with so many cages and cells, he kept speaking to illicit further reaction. "I can be a gracious commander."

This time the mocking laughter was followed by a comment. "A gale force wind is a better commander." In a nearby cage sat a lone Guardian. His silver hair, thin beard and ruddy complexion showed the dirt of being trapped underground for over a century. The clothes were soiled and unkempt, yet with no signs of abuse. The bright sea-green eyes had not dulled in their obstinacy.

Dagar approached the cage. "Gulliver, I should have known."

The sea Guardian shrugged with indifference. "What you know doesn't matter to me since it could fit on the head of mortal's pin."

With a low throaty growl, Dagar accosted Griswold, "Why hasn't he been reconditioned?"

"I thought to deal with the weaker ones first to build up your forces. Then I can take my time and pleasure with those more stubborn."

"You don't scare me, Gristle," scoffed Gulliver.

"Griswold!"

"You look like all fat to me."

Griswold moved to grab the cage when Dagar stopped him.

"He purposely incited you."

"Better listen to your *gracious* commander," Gulliver said with a jeer.

Griswold jerked away, which made Dagar snap a command in the Ancient language of the Guardians. "*Griswold, sguir!*"

He stiffened as if frozen, though snarled at Gulliver.

"His time will come." Dagar looked around the chamber to once again speak. "All of you will face reconditioning. The extent of which will be determined by your attitude. In the end, you will either yield, or cease to exist," he said the last sentence directly to Gulliver.

"Then do it now, for some of us will never turn," said a new voice.

Dagar spotted the speaker in cell carved out from the Cave wall. The youthful-looking, blond-haired warrior with light translucent blue eyes wore a soiled uniform. He was not alone in the cell. The other Guardian warrior appeared older with grey hair and light brown eyes. He showed signs of abuse. He lay on the carved out portion of the wall used for a bed. He reached to touch his younger companion's arm in warning.

"Don't provoke him."

"Listen to Cyril, Mahon. You don't want to make me angry." A toothy fake grin crossed Dagar's lips.

"You don't frighten me."

Dagar sardonically smirked. "We'll see if that pompous attitude changes after your first taste of reconditioning. I hear Cyril's been taking your punishment all these years." He signaled Griswold to the cell door.

Griswold muttered under his breath and flicked his wrist. Without touching the cell, the door opened by itself. He entered.

56

"No!" Cyril painfully tried to rise.

With a gentle hand, Mahon stopped Cyril. He flashed a reassuring smile. "It's all right. I'm not afraid. Jor'el will strengthen me."

Cyril sneered when Griswold took hold of Mahon. "You'll regret this, Griswold, I swear."

Griswold seemed to ignore Cyril as he jerked Mahon out of the cell. The younger warrior offered no resistance. Griswold waved his hand to slam the door shut. A loud click sounded when it locked. He spoke to Cyril. "I'll pretend he's you so when I bring him back, you'll see how much I think of your idle threat."

"You know he means it!" said a pitiful voice from the adjoining cell. He lay on a stone bed with numerous severe injuries.

"Easy, Elgin." Vidar knelt to comfort Elgin. Vidar also suffered abuse as told by fading welts on his face. The copper eyes of the premier Guardian archer sent a cautious glance Cyril.

Understanding Vidar's expression, Cyril said, "Listen to Vidar, Elgin, and be at ease."

"Ay, you won't hear me make a sound," said Mahon to Vidar and Elgin's cage.

Griswold snorted a laugh. "We'll see about that, puny warrior." He shoved Mahon toward the main reconditioning portion of the chamber.

Dagar moved to Vidar's cell. "Pride won't get you anywhere."

Standing, Vidar only reached seven feet tall, which made him six inches shorter than Dagar. "Where did pride get you? Oh, ay, confined for your crime of rebellion."

Dagar's eyes narrowed. "I might just see to your reconditioning personally. Or better yet, have you watch while I take a turn with Elgin and then end his miserable existence!"

"No!" Vidar seized the cell bars. He fell back when searing pain shot through him.

Dagar laughed at Vidar's misfortune. He left.

"Vidar?" asked Elgin.

"I'm all right," he groused in discomfort. "I forgot the bars were stygian metal. My hands will be numb for awhile, but I'll survive."

"For how long is the question. You can't protect me forever."

"We protect each other." At movement from the adjoining cell, Vidar watched Cyril sit by the door. "You know Mahon meant it. We won't hear him."

"Ay, Avatar trained him well, only he's not here. When assigned as my second-in-command, Mahon became my responsibility."

"Then just be ready to help him when Griswold is done."

Agitated, Dagar left the reconditioning chamber with Tor. "Seven recruits is not good enough after so long. Witter and Altari complain of needing more troops to continue the campaign against the Fortresses."

"You know Griswold is doing all he can. Several hundred have succumbed rather than yield. It wouldn't go well to lose too many."

"It's not the numbers! Ram is proving a less forceful king than I hoped. In fits and starts he takes control."

"Because he is hesitant to act against Razi."

The statement made Dagar slam a fist into his palm. "I should have separated them at birth rather than let them get too close."

"All part of your plan so they would rely on each other. Razi's betrayal was unforeseen. You couldn't have calculated for that."

Dagar's glare turned so lethal that Tor took a step back. "I suspected a spy."

"Barrion acted on his own. Kell wouldn't have sent a spy since he considered you his friend—" Tor stopped when Dagar seized his throat, cutting off his air.

The brightened mahogany eyes narrowed with malice. "Don't ever use *his* name in my presence! I may sometimes miscalculate, but I have always been more clever than the venerated captain!" A hard shove sent Tor flying across the room and into the wall. "Don't forget that, or mention *his* name again!" Dagar shouted loud enough to echo in the room. "Let it be known that *his* name is forbidden to be spoken in my presence!"

Tor rubbed his throat. He spoke in raspy voice. "I will make sure everyone knows."

"Tell Griswold to send the new recruits immediately to Witter and Altari. Training can come later. The present situation must be dealt with. And," he added when Tor went to depart, "double his effort in reconditioning, I want more troops!"

In the heart of Dorgirith stood a fortified manor house. To an individual who ventured into the forbidden forest, finding a house would be surprising due to the isolated location. Upon closer inspection, a cold, dark sense of evil emanated from the house.

In the main room, Witter and Altari reappeared with Magelen. The mortal swayed from wooziness, since their bodies were ill-fitted for dimension travel. Altari held Magelen for recovery. Witter called for a former woodland Guardian by the name of Cassius.

He hastened to the summons. "Commander. Grand Master."

"What news of these intruders?" Witter asked.

Cassius grew cautious in reply. "They were joined by three others, who killed the lions."

"What?"

Cassius became fretful of the Warrior's anger. "Knights perhaps, I don't know! According to the ravens they killed the lions."

"Where are they now?"

"I don't know."

Magelen regained command of his senses. "They cannot be allowed to escape with news of victory. If it is believed one can survive Dorgirith then others will come."

"Dispatch the *madah-dune* to track and destroy them," said Witter.

They heard the caw of a raven. It landed on a ledge outside a nearby window. Cassius opened the window. He briefly spoke to the raven in the Ancient. The bird replied with caws and cackles. He dismissed the raven before returning to the others.

"Sir Dunham and a dozen of his men are encamped on the border."

"Dunham? Now, what would he ..." began Magelen. "A boy and girl," he mused then spoke aloud. "They must be his children." A caustic smile appeared. He amended his order. "Have the madah-dune capture the children and bring them to me. Kill the others."

"Why?"

"To use as leverage against Dunham. He is stubborn but a man of his word. If I offer assistance to recover his children lost in the dangerous wilds of Dorgirith, he will be more agreeable. With him subdued, others will follow."

"Consider it done, my lord." Cassius bowed and left.

Chapter 6

GARRICK AND MADDY SLEPT ON THE GROUND BESIDE THE LOG where Tristan sat. She still wore his cloak. Karryn sat on the ground with her shoulders and head against the log between Ethan and Tristan. Her hood was up with the cloak closed, as she too slept. The squires remained awake. Tristan carefully tended the fire, mindful not to disturb those who slept.

A ready bow lay across Ethan's lap. "The night is unusually still," he whispered in wariness. "Not even a breeze stirs the trees. Nor do I hear sounds of night creatures. Something is lurking, something even the animals want no part of."

Tristan stopped tending the fire at Ethan's last statement. His eyes shifted to look around. A howling began, low at first then grew in deafening painful volume. Maddy, Garrick and Karryn woke, startled.

A nearby raven and several owls flew from the trees in fright. Tristan gritted his teeth against the noise to rise and draw his sword. Ethan stood ready to shoot at the first sign of movement. His knuckles turned white in gripping the bow to withstand the earsplitting noise. Karryn managed to rise to her knees with dagger in hand.

Out of the darkness, six wolf-man beasts charged them. The beasts stood nine feet tall on two legs yet completely covered in fur. The heads resembled wolves with snarling, drooling fangs, and large hands with sharp claws. Each wielded a spiked club.

Ethan fired, striking one in the chest. The wound briefly slowed its advance. He went to reload when the beast seized the bow. Ethan wouldn't let go. The beast tossed him sideways when it ripped the weapon from his grasp. The beast snapped the bow in half. It then yanked the arrow out of its chest. It raised the arrow to strike Ethan. He noticed the attack and rolled away to avoid being impaled. The force plunged the arrow into the ground up to the feathers. The beast tried to pull the arrow from the ground but the shaft broke.

Karryn dodged a swiping paw. The paw hit her shoulder with such force it sent her sideways to ground, knocking her unconscious.

Tristan ducked beneath the club of another beast. His defensive swing caught the beast in the back of the leg. It staggered yet remained on its feet. The backward swing of the club clipped Tristan in the chest. He fell backwards off his feet into a tree. With wind knocked from him on impact, he collapsed into a crumpled heap. He struggled to breathe.

"Tristan!" Maddy screamed when a beast seized her. She struggled as the strong hold squeezed the air from her lungs. She fainted and went limp in its arm.

Another beast knocked Garret's sword away to seize the boy. The two carrying Garrick and Maddy made barking sounds before hurrying into the woods. The other beasts followed.

Ethan scrambled to retrieve his bow. Broken! He tossed it aside then made his way to Tristan. "How badly are you hurt?"

Tristan held onto Ethan in an effort to sit up. "It knocked the wind out of me. Karryn!" He motioned to where she laid.

Ethan left Tristan. Karryn remained unconscious so he made a quick survey to determine her injuries. "I don't see any wounds." Hearing her moan, he encouraged her to wake by lightly tapping her face. "Karryn." She jerked awake, her eyes wide in fear. "Easy. The beasts are gone."

He helped her sit up. She took a couple of deep breath before speaking. "What were those things?"

"No creature I've seen before."

She glanced around. "Where are Maddy and Garrick?"

"The beasts took them and headed north."

Tristan joined them. He gingerly touched his chest when taking a breath to speak. "Karryn. Are you well enough to continue?"

"If the beasts didn't stop, me you won't." Upon standing, she immediately doubled over in pain.

Ethan caught her for support. "Take a moment or two for recovery."

"No." She forced herself to straighten up. "We could lose them."

Ethan cocked a confident smile. "I'll find them." He observed Tristan's grimace of pain. "What about you? Can you continue?"

"Ay. I'm only sore, nothing broken." Tristan retrieved his sword. He heard muffled voices to the south. "More creatures?"

"No, it sounds like men." Ethan listened for a moment then smiled. "Hadwin." He began to move in the direction of the voices when Karryn stopped him.

"What about Maddy and Garrick? And where is your bow?"

"A beast broke it. While I can find them, we can cover more ground with help."

After a half mile, Ethan stopped and recognized the man. "Master Hadwin!"

The master-at-arms looked in their direction. "My lord! The squires!" Hadwin became perplexed. "Lady Karryn?"

"Surprised us too," said Ethan with a chuckle.

Dunham took note of their pale faces. "Run afoul of trouble?"

"Some beasts attacked our camp, knocked out Lady Karryn and Tristan, and smashed my bow. They took Lady Madelyn and Master Garrick. We were about to pursue when we heard voices," replied Ethan.

"Which way?"

"North."

Dunham motioned to one of his soldiers. "Give Ethan your bow." Once the weapon was exchanged, Dunham said to Ethan, "Lead on."

"The lady is coming with us?" Hadwin asked Dunham about Karryn.

"The lady can handle herself."

Maddy jolted awake when dropped to the ground like a sack of potatoes. A beast still held Garrick. Two others were wounded, no doubt by Ethan and Tristan. Stopping meant the squires and Karryn may be able to catch up with them. Then again, she had no idea how long she was unconscious; how far they traveled; or if Ethan, Tristan and Karryn were capable of pursuit. She recalled Tristan being knocked into a tree. Ethan might follow, if he could. He would first see to Tristan. After all, they came together into her father's service ten years ago, and were inseparable. Karryn's appearance and ability proved surprising. There may be no rescue. The thought made her inwardly shiver. Decidedly angry vocalizations drew her attention.

Maddy caught Garrick's frightened glance. Whereas it would be so easy to blame him, she couldn't. With the possibility of no rescue, she needed to stay calm. "Where are you taking us?" she demanded, even though she didn't know if the beasts could understand her speech.

The one with the chest wound, growled and bared fangs at her.

She swallowed back her fear to say, "You don't frighten me."

The beast raised a hand. She shrunk back against the tree. It didn't strike. At that moment, she realized it understood and made the threatening gesture to silence her.

"Maddy?" clamored Garrick.

"I'm all right. They won't hurt us. I think they are supposed to take us someplace."

"How can you tell?"

The wounded beast made barking, growling noises to its companions along with gestures suggesting time to move. Maddy heard Garrick grunt when subdued by the beast to be picked up again. The beast reached down for her. She made a motion to resist. In actuality, she broke one of the small lower branches. She gasped for air when it snatched her in such a way that wrenched the air from her lungs. Once again, she nearly swooned before catching her breath. They were on the move.

After retracing their steps to the north side of the hollow, Ethan knelt to scan the ground with his eyes and feel with his fingers. "The tracks belong to the beasts. I see no sign of Lady Madelyn or Master Garrick. At least not footprints, though these tracks are heavier."

"I saw one pick up Maddy before being struck aside," said Tristan.

"Quicker to move when carrying something than keep a struggling prey in tow," said Hadwin.

"Prey?" chided Dunham in great offense.

"I didn't mean that the way it sounded, my lord. I meant wherever they are heading, it would be faster to carry than drag them along." Hadwin cursed under his breath at realizing his explanation didn't help.

"I'll find them." Ethan followed the tracks. He traveled another half mile before stopping where the beasts had rested. He squatted to feel the ground then scrambled a short distance to a tree. He grinned upon inspecting the broken branch. "They left us a sign to follow."

"Are you certain?" asked Dunham.

"Ay, my lord. Master Garrick sat there," he pointed to the spot. "His boot prints suggest slipping or tripping. The lady, here. And not easily seated by the look of the disturbed ground. She broke this for me to find." He lifted the branch.

"How do you know it wasn't broken in passing?"

Ethan stood. "Too low and close to the trunk to be caught on either fur or boot."

"By the heavenlies, you are good."

"Let's just hope I'm good enough to find them safe and whole."

"Which way?" asked Tristan.

"Deeper into the forest."

"I wonder why?"

"Whatever the reason, it will go ill for them when we find my children," said Dunham.

For what seemed like a couple of hours, the beasts traveled with Maddy and Garrick. The light of dawn penetrated the dark of the forest. Maddy tried to get comfortable as the beast's arm hurt her side. It carried her in a manner more advantageous for itself than any comfort to her. She had only been successful once more in leaving another sign to follow. Then again, she didn't know if it would help.

In the midst of clearing stood a manor house. What a strange place to find a dwelling. The more she looked at the house, the more fearful she became. A cold, dark sense of foreboding forced her to look away or be overcome with illness.

Inside, the small amount of daylight filtering through the windows exposed bare walls. A sense of coldness enveloped everything. The beast let her down. She shivered, more from trepidation than an actual chill.

"Maddy?" Garrick looked scared. A red welt raised on his face from earlier.

"I'm all right. What about you?"

"I want to go home!" He tried to approach her when the beast jerked him back.

"Don't hurt him, he's just a boy!"

"A boy who is a trespasser." Magelen entered from a doorway across the room. Cassius, Witter and Altari accompanied him.

Maddy gasped in alarmed recognition of Magelen. Her uneasy glance shifted to the Shadow Warriors before returning to Magelen. "What do you want with us?"

"Me? I could ask the same question since you invade my home."

"We didn't mean it. It was accidental."

Magelen laughed with mockery. "That's not what I was told."

The curious statement made Maddy ask, "Told by whom?"

"By all that surrounds," he said with exaggerated gestures. "The forest is alive. It says you are intruders. A very pretty intruder, but an intruder nonetheless." He caressed her face. She whimpered in apprehension.

"Don't touch my sister!" Garrick tried to sound brave.

"You should have kept her home rather than let her trespass."

"It's my fault! Maddy tried to stop me," admitted Garrick, upset.

Magelen smiled with sarcastic spite. "Hardly neighborly of Sir Dunham to let you wander about disturbing others."

"He didn't know!" Garrick blurted out.

"Hush," warned Maddy. She sent a cautious glance to Magelen.

Magelen made Maddy face him. "You recognize me. Tell your brother who I am." She attempted to remove her face but he wouldn't yield. He turned her to face Garrick.

"Grand Master Magelen, the King's counselor," she said.

Garrick paled with fear.

Magelen brought her around to face him again. "You make me sound so ominous, my dear lady. I find you fascinating." His gaze grew lecherous as the corners of his mouth turned into a lustful smile. "Although, I must say I prefer you in a gown than breeches, Lady Madelyn."

His wanton look made her quiver with dread. She forced herself to speak. "What you think of me is of little concern when my father hears of this."

"Oh, but it will. Sir Dunham's stubbornness is exceedingly irritating, to the point of exhausting royal patience. Something must be done to avoid unwanted action."

Despite the frightening circumstances, Maddy's anger rose. "You threaten my father?"

"No, my dear lady. I wish to help him. You *accidentally* coming here may provide me the opportunity." He spoke to Cassius. "See Master Garrick is made comfortable *downstairs* while I continued to speak with the lady."

Cassius signaled to the beast, which in turn picked up Garrick to follow him.

"Maddy!" Garrick tried to resist the beast.

She broke free of Magelen's hold. "No! Garrick!" Witter and Altari blocked her path. She heard Garrick's muffled cries. "If you don't release him, nothing you say to me will help you with my father!"

"You're very much mistaken, my dear. You will help me more than you realize." Magelen gazed up and down at her. "Breeches are so unbecoming. Commander Altari will escort you to my personal chamber. There you will find more suitable clothes. When you are comfortable, we shall talk some more."

The disturbing implications kept her mute. She recoiled when Altari took hold of her arm. She didn't know which felt more unnerving, the beast, Magelen or the Shadow Warrior's cold grey eyes. She bit her lower lip to keep her emotions mute. Silent tears of fear fell, as Altari escorted her upstairs to the chamber.

"It's dark," she said in a quivering voice.

He lit a lantern. "You'll find what you need in there." He indicated a wardrobe.

The chamber appeared no different than the rest of the unwelcoming, frigid home. She rubbed her arms to ward off a chill. "It's too cold to change clothes."

Altari went to the hearth with wood already in place for the night's fire. He knelt and spoke under his breath before touching a match to the wood. Immediately, a roaring fire sprang to life.

"How did you do that?" she asked in wonder.

"Dry wood catches fast. Now get changed."

"Not with you in the room."

He glanced around. "No way for you to escape. Besides, you wouldn't get far. I'll be right outside the door."

For a moment Maddy trembled with indecision. She understood Magelen veiled reference to *speaking*. Although she had never been with a man, she knew that if he succeeded, he would have leverage against her father. Marriage by force was used as a means to get what one desired.

She and her father spoke of marriage. Not with anyone specific more in general terms. He enjoyed teasing her about Tristan. Though highly favored, Tristan lacked position and property to make a suitable husband. Still, when he killed the lion to save them none of that mattered. *Garrick* she thought, bringing a new wave of fear. What would become of him if she refused? Her knees grew weak and forced her to sit on the bed.

"Jor'el, please help me! Don't let this evil scheme succeed—"

Maddy stopped at hearing noise from across the room. Cautious, she moved to the wardrobe since she couldn't tell if the sound came from behind or inside of it. At another sound, she threw open the doors to confront whatever hid inside. To her surprise, she found only nightclothes, both male and female. Overcome with disgust, she shut the wardrobe.

She started to cry out at seeing a very tall man beside her. He wore the brown and gold uniform of her father's soldiers along with a handsome sword. His hand quickly covered her mouth. He put a finger over his lips for silence. It took her a moment to take stock of him. He stood taller than Tristan but shorter than the Shadow Warrior making him around six feet, eight inches. His hair and goatee were bronze. His bright silver eyes were kind and reassuring compared to the cold grey of the Shadow Warrior.

Altari's voice came through the door. "Are you all right, my lady?"

The man glared at the door, then warned her with another cautious gesture. With a vigorous nod, she agreed. He released her to reply.

"I'm fine. Just deciding what to wear." She saw him smile with approval.

"Let me know when you are ready."

"I will."

He crossed to the other side of the room. He felt along the seams of the paneling. She watched, curious, then her eyes darted back to the door.

"Hurry," she urged.

He ignored her, until he found what he was looking for. Both froze at hearing Altari address someone.

"My lord, she is still dressing."

She covered her own mouth to stop an outcry. He slid open the panel, snatched her hand and they disappeared into the wall with the panel sliding closed behind them.

Meanwhile, Cassius lead Garrick into the cellar and down a damp, dingy hallway. Witter accompanied them. Doors leading to rooms lined one side of the corridor. The other side was an exterior wall with two small windows ten feet off the floor; too small for escape, but enough for light and air. From behind several closed doors came horrid animal sounds, making Garrick jerk around in looking for the source. He stopped at hearing one high ear-piercing screech. Witter nudged him forward. Garrick paled in fright at the formidable Shadow Warrior with the nasty scar and menacing glare. He seized Cassius' sleeve.

"Where are you taking me? And what are you going to do to me? To my sister?"

"If you and your sister cooperate, then nothing will happen."

Garrick jumped in fear at a howling of agonizing pain. This time he stopped in front of an open door. Several wolves or dogs of some kind were chained to the far wall. The room contained a table the top of which contained iron fetters. Shelves lined the far wall. Vials of various colored liquids and surgical instruments filled the shelves. Something moved to one side. He caught sight of a man-like beast, hideous in feature. One of the dogs lunged toward the door, growling and snarling. Only the chain kept it from attacking. In sheer terror, Garrick backed into the far hallway wall. His breathing labored and heart racing.

Cassius and Witter remained unfazed by his reaction. Cassius casually announced, "Your room, Master Garrick."

The boy turned in a panic from the open door to the room Cassius indicated. "Next to this?" He pointed to the room.

"The accommodations not to your liking?" he asked in mockery. "Perhaps other arrangements can be made after Grand Master Magelen speaks to your sister."

"What could Maddy tell him to make him change his mind?"

He laughed with high ridicule. "You will learn soon enough."

Witter shoved Garrick into the room. Cassius slammed the door then locked it.

"Hey! There's no light in here," called Garrick through the door. "Hey!" he shouted again when they didn't respond.

Cassius and Witter started to leave when Witter seized the hilt of his sword. Cassius braced himself against the sensation. "A Guardian? Here? How is that possible?"

70

Witter raced from the cellar to Magelen's private chamber. Magelen had joined Altari. "Who?" Witter demanded.

Altari hissed the name, "Avatar! He took the girl."

Witter made a low throaty growl of anger.

At their piqued reactions, Magelen asked, "Who is Avatar that he upsets you both?"

"The obnoxious protégé of Kell, who usurped me and took my position!" said Altari.

"Why would Kell send him for a girl?"

"Kell has been neutralized since the Great Battle. Jor'el probably sent Avatar, which means we must stop him from leaving!" The Shadow Warriors rushed from the room.

Maddy held tightly onto Avatar's hand. He led her through the dark passageway down steep, narrow steps. She couldn't see well. The smell told her it was a damp earthen tunnel. He seemed certain of where he headed.

"Can you see?"

"Well enough to get you out of here. There is light up ahead."

She jerked on his hand to stop him. "Not without Garrick."

"Garrick?"

"Surely you know we're both here. Father must have told you."

Avatar balked in reply. "Eh? No, actually. Where is he?"

"Downstairs. We were separated upon arrival. I won't leave without him."

Avatar pursed his lips at her declaration. "I will get you to safety then return for him."

Both flinched at the screeching noise, she in fright and he to make defense. Avatar listened to the fading screech then gently urged her to continue.

"I promise, I will return for him once you are safe."

Without further objection, Maddy went with Avatar. She clung to his arm using both hands; more for maintaining balance since the steps grew steeper. The stairs ended inside a small room. Natural light came from behind a door on the opposite wall, indicating an exterior door.

Avatar grinned. "I told you I could see to find a way out." He opened the door enough to survey the area. Hearing the bird screech again, he glanced up. A large grotesque black vulture with rotten flesh and feathers circled overhead. The wingspan was ten feet. "That can't be good," he groused.

"What?"

"Never mind. Going this way is out of the question." He began to steer her back into the tunnel when he became alert. "They're coming." He seized her and spoke in the Ancient, "Sleep!" Immediately she fell asleep into his arms. In a flash of white light, they vanished.

The exterior door flung open. The Shadow Warriors entered with swords drawn.

"We're too late!" swore Altari.

"We can track him or send the hunter-hawk after him." Witter indicated the circling bird.

Altari shook his head. "If he left with only the girl that means the boy is still secure. He'll be back, and we'll be waiting."

Chapter 7

ETHAN STOPPED UPON SPYING THE MANOR HOUSE. TRISTAN WAS at Ethan's shoulder. Dunham came alongside while the men gathered behind them.

A disconcerted expression appeared on Tristan's face. "What place is this?"

Ethan answered in a hushed, uneasy tone. "I don't know, but this is where the tracks lead."

Dunham clenched the neck of his tunic. His eyes narrowed in focus on the house. "Evil lives here."

"The Dark Way," Tristan swore under his breath. He tightened the grip on the hilt of his sword.

Dunham signaled to Hadwin, who in turn used hand signs to dispatch the men around the manor house. All had swords, daggers and bows ready. Hearing high-pitched screeching from overhead brought the deployment to a halt. The hunter-hawk appeared and circled the manor.

"By the heavenlies, what is that?" asked Hadwin.

"Nothing from heaven," said Dunham. "Keep to the trees until time to move."

Karryn recoiled in fear. Ethan caught her arm in support.

"Remain here when we move," he said.

"How am I safer here with that thing flying around and those beasts on the loose?"

He couldn't argue so he said, "Stay close to me."

The hunter-hawk disappeared from view.

"Now!" shouted Dunham.

They rushed the house from various directions. Dunham, Hadwin, Tristan, Ethan and Karryn entered through the unlocked front door. Inside the main room, wolf-men attacked them. Dunham aptly handled the beast he fought.

Ethan killed one with an arrow to the face. He wounded a second between the shoulder blades when it attacked Hadwin. The beast turned to deal with Ethan. Karryn's dagger struck hilt deep into its throat. It didn't make a sound when it fell. Confident the beast was dead she used both hands to jerk out the dagger.

A beast seized Tristan. It swung him around into Ethan's line of sight. Ethan barely reacted in time to shift his aim. The arrow ripped Tristan's sleeve in passing to strike the beast in the body. It released Tristan.

"Find Madelyn and Garrick!" Hadwin ordered the squires.

On the other side of the room, stairs led to different levels. "I'll go up, you go down!" said Ethan.

At the top of the stairs, Ethan made quick assessment of the hall with six doors, three on each side. He went to the closest room calling, "Maddy. Garrick?"

"Looking for someone?"

Ethan raised his bow in response to the question.

Magelen stood at the end of the hall. "Not polite to come into someone's home armed. Then again, you were not invited."

"Tell me where they are and I'll let you live."

"Arrogant knave!" Magelen seized the talisman and spoke in the Ancient, *"Teine!"*

Instantly, small flames appeared on the bow. Feeling the burn, Ethan dropped it. He reached for his sword. He felt the same burning upon touching the hilt.

Magelen spoke in the Ancient and flung his hand out at Ethan, *"Cuileag!"*

Ethan flew backwards off his feet. He tumbled down the stairs to the foyer floor. The impact rendered him unconscious.

Karryn rushed to him. "Ethan?" Fearful at lack of response, she grabbed him. "Please don't be dead. Ethan." He groaned then blinked before opening his eyes. "Thank Jor'el."

Dunham and Hadwin arrived to help examine Ethan for injury. "Where are you hurt?"

"Everywhere," Ethan replied with a grunt.

"Can you stand up?" asked Hadwin.

"I think so."

Karryn and Hadwin helped Ethan to his feet.

Dunham noticed Magelen at the top of the stairs. "What are you doing here, villain?"

"This is my home, and you are unwanted guests!" Magelen reached for his talisman.

Dunham pointed his sword at the Grand Master. "By Jor'el's power, don't touch it!"

Magelen flinched when his hand immediately fell from the talisman to his side. He tried to cover his reaction with an angry rebuke. "You presume to order me in my own home with some ancient threat?"

"Don't think for a moment I can't fulfill that threat, creature of darkness." Dunham revealed a medallion he wore tucked under the neck of his tunic. The figure was an eagle with wings up. Its talons held a crown with a sword through the center.

Surprised recognition passed over Magelen's face before meeting Dunham's intense glare. Magelen tried to regain his composure. "You have overstayed your welcome, my lord Dunham."

Witter and Altari arrived with their swords drawn.

"*Sguir!*" Dunham commanded in the Ancient.

The Warriors' eyes narrowed in angry regard of his medallion, as they were compelled to obey.

"Commander Witter!" insisted Magelen.

The Warrior's taut features showed his fury at the inability to respond.

Dunham quelled a rueful smile to address Magelen. "Where are my children?"

By now, Magelen regained his composure. "I don't know. Have you misplaced them?"

"I know they came here, my lord," said Ethan.

"Take your mistaken squire and leave or I will report this unwarranted invasion to the King!" When Dunham hesitated, "Commander!" Magelen again shouted at Witter.

Armed with both daggers, Karryn stepped beside Dunham to make defense. Neither Witter nor Altari moved. The Warriors continued to stare at Dunham's medallion.

Dunham tucked the medallion back under his collar. He touched her shoulder. "We're leaving."

"My lord—" began Ethan in protest. He stopped when Dunham grabbed his arm, which made him flinch in pain.

"Karryn, help me with Ethan," said Dunham.

Hadwin kept his sword ready to insure safe withdrawal.

Magelen quickly descended to the threshold. He hissed with anger at the Warriors before accosting Dunham. "Wait! Where is your other meddlesome squire?"

Dunham paused long enough to answer. "With my men. He became injured earlier."

To the reply, Ethan curbed a smile.

Magelen slammed the door shut.

In the cellar, Tristan cautiously moved along the corridor. He heard animal noises behind closed doors. He resisted the desire to investigate by focusing his attention on finding Garrick. However, it became increasingly hard to ignore whimpering animal sounds or unfamiliar pitiful cries.

Near a hall window, he heard Hadwin call for retreat. Why would he do that? Had Ethan found Maddy and Garrick? Tristan began to head back when Magelen shouted his question about the other *meddlesome squire* and Dunham replied. By the exchange, he understood they had been discovered. It would be up to him to find Maddy and Garrick.

Turning from the window, Tristan spied an open door from which came more noises. This time, he didn't resist. He entered. Two canines were chained to the far wall. One growled at him, the other remained lying on the floor whimpering. At hearing human groans, Tristan stepped further into the room. To his left stood a cage. He froze in horror at the sight of what appeared to be a man with some canine features, yet not fully like the beasts that attacked them.

The man/beast lurched forward in the cage. It thrust a hand through the bars to seize Tristan. In retreat, Tristan fell into the table, which caused the iron fetters to rattle. The growling canine charged him, only to be jerked back by the chain. In a panic, Tristan hurried from the room and slammed the door closed. He held onto the handle to catch his breath in hopes of stilling his racing heart.

"Surely this place is cursed," he murmured, unnerved.

A screech startled him. He listened to more screeching. It didn't sound like any bird he recognized. When the noise faded, him heard sobbing and sniffling. Definitely mortal and close, perhaps in the next room. He approached the door to listen. Not only mortal, but also young.

"Garrick? Maddy?"

"Who's there?" said a small, quivering voice.

Tristan flashed a smile in recognizing Garrick's voice. "Tristan. Are you hurt?"

"Tristan!" the boy shouted.

Something hit the door from the other side. "*Shh!* Not so loud. I'll find a way to get you out."

"Hurry! It's cold and dark in here."

Tristan searched nearby for something to undo the lock. His stopped at the sound of running feet. He raised his sword for confrontation. To his befuddlement, a very tall man with a goatee wearing Dunham's uniform arrived. He didn't recognize the man. "Who are you?"

"Someone who wants to help. I was told the boy is down here."

"Tristan?" called Garrick, fearfully.

He didn't immediately answer. He stared into a pair of silver eyes somehow comforting and strengthening at the same time. "The door is locked."

Avatar smiled. "I'll take care of it." He knelt to shield the lock from Tristan's view. He muttered under his breath and pretended to fiddle with the lock. Click. "It's unlocked now."

"How did you do that?"

"A little trick I picked up over the years." Avatar opened the cell door.

Trembling and sobbing, Garrick rushed out to embrace Tristan.

"Easy. We still have to find Maddy."

"The lady is safe," said Avatar. At the sound of commotion outside, he urged Tristan and Garrick in the opposite direction of the stairs. "Quickly."

"The stairs are that way," insisted Tristan.

"There is another way out, one less guarded. Take a right at the next corridor."

The corridor ended. "Now where?" asked Tristan.

"That door." Avatar pointed, then turned around at more noise. "Hurry! Inside." Once they were in, he shut and barred the door with a heavy beam that would normally take two men to lift. He took a deep breath at the effort required to brace the door.

Shafts of light filtered through the planks of the door. "It's a store room," said Tristan.

"Root cellar to be exact." Avatar put up a hand for caution before mounting the three wooden steps to the cellar door. He paused to regard Garrick's unnerved state. The terror in the boy's eyes went deep while his whole body trembled uncontrollably. "You'll have to help him, so put up your sword," he said to Tristan concerning Garrick. "When I open the door, run for the woods and immediately turn south. There is a cove where you will find the lady waiting. Continue south until you're out of the forest."

"What about you?"

"Never mind about me." Again Avatar glanced with compassionate at Garrick before speaking to Tristan, "Get ready." He opened the door and lifted Garrick outside. "Go!" he urged Tristan.

Frightened beyond measure, Garrick didn't move. Tristan snatched Garrick's and practically dragged him away.

When the bird caught sight of the mortals, Avatar drew his sword. He stepped out into the open intent on getting the creature's attention when …

"Going somewhere?"

Avatar whirled around to face Witter and Altari. He cracked a smile of bravado. He rose to his full height of seven and half feet. "I wondered if you two had gone into hiding."

"Your arrogance will finally be your downfall," chided Altari.

A twinge of regret passed over Avatar's face. "I once felt pity when I saw you being tortured. Not, now, not after betraying Kell!"

"Kell cast me aside in favor of you!" Altari launched at Avatar.

Sparks flew when their swords met. Avatar slipped, unable to hold his ground. He stumbled backwards. Altari charged. Avatar parried the attack. He struck Altari in the back of the shoulders with the hilt of his sword. The Shadow Warrior went sprawling to the ground. Again, Avatar had to catch his breath at the effort it took to do battle. Witter attacked. Avatar barely maintained his balance in the exchange of heavy blows.

Altari recovered to join Witter and advanced on Avatar. The diving bird made them break apart. Not good, Shadow Warriors and a creature. Normally that wouldn't be a concern, but something affected his strength and abilities. He had one option to avoid more trouble. He vanished in dimension travel.

Tristan and Garrick continued in the direction Avatar indicated. Tristan wasn't sure how far to the cove but determined to get Garrick to safety and find Maddy. He glanced over his shoulder. No pursuit came from the house. After another two hundred yards he spotted a clearing. Could that be the cove? He hoped so. He nudged Garrick forward then slowed to look over his shoulder again. This time he wondered about the soldier. Tristan turned at hearing Garrick yelp and a female cry out.

Maddy appeared. "Garrick!" He clung to her and wept. She also shed tears of relief.

Tristan rushed over. He touched her shoulder to get her attention. His eyes filled with tender concern. "Maddy? Are you hurt?"

"No, thanks to one of father's men. He went back to fetch Garrick."

"Ay. He helped us." Tristan looked toward the manor house. "I thought he was right behind me."

Garrick continued to sob.

"We can't stay here and wait." Tristan went to take Garrick's hand. The boy balked, unwilling to let go of Maddy.

"I'll help him," she said quietly to Tristan.

"We must move quickly. Do you understand, Garrick?"

The boy nodded, his cheeks wet with tears.

Tristan pointed south. "Continue going straight and don't change course. I'm sure Sir Dunham didn't go far and is waiting for word from me. I'll be right behind you."

Garrick proved clumsy in step for clinging to Maddy with both hands. She tried to encourage him. "We must make haste to find Father." She moved from his grasp to hold his hand.

<hr />

When Avatar reappeared, he fell to his knees in exhaustion. After taking a few deep breaths for recovery, he noticed the trees. He remained in the forest. Why hadn't he gone further in his travel? And why did he feel so weak? He hadn't used his special power, just normal strength along with simple abilities for the rescue then to fight Witter and Altari. Of course, if Dorgirith is a source of power for the Dark Way that could account for his drain of energy. Logically, the further away he travelled from Dorgirith, the more his strength should return.

It took a moment to gauge direction. Perhaps the clearing to the southeast was the forest border. Upon standing, the weakness felt greater than he anticipated. He willed his legs to move.

At the clearing, the hideous bird dove at him. Avatar raised his sword in time to make defense. The bird veered off for another attack. Avatar looked for a place to either hide or made a stand. The clearing ended at an outcropping overlooking a meadow, which he reckoned to be the Southern Forest. Once in the meadow, he should be far enough to regain his strength and deal with the bird-creature.

He reached the outcropping when the bird attacked, and this time with talons outstretched. Avatar's foot slipped on rocks near the edge. He managed to land a blow that severed one talon. When it snapped at him in retaliation, he lost his balance. He caught himself on a boulder to keep from falling over the edge. An arrow flew past his head to impale the bird's body near one wing. Enraged, it stuck Avatar with its tail, sending him over the ledge. The same time Avatar fell, another arrow pierced the bird's throat and killed it.

Avatar didn't stop tumbling until he reached the bottom. He remained conscious while every inch of his body hurt. When hands grabbed him from behind, he jerked to resist. The hands proved persistent, and followed by a voice.

"Easy, Avatar."

He stared in dazed wonder at who held him. "Armus?"

"Ay." Armus smiled. He helped Avatar sit up.

"Nice of you to drop in for a visit." Wren knelt beside Avatar.

Avatar sent a sarcastic smirk to Wren. "I was handling it just fine until your shot made it angry and sent me falling!"

She snorted with irony. "A fine thank you for saving your life. I'll remember that next time a hunter-hawk attacks."

"Is that's what it's called? Never seen one before."

"One of Dagar and Magelen's latest creatures."

"Who is Magelen?"

Wren regarded Avatar with skepticism. "The mortal counterpart of Dagar who lives in Dorigirth."

"I didn't see him. I did encounter Witter and Altari during my mission," he chided.

"Is that why you changed uniforms? To facilitate your mission?" asked Armus.

Avatar glanced at the uniform he wore. He shrugged. "I hadn't noticed the change. Jor'el sent me in response to a prayer for help from a mortal female."

"Maddy," said Wren, hopeful. "Is she safe?"

"I believe so. I left her hidden before going back for the boy, her brother she said. Although I encountered another mortal, a soldier, I think. I got them out of the house and sent them to find her before encountering Witter and Altari. Fighting them, I noticed my strength waning. I made a quick exit only to confront that hunter-hawk creature."

"Reduced strength is part of our punishment," Wren groused.

"What punishment?" Avatar asked in confusion.

She looked incredulous. "You don't know about that either?"

"He's been in the heavenlies for a hundred and fifty years," Armus reminded her.

"A hundred and fifty years?" echoed Avatar with surprise. "The last thing I recall is being in the infirmary of Melwyn after the battle with Dagar."

"Much has happened since then. Can you stand? We should be leaving."

"I think so." Avatar had trouble getting to his feet so Armus helped him. Once standing, his legs trembled. He grabbed onto Armus to remain standing. "Why should this punishment rob us of our strength and abilities that I feel so weak? I did a simple dimension travel then battled a few malcontents."

"Come, let's find a place for you to rest and we'll explain." Armus held onto Avatar as they crossed the meadow to a sheltered grove.

Feeling Avatar's weight grow due to fatigue, Armus allowed him to sit on log. Avatar appeared slightly pale.

Wren reached into her pouch. "I'll mix a strengthening tonic to help your recovery."

"I'd rather have an explanation."

"You'll get both." Armus sat beside Avatar. "Because of Dagar's rebellion, Jor'el punished us with banishment from Allon. Well, all but twelve of us. You were taken from the infirmary back to the heavenlies in the recall. Those of us who remain are reduced to half-strength, and forced to watch in obscurity. We can only aid those of the remnant when allowed to do so. You're coming is the first help sent from the heavenlies in all these years."

"I know where I've been, I just didn't know why or for how long. Who remains?"

"Valmar watches the Highlands, Gresham in Midessex, Mona, the North Plains, Zinna, the South Plains, Wren, the Southern Forest, Barnum, the Northern Forest, Jedrek, the Delta, Eldric, the Lowlands. Chase is still the West Coast, with Priscilla in the East. I watch the Meadowlands and Kell the Region of Sanctuary."

"Witter and Altari remain."

"As do most of the Shadow Warriors."

Avatar took the cup Wren offered. He grimaced when finished with the tonic. "That's awful."

"Don't complain to me. It's one of Eldric's remedies," she said of the prime Guardian physician. She took back the cup.

Avatar continued to question Armus. "What are Shadow Warriors?"

"Don't you remember my encounter with Tor in the Northern Forest? I told him he had become nothing but a shadow warrior for following Dagar, lurking in caves and hiding in shadows to attack." Armus shrugged. "The denouncement seems to have stuck for a name. In fact, Tor used it to call his troops during the final assault."

"Ah, now I remember."

"Good, because I wondered if senility set in during your lengthy holiday," she said.

Avatar huffed with sarcasm in turning from Wren to Armus. "I see her attitude hasn't changed."

"Without you as a counter, she's gotten worse. Why do you think Kell has her in the wilderness by herself?" said Armus in matching humor.

"Because neither of you can match her wit."

Armus heartily laughed, much to Wren's chagrin.

"We're wasting time. Let's see if Maddy and Garrick are safe," she chided.

"If you are allowed to remain, you need to speak to Kell." Armus grinned in his survey of Avatar. "Of course, a change of uniform is in order."

"If she hasn't poisoned me so I can make the change."

"One more remark like that and I will," she retorted.

Armus chuckled. "I've not exhausted my powers or drunk her concoction." He placed a hand on Avatar's shoulder and spoke in the Ancient; *"Laoch aodach."* The brown and gold livery changed into the Guardian warrior uniform identical to what Armus wore. "That's better. Now let's see if they made it out safely."

Angry, Magelen accosted the Shadow Warriors upon their return to the manor. "Well?"

"Gone," said Witter.

"Dispatched?"

The Warriors exchanged wary glances before Altari replied, "No, he vanished in dimension travel while the mortals escaped."

Magelen was irate. "Why haven't you gone after them?"

"The hunter-hawk will deal with Avatar. To pursue the mortals is unwise."

Magelen continued his hot argument. "We've been discovered! Dagar will not be pleased when learning a Guardian helped them escape."

"Avatar's arrival was unexpected. The mortals killed the madah-dune."

"How? That should not be possible."

"They are creatures, not immortal, thus can be killed," said Witter.

"Besides, it was your idea to capture the children to use against Sir Dunham. We suggested the madah-dune kill them. All of this could have been avoided," chided Altari.

Magelen's great agitation turned to suspicion. "So, you didn't pursue them to make me look incompetent to Dagar?"

"No! By Avatar's arrival, we don't know if there are more Guardians nearby. We may have driven him off, or he could be a scout with Kell and others laying a trap using him for a lure. It isn't worth the risk for two mortal children."

Magelen fiercely snarled. "His intervention is most disturbing. Dagar is right, something uneasy stirs." A small smile crossed his lips. "Perhaps I can convince him that this failure may actually prove useful."

"How?" Witter asked.

"By exposing the return of the Guardians. What began as mere childhood mischief, actually unmasked the enemy's movements. Come. We return to Ravendale."

Chapter 8

DUNHAM, HADWIN, KARRYN AND THE OTHERS HEADED SOUTH toward the border of Dorgirith. Ethan lagged behind, occasionally watching for signs of Tristan. Frustrated, he finally spoke.

"My lord, aren't we going to wait?"

"No."

"We can't just leave!"

"Do you think I want to leave without my children? We have no choice. If we linger, Magelen will grow suspicious and use his powers against us. How will that help them?"

"Let me go back—"

Dunham seized Ethan to prevent departure. "I understand your loyalty to Tristan, but it is too risky for everyone."

Ethan stiffened with alarm. His head turned about to spy activity in the trees. "Something moves!" he said in warning. "Everyone be still." He crouched with Dunham beside him. The men also took cover.

"What is it?" Dunham whispered in Ethan's ear.

Instead of answering directly, Ethan cupped his hands over his mouth. He made an animal call. The movement stopped, shortly followed by an answering call. Ethan made the call again. Another reply. Ethan smiled at Dunham. "Tristan." He stood and waved.

Dunham's breath caught in this throat. "Maddy. Garrick!" With open arms, he embraced his children. "Thank Jor'el!"

"We must not linger, my lord," urged Hadwin.

"Ay. Let's leave this cursed place." Dunham ushered his children forward.

They hurried from the forest to the campsite near the log. The sun was well past mid-day. Maddy bit her lip in concern, as she watched the soldiers gather the horses. "I don't see him."

"Neither do I," said Tristan.

"Who?" Dunham asked.

"The soldier who rescued me then went back for Garrick and Tristan."

"I didn't recognize him, though he wore your livery," said Tristan.

She grew fearful. "Has he fallen?"

Dunham did a head count. "No, my men are accounted for."

"All?" Tristan did his own observance of the soldiers.

"Hadwin. These men are all who accompanied us, correct?"

"Ay, my lord."

"Any new recruits?"

"No, my lord. Why?"

"There was another, Father," she insisted. "A very tall man with a beard and light eyes." She became thoughtful with recollection. "Unusual silver eyes, beautiful in color and appearance. He was kind, brave and made me feel safe."

Curious, Dunham studied Maddy during her description of the man. He gently took her by the arm to help her. "Mount your horse."

"But, Father."

"Mount," he kindly said. Once she was astride, he spoke privately to Tristan. "Stay with her."

"Are you concerned about this mysterious soldier?"

Dunham fought a smile and shook his head. "No, just keep watch. Magelen is crafty." He mounted his horse. He noticed Ethan move to ride beside Garrick. The boy sat on his pony, shying away from all eye contact while clenching the reins. Dunham moved to his horse to Garrick. "Are you ready to go home?" Garrick didn't look at him. He simply nodded.

At Garwood, Hadwin, Ethan and Tristan waited in Sir Dunham's private study. Most of the construction was done save for plaster work, painting and new furniture. Odd pieces of older furniture served for the time being. No one showed interest in the décor or construction.

Dunham entered. "Maddy is seeing to Garrick. He still hasn't spoken. Perhaps, he's fearful of my reaction. I'm just grateful they are alive."

"He may speak to Lady Madelyn after some rest." Hadwin tried to sound encouraging.

Dunham's dismay showed on his face and in his voice. "I've never seen such a frightened, vacant look in his eyes before. Even when their mother died he didn't look so unnerved. He cowered from Alger. He raised the dog from a pup and is his favorite of all the hounds. Why would he do that?"

"I believe I know why." Tristan spoke in unsettled tone.

Dunham observed the young man's affected features. "It disturbed you also."

Tristan gathered his emotions to speak. "I saw unimaginable horrors in the cellar where they put Garrick. The wolf-like creature that attacked us is the result of some unnatural experiments between men and wolves."

"You saw this?" asked Hadwin with some skepticism.

"Ay." Tristan again fought to maintain his composure. "I found Garrick in a room next to the one containing surgical instruments and vials. Two animals were chained, one wolf and one dog. Both showed signs of abuse." He paused due to the disturbing recollection. "In a cage, sat a beastly man. At least he possessed most of the features of a man, with skin and hands, but the face of a wolf. He lunged and tried to grab me through the bars. I backed away. That's when the chained wolf made for an attack. Fortunately, it couldn't reach me. I left as quickly as I could. After that is when I discovered Garrick in the next room."

Dunham listened with dread at the unmistakable implications. "You think Garrick saw what you did?"

"Very likely, for the door stood opened with most things in full view. I never felt such cold evil, horror and repulsion before, and I'm a grown man. The affect upon a boy—" Tristan stopped, unable to speak his opinion.

Shaken, Dunham sat. "He may never be right in mind again."

"I didn't say that, my lord!" insisted Tristan, stirred to compassion by Dunham's distress. "He may just need time to recover."

"I pray you're right." With renewed anxiety, Dunham asked, "What of Maddy? Did she see any of it?"

"I don't think so. She said they were separated."

Dunham relaxed with some relief.

"You found her in a cove?" asked Ethan.

"Ay, just like the soldier said. Actually, Garrick stumbled upon her."

"About this soldier," began Hadwin He stopped when Dunham chuckled. "My lord?"

"You won't find him. None of us will."

"Why do you say that?"

"Because I don't believe he is mortal."

"A Guardian," said Tristan with certainty. "I thought his appearance unusual. When I looked into his silver eyes, I felt the same peace Maddy spoke of, even to the point of trusting him without question."

"There haven't been Guardians in Allon for well over a century," refuted Hadwin.

Tristan sent Ethan a private gleeful look before replying to Hadwin. "That we know of."

"He's right," said Dunham. "I prayed for Jor'el to protect my children and He heard me. Surely, this is a sign our plan will succeed."

"Isn't that jumping to conclusions?" asked Hadwin.

"No," said Dunham, his excitement growing. "I thought Garrick running off would cause another unnecessary delay. Now I see it brings a good omen."

Hadwin didn't appear convinced. "My lord, I don't wish dispute you, but the others may not be so agreeable. Total success is dependent upon their help. Some may view this incident as a reason to abort the plan."

"Abort? I think not. Although I will not bring Maddy, as the king requested."

"When did he make such a request?" asked Tristan.

"In a dispatch I received yesterday before all this happened. For some reason he made a pointed request for Maddy's presence. Not now, not with Garrick so traumatized. Nor would I ever consider bringing her to Ravendale."

"The king probably sent the request due to prompting. Magelen may have discovered the plan, or at least gotten wind of it and means ill for the lady," Hadwin spoke with emphasis.

"Which is why I won't bring her," said Dunham stoutly.

"He could have done her harm in Dorgirith," said Ethan.

Dunham grinned. "Divine intervention stopped him."

Hadwin continued his objections. "What about the venison? No one saw who brought it, though Lady Madelyn claims the woman from the forest did. She could have lured Master Garrick to Magelen."

"My dear Hadwin, you are seeing trouble where I don't believe any exists. This woman has helped my children on several occasions. Why suddenly turn against them?"

"To gain their trust. Magelen knows what influence you have over the other lords. This summons was *not* sent without a purpose."

"No, indeed. Not after capturing Lord Razi to silence him!" chided Tristan.

Dunham placed a hand on Tristan's shoulder in a calming signal. He spoke to Hadwin. "I am well aware of royal suspicion. However, Ram is old and feeble. To stop Magelen and the Dark Way from seizing total control through Ramsey, now is the time to act. I will not back down!"

"The cost could be great. Remember your father's friendship with the Vicar cost his life!" Hadwin spoke in firm challenge.

"What?" Tristan asked only ignored, as Dunham confronted Hadwin.

"Do not speak to me of my father! If you have objections to my decision you can consider yourself discharged."

The declaration stunned Hadwin, Ethan and Tristan.

90

The master-at-arms stuttered in reply. "My lord, you misunderstand. I would be remiss in my duty not to speak my mind when I believe an act could be harmful or detrimental to you and your family."

"My lord, in the past you have tolerated objection without such a vehement reaction," said Ethan.

Dunham's rigid gaze shifted from Ethan to Hadwin, where it lingered a moment. His focus then moved to Tristan. The young man appeared visibly concerned. Tristan's reaction helped Dunham regain his composure and speak with more control. "Perhaps, I reacted in haste. Yet, understand, I will follow through with or without your approval," he said pointedly to Hadwin.

"Ay, my lord."

"How long to prepare for departure?"

"Two days at least."

"Then make haste."

"You would leave your children vulnerable?"

"Of course not, man!" Dunham's temper flared again at Hadwin's question. "They will stay at the Fortress until all is over. Perhaps Master Reagan can help Garrick recover. We'll see them situated on the way. Now, go." He made a curt wave of dismissal.

"My lord?" said Tristan with prompting.

Dunham's regard turned sympathetic yet he waited for Hadwin to depart. "Ethan, shut the door." He then spoke to Tristan. "There are things I neglected to tell you."

"Indeed! I knew our families were close but not to such an extent."

"Other families are also close. Karryn's family for example."

"Karryn?" echoed Tristan, surprised by shift in focus.

"It's obvious she's not the governess he claimed," said Ethan.

Dunham chuckled. "No, rather the result of an impromptu plan after my wife's sudden death. With Joan alive, I was certain of things at home, of confidences and safety. Not so with Maddy. She is inexperienced and naïve. Thus I sought a person I could trust, who possessed certain capabilities and the wherewithal to use them if needed. Karryn is that person. Fortunately, she and Renfrow agreed."

"Renfrow's daughter. Little freckled-faced, pigtailed Karryn," Ethan mused, more to himself than anyone.

Dunham heard and laughed. "No longer little, freckled or wearing pigtails."

"I knew her name sounded familiar, only I dare not believe—" Ethan's voice trailed off.

"You know her?" asked Tristan.

"So do you. Although you were seven when she and her father visited your grandfather," said Ethan with discretion.

"How old was she?"

"Ten."

Still befuddled, Tristan shook his head. "Since she is Renfrow's daughter why haven't we seen her since then? The baron has been here or at Dunlap a number of times."

"Our meetings are usually in secret, so he never brought her," began Dunham. "You have only journeyed twice to the North Plains, with the last time being eight years ago. As squires, duties don't allow you to venture inside another manor without permission. Still, you may have caught sight of her without realizing it."

Ethan again spoke under his breath. "So changed from a girl into a woman that I didn't recognize her."

"Who? Karryn?" asked Tristan.

Ethan waved off Tristan to address Dunham "She avoided answering Lady Madelyn's questions at Dorgirith. What about now?"

"She will say enough to satisfy. Her discreet, silence nature is one of her greatest attributes." Dunham's grin faded into sullenness. "In the meantime, I hope they can get Garrick to speak. Attend me later."

"My lord, what about my family?" asked Tristan.

The disagreeable frown showed Dunham was no longer in the mood to speak. Ethan guided Tristan from the study.

Upstairs, Garrick curled up on his bed clutching a pillow as he slept. Maddy couldn't blame him after what happened. The whole situation proved frightening and disconcerting. Still, his behavior troubled her. Since being reunited in the forest, he hadn't spoken a word. He nodded when addressed while his forlorn expression and lack of speech worried her. By nature he was talkative, even obstinate. His horrified reaction to Alger surprised everyone. Karryn and Floyd, the butler, tried to aid Maddy. Before falling sleep, Garrick would not even answer simple questions and avoided eye contact.

"Get some rest. We'll stay with him." Karryn spoke to Maddy in a tone not to disturb Garrick.

"No, I'll remain. I've never seen him like this, terrified into silence."

"Sight of those creatures is enough for an adult."

Maddy cast a glance up and down at Karryn. "You too are a sight. Why didn't you tell me you could handle a weapon?"

Karryn shrugged. "There isn't much to tell."

Maddy grew incredulous. "You dress like man and are lethal with a dagger. How is that not much to tell?" Since her volume rose, Karryn placed a finger to her lips for silence and motioned to the sleeping Garrick. Maddy drew Karryn away from the bed. "Answer me, where did you learn such skill?"

"My father taught me how to defend myself."

Maddy scowled with frustration. "Can you not speak more than one sentence at a time even when an explanation is due?" For a moment Karryn stared at her. Those hazel eyes reflected a self-containment Maddy admired, along with a prudent gleam she found frustrating. "Karryn?"

"The lessons you need are domestic not martial."

"Oh!" Maddy stomped her foot. "What a vexing companion you are with your carefully worded answers! At least Ethan deals forthrightly with Tristan."

"I'm sorry my soft-spoken nature displeases you."

"Not soft-spoken rather guarded, even secretive."

Karryn offered no answer, which increased Maddy's vexation.

"Even when scolded you make no defense or appear put out. Have you no feelings at all?"

Pricked, Karryn withdrew from Maddy.

"I'm sorry; I didn't mean to wound you." Met with more silence, Maddy moved to stand in front of Karryn to get attention. Misty eyed, Karryn avoided looking at her. This deepened Maddy's remorse. "Truly, I am sorry. I spoke rashly. The whole situation is disturbing. Please, forgive me. I don't think you are unfeeling."

Karryn wiped the tears from her face.

"Ah!" screamed Garrick and bolted up in bed.

Maddy rushed to him. He trembled with terror while his breath labored. "Garrick, easy! You are home. All is well." She tried to calm him by holding him and speaking soothing words.

Hearing a dog whimpering at the door, Garrick pulled away from her. He drew his knees to his chest and buried his head.

"It's only Alger, young master," said Floyd.

Garrick wildly shook his head.

"Alger won't hurt you," said Maddy. Garrick kept shaking his head. "Very well. Floyd, take Alger to the kennel," she said. After the butler left, she returned her attention to Garrick. "I had cook send up your favorite treat, gingerbread and some tea. The tea might be cool by now. I can send Karryn for another pot."

Garrick just shrugged.

Karryn fetched the plate of gingerbread from a side table to give Maddy. Garrick didn't take the plate, so she went to feed him. At first he resisted.

"I know you're not a child, but you must eat something."

He flinched in fright when the door opened, then relaxed at seeing Dunham.

"Eating, I see. A good sign," said Dunham with a kind smile.

94

"Not yet. He's being stubborn, as usual." Maddy tried to be humorous. Garrick huffed and lay back down, clinging to his pillow. "Garrick," she began in apology.

Dunham touched her arm to motion her away. "I gather he's said nothing."

"No. I had Floyd take Alger to the kennel. He kept whimpering to come back in, only Garrick is too afraid."

"Tristan believes Garrick's rejection to Alger is because of the wolf-men. I think he is right."

"Oh, I hadn't thought of that. Poor Alger won't understand."

"The dog is the least of our worries. Shortly we must leave for Ravendale. I can't put it off any longer. You, Karryn and Garrick will stay at the Fortress until our return."

"Why? Garrick is scared enough and he's comfortable here."

"This has nothing to do with his comfort, rather safety. Perhaps Master Reagan can help restore his spirit."

"I can do that. I was just about to get him to eat when you arrived."

Dunham spoke with gentle reassurance. "This is not a dispute concerning your care, merely precaution."

"Who will oversee the construction while we are gone?"

"I trust Marlow. No more arguments. We leave in two days."

"Two days? No, Father!"

"I said no argument." His voice started to rise. He lowered it after casting a concern look toward the bed. "You must heed me in this, for both your sakes." He encouraged her to observe Garrick. "In the meantime, see if you can get him to eat and talk."

"I'll try," she said with reluctant submission.

With a last sympathetic glance at his son, Dunham left.

Maddy managed to coax Garrick into eating half of the gingerbread without assistance. However, speech was not forthcoming. When Floyd returned, Maddy and Karryn tried to leave. Garrick became agitated so they remained.

Maddy thought going to the Fortress was totally unnecessary. After all, much had been made of her being mistress. This would to be the first time Dunham left her in charge. What better way to prove her capability than during a crisis? The problem was convincing her father. Usually she enlisted the help of her mother or maid or ... she smiled, *Tristan*. Ay, he could speak to Dunham in ways she could not. At first opportunity, she would seek him out and enlist his help.

Chapter 9

TRISTAN SAT ON A TACK BOX IN THE STABLE TENDING TO THE harness. After the argument between Hadwin and Dunham, he needed work to calm his agitated mind. He knew of the friendship between his family and Sir Dunham's family, but not such extreme circumstances. His presence at Garwood posed danger to Dunham, Maddy and Garrick. He always knew of some risk. However being young and shielded, the reality of how dangerous felt abstract. Since his grandfather's capture, the formulating of the plan and the harrowing experiences of Dorgirith, the abstract became reality. The conversation made him grapple with the possible cost.

Dunham's staunch resolution to continue with the plan, helped to lift Tristan's spirit. Like his father and grandfather, Dunham proved to be a man of deep conviction. In Dorgirith, he stared in the face of evil and did not yield. Tristan faced the same challenge. He too felt a strong desire to defeat evil in protection of the innocent.

Deep in thought as he polished a saddle, he didn't realize someone had arrived. At the clearing of the throat, he noticed Maddy. Though now clean and wearing a day dress, her expression showed distress. Not good after what just happened. Tristan set the saddle aside to stand.

"Is something wrong?" he asked.

"Father says Garrick and I are to be installed at the Fortress while you are away to Ravendale."

He grinned in relief, thinking it might be more serious. "That's right."

"Why?"

Tristan pursed his lips with consideration. He knew she hadn't been informed of the plan, thus searched for an answer. "I'm sure he gave you a reason."

"He said it is best for Garrick. I argued how I can take care of Garrick here. It's unnecessary to go to the Fortress. Father didn't agree."

Tristan put up a saddle to stall a reply, as he once again considered his words. With the situation tenuous, he must be careful. "If your father insists, who am I to dispute him?"

"Oh, stop treating me like a child!" Maddy chided.

"I didn't mean to. It's not my place to contradict your father. In fact, I support him where your welfare is concerned."

Maddy fought to contain her annoyance. "I appreciate that more I can say, but I'm tired of being treated like a little girl. I'm the lady of the manor. It is my right to know!"

Tristan swallowed back his anger at her demanding tone. However, when she glared indignantly at him, he spoke in rebuke. "This is an argument you should have with your father not me." He started to walk past her to exit the stables when she grabbed him.

"I want to know and I want you to tell me!"

Her newfound independence grew irksome. However, he couldn't blame her. They were withholding information, thus he tempered his words. "I'm not at liberty to discuss it."

Her tone changed from frustration to entreaty. "Please, Tristan! Can't you see how difficult this is for me? I need your help."

Her plea softened his expression into a smile. "You've always had my help, Maddy."

"Along with your affection?"

To this question, Tristan grew awkward. He couldn't deny he feared for her safety, nor his relief at finding her alive. Although growing up together the last ten years, they never expressed affection. He fumbled over his words. "That would be presumptuous of me to say." He immediately regretted his reply when she winced with dismay.

"At least your friendship?"

He widely smiled at the chance to quell her concern. "Of course."

"Then for friendship, please tell me what is happening?"

So soft and tender was her regard of him that his inability to respond gnawed at him. "For your sake, as well as my duty to your father, I cannot." He gently touched her cheek.

With angry disappointment, she slapped away his hand. "How cruel you are to toy with my affections then deny me!" She marched from the stable.

"Maddy!" Tristan rushed after her. He dodged construction and preparations for departure. He finally caught her in the yard busy with the activity.

Pride wounded, she jerked away. "Lady Madelyn to you, squire!"

Tristan's jowls flexed at the rebuke done in the open for all to see. "My lady. Forgive my impertinence." He bowed. She continued her trek to the house.

Ethan sat on a nearby bench tending his bow in pretense of not observing. His chuckle gave him away. Tristan slapped the bow in passing back to the stable and said, "If you ever hear me say I like her, shoot me!"

Ethan followed. "Actually, it would be one of the smartest things you ever said, not to mention the waste a good arrow."

"What?" Tristan kept walking even when Ethan drew alongside him. "Oh, what do you know about women anyway? You can hardly engage one in conversation without tripping over your tongue with ill humor."

Offended, Ethan grabbed Tristan. "Because I'm so concerned for your welfare that I don't even attempt to win a lady's affection! Who else would look after your ungrateful hide?" He stormed off.

The unusual rebuke stunned Tristan. He hurried to catch his friend. "Ethan, I'm sorry. I don't know why I lashed out. You are a true and loyal friend."

Ethan drew Tristan a short distance from the construction to speak privately. "In many ways our age difference is hardly noticeable, mostly because people don't think I look my age. However, I am older by seven years. Sometimes you forget that. Though in fairness, I sometimes I forget who is the master because of our familiarity."

"I'm not your master."

He looked Tristan squarely in the eye. "You have been my charge for a dozen years. Marriage would interfere with my duty."

"I don't want you to give up any part of your life. If there is someone you fancy, let me know and I will discharge you."

Ethan flashed a wry grin. "Only one person can discharge me from my duty, and it isn't *you*. So until he does, you're stuck with me."

"If for some reason he does, will you still be my friend?" asked Tristan with a goading smile.

Ethan wrapped Tristan in a semi-head lock. "Till my dying day, married or not."

"Is there a woman you fancy?"

Ethan released Tristan. "Once when I was nineteen, I thought—" He waved it aside. "Too many years to speak of it. As for you, maybe I should use an arrow to make you think twice about Madelyn."

"Hah! You'd have to lace the tip with hemlock."

"Unlike a poisoned arrow, it wouldn't kill you to admit you have feelings for her. That is where I failed." Ethan droned the last sentence then shook off his dreary mood at Tristan's interest. "Don't make the same mistake I did and keep your passion hidden. Nor deny it! I saw your reaction when she was in danger. How you watched over her as she slept."

Tristan sighed in resignation. He sat on a pile of bricks. "Maybe. I just feel similar in respect to marriage."

"That you're as dedicated to my welfare?" asked Ethan with confusion.

"No, that it would interfere with duty." When Ethan pretended to be distressed, Tristan added, "Naturally I'm concerned for your well being. As long as Grandpapi is a prisoner and Magelen wields his power, I can't consider marriage. After Dorgirith, I feel more strongly that this plan must succeed!" Passionate determination filled his voice.

Ethan sat beside Tristan to speak with discretion. "I would do anything to free *him*. I couldn't be more grateful to any man. I would still be wandering the woods with no hope of a future if he hadn't found me and took me in."

"I was only four but I remember you were quite a sight, wild and unkempt. A bit frightening, actually. Also much quieter."

Ethan shrugged. "Life was too hard to talk much. Mother did what she could to raise me after Father died. When she passed, an eleven year old on his own in the woods doesn't have much of a future." He grew reflective in speech. "Even though I had been with your family for several years, I didn't understand what your grandfather meant when he placed you in my charge, saying it was the best for both of us. Now I do. It was no accident he found me. Nor has anything happened that wasn't meant to happen." He gazed directly at Tristan. "If we purpose to do something, it's because we were meant to do it."

Tristan contemplated Ethan's statement. "You think we're part of prophecy?"

"I won't go so far as to presume. Not everyone who follows Jor'el is part of prophecy. If we are faithful, the Almighty will direct our paths. Sir Dunham believes Jor'el has done so by way of this supposed Guardian."

Tristan cocked a teasing grin. "I think that's the longest, most coherent, non-humorous statement I've ever heard you speak."

Ethan laughed. "When you admit you like Madelyn then I can say the same about you."

"Tristan! Tristan!" called Dunham. He didn't sound pleased.

"I think the lady has complained," said Ethan. They came attention when Dunham arrived.

"I was about to respond to your summons, my lord," said Tristan.

Dunham cleared his throat then tossed a glance over his shoulder. Maddy stood twenty yards away, looking smug and determined. Dunham cleared his throat again to get their attention. He turned his back to Maddy. He spoke in low voice that did not matching his stern expression.

"I'm supposed to be giving you a piece of my mind for a public display of impertinence, yet I learned you disclosed nothing."

"Ay, my lord," said Tristan, displaying some relief.

"Keep to attention." Dunham shifted warning eyes over his shoulder at Maddy.

Tristan resisted the impulse to look at her.

Dunham resumed in a low voice. "We both seek to protect her, only I'm beginning to wonder just how long we can, and *should*, maintain our confidence."

Tristan became curious and concerned. "My lord?"

"If what I have suspected for sometime is true, and you both have feelings for the other, now would be the time to disclose your past."

Tristan showed genuine surprise. "To Maddy?"

"Lady Madelyn!" Dunham shouted for effect.

Tristan snatched a glance to see her watching them. "My lord," he began in objection, only stopped when Dunham raised a hand.

"Are you going to tell me my suspicions are not true?"

A squeak of laughter escaped Ethan's tightly pressed lips.

"That you don't act upon your feelings for my daughter and in her best interest?"

To this Ethan coughed a guffaw to one side.

"Ethan!" chided Tristan out of the corner of his mouth.

"Why scold your friend when the truth is so obvious?"

"I dare not presume, my lord," Tristan replied in a private voice.

Dunham leaned closer, as if making a stern point when poking Tristan in the chest. "The title is mutual, remember?"

"I have grown to respect you. For that reason, I have withheld my affection rather than trespass upon your good graces and friendship."

"Well said. I believe it is time." Dunham resumed his raised his voice. "Both of you be in my study immediately after supper!"

"Ay, my lord," the spoke in unison.

Tristan and Ethan bowed. They watched Dunham approach Maddy to say, "I made it clear. All will be settled after supper." He steered her away from the squires.

Ethan could no longer contain his humor. He laughed so hard he had to sit in an effort to catch his breath.

Tristan took exception to Ethan's amusement. "It's not funny! What if telling her she changes her mind about me?"

"She likes a lowly squire. Why should learning the truth change her feelings?"

"I don't know!" huffed Tristan. He sat. "I guess I'm not certain this is the right time. I'd rather wait until after we succeed and I take my place."

Ethan let his humor subside. "By then it may be too late. We don't know what the future holds, so why put it off? Would she worry less? I don't think so. At least telling her now can erase all doubts and barriers."

"What you say makes sense. I'm just uncertain."

"You mean petrified about a woman finding out how you feel."

Tristan's frustration came out in challenging questions. "What about your admitted failure? Would you tell the woman you cared about your long held secret?"

Ethan took a contemplative pause before answering. "Ay. There is uncertainty on all sides. At least I would have an answer rather than wondering what could have been if I acted bolder back then." He patted Tristan's leg. A large smile appeared. "I don't have to waste an arrow. Sir Dunham hit the target for me." He left.

Dunham insisted his squires and Hadwin join them at dinner. Garrick kept to his room with Floyd in attendance. A formal dinner required better clothes than a squire's uniform. Both Ethan and Tristan cut dashing figures in finer, noble suits. Maddy and Karryn wore evening gowns with pampered hair and headpieces. Maddy and Dunham sat at the opposite heads of the table. Hadwin and Karryn sat to Dunham's right, with Tristan and Ethan on his left. Topics of conversation remained light, mostly about construction or the hunting season. They avoided Dorgirith or the upcoming journey. Dunham kept it going with his usual cordial manner, made easier by Ethan's wit.

Despite his difficult upbringing, the keen woodsman enjoyed life. Tristan admired Ethan's unquenchable spirit while observing his friend's behavior at dinner. Ethan kept looking across to Karryn, paying her particular attention in conversation. She responded by laughing at his humor with an occasional witty retort of her own. Tristan found himself smiling at their exchange, more for Ethan playing the part of a gallant. He recalled their earlier conversation where Ethan confessed *it wouldn't kill you to admit you have feelings for her. That is where I failed.* Then followed by Ethan's later answer *At least I would have an answer rather than wondering what could have been if I acted bolder back then.*

Back then, Tristan's mind echoed. *Karryn!* Now, it all made sense. Ethan prompted him to speak his heart to Maddy due to his reaction at realizing Karryn's identity as the girl to whom he failed to confess his heart years earlier. True, he suppressed his feelings under the circumstances, similar to what Ethan did. Unlike Ethan and Karryn, whose meeting was infrequent—*infrequent?* Karryn arrived six months ago. Ethan didn't recognize her, at least not enough to speak with confidence. He did with Maddy. Their relationship grew over time into a steady attachment, not a realization of being reunited. Tristan couldn't imagine not seeing Maddy for any extended period of time.

Tristan's gaze lingered on Maddy when she laughed at something Ethan said. At that moment, she wasn't a girl, or even a young maid rather lady of the manor. Catching her eye, Tristan raised his tankard in a gesture of salute before drinking. She deeply blushed in returning his smile. Her reaction made him reconsider Dunham's planned discussion for later. It may be the right time. Still, a sense of doubt, or more rightly, apprehension gnawed at his brain.

After dining, they retired to the study. Dunham, Maddy and Karryn sat while Hadwin, Ethan and Tristan remained standing. Being a formal occasion, they observed protocol.

"A fine meal," said Dunham

"Indeed, my lord," agreed Hadwin.

Tristan watched Hadwin. He might have been agreeable to informing Maddy, but not Hadwin. The master-at-arms acted faithful in most of his duties. However, he recently expressed harsh feelings about the plan, along with his dismissive attitude regarding Guardians. Tristan sent a caution glance to Dunham in regard to Hadwin. Dunham understood.

"Hadwin. Have the preparations for departure been completed?"

"All save the last minute matters, my lord."

"See they are finished tonight. I want no disruptions come the morning."

Hadwin showed surprise at the instruction. "As you say, my lord."

"You expect trouble, Father?" Maddy asked after Hadwin shut the door in departure.

Dunham kindly smiled. "With the matters we must discuss, it is best done in a more private environment."

"Why do Tristan, Karryn and Ethan remain if this is a private matter?"

"Because the matter involves them, not Hadwin."

Maddy looked baffled. "How so?"

"You told me you wanted Tristan to apologize for his rude behavior when demanding him to tell you what I would not. On his part, he acted correctly in keeping my confidence."

"You scolded him earlier."

"In truth, I was preparing him for this evening. What you ask is legitimate, to a point."

"I don't understand."

"The trip to Ravendale is for important business. In the aftermath of Dorgirith, taking you and Garrick to the Fortress is a precaution."

"You already told me that," she spoke with some impatience.

"And that should be sufficient, for it is not your domain unless I, or your future husband, deem it so." Dunham put up a hand to still Maddy's protest. "However, the household is your concern, and that is the issue to be discussed." He rose to pace. His brows furrowed with fatherly disapproval. "You were wrong to go behind my back in an attempt to cajole Tristan into breaking my confidence. You also wrongly rebuked him. I say that to lay the foundation for what is to be told. You referred to him as squire, and for the past ten years he has lived here under that guise. Such is not the case."

Maddy's gaze shifted between Dunham and Tristan. "What do you mean?"

"My father was good friends with Vicar Elias in their youth, so he knew the family very well. He mourned with the Vicar when his six sons and their families mysteriously died. Thirty-three in all, killed or found dead. When they learned Nyomi, the Vicar's wife, became pregnant, they formulated a plan to send her into seclusion to protect her and the child. Unfortunately, she died in childbirth," explained Dunham.

"And the child?" she asked, though sending a quick glance to Tristan.

"Survived. Raised in secret until it became too dangerous for those involved. The alternative plan between my father and the Vicar came to fruition. I agreed to keep to the plan after his death."

"How so?" Maddy's eyes again shifted to Tristan then back to her father when he replied.

"The boy assumed a new role under the guise of training to be a knight."

"You are the Vicar's son," she said to Tristan

"Ay." He saw both her dismay and attempt to digest the news. He had his own questions for Dunham. "So, your father's death brought me here?"

"In a manner of speaking. He learned your location had been discovered and acted to protect you. His success in sending a warning cost his life."

Maddy's eyes grew misty. "You said grandfather died of natural causes."

"I had to tell you something. You were only a child at the time," Dunham spoke with regret.

She didn't look at him rather stared at the floor in a moment of consideration. "Wait," she began with realization. "You said Tristan was raised in secret, and Grandfather sent a warning. To whom, the Vicar?"

"To *my* grandfather, the man who raised me," said Tristan. "Under the circumstances I only saw my father occasionally. My grandfather and I are very close," he said with a fond smile.

"What became of him?"

Tristan's jowls flex with anger. "Captured and imprisoned. With Jor'el's help, that will soon be rectified."

"Is Lord Razi involved?"

Tristan, Ethan, Karryn and Dunham were caught off guard by Maddy's question.

"What made you say that name?" asked Karryn.

All looked to Maddy for an answer.

She timidly shrugged. "Talk among the people at Mother's funeral. I thought nothing of it at the time, simply court gossip I found offensive. A few mentioned Lord Razi. About him being the King's brother. I even heard the Vicar and Grandfather mentioned in connection with him. That is what angered me the most, to link Grandfather with such rumors. After hearing this, it makes me wonder if Lord Razi helped the Vicar to protect Tristan like you and Grandfather."

"Lord Razi *is my* grandfather," said Tristan.

For a moment Maddy stared at Tristan, again absorbing the revelation. "Then you are the King's nephew?"

"Grand-nephew, actually."

"And another he would eliminate if possible," said Ethan stoutly.

"Which is why it's been a closely guarded secret. We only tell you now because of Dorgirith," said Dunham.

Maddy wept. Moved by compassion, Tristan knelt to take her hand in support. "I'm sorry this is such a shock to you."

She shook her head in an attempt to regain her voice. Sympathy filled her gaze. "No. After what could have happened to Garrick, I cannot imagine losing all my siblings and their families as you have."

He smiled with tender compassion. "I know them only by stories. The last one died five years before my birth. Ethan is the closest to a brother I've known."

"Thank you," said Ethan with an easy smile.

"The way you came here together I thought you knew each other before." She motioned to Tristan and Ethan.

"We did. Grandpapi took Ethan in when he became orphaned at age eleven."

Maddy spoke to Dunham. "Now I understand why the Vicar often visits. I thought it due to friendship, now I know the real reason."

"Oh, friendship is involved. Remember, he and my father were childhood friends. Because of that relationship, I've been entrusted with Tristan, to shield him, teach him and prepare him to someday take his rightful place among the *nobility* of Allon." He stressed the word *nobility*.

Maddy smiled a bit sheepish at Tristan. "I supposed I acted foolish by scolding you in public."

He heaved a casual shrug. "I gave you cause. A *squire* did speak too familiarly to a lady."

She giggled. Her humor proved short-lived, being replaced by sympathy. "You may not have known them, but I still can't imagine not being surrounded by family." She fought back new tears.

Tristan tightly held Maddy's hand. "Do not cry for me. I cannot miss what I didn't have. I am distressed by your tears on my behalf."

She wiped the tears from her face and eyes. "Garrick is so changed."

"Ay, but a nightmarish experience you both survived. For that I'm eternally grateful to Jor'el. Garrick just needs time to recover."

"Which is why we are taking you both to the Fortress," began Dunham. "Not only for Garrick's spiritual, emotion and mental health, but Magelen is angry. Without us here for protection, the Fortress is the safest place."

"I understand, but," Maddy turned with trepidation to Tristan, "if you go to Ravendale will it pose a danger to you because of your father?"

"That's a possibility—"

"Don't go! Come with Garrick and me to the Fortress," she pleaded with urgency.

Tristan tightened his grip on her hands. "I'm not afraid. Jor'el has protected me all these years. I must go."

"Why?"

Tristan grappled with how much to reveal. Anything more could place her in further peril. "I can't say. Please, Maddy, trust me," he said over her beginning objection.

She turned imploring eyes to Dunham. "Father, tell me to come."

"I can't and I won't. This is something you must trust to all of us."

Tristan gently turned Maddy to face him. "Trust us to Jor'el."

She flung her arms around his neck and wept.

"It appears you were right, my lord," said Ethan quietly to Dunham.

"I usually am."

Karryn approached Maddy. "He will be kept safe."

Maddy wiped her tears away. "Where do you fit into this? Since you weren't brought here solely for your domestic skills."

Dunham laughed. "Karryn knows the ways of a manor, but no, I sought out someone with other skills."

"Why not tell me?"

"For protection. Times are dangerous. And for her other skills, I am in her debt." He spoke earnestly to Karryn.

"My lord, you owe me nothing," she said.

"You are as modest as you are trustworthy and discrete. The lives of my children are precious to me. I will remember your service."

"We are united in purpose. Debt should have no bearing only mutual diligence to see the task to completion."

Dunham smiled, wide and pleased. "My dear Karryn, you do your father credit. He would have no more pride in your words and deeds if you were a man."

"The rest of us would be the worse without such charming tenacity," said Ethan.

The compliment brought a flush to Karryn's cheeks and a retiring smile to her lips.

Dunham heartily laughed. "A night of firsts! You speak with unusual eloquence and she blushes." He brought his humor under control. "I believe enough has been said. There are still preparations to be made so I bid you all good-night."

"My lord. Ladies." Ethan bowed.

Tristan followed Ethan's lead in saying goodnight. They headed for the servants wing. "Don't you want to wait and bid Karryn a proper good-night?" teased Tristan.

"What gave you that idea?" asked Ethan, his tone a touch annoyed.

"Oh, don't play coy. She is the woman you spoke of earlier."

Ethan grabbed Tristan's arm and hurried inside the room they shared. "Did your confession make you so bold as to forget discretion? Karryn is a lady! I am a woodsman, a commoner," he rebuked harsher than usual for his even temper.

"Her blushing smile showed she does not mind your status. The same as Maddy doesn't mind the change in mine. Remember she gave her affection to a squire, not a lord."

"You are impertinent!" said Ethan in half-hearted, awkward protest.

"I'm also right."

In avoidance, Ethan began to undress by unbuttoning the doublet.

Tristan wouldn't be put off. "I followed your advice. Will you do so with Karryn and amend past regrets?"

In a pained drone, Ethan spoke. "It maybe eight years too late."

" '*In these uncertain times at least you wouldn't be wondering about what might have been rather know for certain.*' " Tristan quoted Ethan.

Ethan scowled at his words used against him. "Keep going and I will use a hemlock tipped arrow to shut you up!" At Tristan's intense prompting stare, Ethan became frustrated. "We leave in the morning. There is no time to woo or win a woman, despite confessing to the past." He jerked off his shirt and threw it into the chair.

"I feel a weight lifted for telling Maddy. Don't let any more time pass. If you have the opportunity before we leave them at the Fortress, speak to Karryn."

"*If* there is an opportunity."

"I'll pray for Jor'el to make it so."

Ethan snorted a chuckle at Tristan's tenacity. "Very well. If the Almighty grants it, I will speak to her."

Chapter 10

UPON RETURN TO RAVENDALE, MAGELEN LEARNED RAM RETIRED for the night with instructions not to be disturbed. This suited Magelen since he wanted to speak with Dagar. Altari and Witter waited a few steps away while Magelen stood before the basin to summon Dagar. The water around the sod began to boil. Steam rose. Dagar's image appeared.

"Why do you summon me? Have you dealt with the intruders?"

"In a manner of speaking, my lord."

Dagar's gaze narrowed in suspicion. "Explain that answer."

"The boy and a girl were Sir Dunham's children."

"Dunham?" said Dagar, intrigued.

"Ay. The others you sensed were his squires. Dunham eventually followed with some men to retrieve them—after I ordered their capture."

"Capture?"

"I intended to use the children to persuade him of the folly of his continued resistance. Alas, we ran afoul of interference, which resulted in a confrontation."

Dagar's ire kindled. "So he freed them while discovering the facility."

"In a manner of speaking, my lord."

"Hang that phrase! What happened?"

"During the confrontation, six madah-dune and a hunter-hawk were killed."

"How did they manage to ..." Dagar's face grew virulent. "They were not alone, were they?"

"No, my lord." Magelen motioned for Witter and Altari to step forward.

Dagar demanded of the Shadow Warriors, "Who?"

"Avatar," said Altari.

Dagar let out a tremendous bellow of rage. "Curse that troublesome wretch! I should have destroyed him when I had the chance."

"My lord, the enemy has shown his hand," said Magelen.

Dagar's guarded focus returned to Magelen. "What do you mean?"

"Is it not mentioned in prophecy that the Guardians will return? Avatar's interference may signal the event. We can use his appearance to be prepared."

Dagar's sneer found Witter and Altari. "Was he at full strength?"

The Warriors exchanged uncertain conferring glances before Witter replied. "Hard to tell. Our encounter was brief, though he helped them to escape."

"Any reports of other unusual encounters?"

"No, but we haven't inquired since we just returned from Dorgirith."

"Do so! The suggestion has merit, *if* others report similar encounters." Dagar asked Magelen, "What of Ramsey? Is he in agreement?"

"Ay, my lord. In turn, he spoke to his wife. Being convinced this will ensure her husband and son's future reign, she is willing to bear your child and give him to me to raise when weaned."

"Ay, Carnel will be king after Ramsey. Ram must not survive the night so all can happen as planned."

Magelen reminded Dagar, "Ram summoned the lords. They are expected within a week. He also took my suggestion of requesting the more troublesome ones to bring their daughters for the purpose of bestowing royal favor."

"You mean as bride for Carnel?"

"Ay. The favor could be used to thwart Dunham by choosing his daughter."

A wicked, cunning smile appeared on Dagar's face. "Correcting your earlier failure as well, I assume?"

"Unforeseen complications due to Avatar, not my failure. It would be best to wait until after the meeting of the lords to report the king's unfortunate death."

"Why? They can swear allegiance to Ramsey."

"They are aware of Lord Razi's imprisonment. His death along with the King will be highly suspicious."

Dagar thought for just a moment. "Ram will not survive the night," he said emphatically. "As for Razi, if he can be used in convincing them to swear fealty to Ramsey, then so be it. *But* he too will eventually die."

"Of course. However, my lord—" Magelen hesitated at receiving a withering glare from Dagar for another objection. "Ram suspects poison. He ordered his food and drink tasted before touching any of it. He made references that strongly suggest I am responsible, which I denied. I need another means that will not give credence to those suspicions."

Dagar spoke with impatience. "What is the talisman for, Magelen?" Both the talisman he wore, and Magelen's, began to glow. A malicious smile appeared on the dark lord's face.

"I realize the connection to your power. However, each time I serve as a conduit, it takes tremendous effort to withstand the effects. I am part mortal."

Dagar instructed the Warriors, "See he is given a strengthening tonic before and after the deed is done."

"Ay, my lord," said Witter.

Dagar disappeared. The steam cleared when the water ceased boiling.

"That went better than expected," said Altari.

"Speak for yourself!" Magelen waved them away. "Do as he orders."

Tor entered the main chamber to find Dagar in a foul mood. "Trouble?"

"Apparently what I sensed in Dorgirith was the presence of a Guardian—Avatar." Dagar fiercely sneered.

"What? How?"

114

"The *how* doesn't matter! He helped Dunham, his children and squires to escape the facility."

"What are you going to do about it?"

Dagar paced, his face hard in consideration. "When he and Mahon discovered I gained control of this cave, I tried to use Mahon to bait a trap for him."

Tor cocked his head to the contrary. "He may have given up hope of Mahon's survival. A similar trap won't work a second time. Despite his galling character, Avatar is no fool."

"Ay," grumbled Dagar in agreement. "In all these years, I have yet to get a distinct sense of any Guardian. Yet I can't imagine Jor'el not leaving at least *him*, or Armus, to aid the mortals. Avatar is the first sense I detected. There may be more, and baiting a trap could give away our position. Thus far we've been successful in keeping the Cave hidden beneath the bowels of Ravendale. It must stay that way until we can determine if Avatar is alone or the Guardians are returning. *His* reappearance will pose a greater threat than his irksome protégé."

"Dispatch the new recruits as scouts. Let them prove worthy of their new oath."

Dagar flashed an irritated smile. "I was about to issue the order. If they fail, tell Witter and Altari to destroy them. That way we're not risking any of those who have proven loyal."

"Consider it done." Tor left.

In the torture portion of the Cave, Griswold put up a spurean whip. Mahon stood between two natural pillars, stripped to the waist. Chains on his wrists stretched his arms out while fetters bound his ankles to the pillar. His entire back, shoulders and upper arms were covered with vicious, bloody lash marks. In pain and exhaustion, Mahon head hung. He seemed unconscious. In reality, he remained awake with his eyes shrouded. He needed to rest. It took great effort to remain silent. In fact, being mute infuriated Griswold, who put the full force into several frustrated blows. Those final lashes nearly broke Mahon's silence. He bit his lower lip so hard it tore open and bled heavily.

"Any success?" Mahon heard Dagar asked Griswold. He took a careful peek. No need to give any sign of being awake.

"No," groused Griswold. "He is indeed stubborn."

Mahon let his head fall when Griswold motioned towards him. Hearing footsteps draw near, he closed his eyes. He knew by the voice Dagar lifted his head.

"He may need a more concentrated effort. Unfortunately, you don't have time."

Dagar roughly released Mahon's head. He kept his eyes closed, yet curious as to the reason of Dagar's statement. By the footsteps, Dagar drew Griswold aside. Mahon didn't know if he had the strength to stretch out his hearing. He took a deep breath, and ever so gently, tried.

"We had an unexpected visitor to the facility," Dagar was saying. "Avatar."

Hearing the name of his good friend and mentor, Mahon quelled an impulsive smile.

Griswold growled, loud and angry. "What was that wretched excuse for a warrior doing there?"

"Rescuing some mortals from Magelen, but that's not important. What *is* important is his arrival after a hundred and fifty years."

A hundred and fifty years? Hard to gauge time in the Nether Cave, though Mahon didn't imagine so many years had passed. That would make him one thousand and sixty years old and Avatar just over fourteen hundred.

Dagar kept speaking. "It could be the beginning of their return or a solo mission. I'm not certain which. I dispatched scouts, but if Avatar's *mentor* shows up, there will be conflict. Our ranks are not enough. I need more recruits, quickly!"

Griswold's wicked chuckle grew louder. Mahon determined the larger Guardian was returning. Suddenly someone grabbed a fist full of his hair and pulled back his head. He kept his eyes closed despite the pain of feeling like his scalp was being ripped off.

"It would be wonderful to turn this one and send him to kill Avatar."

At Griswold's statement, Mahon battled the impulse to lash out and maintain the illusion of being unconscious. Not that he could act while chained or had the strength in his current injured condition, just sheer anger at the threat.

"No, Avatar is too clever. If Mahon shows up without any explanation, he'll be suspicious," said Dagar.

"Of his protégé?"

"Despite prior relationships, any warrior would proceed with caution. For now just keep him under lock and key. If the situation changes, he may prove useful."

"If you say so." Griswold shoved Mahon's head back down.

Mahon heard the rattling of chains as Griswold undid his ankle fetters.

Dagar spoke again. "Concentrate on the weaker ones. I need recruits!"

Mahon heard the hurried footsteps of Dagar's departure. Griswold now removed the fetters holding his arms. Keeping up his pretense, he allowed each arm to fall limp. Mahon leaned forward and bumped into Griswold. The large Guardian caught him then dragged him across the chamber. At one point, Mahon wished he were unconscious due to the pain of injury. At the clicking, he suspected the cell door being unlocked.

"Griswold!" he heard the threatening voice of Cyril.

"Out of my way, maggot, or I'll snap his neck."

Hearing the squeak of hinges, Mahon guessed Cyril moved. Griswold brought him inside and dumped onto the hard, cold floor. The cell door slam shut.

"Mahon?" he heard Cyril's concerned voice near his left ear.

"I'm all right," he whispered. His eyes remained closed. "Is he gone?"

"Ay."

Mahon gingerly pushed himself up in an attempt to sit. He experienced more pain than anticipated.

Cyril held him steady. "You're not all right, lad."

"No, I am. So will all of you after hearing what I learned. "Help me sit near the bars to Vidar and Elgin's cell." Mahon made certain to sit with his back to the chamber. "Pretend to examine my back while I speak," he quietly said to Cyril.

"No pretense with half your hide gone."

Mahon flinched in pain. "Vidar, Elgin," he lowly hissed between attempts to withstand Cyril's examination.

"Mahon, you look awful," said Elgin in distress.

He grinned with bravado. "I'll be all right. I told you I wouldn't make a sound."

Through the bars Vidar noticed most of the skin torn and some muscle exposed. "I'm amazed you made good on that statement."

"Prepare for more amazement. We've been here for a hundred and fifty years."

"What?" Elgin spoke a bit too loud. Vidar nudged him quiet.

"How did you learn that?" asked Vidar in a subdued voice.

"Apparently, *my old friend* upset Dagar's plan," said Mahon with a discreet smile. They understood. "Needless to say, Dagar's angry. He dispatched scouts to determine if *he* is alone or *another* is also back."

"Kell?" asked Elgin, cautious, but hopeful.

Annoyed by the pain of Cyril's continuing examination, Mahon waved Cyril to stop. "Dagar fears conflict before he is ready."

"That means he also suffered great losses at the battle," said Vidar.

"Ay. He ordered Griswold to get him more recruits."

Elgin paled in distress.

"You know I'll do what I can to help you," Vidar assured him.

"More than that," began Mahon with eagerness. "If this *is* the return, we won't have to endure this cursed place much longer. Conflict will be the end of Dagar ... and this," he carefully motioned at the chamber. "We must remain strong and ready for when the time comes."

118

"You're a warrior, stronger than I am to begin with," said Elgin in protest.

"Look at his back," insisted Cyril. "It wasn't his strength that endured such a vicious a beating tearing hide and muscle."

Elgin dared a glance and gasped in horror.

Mahon caught Elgin's eye. "I did it with Jor'el's help. Something you too can do since you have access to the Almighty's strength the same as I. Our caste doesn't matter." His voice grew weak and weary. In fact, he shivered, a sign of great injury since temperature didn't affect Guardians.

"Enough, lad. You need to rest." Cyril started to lift Mahon to help him to the carved out stone bed, but Mahon wouldn't move.

"No. I think I'll lie here."

Cyril stopped him. "Not on the cold floor."

"The stone bed is warmer?" Mahon tried to be humorous.

Cyril took off his tattered tunic to place it on the floor. "It's not much, but should provide some protection."

"Here" Elgin removed his intact jacket. He carefully passed it through the bars to Cyril. "Can you put Vidar's tunic over him?"

"Not with open wounds." Cyril placed Elgin's jacket on top of his.

Mahon carefully lied down on the jackets where he immediately fell asleep.

Chapter 11

R AM SUDDENLY AWOKE IN THE THRONGS OF GREAT PAIN. He began convulsing on the bed. In a loud exclamation he called; "Razi!" then became still. From his ashen face, vacant eyes stared at the ceiling.

A guard and the royal chamberlain rushed in. Both apprehensive.

"Sire? Your majesty?" the chamberlain asked. He felt Ram's forehead then his neck for a pulse. He shook his head. "Did you hear nothing before this?"

"No. All was quiet until a moment ago."

"Fetch the physician so he can determine the cause of death. I'll speak to the Prince and send word to Grand Master Magelen."

Magelen, Ramsey and his thirty-year-old son Carnel arrived at the King's chamber. Magelen and Ramsey took their time in coming as told by the fact Magelen appeared fresh with no signs of exertion. Ramsey was fully dressed. Carnel looked heartbroken, his eyes woeful upon his grandsire.

"Well?" asked Ramsey.

The royal physician paused in his examination to reply. "His heart gave out, Highness. Despite my urging, he refused to take his medicine before bed. He rambled on about poison. I assured him my remedies are safe. I even took a drink to show him. He still refused. The chamberlain can confirm my story. He witnessed the entire exchange."

"Indeed, Highness. The King became agitated in his delirium," said the chamberlain.

"The Prince knows the King's mind was prone to fits of delusions," said Magelen.

"I wish I could have done more," droned the physician.

"He was old. His time had come," said Ramsey, a bit more dispassionate than appropriate by the offended reactions of the physician and Carnel. Ramsey tempered his tone. "I meant he lived a full life. Even a gifted physician cannot alter the fate when one's appointed time has come."

Carnel rolled his eyes at the flimsy excuse.

Magelen escorted the physician to the door. "Be at ease, and return to your home."

"My service is terminated?"

"For this evening. Once His Highness is crowned, he will evaluate all his father's servants. He shall either reward them or judge them accordingly."

Alarmed, the physician stopped in the threshold. "Judge? I have always tried to protect the king's health. Truly, Highness," he pleaded.

"At the appropriate time you may speak." Magelen shoved the man to a guard, who took charge of the physician for leaving.

Ramsey spoke to the chamberlain. "Begin making the arrangements. I must inform my wife. Carnel. Magelen." They left with him.

On the walk back to Ramsey's chamber, servants bowed to offer condolences. Ramsey didn't acknowledge them. In fact, he had difficultly keeping a stoic façade. That was until he entered his chamber where his wife, Beryl, waited. She flinched in nervousness when he heartily laughed.

"It is done at last!"

Carnel consoled his nervous mother. His presence helped her muster the courage to speak.

"When will you be crowned?" she asked Ramsey.

"Immediately, of course."

"So soon?" asked Carnel in surprise. "He just died!"

"Allon must have a king."

"I don't dispute that. Can there be no mourning? No respect shown to the dead?"

"Highness," began Magelen, to which Ramsey sharply turned. He corrected his address, "I mean, *Your Majesty*. Whereas I agree a quick coronation is welcomed, the Prince's suggestion has merit. In a few days, the lords will arrive. This occasion offers you the stateliness and grandeur a private coronation would not."

Ramsey sarcastically chuckled. "Not to mention bringing the more disagreeable ones into line." Magelen widely smiled so Ramsey continued. "They will not find me a doddering old fool plagued by paranoia. Ay, a grand coronation. Those who do not swear allegiance will not leave Ravendale alive!"

"At least in prison for trial, Majesty."

"You dispute me already?"

"No, Majesty. However public trials and executions would provide a stark declaration that a new reign has begun."

Carnel became concerned at the implication. "Would you have Lord Razi included in these trials?"

"Not at first, Highness."

"Why?" Ramsey demanded. "He's been a thorn in our side for years! Father shielded him, while *he* offered nothing but platitudes, no useful information."

Despite Ramsey having a more explosive temper than Ram, Magelen maintained his composure. "His presence can corral the more disagreeable lords. Once his usefulness is exploited, he is expendable in whatever manner you choose."

The suggestion pleased Ramsey. He cocked a cunning smile. "I shall pay my uncle a visit to make him aware of the situation."

"Now?" asked Carnel.

"Of course. What better time than to catch an enemy unaware. Come, you may enjoy this." Ramsey headed for the door. When Magelen followed, he stopped him. "Just my son."

In the dungeon, Razi bolted up out of a sound sleep at hearing his name. "Ram?"

For a moment, he sat on edge of the cot trying to determine the source of terror concerning his brother. In his heart, he feared the reason. They had been at odds since that fateful day when both were eighteen and Ram discovered Razi secretly married Janel. Their relationship continued to deteriorate during Ram's reign. It accelerated when Magelen became Grand Master forty years ago and targeted his family for destruction.

Razi recalled that during Ram's last visit, he spoke about deadly consequences should he die. Thought of death didn't trouble Razi. He lived a long life. His concern the last twenty years was his grandson's survival. As long as Tristan lived and was safe, nothing else mattered. A terrifying thought struck him. What if Ram's death meant Magelen learned about Tristan? Being rid of Ram, Razi and Tristan meant that Magelen and Dagar would have free reign. The thought brought tears to Razi's eyes.

"Please, Jor'el, spare him. I can't lose any more, and you promised," he prayed in a quivering voice.

Razi became startled at hearing voices followed by the jingling of keys outside the door. He quickly wiped away the tears. He stood when the door opened. Light from a lantern temporarily blinded him. The only light in the cell came from the dim moonlight filtering through the cell window. He shielded his eyes to allow them time to adjust to see who entered.

Murdock remained by the door holding the lantern. Ramsey stepped further into the cell. Carnel accompanied him. This was first time Razi had seen his nephew and grandnephew since Ramsey presented him like a trophy to Ram. While the father looked smug, the son appeared apprehensive.

"What do you want?" Razi asked, wary.

"Is that anyway to greet family? Or better yet, your King?" rebuffed Ramsey.

"King?" Razi's brows level with realization. His voice barely rose above a whisper. "So what I sensed is true. Ram is dead."

"Died of heart failure."

Ramsey's contempt annoyed Razi. "You don't sound grief stricken about your father's death."

Ramsey sardonically laughed. "Or you, your brother, my lord uncle." The term *uncle* laced with scorn.

Pricked, Razi began to respond yet caught sight of Carnel's careful shake of his head. The young man definitely ill-at-ease. What a contrast between father and son; one scornful and the other sympathetic. Razi assumed a benign attitude.

Ramsey noticed the exchange. "Don't pretend, *Uncle*. I brought Carnel to see the real you; a pompous, stubborn old man who can't stop pretending. What were you going to say? That you loved the brother you betrayed so long ago?"

Razi glared at Ramsey. "You don't know what you're talking about."

Ramsey shrugged with inconsequence. "Maybe not since I have no siblings. It doesn't matter now. He's dead and I'm King. You will deal with me, *Uncle*."

Razi mimicked Ramsey in tone and inflection. "You think that fact will change my stance, *nephew?*"

"Oh, it will," said Ramsey with dreaded certainty. "You see, my father summoned the lords to Ravendale with the intention of restating their allegiance. Now, they will witness my coronation while swearing fealty to me. Your voice will help to persuade those less agreeable, such as Baron Kaleb, Baron Renfrow and Sir Dunham."

Razi's brows knitted at Dunham's name. "Why should I do that?"

"Because if you can't convince them, I shall permanently relieve them of their positions, confiscate their goods and lands—or worse." Ramsey's voice grew threatening and eyes narrow.

Razi forced himself to keep his wits by way of a shrug. "You place too much dependence upon my influence, nephew. Why should they listen to me?"

"Stop the pretense!" snapped Ramsey, his patience exhausted. "You know as well as I how they always favored you over my father. Well, I won't stand for it—from you or any man! *I am King* and will rule supreme."

"Only with Magelen's help."

Ramsey seized Razi and struck him with a vicious backhand. The force of the blow split Razi's lower lip. Ramsey's hold kept Razi on his feet when the older man's knees buckled. "You will not dispute me like you did my father!"

The violence dazed Razi. At his advanced age, it was difficult to recover from such an unexpected blow.

Carnel intervened. "Father! You said he is an old man. Will you strike him dead before he can help you?"

Ramsey sneered at Carnel. He roughly released Razi. Stumbling, Razi steadied himself by throwing a hand against the wall to remain standing. He touched his painful lip and felt blood.

Ramsey continued his bully manner. "Did I forget to mention Elias?"

The question confused Razi, as he still tried to recover from the blow. "Elias?"

"Surely you remember the Vicar, *your son*? His fate is also dependent upon you convincing the lords."

Understanding the reason for a switch in tactics, Razi straightened. "Elias, or any man honored as Vicar, is protected by divine law from reprisal!"

"Then you admit he's your son."

"I admit nothing! However, if you harm him, you will personally answer to the Almighty for a crime against his appointed one."

This time Ramsey's fierce blow sent Razi falling backwards, striking the cot then the floor. On the verge of unconsciousness, Razi couldn't move. Ramsey left.

Carnel flinched and Murdock clenched his fists at the abuse. However, both remained in their places.

Carnel heard his father bark his name from the hallway. "I'm truly sorry about Grandfather," he said to Razi before leaving.

Murdock locked the cell door.

Ramsey confronted Carnel. "What was that about?"

"Would you kill him before he can help you? You agreed with Magelen about his usefulness. If he dies at your hand, the lords won't be so agreeable. Maybe even revolt!"

"It won't be anything else, would it?"

Carnel's brows knitted in trepidation. "Such as what? Defy you? No. I just forgot how much he looks like Grandfather and momentarily caught off guard."

The explanation only mildly satisfied Ramsey. "He did spoil you." He turned on his heels to mount the steps leading from the dungeon.

Anger and compassion crisscrossed Carnel's face. "Murdock."

"I'll take care of his injuries immediately, Highness."

Fighting agitation, Carnel made his way to his mother's chamber. Her anxiety matched his disturbance.

"Oh, Carnel, everything is happening faster than I thought."

"Father inflicted violence upon Razi." His face took on an expression of recollection. "He looks so much like Grandfather that I felt sorry for him."

Beryl seized Carnel's arm to get his attention. She spoke in low, urgent voice. "Razi isn't the issue. Your father and Magelen are! I may be able to placate Ramsey, but Magelen should not be provoked."

"The man is insufferable! He plagued Grandfather to death."

"*Shh!*" she urged. "He is also powerful."

"Powerful enough to make you agree to the arrangement?"

Though visibly wounded, pride made her square her shoulders. "It will secure your reign as well."

Carnel didn't hide his scornful ridicule. "To have an illegitimate half-breed brother watching my every move like he does father?"

Beryl jerked his arm in warning. "Beware, his spies are everywhere!" Her eyes darted to the door.

Carnel took his mother by the shoulders to make her look directly at him. "If you can tell me that you do this of your own free will and are not coerced then I will be silent." His question and probing gaze were too much. Beryl shied away with a whimper. He gently turned her face back to him. "Just as you do not want to do this, I cannot ask any woman who would be my wife to make such a sacrifice by bearing a child of the Dark Way. So understand, if that is the price to secure my throne, I will not marry."

A thin smile quivered before she suppressed it. "Do not say so openly to your father, for he will order you to marry for it is your duty as heir."

"One problem at a time, Mother."

Chapter 12

IN A VAULT UNDERNEATH THE TEMPLE, WREN AND AVATAR WAITED for Armus to fetch Kell. Avatar sat on a stone bench where two walls intersected to create an "L" shape. He had his back against one wall, feet up on the bench, relaxed and at-ease. He watched Wren pace the chamber. She greeted his return with her usual cutting sarcasm, which he countered in like manner. Being contemporaries in the group of Guardians created after the Originals, they competed with good-natured banter. However, behind her sarcasm he noticed an unusual edginess and agitation in her mannerisms. After several moments he spoke.

"Why are you so nervous?"

"I don't like being away from my province."

"You never complained about it in the past."

She shot him a harsh side-glance, speaking in a tone that matched her expression. "Now is not like in the past! You've been gone too long to fully explain the changes that have happened."

Avatar swung his feet onto the floor to sit up and give his full attention. "Try me."

Wren regarded him in momentary consideration. "Many mortals have embraced the Dark Way. They have forgotten Jor'el, or at least don't want to acknowledge the Almighty's existence for fear of reprisal from Ram and Magelen. To them, *we* are myths, legends, something to be scoffed at or dismissed all together. Meanwhile, we stand by watching everything we helped govern be torn down or destroyed! I don't think you can understand the torment of that." Passion filled her voice.

Rather than being provoked by her concluding statement, he stood to speak in a consoling tone. "I was at the Great Battle, remember? I *do*

128

know what it is like to see everything destroyed. I may not have witnessed the aftermath, but it doesn't mean I can't sympathize."

Wren heaved an audible sigh to let her passion subside. "I'm sorry for lashing out. I've seen too much waste and apathy among the mortals. It gets to me sometimes. Although I admit, it is good to know you helped when Armus and I could not."

Avatar roguishly smiled. "That is an admission worth returning to hear."

"If you tell anyone I said it, I'll deny it," she returned with her normal banter.

"Deny what?" Kell appeared in the threshold with Armus behind him.

Wren flushed with embarrassment. "We didn't hear you."

Kell chuckled. "I can move silently." He embraced Avatar. After parting, he said, "It is good to see you after so long."

"It's good to be seen from what I've heard."

"Only I don't know for how long you'll be among us again," groused Kell. He averted his eyes.

"What do you mean? I'm here." Avatar flashed one of his rakish smiles. He tried to catch Kell's glance, surprised by the abrupt change from gladness to downcast. Even though he saw an impulsive grin to his humor, Kell continued to avoid eye contact.

Kell paced. "The situation is tenuous. Ram is dying and Razi imprisoned. True, Razi's son, Vicar Elias, is diligent in his effort to rewrite Verse and Prophecy. However, the fate of the mortals hangs by a thread! Magelen utilizes the Dark Way and Shadow Warriors to impose Dagar's will. I fear Allon is on the brink of total collapse."

Avatar shot Wren a level glance. "I know about Witter and Altari, but what I've heard wasn't that dire."

Kell paused in pacing just long enough to wave a hand. "Don't be cross with Wren. I just left Gresham in Midessex where I learned what I told you. Communication between us is more difficult with our diminished powers. Gresham also said Ram summoned the lords in an effort to regain their allegiance. However, in his present health, the outcome is unknown."

"What can we do?"

Kell shook his head. "Not much, I'm afraid. Any hope lies with the remnant. There are a few particular mortals who bear watching and protecting. One such group is the house of Sir Dunham, his children and two squires—the ones you helped to escape from Dorgirith." Though he motioned at Avatar, he still didn't look directly at him while pacing. "It is a little known fact that one squire is actually Elias' son, Razi's grandson." Pensive, Kell stopped and lowered his head. "Since the Great Battle, I've not been able to speak to Razi or help him as I promised." With determination he declared, "Tristan will survive! By all in heaven, I swear it, whether he is the son of prophecy or not. The daughter included in the prophecy is not yet alive, so I have my doubts, but there is a sense of change coming."

Avatar looked baffled. "Son and daughter of prophecy? I don't recall that."

"New revelation from Jor'el since the battle. He won't abandon his faithful."

"How does that explain my return?"

Kell acted hasty in his reply to the point of distraction. "Our restoration is linked to the daughter. That's why your return may only be temporary. Once this change has occurred, you could be recalled."

"Then I suppose I'll enjoy being here while I can."

"There is no enjoyment in being spectators!" snapped Kell.

"I was being facetious," said Avatar, taken back by the outburst.

"Now is not time for it."

Indeed, Kell acted unusually terse, and that concerned Avatar. From the day of his creation, he apprenticed under Kell and Armus. While most Guardians had one mentor, he learned from the best of all Guardians. He then mentored Mahon before assuming the position as the captain's aide. Together, he, Kell and Armus comprised the High Trio in command of all Guardians. It was an honored position for anyone not among the Originals. For Kell to first be glad to see him then switch to intense preoccupation and irritation could indicate more happened in Midessex than he said.

Avatar tossed a questioning glance to Armus. The second-in-command heaved a shrug of ignorance. With no immediate answers regarding Kell's state of mind, Avatar assumed a formal attitude. "What do you want me to do, Captain?"

"Help Armus keep watch over Sir Dunham and the squires."

"I thought I was doing that?" asked Wren.

"With the lords summoned to Ravendale, Dunham may leave his children at Garwood or take them to the Fortress. Either way, they will be vulnerable. After what happened in Dorgirith you need to remain in the province."

"Then I should return."

"All of you return together, and quickly."

"So it wasn't just due to my diminished strength they aided me in dimension travel. It's now normal for two or more to travel together," said Avatar.

"Advisable, since it drains our energy," said Armus. "Mostly we travel on foot. We can still cover more distance than mortals on horseback. The diminished energy also makes sharing information a more hazardous process." He sent a circumspect glance at Kell. The captain remained distracted.

Avatar gave Armus a nod of comprehension. Again, Kell didn't notice. "One more question before we leave, Captain. Any word on Mahon, Vidar or the others?"

This time, Kell looked directly at Avatar. "I'm afraid not. I'm sorry."

Avatar noticed Wren's dejection at the answer. As Mahon was his protégé, she was Vidar's protégé. Their capture by Dagar's forces came as a harsh personal blow. "Well, if I get my hands on either Witter or Altari, I'll learn some answers."

"I would welcome that, only don't take unnecessary risk."

Avatar roguishly smiled. "Who, me?"

Again, Kell scowled at the humor.

Wren intervened. "It's no use, Kell, you know he's incorrigible." She took Avatar's hand for the dimension travel. Armus held onto Wren's shoulder.

"Jor'el be with all of you," said Kell.

"And with you," they said in unison then spoke, "*Siuthad!*" before vanishing.

Wren, Armus and Avatar took up position on the western horizon to observe Garwood. Fires and torches illuminated the construction areas were workers gathered. The warm glow of lights came from behind curtains of the house.

"What's wrong with Kell?" asked Avatar.

Armus shrugged. "He must have learned more from Gresham than he said. He was preoccupied when I found him."

"That's obvious."

"Ay, but he perked up when I told him of your return. Although it didn't last long, so the problem must be quite burdensome."

"Especially if he won't tell you." Seeing Armus frown, Avatar changed the subject. "What about these mortals who bear watching?"

"I don't know all the details of how the squires came to be with Sir Dunham, only what Kell said about Tristan being Vicar Elias' son—his *last* son," Armus said with heavy emphasis.

"How did the others die?"

"Killed by various means, none of which were natural." Armus' expression turned fierce.

"I take it by your reaction, you couldn't interfere."

"No! Tristan is the exception because of Jor'el's promise to Razi and Janel."

"What promise?"

Wren chuckled at the question. "You're ignorance is quite amusing."

Armus scolded her. "This is difficult enough for those of us who know what has happened. Avatar obeyed Jor'el's order, and came totally

132

blind into a dangerous situation where he immediately faced Shadow Warriors and creatures of infrinn! The least we can do is provide him with information."

Seeing Wren subdued, Avatar kindly spoke. "I understand her enjoyment. I'd probably do the same after going so long without lighthearted diversion. Besides, I can best her any day regardless of the situation or lack of information."

Armus looked along his shoulder at Avatar. "She's right, you are incorrigible. But," he forestalled her rebuttal quip, "there is information he needs to know."

"I mean to tell him what you couldn't about Sir Dunham." Armus yielded so Wren continued. "He is the son of Elias' childhood friend, thus acquainted with the history of the Vicar's family. That is why Tristan went to train with him rather than stay any longer with Lord Razi."

"You mean after Razi was captured?" asked Avatar.

"No, Tristan went to live with Dunham ten years ago. Ramsey captured Razi five years ago."

"Ramsey is Ram's only son, and quite eager for his father's death," explained Armus. "Magelen is his royal advisor, who takes the title Grand Master."

"Of the Dark Way," said Wren, preempting Avatar's question.

"So he serves both the King and Dagar," Avatar said in summation.

"Ay. His command of the Dark Way is considerable. Which is one reason we must be cautious."

"And also why we couldn't enter Dorgirith due to our limited capacity," added Armus.

Avatar furrowed his brows while listening. "The female, Maddy, said something about Magelen wanting to use her and her brother against Sir Dunham, why?"

Armus replied, "Dunham is very influential among the mortal lords. If he can be silenced or persuaded, then convincing the others to swear allegiance will be easy. Hence the summons."

Avatar pursued the line of thinking. "Could Magelen have planned the capture of the children to coincide with the summons?"

Wren shook her head. "No, venturing into the forest was Garrick's idea. His headstrong nature is of constant vexation. Since their mother died six months ago, he has grown worse. I've tried numerous times to corral him when he's gotten too near Dorgirith. Alas, I can only do so much without revealing my true identity. In fact, I went to Garwood in disguise when I sensed trouble. Shortly after, Garrick left."

Thoughtful, Avatar stared at Garwood. "Will Tristan go with Sir Dunham or stay with Garrick and Maddy?"

Wren chuckled. "His heart would stay with Maddy, but his duty compels him to go."

Avatar flashed a teasing grin. "Meddling in mortal affairs of the heart again, are you?"

She flushed, abashed by his jesting. "No!" Hearing Armus laugh, she accosted Avatar. "He bears watching because going to Ravendale could reveal his identity. Anything happens to him and Jor'el's promise is threatened."

"Back to my earlier question, what promise?" insisted Avatar.

Armus curtailed his laughter to answer. "From Razi and Janel's descendants, will come a son to take back what was lost, along with a daughter to help restore the Guardians. If Tristan dies, the line stops with Elias."

"Ah," said Avatar with understanding. "I wondered what Kell meant."

"Anxious for us to be on our way, and possibly due to what he learned from Gresham."

"What about Witter, Altari and the Shadow Warriors, any idea of their numbers?"

Armus shrugged. "Enough to force us to inaction most of the time."

"Which is why your arrival is hopeful. Maybe now we can be more than spectators," said Wren.

"Don't get your hopes up," cautioned Armus.

"Why not? Don't you want to get back at them for over a century of abuse and crimes against the mortals? Not to mention the Great Battle," she challenged Armus.

"Of course, but Kell doesn't know if this is the time or not. He said so when mentioning the Daughter of Allon. He isn't aware of her existence."

"Is that the name of the promised daughter?" asked Avatar.

"Ay. Kell delivered the latest prophecy to Elias in a dream. For now, *much* depends upon Tristan's survival," said Armus emphatically.

"That we know of," insisted Wren. "What if not all of Elias' grandchildren were slain? If one or more unknowingly survived and are also in hiding?"

Armus considered her theory. "Possible, though I assume Jor'el would at least tell Kell to protect the child."

"Not if having Kell focus on Tristan could be a ruse to keep the real heir hidden from Magelen and Dagar."

Armus took exception to the theory. "That's stretching the situation to suggest Jor'el would purposely keep Kell ignorant about a highly critical matter."

"It's a viable possibility," she insisted.

Armus adamantly shook his head. "I don't agree with the assessment. *Nor*," he stressed to stop further argument, "does it change our assignment. Let us concentrate on that and leave the speculation for another time."

"He's right, Wren," began Avatar. "Your suggestion has some merit. However, Kell being ignorant is highly unlikely. And why send me? My arrival would hardly facilitate the ruse. In fact, Dagar probably knows I'm here, so there goes any form of secrecy."

"Your presence always did complicate matters," she dryly quipped.

"Thank you," he said with a wide, pleased smile.

"They are turning in for the night." Armus indicated the dimming lights at Garwood.

Wren readied her crossbow. "I'll watch the eastern road. Can you both stay out of trouble while I'm gone?"

They just stared at her, to which she moved off.

On the border of Dorgirith, a bright, large flash of white light pierced the darkness. From the fading glow, Nari, Roan, Indigo, Cletus and Bern emerged. All wore the black Shadow Warrior uniforms, and fully armed.

"I don't know that working in a group is what Dagar had in mind when he issued our orders to scout out Guardians," said Bern.

"Our orders are to deal with Avatar," said Nari stoutly.

"So? One warrior against all of us," said Cletus with flippancy.

Nari glared crossly at him. "An important fact left out of our instructions: Avatar is a member of the High Trio!"

"I wondered why his name was familiar," said Indigo.

She continued her assessment. "He's older than all of you. Despite what Witter and Altari say about his insufferable character, his high rank makes him very formidable."

"Have you ever dealt with him?" asked Cletus.

Roane made a scoffing laugh, to which he promptly received a jab in the ribs from Nari.

"I take it she has," commented Bern to Cletus and Indigo.

"He bested her every time they met in mock combat," said Roane.

"Nari? An undefeated Original?" said Bern with hint of sarcasm

"Fan out!" Nari snapped. "Be careful in sensing which way he went." She sent Roane on his way with a hard shove.

Wren just arrived on the eastern road two miles from where they found Avatar. She spotted someone just before the individual disappeared behind a rock. Wary from the earlier encounter, she carefully made her way closer to determine identity. Although Guardians could sense each other over distances, the strongest sense happened within a mile, thus she erred on the side of caution by stopping after half a mile.

With bow ready, Wren knelt behind a tree to get a clear view. Darkness didn't affect a Guardian's eyesight. A very tall male all clad in black. A Shadow Warrior. The assessment became confirmed when a flash of white light appeared. Two more Shadow Warriors arrived. Not good! Not so close to Garwood. Wren drifted into the woods then rushed back. Her sudden arrival brought Armus and Avatar to their feet, armed and ready.

"We have visitors," she announced. "Three Shadow Warriors investigating the outcropping where you fell," she said to Avatar.

He cocked a lopsided grin. "So my appearance generated interest."

"We can't let them approach Garwood," she rebuffed.

Avatar chucked. "That's not their intention. They're looking for me. So, I'll oblige them as a diversion." He began to move off.

Wren seized Avatar's arm. "Just like that? No plan, no backup?"

"If either you or Armus appear, they'll know the mortals of Garwood are of interest to more than one Guardian."

"Scouting for you but ferreting out any more. Makes sense," said Armus. "But, under the circumstances three to one aren't good odds."

"Neither were Witter, Altari and a hunter-hawk, but I'm still standing," Avatar said with bravado.

"Can I shoot him?" Wren demanded of Armus.

"Later. After he's drawn them off," he replied to her then to Avatar, "You're not going without backup. We'll stay far enough away not to be sensed. With diminished strength, taking on Shadow Warriors single-handed is a bad idea, regardless of what you did before."

Chapter 13

BERN AND CLETUS JOINED INDIGO AT THE OUTCROPPING. THEY watched Indigo kneel to feel the ground.

"There is a strong sense of a Guardian presence," said Indigo. He moved to the edge. "Look!" He waved over Bern and Cletus. He indicated the dead hunter-hawk lying on a ledge just below the outcropping.

"What it is?" Cletus asked.

"My guess is something of Magelen or Dagar's creation."

"Perhaps it destroyed Avatar," said Bern.

"Not with an arrow through its neck." Indigo climbed down to the ledge to examine the hunter-hawk. "By the force of the shot, it came from a Guardian."

"Other than Avatar?" asked Bern.

"Possible."

"I only sensed one presence."

"As do I," added Cletus. "Witter said Sir Dunham and his men were present, and one armed with a bow. That would account for the demise of the creature since we can't sense another Guardian."

Indigo climbed up from the ledge. "He would have to be one strong mortal to inflict such a wound."

"Avatar could have used the arrow in self-defense, thus accounting for the wound," said Bern.

"Either way we need proof," said Indigo.

"How? We sense them or we don't," said Cletus.

"I don't know—" Bern became alert. "Avatar's nearby!" He and Cletus moved in the direction of Dorgirith when Indigo's shout stopped them.

"There! Across the meadow. I saw him just before he entered the woods," said Indigo.

"I'll fetch Nari and Roane," said Cletus.

"No," said Bern. "It will take too long and we'll lose his trail." He spoke to Indigo, "Dimension travel us to where you saw him."

All three held onto each other and disappeared. When they reappeared on the other side of the meadow, Indigo led them into the woods. After several hundred yards, he stopped.

"What's the problem?" asked Cletus.

"This is too easy." Indigo warily looked from side-to-side. He cautiously moved forward. "It's as if he wants us to follow hi-i-i-m-m-!" Something beneath his feet snapped, ensnared his ankles, jerked him into the air and slammed him against a tree. Unconscious from smashing his head into the trunk, Indigo dangled upside down.

Bern and Cletus jumped out of the way. They drew their swords to confront trouble. Bern moved toward Indigo.

"Careful," warned Cletus.

Bern found a wound on the back of Indigo's head. He opened Indigo's eyes. No reaction. "He'll be out cold for a while."

Cletus surveyed the trap. "Nari's right, Avatar is clever. He must have known we were following to have set a trap so fast."

"We'll just have to be more clever, and careful." Bern signaled to continue moving.

After a mile, they reached the edge of the woods overlooking a ravine. A small river ran through it with several waterfalls that dropped in elevation. Bern's eyes narrowed in studying the river.

"Why are you stopping? I don't sense he changed course," said Cletus.

"This is an offshoot of the Deigh River that runs from the Highlands along the border of Northern and Southern Forest."

"You think he crossed into the Northern Forest? Why? Dunham lives in the Southern Forest."

Bern shrugged. "Maybe luring us away or is trying to avoid capture. It's hard to tell."

Cletus closed his eyes. His furrowed brow showed the effort of his attempt. With a growl of frustration, he opened his eyes. "I don't sense him anywhere nearby."

"We know he came this way." Bern descended into the ravine. He paused at the water's edge. The river ran fast due to the autumn rains.

"It can't be that deep," said Cletus.

"It's not the depth that concerns me." Bern waded into the water until it covered his ankles. He prodded the area about him with his sword.

"You think he set a trap in the water?"

"It won't be seen, now would it? I'll cross first. Follow my path exactly."

"We could just dimension travel across."

"And if he's waiting on the other side when we reappear?"

"I didn't sense him," Cletus insisted.

"Our assignment is the capture him. We go this way." Bern advanced two steps into the water then prodded again with his sword. Each time he took several steps before using his sword to poke the bottom. Steadily the water increased to his waist in the center of the river. Then it happened. He went under.

"Bern!" Cletus impulsively stepped forward into the water.

Bern became visible when the current pushed him downstream and over one of the small waterfalls. Cletus ran along the shore trying to keep track of Bern. He peered over the falls. His eyes scanned the churning water when he couldn't see Bern. A black figure popped to the surface then floated to the opposite shore. Bern appeared to be unconscious. Cletus noticed a quiet pool near the far end of the waterfall. He headed there with the intent of crossing to Bern. He stepped into the water when he heard ...

"Going somewhere?"

Cletus turned about to find—Avatar! Annoyed, Cletus clenched the hilt of his sword. Being so preoccupied, he didn't sense any approach. "You're going to regret what you did to Indigo and Bern."

"I simply gave a few inept Shadow Weaklings a lesson in tracking. You should thank me."

"This is my thanks!" Cletus attacked. They exchanged several strong, vicious blows. The force of Cletus' attack drove Avatar back a few paces. "Looks like you need remedial lessons in fighting."

"No, just conserving my strength against a lesser opponent."

Cletus attacked again. This time, Avatar didn't budge. He soundly turned Cletus aside. Cletus proved persistent by attacking a third time and a fourth time. After the fifth exchange, each showed signs that such a forceful battle was draining. On the sixth attack, Avatar slipped at the water's edge and fell into the pool. He briefly went under. He surfaced, only unarmed. He searched the water for his sword.

Cletus moved to accost Avatar when he noticed Bern coming in behind Avatar. Bern seized Avatar just as he reached under water to retrieve his sword. They wrestled. Bern got the upper hand. He strained to hold Avatar under water. Bern fell backwards when Avatar bolted to the surface, gulping for air. Avatar staggered back a few steps in an attempt to recover his breath. Cletus entered the water.

With Warriors coming for him, Avatar dove beneath the surface. A powerful explosion of thunder came from underwater followed by a lightning bolt shooting straight up. The force sent Bern and Cletus flying out of the pool. Both slammed into a boulder on the Northern Forest side of the river. They lay in an unconscious heap.

Avatar broke the surface, desperate for air. He sloshed out of the water up the Southern Forest bank. He collapsed in exhaustion. He jerked when something took hold of his arm. He tried to lift his sword but didn't have the strength to resist or fight. He relaxed at recognizing a Guardian warrior with a grizzled beard equal in bulk to Armus.

"Barnum," he said in weary relief. He struggled to raise his head in an attempt to look around. "Where are they?"

"Unconscious for the moment. You're on the verge of joining them."

Avatar fought to stay awake. "No. We need to get out of here before they recover. They can't see you." He made a feeble attempt to stand so Barnum pulled him to his feet.

Wren and Armus arrived. Armus helped to support Avatar on the other side. Wren fetched his sword. She stuck it in her belt. She lowly spoke the Ancient. Taking a deep breath of recovery from expending energy, she ran after the others.

They managed to travel a little over a mile before Avatar fainted. His face was pale and cool to the touch. Wren hurried to mix another strengthening tonic. He woke to her urging, only groggy and incapable of drinking on his own. Barnum elevated Avatar's head when she held the cup for him to take measured sips. Once finished, Barnum gently laid Avatar back on the ground where he closed his eyes.

"What was that all about at the river?" asked Barnum.

"He led Shadow Warriors away from Garwood. We followed as backup, only we couldn't get too close. They were sent to track him while scouting for any other Guardians," said Armus.

"That explains his anxiety about leaving the pool."

"Ay. If they sensed us, they would know he wasn't alone."

"They can when they wake up." Barnum motioned toward the river.

Wren shook her head. "I used some of my power to cover our essence. It wasn't a complete cover since they need to sense Avatar or become suspicious. What brought you here?"

"Aside from the fact it's the border to my province, I sensed trouble and the Dark Way."

Avatar lowly moaned. His eyes open when Wren touched his forehead. "What concoction did you give me this time?"

"Well, your mouth is working again. Your temperature feels better too," she said.

"We should return to Garwood for full recovery." Armus lifted Avatar to his feet. Wren stood on the other side to help support him. "Remain alert yet out of sight until the Shadow Warriors are gone," he told Barnum. He, Wren and Avatar disappeared in dimension travel.

⁓⁕⁓

Reappearing at the western vantage point near Garwood, they discovered Kell waiting. Wren and Armus lowered Avatar to sit on the ground in such a way as to lean against the log.

Concerned, Kell knelt to examine Avatar for wounds. "What happened?"

"I decided to take a swim. Quite refreshing, actually," Avatar replied in his normal wit. Kell wasn't amused so he added, "No wounds, just exhaustion."

"I gave him a strengthening tonic," said Wren.

Kell sharply rebuked her. "That doesn't answer my question!"

"Easy, Kell. I'm all right," said Avatar. At Kell's irked glare, he explained. "I led three Shadow Weaklings on a merry chase, complete with traps. Only I ended up fighting two and using my power. I'll recover. They however, will be very sore for a while."

The answer baffled Kell. "They escaped your power? How? Lightning destroys."

"Well," began Avatar, tentative, "not when used underwater."

"What?"

"I said I went for a swim, just not voluntarily."

Kell grunt with great annoyance. "Who were they?"

"I don't know. I've never seen them before."

Kell looked to Armus for an answer.

"I didn't recognize them either."

Avatar gripped Kell's arm to get his attention. "Kell, what is wrong? You've been distracted and unusually surly since I arrived. Did Gresham provide some information you haven't told us?"

"No! I told you everything."

"Kell," began Armus in a coaxing voice. "We know something is troubling you. Why avoid telling us what it is?"

Kell pursed his lips, the conflict evident on his face.

"If this is a private discussion with your second-in-command and aide, I can leave, Captain," Wren spoke with deference and formality.

With a resigned sigh, Kell moved from kneeling to sitting beside Avatar. "It's not private. It's something I wish were different. In fact, I tried to make it so by assigning you to help Armus and avoid what was supposed to happen," he said to Avatar.

Perplexed, Avatar looked along his shoulder at Kell. "Once more with clarity. You *knew* I was going to face Shadow Warriors? That I was *supposed* to face them?"

Kell held Avatar's gaze. "You weren't sent in answer to a prayer, rather as a decoy."

"Decoy," repeated Avatar, digesting the interesting news.

Kell continued. "Your arrival was meant to draw Magelen and Dagar's attention so the rest of us can act freely in our assignments. I tried to avoid employing you that way with a reassignment, only you ending up fulfilling Jor'el's task anyway."

Overwhelmed by the revelation, Wren sat on a log opposite Kell and Avatar. "That means he is deliberate bait for Shadow Warriors."

"Thanks for stating the obvious," said Avatar with a wry snicker.

"It's not funny! You don't know how ruthless they've become," she insisted.

"No, I have a pretty good idea." Avatar turned to Kell. "Why didn't you tell me this before? Why avoid it?"

"Because the last time I employed you against Dagar, you were nearly trapped in the Nether Cave. As it was, Mahon became a prisoner. At present only twelve of us remain to defend Allon. I can't afford to lose any more to him. Dagar's spleen would have no bounds if he got his hands on you."

Avatar quelled a grin. "Kell, I appreciate your friendship and attempt to shield me. Yet as captain, you know Jor'el will not be thwarted. This incident proves that. Nor do I fear Shadow Warriors or Dagar. You must accept that going into the Cave was *my* choice. It provided vital intelligence about the creatures of infrinn. Granted, it didn't work out as we hoped, and I feel responsible for Mahon's capture, but it was a necessary risk."

"I have accepted it. You asked me why I was avoiding this assignment. I gave you my answer based upon the present situation in our reduced capacity. I don't want to take the same risk I did before."

"I agree with Kell," said Wren. "It's a greater risk now. Don't take it lightly."

Avatar ironically chuckled. "Don't misunderstand; being chased and nearly drowned isn't exactly what I want to do. I'd rather stand and fight. However, someone once told me that my tracking and evasive skills far exceed Dagar."

Kell snickered. "In the future, I should parcel out my compliments with more care."

Armus grinned. "I'll remind you of that. For now, are you rethinking our assignments?"

Kell slowly nodded. "You and Wren continue as before. You," he said to Avatar, "find a way to keep the Shadow Warriors from following or harassing Sir Dunham and his squires when they leave."

Avatar mischievously smiled. "No need. Those Shadow Weaklings aren't going to be happy when they wake up. They will be hunting for me."

Wren undid the pouch from her belt and held it out to Avatar. "You'll need this. There are three doses of the strengthening tonic left, some salve for wounds and herbs for pain." She caught his hand to delay his taking it. "Just promise to use the contents sparingly."

"With Jor'el's help, they'll be in need, not me." Avatar fastened the pouch to his belt.

At the manor house inside Dorgirith, Nari, Roane and Cassius tended to Indigo, Bern and Cletus. The latter two were sore and fatigued. Indigo suffered a large gash to the head, resulting in a concussion.

"You two are fortunate to survive an encounter with Avatar's power. I heard he took down forty at one time during the Great Battle," said Nari.

"He did. I witnessed it from a short distance away," said Cassius. He finished tying the bandage on Indigo's head.

"The only other time I felt this weak happened after the forced dimension travel sent us to the Cave," grumbled Bern.

"And made us prisoners," chided Cletus.

"This could have made you dead!" she snapped. "Next time, be more careful. I warned you about Avatar. Now maybe you'll listen."

Bern and Cletus both glared in annoyed offense. Indigo wasn't capable of much reaction. The head wound made him listless.

"This should help with the pain and give you some strength." Roane gave a cup to Indigo, who took it and drank.

"What now?" Bern asked.

"Once Indigo is recovered, we pick up the search for Avatar. Unless you sensed other Guardians while following him," replied Nari.

"No."

"The arrow," said Indigo in a droning voice.

"What arrow?" Roane asked.

"A hideous bird creature with rotting flesh and feathers was killed by a arrow through the neck near where we sensed Avatar," said Bern.

"A hunter-hawk. Witter and Altari sent it after Avatar," said Cassius, who then asked, "What kind of arrow?"

Bern shrugged with indifference. "Nothing unusual about it."

"Witter said one of the mortals was armed with a bow," said Cletus.

"Ay, one of the squires," chided Cassius.

"You think a mortal killed it?" asked Roane.

"They killed six madah-dune. Magelen and Dagar were furious"

Skeptical, Roane asked, "Mortals killed them? How is that possible?"

146

"Dark Way creatures aren't immortal. Powerful, ay, but can be killed like any normal creature," replied Cassius.

"Since there is no other Guardian presence, it confirms Avatar is alone," said Bern.

Nari tugged on her lower lip in consideration. "I don't know if I'm ready to report that to Witter and Altari just yet."

"Why? They couldn't stop Avatar," said Cassius.

"Which is why *we* were given the task of destroying him. This is a test of our newfound strength and loyalty."

"You believe that?" Cletus asked Nari.

"Of course! I've known Dagar since the beginning. Even as a Trio Leader, he tested those assigned to him to learn their strengths, weaknesses and loyalty. More than anything, he seeks revenge."

"We know. He didn't rebel against Jor'el for fun," chided Bern.

"No, revenge against *Kell*," Nari said emphatically. "If he can't engage the captain directly, he will destroy those closest to him: Armus and Avatar. Of course, Dagar always found Avatar's manner irritating from the moment of his creation. So until we succeed anything less will be viewed as failure. Any of you wish to report an incomplete mission?" She turned intense eyes on her Shadow Warrior companions.

"The consequences are further reconditioning, or worse," warned Cassius.

Bern firmly took Indigo's shoulder. "Hurry up and recover. We can't let him get too far ahead."

"Just as long as I have the first chance at him."

Chapter 14

AN HOUR BEFORE DAWN, KARRYN LEFT THE SMALL CASTLE chapel. She began to cross the compound intent on returning to the main house.

"Good morning," said Ethan. His greeting startled her. "I didn't mean to frighten you."

"I didn't know you were there." She spoke after taking a breath of recovery.

"I was on my way to the stables when I saw you. Trouble sleeping?"

"Ay. Coming to the chapel helps on those occasions it happens."

"I know. I've observed your habit."

Curious, she asked, "Why haven't you said anything before?"

Ethan smiled. "A funny question coming from one so quiet as you. Unlike me, who is accused of speaking too much." When she shied at his humor, he added an explanation in a more sincere tone. "I didn't want to interrupt your meditation and prayer. Are you feeling better?"

"Ay." She met his eyes. Even in the torchlight of the courtyard his gaze lingered on her, almost reminiscent. "You have looked at me strangely of late, why?"

"I thought I recognized your name when you first arrived. Since Dunham told us your father's identity, I've tried to see the girl I met so long ago." He touched her hair. "No pigtails, no freckles." He lightly tapped a finger on her nose.

Karryn laughed. "I haven't worn pigtails since I was thirteen. I still have a few freckles. You haven't changed much."

"No?" he asked with an ironic chuckle. "I'm a man now, not a teenager."

"I mean I would recognize you anywhere at any time."

"So why haven't *you* said anything before?" he teased in mimicking her question.

"Because as you and others are so quick to point out, I don't talk much." A tremor of hurt crept into her voice.

Ethan immediately became regretful. "I didn't mean to offend you or make light of your quiet nature."

Karryn sighed with lament. "No. It's me. People often mistake my silence as a fault and lack of feeling." She turned aside when to deal with her frustration.

Using a gentle hand, Ethan turned Karryn to face him. She avoided eye contact. "I'm accused of the same lack of feelings for the opposite reason. I use verbosity to sometimes mask my true sentiment. I believe your silence does the same in acting as a shield."

She gazed at him with wonder in her eyes. "Ay. There are times I fear to speak what I feel."

"What do you feel now? At this moment."

"I ... I -" Overcome by timidity, she tried to pull away.

Ethan wouldn't let her leave. "You have nothing to fear from me." She didn't answer, so he said, "I'll tell you what I feel. That meeting again as adults there are things left unsaid from our youth."

She darted him a glance. "Maybe," she spoke in an almost whisper.

Encouraged, Ethan continued, hoping to promote more of a response. "I remember a shy ten-year-old girl, I thought was the prettiest I had ever seen. Her bright auburn hair shining in the sun, large hazel eyes so unpretentious and the most freckles I recall seeing on anyone. I couldn't count them there were so many." He made an inspection of her face as if counting. "Most are gone now."

She giggled in shy amusement. "For years my father teased me about using my face to make a map of the constellations. I can't say I'm sad they're gone."

He smiled. "The girl is now a beautiful woman."

A blush rose to her cheeks.

"So this is where you are." Tristan's lighthearted tone told his mood.

Karryn took advantage of Tristan's arrival. "I need to help Maddy with Garrick. Excuse me." She withdrew.

Ethan watched Karryn moved to the house then sent a narrow glare to Tristan.

Apologetic, Tristan asked, "Did I interrupt something?"

Ethan didn't answer, rather headed for the stables.

Tristan followed. "I did interrupt. I'm sorry. Did you tell her? What did she say?"

"Tristan!"

"What?"

"Shut up."

Dressed and ready for departure, Dunham entered the kitchen. To his surprise, the staff was hard at work under Maddy's direction. He fought a smile when she spoke to him in a nonchalant manner.

"Breakfast will be ready soon. I'm having provisions packed for your journey."

"Well done. What of Garrick? Is he awake yet?"

"No. I was tending to this before waking him."

A gentle smile crossed his lips. He placed a hand on her shoulder. "I'm pleased at how well you are handling this now."

"I'm trying. Although I still wish you'd tell me why Tristan has to go with you."

He drew her away from the activity. "That is better left for a private matter, and not for open discussion."

Maddy bit her lip, abashed.

"See to Garrick. Cook and the rest can finish here." Dunham escorted Maddy to the back stairs, after which he made his way outside.

In the courtyard, Hadwin, Ethan, Tristan and fifty men prepared for departure. Being an official court visit required all the pomp and necessary trappings of nobility. The men wore their best livery. Dogs served for hunting and to ward off night predators. Heralds carried banners representing the house of Sir Dunham of Garwood, replacing the old Dunlap standard. He specifically ordered the new banners to show the change.

Hadwin bowed. "We should be ready to leave in an hour, my lord."

"Maddy is seeing to Garrick. I don't want to rush him if it causes undue angst."

"Then we leave at your convenience."

Dunham's eyes scanned the men until he spied Tristan by his horse. He approached the young man. "Any second thoughts this morning?"

"I settled any doubts long before today."

"Including Maddy?" Dunham gently probed.

At this question, Tristan stopped fastening the harness. "I won't deny being hesitant about telling her. Now that she knows, I'm relieved."

"You feared she would reject you."

Tristan slightly balked then admitted, "Ay."

Dunham smiled. "The thought never crossed my mind. I've watched you both for years. Love doesn't always come like a lightning bolt from the sky, making one giddy or out of their mind with desire. Sometimes it is slow, almost imperceptible, yet when discovered, is surprising how deep the bond is. She would no more reject you than you could turn your back on her."

"Which is why I'm relieved. I hoped, but didn't presume."

"Then let us make certain the plan succeeds so you can officially ask, and I grant her to you in marriage."

They heard delighted laughter coming from the other side of the horse. Ethan used a rag to buff his horse's saddle. Dunham chuckled and clapped Tristan's shoulder.

With a merry twinkle in his eye and mirth in his voice, Tristan said, "My lord, what about Widow Sorah for Ethan?"

"What?" Ethan asked with astonishment. "She's twice my age."

"And the only one who will tolerate you," quipped Dunham as he left.

Tristan heartily laughed. A rag hit his face. Tristan removed the rag. He saw Karryn standing across the yard. She smiled at him then her gaze turned to Ethan when it lingered a moment. She entered the house.

Tristan approached Ethan. "You did tell her." He slapped the rag into Ethan's hand.

"Only *you* interrupted before she could tell me anything in return."

Garrick offered little cooperation in waking, eating some breakfast or getting dressed. However, he didn't fight Maddy or Karryn. Maddy wasn't sure what to make of it. She told him they were going to the Fortress, a place he complained about in the past. Not that he disliked the priests; everything was just too formal for him. This morning he made no reaction, either in feature or physical movement to what Maddy said.

Finally, exasperated, Maddy sat Garrick on the bench at the foot of his bed. Intent on getting a response, she made him look at her. "Garrick, please, I need you to speak to me. You know we're going to the Fortress, correct?"

He sluggishly nodded.

"No, speak, Garrick, please."

To this request, he looked away.

"Oh, why are you being so stubborn?" She made him look at her again. "I know this is difficult for you but Father believes Master Reagan can help you. So do I. I don't like seeing you like this." Her voice broke with a quiver.

Karryn answered a knock at the door. Tristan entered. He grew sympathetic toward Garrick and asked Karryn, "How is he doing this morning?"

"Well, he's not fighting going to Fortress," she tried to sound encouraging.

Tristan approached the bed. "Your father sent me to tell you all is ready for departure, if Garrick is ready," he said to Maddy.

"I don't know." She asked her brother, "Are you ready, Garrick?"

The boy didn't reply, rather his gaze shifted between Tristan and Maddy.

"We should be going." Tristan gently took hold of Garrick's arm. The boy didn't pull away yet seized Maddy's hand.

"I'm coming," she said with a kind smile. "So is Karryn. You won't be alone."

Garrick walked between Tristan and Maddy, clinging to both of them. His face remained expressionless. As they approached the horses, an excited barking began. Alger broke from his handler and ran toward Garrick. Terrified Garrick screamed and hid behind Maddy. Tristan intercepted Alger. The dog happily wagged its tail, as it kept barking in Garrick's direction.

"Take him to his pony," said Dunham to Maddy and Karryn.

Tristan knelt to hold Alger's collar. He petted the friendly dog.

The handler came to get Alger. "He didn't mean anything, my lord. He's just excited."

"I know. The dog is not to blame. Put him back in the kennel. We'll take the others."

He took Alger from Tristan.

"I wonder if it's just Alger or all dogs?" said Tristan.

"It doesn't matter where fear is concerned. Let us pray Reagan can help him." Dunham steered Tristan to the horses.

The herald took the lead, followed by Sir Dunham with Maddy, Garrick with Karryn. Garrick clenched the saddlebow. He stared straight ahead. Karryn held the reins to lead his pony. Ethan and Tristan followed them. Next came Hadwin, soldiers, and lastly the wagon of provisions and the dogs.

It took most of the night for Avatar to recover. Kell remained with them. A sense of anticipation kept everyone silent. Even when the mortals left Garwood, they didn't speak. That was until all grew tense with the sensation of Shadow Warriors within range.

"Time to draw them away again," said Avatar.

Kell delayed Avatar's departure to ask Wren, "Will you be able to sense when he is successful so we can leave?"

"Ay, along with covering our essence when we depart."

Kell said to Avatar, "Jor'el be with you."

Avatar simply smiled and headed north. Since it took hours to recover his full strength, he didn't have the opportunity to lay traps. He had to be attentive and swift. This would be spot and chase until he could reach a point to deliberately lure them like earlier. With dimension travel being more difficult, it would be a last resort to conserve his energy.

Fortunately, being on higher ground, he spotted them before they saw him. Only this time, he counted five Shadow Warriors, including one very familiar looking female—Nari. When they became alert, he pretended to be evasive in movement. Upon hearing a voice raised in alarm, he took off at a run, faster than any mortal or horse.

Avatar turned northwest toward the Region of Sanctuary border. After all, isn't that where a Guardian of Jor'el would head, to the Temple? By the sounds, they followed. He hoped none of them were faster on foot than he.

The short ride to the Fortress of Garwood was made in silence. Garrick's condition caused uneasiness. Several exchanged glances of distressed concern passed between father and daughter. Despite his hands-off approach in some areas, Maddy knew he loved them. He rarely interfered in sibling squabbles, preferring them to work out any differences. He did not fully abdicate Garrick's training to Hadwin, Ethan and Tristan, rather wanted the boy to receive instruction like a normal soldier. Lessons in court etiquette, history, faith, respect and personal responsibility to Jor'el's laws, those he conducted.

Maddy heard expressed regret in his handling of Garrick since Dorgirith. She couldn't fault him entirely. Many times they circumvented their parents wishes. She buried herself in books while Garrick grew mischievously inventive in avoiding responsibility. Now, in their own way, each reaped the consequences of their own devices, she in conflict with servants when asserting her authority and Garrick ... Oh, poor Garrick! Frightened into silence by a hideous encounter with the Dark Way! Neither she nor her father was capable of handling such a condition. Despite initial resistance, for Garrick's sake she couldn't wait to get to the Fortress.

She sat so deep in thought it surprised her to hear a call to halt. They arrived. The simple construction consisted of weathered yellow stone framed by timbers. The main tower stood in the middle of the rear wall.

At the height of Jor'el's reign among the mortals, each major city of the twelve provinces had a Fortress to serve as a regional place of worship. Smaller ones were common among the countryside. Since Jor'el withdrew his presence after the Great Battle, many Fortresses became abandoned or neglected. Few viewed them as places of sanctuary or encouragement. Dunham's family never wavered in their support of the Fortress of Garwood or belief in Jor'el. This was one reason Dunham chose the site for his new castle, to protect the access road.

Dunham, Maddy, Garrick, Karryn, Ethan, Tristan and Hadwin entered the small courtyard. Ethan and Tristan dismounted in customary fashion to tend their lord and ladies.

Master Reagan and eight priests greeted them. A wiry man of fifty with balding red hair, a gentle soul as told by his congenial smile and friendly blue eyes. "My lord, welcome. Ladies."

Maddy flashed a distracted smile, her focus on Garrick. He warily eyed the compound. "It's all right, Garrick. We'll be safe here."

"Indeed you will, young master," said Reagan with a large, open smile.

Garrick caught Reagan's eyes. He appeared to relax.

"Help him down." Reagan instructed a priest.

Garrick balked, so Tristan intervened. "Let me help him. Until he's settled," he added to Reagan's curiosity. "Come, Garrick." The boy willingly dismounted and held on tight to Tristan.

Ethan aided the ladies to dismount.

"Their quarters, please, Master Reagan," said Dunham.

155

"This way, my lord. Ladies."

"Remain here," Dunham told Hadwin before going inside.

Ethan gave the reins of Karryn, Maddy and Garrick's horses to the Fortress servants to take charge. He noticed a lone priest beckoned to Hadwin. "Someone you know?" he asked.

The question briefly stymied Hadwin. "A cousin. To your duty with Sir Dunham." He nudged Ethan on his way.

Inside, Ethan joined them in going upstairs to the best rooms available. For being a smaller Fortress, it benefited from the family's patronage. The rooms were well furnished and decorated. A fire in the hearth chased away the chill of the late autumn morning.

"These adjacent rooms are connected by this door," said Reagan. "There is also a room across the hall; smaller, but also well furnished."

"I'll take the room across the hall, so Maddy can be near Garrick," said Karryn.

"These will serve well. Thank you," said Dunham.

"No thanks are necessary, my lord. Be assured, your children are in safe hands."

"I never thought otherwise."

"I will see Lady Karryn is installed." Ethan escorted her from the room.

Dunham spoke to Maddy. "Look after him and yourself."

"I will, Father, I promise." She hugged him.

After embracing Maddy, Dunham regarded Garrick with some apprehension. He attempted to sound encouraging. "Look after you sister." The boy didn't reply. Dunham turned to leave. Someone seized him. Garrick trembled, his grip tight. For a long moment, Dunham held his son then knelt to take Garrick by the shoulders.

"I must leave, but you will be safe with Master Reagan. Maddy is with you." Dunham grew frustrated at seeing the fear in his son's tear moistened eyes. "I don't know if you understand that I go to do what is for the best for all of us. Trust me and stay with your sister." To this, Garrick nodded. "I love you." He kissed his son on the forehead and left.

Garrick took Tristan's hand, his gaze imploring.

"I too must leave. And like your father, I will be back," Tristan said the last sentence turning to Maddy. She fought against weeping.

"Come, Master Garrick, I have a surprise for you." Reagan took the boy's hand. "I remember you like gingerbread. My cook made some special just for you."

Garrick went with Reagan. He looked back over his shoulder to Maddy and Tristan, only they regarded each other.

Maddy started weeping. Tristan held her. "You'll be safe here."

"My fear is for you."

"Don't be. I'm not afraid. Truly," he insisted at seeing her skepticism. "For some time, I have sensed in my spirit that I must do this." His voice grew resolute. "I can no more bear seeing what has become of Garrick than you and your father. As I've grown to love you, I consider him my brother. What we do will help him, and everyone, for a better future. So, please trust us and pray that we succeed."

"I do trust you and I also love you." They kissed. Hearing a happy exclamation from the other room broke them apart. "Garrick?"

"Sounds good. Go to him." Tristan ushered Maddy to the adjoining door. He quietly withdrew.

To her pleasant surprise, Garrick eagerly ate the gingerbread. "How did you get him to eat so eagerly?" she asked Reagan.

The headmaster gave her a private smile. "I told cook to add some hard cider to the gingerbread while the tea is a mixture of hawthorn, mint and trefoil. All are good for enlivening the soul and strengthening the heart. With Jor'el's help, we will make your brother whole in body, mind and spirit."

Tears of hope and gratitude swelled, as Maddy watched Garrick consume the gingerbread and drink the tea.

Across the hall, Ethan inspected Karryn's room. He made sure the door and window could be properly locked. "Secure enough."

"I'll be fine. What about you?"

He held her hands to gaze into her eye. "We didn't finish our conversation. Please, tell me your feelings before I must leave."

Karryn slightly shied before starting to speak. "I'm glad to once again meet the boy I thought the most handsome I had ever seen; with dark hair, pretty green eyes and an endearing smile."

Ethan lifted her chin to fully meet his gaze. "Who would have thought after so many years we would remember our first impression of the other so vividly?"

"I never forgot. I watched you each time you came to the North Plains. Secretly, being too shy to let you know."

He cocked a smile. "Oh, I knew. Yet, with the differences in our stations, I dare not hope so pretty a girl could like me. A girl I never forgot." He tenderly caressed her cheek.

"Station doesn't matter when the fate of Allon hangs by a thread. Courage, mettle and faith are needed. I know a woodsman squire who possesses those qualities."

"My lady," Ethan said in ardent respect and kissed her hand. Distracted voices in the hall, prompted him to say, "Jor'el keep you safe until meet again, and if you consent, never to part."

She tenderly smiled. "I consent."

"Ethan!" called Dunham from the hall.

Moved by impulse, Ethan kissed Karryn before rushing from the room.

Chapter 15

THE ONE HUNDRED MILES FROM GARWOOD TO RAVENDALE normally took four days of traveling on horseback at a good pace. Before the Great Battle, two Guardians protecting fifty-four mortals was not a problem. Nowadays, Wren and Armus had to conserve their energy, using just enough power to avoid detection. Such necessary stealth made the task frustrating.

From the shelter of a knoll, Armus and Wren watched Dunham's group cross the river plain from the Southern Forest into Midessex.

"If needed, will you be able to place a defensive shield around them to repel any creatures of infrinn?" asked Armus.

"I can, if it becomes necessary. However, the amount of energy needed will give us away."

His expression grew considerate of the mortal group. "We can't take any chances with Tristan's life."

"You doubt Avatar will succeed?" she said in her provoking humor.

Armus snorted a laugh. "No. You doubt him at your peril."

Wren laughed. Her was mirth short-lived as a sense of danger made them both tense. She held her crossbow aimed at a spot due west of the knoll toward a patch of tress. Armus drew his sword at the silver flash of a blade from behind a tree. An individual stepped out to wave the blade in a beckoning manner.

"Gresham." Wren lowered her bow.

Armus used his sword to acknowledge the signal then sheathed it.

"I hope they didn't notice the glint of steel between you two," she said of the mortals.

"They'd probably mistake it for bandits or outlaws. Remember, we're legends."

They circumvented the procession to meet Gresham. Being an Original made Gresham a peer of Kell and Armus. He had white hair and violet eyes. As a member of the vassal caste, he stood the same height as Wren at seven feet. Known for his elaborate taste in clothes, he toned down his attire since the Great Battle to fit his new covert role.

"How goes it?" he asked.

"Well, so far. Any trouble in the province we should know about?" replied Armus.

"No. Despite the increase in traffic, all is quiet."

"Have any of the other lords reached Ravendale yet?"

"Baron Renfrow should arrive in another day, along with Sir Cavan and Baron Kaleb. The rest are reported on route."

Considering the information, Armus looked to Dunham's group a mile behind their position. "Scout ahead. We need to keep any disturbance from impeding the journey."

"Doing that will prevent me from keeping account of the other mortals," said Gresham.

"Can't be helped. Sir Dunham's group must reach Ravendale safely." Armus continued his observance of the group.

Gresham followed Armus' interest. "I gather there is someone or something of importance among the mortals."

"Ay. More than that I cannot say. If you see Kell, ask him."

Gresham cocked a wry smile. "Hearing that from the second-in-command satisfies my curiosity."

Armus snickered, and glanced to Gresham. "Since when?"

"Since I became stripped and left for bare." Gresham made an elaborate gesture of his clothes.

With a smirk, Wren surveyed Gresham. "I think it's an improvement. I can look at you without being blinded by garish trinkets."

"Well, no one can tell you from a tree," he countered.

"Thank you. That is a great compliment for a hunter."

Armus laughed. "Now, go. Keep the way clear."

For a vassal, Gresham moved surprisingly quick as he faded into the forest out of sight.

"His skill would have impressed Vidar," quipped Armus. He noticed Wren's mood immediately changed to dejected. "Sorry, bad humor."

"No need to apologize. I occasionally experience twinges of sadness over his loss."

"We all do; Kell most of all. He is the captain."

"At least you and Avatar survived." Wren spoke more harshly than intended so she quickly added, "I didn't mean to sound resentful."

Armus graciously smiled at her. "I understand your feelings about Vidar. Perhaps *you* can understand Kell's reluctance to employ Avatar as Jor'el ordered."

"Oh, I do. What I meant is you still have the opportunity to speak to each other, say how you feel. Our last words were a dispute in the heat of battle." Wren's expression turned downcast with recollection. "Vidar ordered me to leave but I wanted to cover the retreat. He shoved me toward Ridge with orders to fall back. When the wyvern released its concussion bomb, Ridge and I dove for cover. After the light and noise faded, we discovered Vidar was gone."

Sympathetic, Armus placed an arm around Wren's shoulders. "We only heard he fell during the bombardment. I'm truly sorry, Wren."

She struggled to gather her emotions. "I don't know why your comment upset me. Vidar would have been impressed to see Gresham wearing subdued clothes and learning to move in the woods unseen."

Shouting drew their attention back to the procession. "We best take to the trees for surveillance," Armus said.

Dunham and Hadwin rode behind the heralds. Ethan and Tristan followed Dunham and Hadwin.

"My lord!" Hadwin pointed to the knoll in time to catch a fleeting glimpse of Armus before he disappeared into the trees. "I think we're being watched."

"I hope we are."

"You hope?"

Dunham chuckled. "Since Dorgirith, I have prayed for the divine protection to continue."

Tristan studied the knoll. "It maybe the same one who helped us. I can't tell for certain at this distance."

"We should find out." Hadwin turned in the saddle to issue orders.

"No!" Dunham's voice made Hadwin stop. "If it is the Guardian, he won't be found unless he wants to be. Besides, why trouble him if his task is to watch us?"

Hadwin peered quizzically at Dunham. "My lord, you take a great risk by placing such unfounded faith in this Guardian. *If* he truly is one."

"Have you been with me so long that you don't know the substance of my faith?"

"I do not dispute your faith in Jor'el. However, there is too much at stake to say with certainty that a stranger you've never seen is a Guardian."

"I saw him!" said Tristan with certainty. "After looking in his eyes, I can say with certainty he was Guardian and not mortal."

"How? Have you seen a Guardian before?" Hadwin's tone turned sarcastic.

Tristan fell silent with reticence so Dunham spoke.

"Faith is trust in something unseen. None of us have seen Jor'el, yet we acknowledge his existence by witnessing his essence in people, animals and nature. He created Guardians before mortals and Allon. Although they no longer dwell among us like they once did, that doesn't nullify their existence. I believe Tristan saw a Guardian, as did Maddy and Garrick. Three who witnessed the same cannot be wrong."

"If you say so, my lord." Hadwin didn't sound convinced.

"I tell you he was a Guardian!" insisted Tristan.

"Tristan." Dunham shook his head in warning.

"No, he—"

"Tristan!"

The young man clamped his mouth at the more forceful rebuke. His expression displeased at complying.

Dunham spoke to Hadwin. "Send out scouts for tonight's campsite."

The master-at-arms turned his horse to leave the group.

With Hadwin gone, Tristan continued his objection. "His doubt is unacceptable."

"His *doubt* isn't aimed at you. It's aimed at the divine," Dunham spoke with emphasis. "I appreciate your zeal, but you cannot argue someone into believing. Many believe without seeing while others only after seeing. Sadly, there are those who won't believe even when their eyes and senses tell them reality."

"You feel Hadwin is among the latter group?" asked Ethan in a tone more suggestive of a statement than question.

"Ay. It pains me to think so after so long. He is a practical man; always has been."

"Grandpapi says practicality and faith can co-exist," said Tristan.

Dunham chuckled in agreement. "There must be practicality to life in order to survive. A concept Maddy is learning. Hopefully she will master it soon enough—for your sake."

Tristan flushed with embarrassment, which made Ethan laugh.

Dunham looked to where Hadwin carried out his orders. His voice changed to resolution laced with regret. "If the situation grows touchy, I might reconsider bringing him into our confidence."

"No!" said Tristan hastily. At Dunham's frowning reaction, he added, "Not that I distrust him rather his latest arguments are worrisome. Being so practical leaves little room for faith. I wonder if we can depend upon his full support. You just expressed similar sentiments."

"In regards to faith, not his trustworthiness or dependence."

"With all due respect, my lord," began Ethan. "He made it plain he would speak out in opposition. Can that be contained if he were fully informed? One wrong word at the wrong time ..." Ethan didn't finish, he didn't have to; Dunham understood.

Four men rode past them to the head of procession.

Hadwin returned. "Scouts are dispatched, my lord," he said.

By the time Dunham and his men made camp, they traveled eighteen miles. To make Ravendale in four days meant traveling twenty-five miles each day. Stopping at the Fortress caused the delay. This made it necessary to make up the distance during the rest of the journey.

Tristan prepared Dunham's accommodations inside the tent. Loud voices interrupted him.

"My lord, listen to reason!" Hadwin argued when he and Dunham entered.

"I have listened. I just don't agree," replied Dunham in a reasonable, calm tone.

"Then let me return to the Fortress—"

"Return? Why?" asked Tristan, interrupting.

Hadwin ignored him to continue speaking to Dunham. "It's the only way to be certain."

"Certain of what?" asked Tristan again, only this time in a more demanding tone.

Hadwin confronted Tristan. "Is his lordship's supper ready?"

"Ethan went to fetch it."

"Then tend to you duties, squire, and leave matters alone that don't concern you!"

Piqued, Tristan went to reply when Dunham ordered him to, "Help Ethan."

In long hasty strides, Tristan went to the cooking area to find Ethan. "Is it ready yet?"

Ethan cocked a curious brow at Tristan's surly tone. "Almost. Can you cook any faster?" he tried some levity. It didn't work so he asked, "What's wrong?"

"Hadwin. He argued with Sir Dunham about returning to the Fortress."

"Why?"

"That's what I asked. Hadwin rebuked me then Sir Dunham told me to help you fetch supper. If something's wrong at the Fortress or with Maddy I want to know."

Ethan received the tray of food from the cook. He didn't speak until they were away from the area. "Hadwin doesn't know of your personal concern for Maddy. Besides, she is Sir Dunham's responsibility until he gives her to you."

Tristan flushed at the statement. Hadwin rushed from the tent and mounted his horse. Ethan's elbow jabbed Tristan to get his marked attention off Hadwin.

"Can't let the food get cold," said Ethan. Inside the tent, he placed the tray on the small portable table to begin serving Dunham. "My lord, may I inquire why Master Hadwin left?"

"He wants to make certain Maddy and Garrick are well installed."

Tristan became alarmed. "Why? Has there been word of trouble?"

"No," said Dunham with a reassurance. "He's not convinced we have Guardians watching us. Instead, he believes they are agents of Magelen. I disagree."

"But you're letting him go back!"

"If it eases his mind he may be more receptive in matters of faith. He can be quick and rejoin us before we reach Ravendale. I see no harm in it. Now, join me." Dunham motioned to the table.

Ethan brought enough food for all. He spoke after pouring a drink for Dunham. "He'll probably find out from his cousin that all is well."

"Cousin?" asked Tristan.

"The brooding priest with the limp. Although I can't recall his name."

Dunham swallowed his drink. "Malik? He's not Hadwin's cousin. He has no living relatives."

Ethan paused in handing Tristan a cup to regard Dunham. "Hadwin said they were related when I asked if he knew him."

"When was this?" asked Dunham.

"At the Fortress when we arrived with the ladies and Master Garrick. The priest beckoned to Hadwin and that's when I made inquiry."

"Why would he lie to Ethan?" Tristan practically demanded of Dunham.

The lord shook his head with befuddlement. "I don't know." He returned to Ethan for confirmation. "He actually claimed Malik is his cousin?"

"Ay. I thought nothing of it at the time or I would have mentioned it sooner."

"You let him go back to the Fortress!" chided Tristan.

Dunham set his jaw at the rebuke, yet tempered his words. "Granted his behavior is puzzling. I can only think of one reason, which has nothing to do with Maddy and Garrick. He simply wants to avoid going to Ravendale. He made it perfectly clear he disagrees with the plan, perhaps this was his way of ..."

"Deserting!" declared Tristan.

Dunham made a slow deliberate nod, almost unable to say, "Ay."

"We'll bring him back." Tristan bolted to his feet.

Dunham snatched Tristan's arm. "There are more important things to be concerned about."

"He has disgraced you!"

"And could betray the plan as easily as he rode from here," added Ethan with severity.

At Dunham's conflict, Tristan insisted, "You know how swiftly Ethan and I can ride."

Dunham released Tristan. "Go. I'll delay slightly, but I can't give you more than half a day. The others will be waiting."

Ethan grabbed his bow and quiver on their way out.

In the shelter of a grove of trees, Armus and Wren viewed the fires of Dunham's encampment. They became alert at first sensing then seeing a flash of white light in the trees behind them. She held her bow ready while he drew his sword. They relaxed at Kell's arrival.

166

"What brings you here?" Armus sheathed his sword.

Kell blinked several times in recovery from the travel before replying. "Is all well? Has anything unusual happened?"

"No. Although the man Hadwin left heading east," said Wren.

Kell's head snapped around to her, alert and concerned. "Back to the Southern Forest?"

"I suppose."

For a moment Kell stared east, past the encampment. He stiffened with alarm. "Wren, return quickly. Something is wrong!"

The urgency concerned her. "What? Maddy and Garrick are at the Fortress."

"I don't know. Just go! I'll remain with Armus."

Wren put up her bow before running off to the east.

"I hope Avatar hasn't failed—" began Armus when both he and Kell flinched. "A disturbance in the transverse?"

"No," said Kell shaking his head. "Avatar's in trouble."

"Go help him. I'll be fine here."

Chapter 16

FOR THE ENTIRE DAY, AVATAR RAN, DODGED AND BARELY ESCAPED the Shadow Warriors. He found the closer he got to the Temple, the more his strength increased. Whether this renewed vigor happened in correlation to being a Guardian of Jor'el, he couldn't stop long enough to determine. Still, the added strength helped in the latest escapade when forced to dimension travel or be captured.

White light faded from Avatar's arrival in the Temple underground vault. He experienced no drain of energy, instead, he felt completely normal. He doubted the Shadow Warriors would dare follow him. He needed time to plan his next move. For the moment he was safe, or so he thought. White light appeared. Avatar drew his sword to confront the new arrival.

"Kell? What are you doing here? I thought you went to Ravendale?"

"I sensed something went wrong." Kell glanced up and down at Avatar. "You appear whole."

Avatar sheathed his sword. "They nearly succeeded. I had to vanish or *poof*—no more decoy. I almost forgot how good Nari is."

"Nari?" asked Kell with surprise that quickly turned to anger.

"Ay. Roane is with her along with the three Weaklings I bested earlier. I thought I could lose them for a moment to consider a new course of action. Lure them again on my terms rather than running. I didn't think they would dare try to get at me here."

"Ay. They are forbidden access to the Temple or Fortresses. You can't wait too long."

"I don't intend to. I thought to move them toward the Highlands. There are enough caves and snowy passes to create some interesting traps." Avatar's gregarious smile vanished at Kell's scowl.

"Act swiftly to be rid of them and return to the Southern Forest. I sense trouble and told Wren to return."

"They couldn't have doubled-back. They are right behind me, so it must be something else." Avatar spoke with certainty.

"Just be quick. I'm going to rejoin Armus." Kell vanished.

Acting quickly was a matter of opinion. Avatar had to consider his next move. Five against one didn't pose a problem for him at full strength. In fact, he often practiced against six warriors in mock bouts. However, that was before the Great Battle and punishment. At present, the Shadow Warriors couldn't come to the Temple while his strength would reduce by half once he left. He hoped remaining to plan his next move didn't affect Wren or whatever trouble Kell mentioned in the Southern Forest.

Avatar recalled Kell saying Valmar still commanded the Highlands. Would his current strength help him to communicate with Valmar? One way to find out. Taking a deep breath, he closed his eyes to stretch out his senses. He searched for Valmar's essence with a message of where to meet. He flinched at making contact with someone. Whether Valmar or not, he didn't know. The inability to make definite identifications proved to be another frustrating sign of the punishment. To find out, meant dimension travel. He hoped whoever waited turned out to be friendly.

Avatar reappeared on the border of the Region of Sanctuary and the Highlands, just north of Lake Joram. This time, he experienced a tremendous drain of energy. His weak legs made him stagger sideways before regaining his balance. The orange glow of twilight told him that he waited longer at the Temple than he thought. He became alert at the nearby presence. Unfortunately, he didn't have the strength for a lengthy fight or take on multiple opponents.

"Valmar?" Avatar asked in a cautious voice.

"Ay, lad. Nice to see you're in one piece. At least I think you are." The Highland Guardian warrior was stouter than Avatar with a thick, glorious mane of white hair and violet eyes. "What brings you back?"

"I'm a decoy."

"Come again?"

"We may soon be joined by five Shadow Weaklings all bent on taking me apart."

"So, naturally you led there here?"

"No, I went to the Temple first. Kell told me to act fast in getting rid of them and return to the Southern Forest. I thought being so cold up here, you needed practice to stay warm."

Valmar made a short, ironic laugh. "What are you luring them away from?"

Avatar spoke in a discrete voice. "Not what, *who*. A knight and his squires."

By Valmar's sudden change to serious, he understood. "Come, lad. I know just the place to set a trap that will keep them busy for quite some time."

"Cover your trail. They are only expecting to sense me. That's also part of the assignment, to keep them from discovering more of us."

Valmar closed his eyes and spoke the Ancient. He then led Avatar from the rendezvous into the foothills, leaving only one set of footprints in the snow—Avatar's.

An hour later, they stopped below the jagged, majestic mountains of the Highlands. The snow depth reached ten inches.

"In another two days, these passes will be inaccessible," said Valmar.

"What is that to Shadow Warriors?" asked Avatar.

"Their strength is also diminished. After expending energy to escape our little trap, they'll have to navigate three feet or more of snow just to get down from here."

Avatar widely grinned. "I like it. Yet, remember, they are following me and not expecting to encounter another Guardian. You being here could cause trouble."

"I don't intend to stay around, just long enough to help you set the trap."

"When this is done, I'll need your help to dimension travel back to the Southern Forest since Kell said it was urgent. Where will we meet?"

Valmar pointed. "That glen with almost no snow is three miles. I'll be there waiting. I can only take you as far as the Northern Forest. From there Barnum can help you."

"That'll have to do. Let's set the trap."

<hr/>

Nari, Roane, Cletus, Indigo, and Bern arrived a mile from the Temple on a hill overlooking the compound. Being night, exterior torches and the soft glow of interior oil lamps illuminated the Temple and grounds.

"Wonderful! We can't get him in there," chided Bern.

"We'll wait for him to come out. When he does, this time I won't miss," said Nari.

Immediately, all five were armed at sensing a presence.

Altari rode a spirit stallion. He jerked the reins to bring the stallion to a skidding stop. "What are you doing here? You're supposed to be following Avatar," he demanded.

"He came to the Temple," said Nari.

"Why are you here, Commander?" asked Roane.

"I was on my way to Dorgirith with new orders for you when I picked up your trail. You're being careless, Nari."

"You said time is crucial in destroying Avatar. We haven't sensed other Guardians. So what if we leave a trail. Who will bother us?"

Altari stood in the stirrups to stare at the Temple. "He left. Heading north."

"We'll get him," she said.

"No. You and Roane report to Cassius, the others will deal with him."

"Why?"

"Because those are your orders! You better correct your insubordinate attitude, Nari. Being an Original has no status in Dagar's ranks. Results matter. Failure means reconditioning or worse! Success means survival and advancement. Understood?" snapped Altari.

"Ay, Commander," she said in a formal, submissive tone, complete with salute.

"Go! Before he gets too far," Altari ordered Cletus, Bern and Indigo.

The three set off in a fast run heading north.

"Dimension travel back to Dorgirith," Altari instructed Nari and Roane. He turned the horse around to gallop south toward the border with Midessex.

Nari glared after Altari; the look on her face unmistakably lethal.

"I wouldn't consider confronting him, if I were you," said Roane in warning. He became the focus of her deadly gaze to which he said, "*Keep your mind on our mission* is what you've always told me."

Nari didn't argue. Instead, she seized his shoulder. "Dimension travel," she said. They spoke in unison, disappeared, and reappeared at the manor house. Although traveling together lessened the draining effects of energy they needed a moment to recover. They didn't get one when Cassius spoke with impatience.

"It's about time. Where are the others?"

"Chasing Avatar, why?" she asked.

Cassius frowned with indignation. "You two will have to do."

"Do what?"

"Curtail Dunham's influence before he reaches Ravendale. He left his son and daughter at the Fortress before departing."

"We can't enter a Fortress," chided Roane.

"We have a confederate who will bring them to us at a pre-arranged rendezvous."

Nari's ire rose. "We were pulled from dealing with a dangerous Guardian to baby-sit mortal children?"

"On Magelen's orders!" Cassius bravely countered. "Avatar is obviously luring you away while the real threat heads to Ravendale."

Nari and Roane exchanged a chided glance. "When do we leave to fetch the children?" she asked.

"At the appointed time. Meanwhile, recover your strength. I'm sure Avatar taxed you."

* * *

Dawn broke. Avatar waited in a cramped crevasse halfway down the slope to watch the pass but not be seen. The trap lay further up the slope. He tried to shrug his shoulders into a more comfortable position. Movement sent some snow falling on his head. He hoped the Shadow Warriors arrived soon so he could relieve the tension in his muscles.

What am I saying? I'm impatient to meet Shadow Warriors?

Avatar moved again. This time a good amount of snow fell on him. He grumbled in annoyance. He attempted to wipe the snow from his face then stopped when struck with a presence close by. He peeked out. Three Warriors trudged up the snowy mountain pass. What about Nari and Roane? All five followed him earlier.

Carefully, Avatar stepped out of the crevasse so as not to draw attention prematurely. He made a quick scan for Nari and Roane. He didn't see them. One of the Warriors wore a bandage on his head. Had to be the one caught in the tree snare since Avatar recognized the others from the river.

With no sign of Nari and Roane, Avatar stepped onto the path. However, instead of drawing their attention as intended, he slipped and slid down the path. He didn't stop until his right foot smacked against a rock buried in the snow. Nothing felt broken, but it hurt. At a shout, he realized they spotted him. He didn't have time to ascertain the extent of his injury, rather move. He couldn't. His foot became wedged in the rock. When he jerked his foot free, the rock ripped through his boot and tore into his ankle. He swallowed back an outcry of pain. He couldn't deal with the wound; he had to get to the safe spot.

Avatar stumbled up the slope; his right ankle painful and weak while the depth of the snow impeded his effort. For a third time, he fell to his knees. The ankle bled profusely. They began gaining on him. Standing, Avatar drew his sword and drove the point into an overhanging batch of snow to create a small avalanche. He hoped to slow their advance and gain time to reach the safe spot. Not waiting to see the results, he used his sword like a crutch to climb the slope. Shouts of annoyance came from below.

Suddenly something large struck Avatar between the shoulder blades. He fell face first into the snow then began to slide down. He lifted his sword and plunged it through the snow and into the ground. Holding the hilt with both hands helped to stop his slide. After pulling himself level with the blade, he attempted to stand. His ankle gave way and he fell back into the snow. The Warriors were a hundred yards behind him. Gritting his teeth against the pain, he jerked the sword free to hasten up the slope as fast as he could. One Warrior shouted in the Ancient.

Avatar turned in time to see a Warrior make a motion of flinging his hand. Avatar dove behind the nearest boulder in time to avoid the impact of a blast. It exploded against the rock. The echoing sound of the blast was followed by a cracking overhead. Snow broke off and headed his way. He had to reach the safe spot now or be caught in the avalanche.

"*Astar et luths!*" Avatar used the Ancient to summon speed. He made it to the safe spot the same moment the avalanche passed him and the Warriors reached the trap.

The force of the falling snow made the ground tremble. The earth collapsed under the Warriors and they disappeared beneath the surface. The avalanche roared over the trap, with snow falling on top of them.

Avatar again summoned speed and ran to the trap. "By Jor'el's will be closed!" He struck the ground with his sword. The earth closed on top of the hole. Snow covered the ground as if nothing disturbed it.

In pain and fatigue, Avatar staggered sideways when he fell onto his buttocks. "Sorry, Wren, I can't keep my promise."

He took the pouch of his belt. After applying the salve to a very deep gash, he used a bandage to bring the cut parts of his boot together over the wound to apply pressure and stem the bleeding. He tied it as tight as he could tolerate.

Muffled voices and thumping came from underground. They attempted to use their powers to escape. Precisely what Valmar predicted. With a satisfied grin, Avatar used his sword to stand. He gingerly put weight on his right foot and flinched in pain. He looked toward the glen. It was going to be a long three-mile walk, even longer to the Southern Forest.

Chapter 17

MADDY TRIED TO IGNORE THE HAND THAT KEPT PUSHING ON her shoulder trying to wake her. She heard a male voice. Was it real or a dream? Suddenly, a hard shove was followed by the command, "Wake up!"

Her eyes snapped open. She became startled at seeing a man beside her bed. She shrunk back against the headboard. She signed in relief at recognizing a priest. "Oh, you frightened me."

"I'm sorry, my lady, but you needed to wake up."

Maddy took a couple breaths to recover her fright. "Is something wrong? My brother?"

The priest frowned with impatience. "There is no time to explain. You and your brother must come with me."

"Why? And what is your name?"

"Malik. But that's not important," he said with urgency. He began to pull down the covers. Maddy resisted by yanking them back.

"I'm not dressed!"

The protest made his frown deepened. "Then hurry! Put on a frock."

Before Maddy could make further inquiry, he disappeared into the other room. Such a rush required an explanation and she would continue with questions when he reappeared. However, knowing the current situation, she rose to dress.

A few grunts and grumbles came from the adjacent room. No doubt Malik had trouble with Garrick. She just finished donning a day dress when she heard a loud "No!" from Garrick.

Maddy rushed into the room. Garrick wrestled with Malik, as the priest forcefully dressed him. She quickly intervened. "Easy, Garrick," she soothed. "What is the reason for this haste?" she asked Malik.

"I'm not at liberty to say."

She stopped helping Garrick to confront Malik. "Then why should we go with you?"

Malik frowned in an attempt to amend answer. "I'm not at liberty to say for *security* reasons, my lady. You would not want me to place your father in further jeopardy by speaking."

Fearful, Garrick seized Maddy's hand. She patted her brother's hand and smiled with reassurance. "Of course not. We would protect him. I'm just surprised it's you and not Tristan or Ethan coming for us."

"Tristan," said Garrick, hopeful.

"Ay, Tristan," Malik said in hasty agreement. "We are meet him outside the Fortress. And without being seen." He seized Garrick's hand to boy pull away from Maddy.

"What about Karryn?" she asked.

The question perplexed Malik. "She was not mentioned. Now come, we cannot tarry any longer." He carefully peeked out into the hall. He saw no one.

"Why outside? Why not come inside? And how could Tristan not ask for Karryn?" she bombarded him with questions.

"*Shh!*" he scolded her. His reply came low and harsh. "I don't know about the other lady, yet there are forces at work which you cannot understand." He tugged on her hand to move quickly.

Once down the back stairs, Malik paused again. Being early morning, not many were up or about their duties. From the back stairs they made their way out to the postern gate.

"Cold," Garrick complained.

"Be quiet," scolded Malik. He opened the gate. "Quick, head for those trees. Tristan is just beyond, waiting. I'll be right behind you."

"Come, Garrick, we're going to meet Tristan." Maddy ushered her brother in the direction indicated.

Malik shut the gate and ran to join them. "Follow me and step lively." He led them deeper into the forest, south of the Fortress.

"Where are we going? Why did Tristan not come to the Fortress?" she demanded.

"I told you, there are reasons. Now no more questions."

Garrick began lagging so Malik pulled the boy forward.

"Through the thicket. You'll see Tristan just beyond." Malik made a shooing motion.

At the front gate, Ethan and Tristan arrived. Both were soiled and fatigued from the night ride. The horses trembled and covered in sweat.

"By command of Sir Dunham, open the gate!" shouted Ethan.

They heard movement from inside the Fortress. It took several moments before the gate opened. Despite being tried, Ethan practically jumped from the saddle to dismount in the courtyard. He accosted the priest who greeted them.

"The priest Malik, where is he?"

"Probably just waking up, why?"

"Has Master Hadwin been here?"

"No."

"Where is Master Reagan?" Ethan continued his questioning.

"At morning prayers in the chapel." The priest pointed across the compound.

"Lady Madelyn?" asked Tristan.

"Still asleep, I suppose."

"Find Malik! And make haste," Ethan ordered the priest.

The priest ran in the direction of the chapel. He passed an upset Karryn in her rush to meet Tristan and Ethan. She wore britches and doublet, fully armed with her hair loose.

"Ethan! Tristan! Maddy and Garrick are gone."

"Where?" Ethan asked.

Karryn shook her head. "I don't know. I woke at hearing voices and discovered their rooms empty. I asked some priests, but no one has seen them. I dressed with the intent of finding them when I saw you both."

Reagan came from the direction of the chapel. "Grady says you are looking for Malik? He wasn't in the chapel so I sent Grady to the dormitory."

"Were Maddy and Garrick with you in chapel?" asked Tristan.

"No, perhaps they are in dining hall for breakfast or still asleep."

"No, they are not in their rooms, and Garrick wouldn't go to the hall," said Karryn.

Grady arrived in a rush. "Master! Franklin said Malik isn't in his chamber or at his morning duty."

"Where has he gone?"

"He didn't know."

The answer didn't please any of them so Ethan ordered Grady, "Search the Fortress! Question anyone who may have seen Malik, Lady Madelyn or Master Garrick!"

Hadwin pushed his exhausted horse through the forest toward the rendezvous. He regretted having to do it this way. Alas, he saw no other alternative to make Dunham reconsider the plan. For his own good and the sake of the children, Hadwin kept telling himself.

The horse stopped in protest, its legs unsteady and breathing labored. Hadwin kicked the animal to make it move. Just a half-mile more! Then, he saw them—two large beings with Malik and the children at the rendezvous. *Shadow Warriors!* What were they doing there? The boy cried out in alarm when a Warrior grabbed Maddy.

"Run, Garrick!" Maddy shouted. She struggled with the Warrior.

Malik followed Garrick. Maddy screamed when the Warrior tossed her aside like a rag doll to race after Malik and Garrick.

Hadwin drew his sword intent on intervening. He kicked the horse. It lunged forward then collapsed to the ground. He tumbled from the saddle. Blood flowed from the horse's nostrils. The red tongue hung out

179

of its mouth. All signs of death. Hadwin became frantic when the second Warrior briefly bent over Maddy before pursuing its companion. Maddy remained on the ground. Hadwin ran to Maddy. He skidded to a halt at seeing the right side of her head and face bloodied. He knelt to feel for a pulse. Someone called to him.

"Hadwin!"

He balked when Ethan, Tristan, Karryn, Reagan and several priests arrived.

"Maddy!" In horror, Tristan dropped to his knees beside her.

Karryn covered her mouth to stifle a sob of dread.

Tristan touched the left side of Maddy's neck then exhaled in relief. "She's alive."

Hadwin's words came choked and hurried. "I tried to reach her in time."

Ethan pulled Hadwin to his feet. "Where is Garrick?"

"I don't know! It wasn't supposed to be like this. Not Shadow Warriors," he stammered, completely unnerved.

Ethan jerked Hadwin. "Get a hold of yourself, man! What do you mean?"

Reagan stopped Ethan from further accosting Hadwin. "We'll learn the answers. First we must find Garrick before they do!"

Ethan shoved Hadwin so hard the older man fell. Ethan knelt beside Tristan. "You and Karryn take Maddy back to the Fortress. I'll find Garrick." He spoke in a private voice to Karryn. "Help Tristan." He left.

Wren didn't slow until she reached the edge of the forest near the Fortress. She felt an overwhelming sense of something dreadfully wrong a moment before—"Shadow Warriors!"

Arming her bow, she carefully entered the woods to track them. She traveled a quarter of a mile when she spotted a priest running after Garrick a few yards ahead of him. A female Shadow Warrior raced past the priest.

Wren raised her bow when the female Shadow Warrior overtook Garrick and seized him. Unfortunately, the action brought Garrick into Wren's line of fire. She held her shot. Another Shadow Warrior arrived and snatched the priest. Again Wren held her shot, not wanting to hit either the priest or Garrick. Voices of shouting made the Shadow Warriors vanish in white light, taking Garrick and the priest. Ethan, Reagan and more priests arrived. Wren lowered her bow to observe.

Ethan was beside himself with angry frustration. "What happened? Where did they go?"

"Some place you won't find them," said Reagan.

"How do you know?"

"Shadow Warriors are servants of the Dark Way—"

"People don't just vanish! I tracked them here." Ethan spoke in hot protest.

Reagan attempted to calm Ethan. "There are forces beyond mortal limitations. Let us return to tend to the lady. We'll get some answers from Hadwin."

The reasoning didn't appear to satisfy Ethan. "Will those answers help to tell Sir Dunham that his son is again in the clutches of the Dark Way? That his daughter is severely injured, maybe dying of wounds?"

Maddy! At the startling news, Wren couldn't watch any longer. She drifted back into the forest. Kell told her something was wrong so she returned as fast as she could. Alas, she failed to reach them in time! If she knew the extent, she would have dimension traveled. No, not with two Shadow Warriors involved. Travel would diminish her energy. Most likely they took Garrick back to Dorgirith. The question is: what to do now?

Suddenly, Wren heard something close by! She raised her crossbow. She fired at the first sight of movement. A thud, not of impact rather someone hitting the ground with an *oofff* followed by loud grumbling.

"By the heavenlies, Wren! What are you trying to do, kill me?"

"Avatar?" she said in horror. She hurried to find him. He lay on the ground, slow in sitting up. "Did I hit you?"

"No, just missed." Avatar jerked his thumb to indicate the arrow impaled in a tree behind him. "You made me move so fast that I wrenched my ankle again."

Wren's discomposure became heightened at seeing his bloody boot and bandage. "What happened?"

"Compliments of the Shadow Weaklings chasing me. I'll live. At least if I don't get shot at again!" He unwrapped the bloody bandage to examine his ankle and didn't notice her distress.

Using disjointed motions, Wren spoke in haste. "I'm sorry! I didn't see you, not after that. I wasn't thinking, just reacting."

"Kell said you needed help." Avatar still tended to his ankle.

"Too late! One is captured and the other possibly dying!"

The statement made Avatar finally notice her great discomposure. "Who?"

Wren had difficultly replying. "Maddy and Garrick."

Thunderstruck, Avatar stared at her before asking, "How?"

"I don't know all the details, but two Shadow Warriors were involved. I arrived to witness them capture Garrick and a priest. I aimed to shoot, but Garrick came into the line of fire so I waited. Hearing the noise of pursuit, they vanished."

"And Maddy?"

Wren struggled with her emotions. "I heard Ethan say she is severely injured, maybe dying." She wiped the tears from her face. "I failed to get here in time!"

Avatar tried to comfort Wren. "I got here as fast I could to help because of what Kell said. I even dimension traveled with Valmar then Barnum." His brows leveled in angry annoyance. "I know I lured the others away! Did you recognize them?"

"No, but the female had short dark hair, and armed with a dagger."

"Nari!" he swore. "The male is Roane. I know they all followed me to the Temple. Only the three I bested before tracked me into the Highlands. I wondered why I didn't see Nari and Roane. They must have doubled back. I'm sorry."

"No need to apologize. Protecting them was my responsibility. You did your job."

"Not good enough since they came back," he complained with bitter regret. Wren battled to regain her composure. Avatar rose to his knees, took her by the shoulders and made her look at him. "You said Maddy is badly injured, which means she is in need of attention. Isn't Eldric among the twelve remaining?" It was more a statement then a question, but one she approved of.

"Ay."

"Do you sense Shadow Weaklings nearby? I don't."

Wren briefly closed her eyes then shook her head. "No."

He held her hands. "I'll take responsibility to tell Kell why we summoned Eldric."

"No, protecting them is my responsibility. I'll answer to Kell."

"We both will."

They closed their eyes to begin concentrating on the summons. After a couple of moments, they separated. Avatar sat back on his rump and off his wounded ankle. Wren rubbed the pain from her eyes.

"Do you think it worked? " she asked.

"You should be asking me that." Eldric, the premier Guardian physician, appeared from behind a tree. He stood the same height as Wren with black hair and pale violet eyes. He replaced his usual blue physician's robes with a more muted suite for their clandestine activities. "You didn't summon me to take care of the warrior's boo-boo, did you?"

Wren bolted to her feet to confront Eldric. "No, it's more serious than that!"

"Steady, Wren." Avatar stood beside her, yet shifted his weight to his left foot. He let the physician know of the severity of the situation by his reprimanding tone and expression. "Even with limited strength and wounded I could deal with you. However, your skills are needed to tend a mortal attacked by Shadow Warriors. As a result, her brother was captured by them."

"Brother? You don't mean Maddy and Garrick, do you?" asked Eldric in grave concern.

"He does. Maddy is at the Fortress," said Wren.

"I'll tend to her immediately." Eldric departed.

"Don't appear as yourself!" called Avatar. He received a wave of acknowledgement from the physician. He hissed in pain and sat to tend his ankle. Wren knelt, but Avatar shooed her away. "Go. Help Eldric. I have your pouch, remember?"

"Honestly, I'm not sure what to do."

"We need to stay because of Tristan. With Shadow Warriors involved they could turn their sights on him and Ethan. I'll join you when I'm done." Avatar grunted again with pain in an effort to tend his ankle.

Wren took the pouch off his belt. "I'll do it. The angle is difficult. Besides, they won't be going anywhere soon. Not until they know of Maddy's condition."

Avatar didn't argue. He leaned back against the tree to let her tend his wound.

⊷ ⋯⋯⋯ ⊶

Maddy lay on a bed in the Fortress infirmary. Tristan sat in a chair beside the cot, clenching her hand. A priest cleansed her head wound. Ethan, Karryn and Reagan waited at the foot of the bed. Reagan heard voices from the threshold. Two priests spoke to a tall, dark headed man with a satchel slung across his chest to hang at his right hip. Reagan approached them

"He says he is a physician passing through. He saw the commotion and came to see if he could help," a priest told the headmaster.

Reagan surveyed the man, who stood above standard height and dressed in dusty travel clothes. "Sir, your arrival at such a time is a strange occurrence."

"Strange or providential, Headmaster?" Eldric looked directly at Reagan. Even in altered form his eyes were a striking bluish/purple.

Reagan quelled a smile. "Providential. Come. We fear she is close to death."

Tristan stood when Reagan returned with the man.

"He is a physician come to help," said Reagan to Tristan's curiosity.

"I pray you can help her," said Tristan earnestly.

"I'll do my best." Eldric removed his satchel. He asked for the priest cleansing the wound to step aside so he could examine Maddy. Eldric opened her eyes to look at each pupil then laid a hand on her forehead. His attention turned to Tristan upon hearing the young man's suppressed distress. Eldric leaned over as if examining Maddy's left side, but spoke so only Tristan could hear. "Be at ease, my lord. I sense this is not unto death." He met Tristan's glance. For a split second, Eldric's eye returned to their natural violet color. Tristan gasped under his breath.

"Tristan?" Concerned, Ethan drew closer.

"I'm fine."

"Are you sure?"

Eldric straightened to smile at Ethan. "I assured him that she is in good hands. Now, please, for privacy sake, leave so we can tend her." He tossed a prompting glance to Reagan.

"Of course. We need to find some answers for you to take back to Sir Dunham," said Reagan to Tristan, Karryn and Ethan.

In the headmaster's study, two guards watched Hadwin. He sat in a chair offering no resistance, rather appeared stricken. He watched in anticipation when the door opened. Reagan, Tristan, Karryn and Ethan entered.

"Lady Madelyn? Is she—I mean will she—?"

"She is being treated by a physician," said Reagan.

Hadwin received a merciless glare from Tristan. Even Karryn's expression was unusually severe. For such a youthful face, Ethan's fierceness made a man's blood turn cold. Hadwin recoiled in his seat, as Ethan's voice matched his features.

"What did you mean this wasn't supposed to happen?"

"I don't know what went wrong. Malik agreed to bring Madelyn and Garrick to me so I could take them to a hidden cottage until this is over. Upon arrival, I saw the Shadow Warriors. Madelyn shouted for Garrick to run. One of the Shadow Warriors threw her aside to pursue Garrick. Malik also went after him."

"Why didn't you help them against the Shadow Warriors?" rebuffed Tristan.

"My horse died out from under me! I swear! I meant to take them to safety!" Hadwin passionately argued.

"Did Sir Dunham know of this plan?" asked Reagan.

Hadwin shook his head with lament. "No."

"He thought Hadwin deserted his service, which is why he sent Tristan and I after him," said Ethan with a disgusted sneer at Hadwin.

"Not deserting! I was trying to help," said Hadwin in desperation.

"By getting Garrick captured and Maddy severely injured?" Tristan seized Hadwin by collar. He gripped so hard that Hadwin began to choke for lack of air. Ethan forced Tristan to release Hadwin. The master-at-arms fell back in the chair gulping for air.

Karryn helped Ethan to ease Tristan away from Hadwin.

"How was it meant to help?" asked Reagan.

Hadwin regained his breath before answering. "I thought..." His voice faltered, so he forced himself to continue. "If he believed they were again in Magelen's hands he would call off this foolhardy venture. In reality, they would be safe!"

"You were going to use them to blackmail him?" At Tristan's rage, Ethan physically intervened to keep him from accosting Hadwin.

"To stop him! For his own safety! For their safety. To protect them."

"Some protection. Garrick is their prisoner! And Maddy—" Tristan jerked away from Ethan in another effort to accost Hadwin. Ethan forcefully drove Tristan back a few steps.

"Easy! Violence won't get us answers. Let Reagan and I handle him."

Karryn added her entreaty. "Ethan's right. Accosting Hadwin won't help Maddy. For her sake, hold your temper."

It took a moment for Tristan's passion to subside enough to nod an agreement.

Ethan released him. Karryn remained with Tristan while Ethan returned to question Hadwin.

"Malik isn't your cousin. So who is he that you trusted him?"

"A priest I've seen for years. He approached me shortly after Lady Joan's death and began talking about the political situation. We agreed it is dangerous for Sir Dunham to continue opposing Magelen."

"Didn't you think it odd for a priest of Jor'el to agree with the Grand Master of the Dark Way?" demanded Reagan.

Hadwin heaved an indifference shrug. "I'm not a believer of either side. My concern is for my lord and his family. It always has been."

"That is what you will tell him: how your stupidity led to this outcome!" Ethan jerked Hadwin to his feet.

Hadwin punched Ethan in the face, which sent him reeling backwards into Tristan. Both fell to the floor. Hadwin seized Karryn in such a way to pin her arms to stop her from reaching her daggers. The guards hesitated to act since he had Karryn. Hadwin forced her from the room.

"Stop him!" Reagan shouted at the guards.

"No! They may hurt Karryn." Ethan scrambled to his feet.

Tristan drew his sword to follow Ethan in rushing from the room.

In the courtyard, Hadwin tried to force Karryn to mount. She put up such a fierce struggle that he shoved her aside to leap onto Tristan's horse. He rode through the gate just as Tristan and Ethan arrived in the courtyard.

"I'm fine! Don't let him get away." Karryn waved them on.

They ran out the gate only to pull up short. Pursuit would be useless on foot. Tristan shouted in anger at the thwarting. Ethan raised his bow.

"He's too far and riding too fast!" protested Tristan.

Karryn, Reagan and the guards arrived to see Ethan release his shot.

Hadwin jerked back on the reins when the arrow struck him in middle of the back. The horse reared. Hadwin landed on his back, which drove the arrow through his body with the arrowhead protruding from his chest.

Ethan, Tristan, Reagan and the guards surrounded Hadwin. Karryn hung back slightly.

Reagan knelt to examine Hadwin. "He's dead."

Ethan spoke with indifference. "Justice is done."

"Not until Malik is dealt with, Garrick found and the Dark Way defeated!" snapped Tristan, his painful sneer a result of heavy emotions.

"None of this will help Maddy recover," said Karryn.

"But it will help the rest of us!"

Tristan's hot rebuff made Karryn recoil. She fought to maintain her composure. Ethan intervened. He placed a comforting arm around her shoulder and chided Tristan.

"Don't scold her!"

Tristan took a steady, calming breath. "I'm sorry, Karryn. I didn't mean it. This is all very disturbing."

"I understand," she said in weak, choked voice.

Reagan motioned to the guards. "Take him back for preparation." While the guards followed his instructions, he spoke to the squires and Karryn. "He may not be a believer, but will be cared for properly. In the meantime, take refreshment before returning to Sir Dunham."

"No, he must be told quickly. Just new horses and food for the journey," said Ethan.

Reagan's sympathetic gaze shifted to Tristan. "Your friend may not agree. I think his grief is deeper than yours."

"No, I do agree," said Tristan in a voice thick. "This doesn't change what must be done, only makes it more urgent. I will go to the infirmary to inquire after Maddy before we leave."

"Very well. Take your choice of any horse." Reagan gave Tristan a smile of encouragement before leaving.

Once inside the Fortress, Ethan stopped Tristan from entering the stables to speak privately. "I don't know what to say about Maddy except I'm so sorry."

Tristan fought his emotions. "To leave the Fortress, she must have trusted Malik with whatever reason he gave her. What harm would a priest do? She convinced Garrick to go since no anyone else could. If only we arrived sooner."

"Maybe if I said something earlier about Hadwin and Malik."

"You couldn't have known or suspected what they were planning."

Ethan said pointedly to Tristan, "Same as *you* could not have ridden any faster. Place the blame where it rightfully belongs."

"I bear some blame. I was here, with the deed done under my watch," said Karryn with pained regret.

"No. It is Dark Way. If I must, I will single-handedly defeat it!" declared Tristan.

"Not singled-handed as long as I'm alive," said Ethan.

"I'm coming too," said Karryn.

"No, it's more dangerous than Dorgirith," said Ethan in dispute.

"Stay and help Maddy," said Tristan.

Karryn's distress became replaced by determination. "I have no skill in the healing arts to help her. But I can help you complete what has been started. That is why I agreed to come to Garwood."

Tristan became confused. "I thought you came to protect Maddy?"

Karryn flashed a modest smile. "She is one part of my agreement. You, my lord, are the other part. Success hinges upon your safety. Like my father and others, I am sworn to that end."

Tristan cocked a grin when she said *others*. "Ethan doesn't agree to you coming."

"This tragedy shows there is no safe place while the Dark Way is allowed to rule."

Ethan grinned with admiration. "She may not speak often, but she speaks truth."

Tristan's gaze lingered on them for a moment. "Fetch the horses while I go to the infirmary."

Inside, Tristan paused to observe the physician tending Maddy. A priest followed instructions, more than likely unaware of whom spoke to him. Like the soldier in Dorgirith, Tristan felt certain the physician was a Guardian. Not the same Guardian since the eyes were a different color. It soothed his soul knowing the Almighty's forces were present during such a dark time, a time when evil reigned unchecked. This evil destroyed his family.

Tristan closed his eyes to swallow back the rising bile of anger. He didn't know members of his family like he did Dunham, Garrick and Maddy. What pain his father and grandfather must have felt, pain they shielded him from—until today. True he felt anger and some grief hearing about his late brothers and their families. He felt more sympathy for his grandfather. He and his father had not spoken of the tragedies. They didn't avoid the subject rather spent time together only when the Vicar came to Garwood. Speaking freely was unwise.

Tristan opened his eyes at feeling a hand on his shoulder. Ethan. At that moment he realized Ethan was right when he said: *If we purpose to do something it's because we were meant to do it.* Jor'el prepared him for this since his birth. He had to see it through no matter the cost. When Tristan noticed the physician staring at him, he moved to the cot.

"It doesn't look so bad after being cleaned," Tristan said concerning the head wound.

"Blood is deceptive. A cut finger can bleed profusely but one won't die from it. The head is the same way; it bleeds easy. All the same, she suffered a very serious injury. Head wounds are tricky things that can affect the memory or faculties. Only time will tell the internal affect of her injuries. Also, from here to here," Eldric touched Tristan's cheek under his right eyes to his right temple, "is broken. It is swollen now, and will become ugly and angry while healing."

"So she may be mentally challenged and disfigured?" It was hard to speak the question, but he needed an answer.

"At this point it is hard to tell. As I said earlier, I will do my best." Eldric eyes gleamed with confidence.

Tristan gripped Eldric's arm. "By Jor'el's mercy, I realize she can be in no better hands."

Eldric leaned closer to whisper, "Jor'el is with you, Son of Razi."

"I know," said Tristan with an unwavering smile of certainty. He leaned down to whisper in Maddy's left ear. "I love you and will return as soon as I can." He kissed her cheek then left with Ethan.

They met Reagan in the courtyard. Three horses were saddled. Karryn was already mounted.

"All is ready for your departure," said the headmaster. He then probed Tristan. "You realize why this was done?"

"To prevent us."

"Will it?"

Tristan straightened to his full height of six and a half feet. "No." He spoke with staunch determination.

"What if I told you that your father will be at Ravendale?"

Tristan grew curious. "Why?"

"A summons went out to all the Headmasters to come for the coronation."

"Coronation?" echoed Karryn.

"This was to be a journey for the lords to again allegiance to Ram," said Ethan, also curious.

"Ram died two days ago. Ramsey will be crowned," said Reagan.

Ethan skeptically eyed Reagan. "Two days? How did you learn the news so quickly?"

Reagan had difficultly suppressing a smile. "Divine messenger."

"The same one treating Maddy?" asked Tristan, eager for confirmation.

Reagan's smile broadened. "No, *the captain* of the old knights."

Tristan barely stopped an exclamation of joy at understanding Reagan's reference.

Ethan nudged Tristan. "We best get started. We have a long ride."

"Jor'el guide all of you," Reagan spoke a blessing.

At the manor house in Dorgirith, an irate Cassius paced in front of Nari and Roane. "How could you be so incompetent? They were mortal children!"

"The girl attacked me," said Roane.

"Oh, like that would really hurt?"

Roane heaved a careless shrug. "Maybe I did overreact."

Cassius stood toe-to-toe with Roane. "You broke her skull and killed her!"

"I assume she's dead, I didn't check—"

"Why not? Even wounded she could be useful."

"We have the boy," said Nari.

"Magelen and Dagar will see it as incompetence to only have one!"

"*You* could also be held responsible since *you* arranged this rendezvous."

Cassius scowled at Nari's suggestion.

"Can't we make up some excuse of mortal duplicity? The girl's injuries happened before we arrived. We secured the boy and priest to prevent total failure and discovery," said Roane.

"Dagar will want full details," insisted Cassius.

"Malik claimed he was to meet another mortal named Hadwin. Something went wrong and Hadwin killed the girl so we did as Roane said, secured the boy and Malik," said Nari.

Cassius looked askew at her. "He'll ask if you killed the other mortal?"

She shrugged. "What difference would it make if we say he did it? How can Magelen confirm or deny our story?"

"He could if the girl is still alive."

"*If?*" asked Roane with offense. "I'm a Shadow Warrior. I didn't check because her survival is unlikely."

"It's still a risk."

"More risky than telling the truth and being reconditioned, or worse?"

Cassius' eyes narrowed with deliberation. "You sensed no Guardian?"

"No," Nari replied. "And unlikely with the others pursuing Avatar."

Cassius slyly pursed his lips. "Using what you told me, I can convince Magelen. For all his craftiness in the dark arts, he is still half mortal and prone to fall for deception. He can take Dagar's anger and leave us unscathed." He turned to Nari. "Are you sure Malik and the boy are secure?"

"Ay. Malik knows his life will be forfeit if the boy escapes."

Cassius scowled. "It would have been safer to bring them here. If Avatar learns—"

"The others are dealing with Avatar," Nari briskly interrupted.

"We could lay a trap for him."

Nari rebuffed Cassius. "I'll forgive that foolish remark since you are a vassal."

"I just thought—" he stopped at hearing her cynical laugh.

"Stop thinking and do as you're told, vassal. Report to Magelen and leave the *thinking* to warriors." She placed a hand on Roane's shoulder. "We're returning to hunt for Avatar."

"Who will guard them—?" Cassius' protest ended when Nari and Roane vanished.

Chapter 18

DUNHAM'S GROUP MOVED AT A DELIBERATELY SLOW PACE, SO Avatar and Wren joined Kell and Armus quickly after leaving the Southern Forest. Avatar did most of the talking when making the grievous report. Wren still dealt with raw feelings.

"I thought all of them followed me," said Avatar with sobriety. "Somehow Nari and Roane doubled back without my knowledge. It may have happened when I stopped at the Temple." He forestalled Kell's anticipated reply, though the captain didn't move to speak. "Perhaps I acted foolish, but I needed time to consider. Nari nearly had me."

"I wasn't going to scold you. In fact, you did what none of us could. The outcome may have been far worse if all five returned," said Kell.

"Ay. At least Eldric is tending to Maddy," said Armus.

"Are you angry that we summoned him?" Wren asked Kell.

"No," he said with a sympathetic smile. "Just considering how difficult this news will be for Dunham. How is Tristan?"

Wren balked, a bit ashamed at being unable to reply.

Avatar placed a supportive hand on Wren's shoulder. "He appeared very determined the few times we observed them. Ethan took down Hadwin with a shot I didn't think any mortal could make, only a keen huntress," he said in an effort to bolster Wren.

"Did Tristan remain at the Fortress with Maddy?" asked Armus.

"No. He, Ethan and Karryn are on their way rejoin Dunham."

"What about Garrick? We can't leave him in the hands of the Dark Way!" argued Wren.

"They probably took him back to Dorgirith," said Armus.

Kell shook his head to the contrary. "No, that will be the first place Dunham suspects. After Avatar's successful rescue, Dagar won't allow a second foray into the forbidden forest."

"They'll find another place to hide Garrick," Avatar said to Wren.

"Won't stop me from finding him." Wren took up her crossbow.

"No—" began Avatar, to which she took great exception.

"I can and I will!"

"I know *you can*. However, doing so will reveal *your* presence. If I make a second rescue, it will infuriate them more. I'm the decoy, remember?" said Avatar with a wry smile.

Wren noticed Kell frown. "Please, Kell, we can't abandon Garrick!"

"It has to be done quickly. There isn't much time, and we can't risk Tristan's life nor possible failure of the plan."

"The only thing that will slow me down is his boo-boo." She jerked her thumb at Avatar.

"I was quick enough to dodge your errant shot. Eluding a few Weaklings will be easy."

Kell voiced his decision with firmness. "Two days. That's how long it will take them to reach Ravendale, *and* the time for you *both* to find Garrick. If successful, leave instructions with Eldric that their presence is to remain a secret, even from Dunham."

"Why? He's their father," said Wren.

"The journey is treacherous. Word may not reach him safely. Such information in the wrong hands could ruin everything. If you are *not* successful in the allotted time, rejoin us. We must be ready to aid Tristan no matter what happens to the others."

"We'll start tracking where I saw them vanish." Wren took hold of Avatar's arm. "Ready?"

In unison they said, "*Siuthad!*" and vanished in dimension travel.

***

Wren and Avatar travelled in an east-by-northeast direction from the Fortress. This made Avatar glance over his shoulders, somewhat baffled.

"Are you certain you're going the right way? Dorgirith is to the northwest."

"That is what I'm being told."

"Told and not sense?"

"I don't *sense* Shadow Warriors for tracking. The animals tell me of unusual activity around Dunlap."

"Where's Dunlap?"

"About fifteen miles from the Fortress. It is the former castle of Dunham's family. They left it for Garwood." She stopped at hearing a cawing. A raven circled above the trees. "Hide!" She pushed him behind a berm over which hung a crooked oak tree.

Avatar stumbled and bit his lower lip at the pain in his ankle. "Why did you do that?"

"*Shhh!*" she warned with a finger to her lips. She carefully motioned him to look up at the raven.

"So? You speak to birds," he harshly whispered.

Despite Avatar's objection, Wren again placed a finger to her lips. For several long moments they waited. Finally the raven flew away. "We can continue."

"What was that all about?"

"Since the Great Battle, ravens are used by the Dark Way thus unresponsive to any communication. Don't you recall us mentioning *Ravendale*, castle of the King?"

"Ay, but I didn't make the connection to the bird as a problem."

"Dagar's attempt to counter the royal eagle by using a fierce scavenger bird."

"Then maybe it should see me," he said with bravado.

"And bring Shadow Warriors down on us? So far, we've been fortunate not to sense them. I prefer to keep it that way."

After several miles, Wren stopped inside the tree line to view the small, fortified castle of Dunlap. It covered two acres. Some decline could be seen from the outside, but the walls and the buildings remained intact. People worked outside the castle.

"It appears some mortals still live here," said Avatar.

"Dunham allows the less fortunate to make use of the castle, or rather what he left behind. They forage for food and seek shelter from the elements. Some may or may not recognize Garrick, though this doesn't seem a likely place to hide."

"Hiding in plain sight might work."

"A priest and nobleman's son would hardly go unnoticed."

A small smile appeared, as Avatar looked along his shoulder at Wren. "How does a Guardian legend appear to mortals when needing information if not in disguise yet still in plain sight?"

She rolled her eyes at the implication. "Armus should have let me shoot you."

"Will you ask them or should I?"

Wren stiffened, not at the question rather alert. She armed her crossbow.

The mortals became alarmed when one shouted "Wolves!" They raced to the safety of the castle. Four wolves came upon the spot where the mortals cleaned newly snared rabbits.

She smiled. "I won't have to ask the mortals."

Wren focused on the lead wolf while it sniffed a rabbit. She spoke the Ancient under her breath. The wolf raised its head to look in their direction. It made a few clipped barks then ran toward the trees. The other three followed it.

"Don't move! Let me handle this," Wren told Avatar.

"I'll just make certain to be ready." He carefully placed a hand on his dagger to draw if needed.

The wolves stopped ten feet short of them. Wren spoke the Ancient. The wolves acted wary at first. The lead wolf growled in an aggressive manner then made a short bark. Wren's tone changed from coaxing to commanding. The lead wolf immediately grew submissive. At the wolf's compliance, Wren reverted to a gentle demeanor. A conversation between her and the lead wolf proceeded.

She translated for Avatar. "He says there are two new people in a shack a mile east. One is very mean."

"Mean? How so?"

Wren questioned the wolf then again informed Avatar. "The bigger one is mean to the smaller one. He also threw rocks at them when they got too close." The yips and barks from the wolf interrupted her. She made several inquiries then again translated. "The smaller one is scared of the bigger one. They don't like the bigger one. Says he smells funny. Not natural."

Avatar cocked his head at the statement. "Priests burn incense. Could the bigger one smell of perfume and not nature?"

Wren inquired of the wolf. "He doesn't understand *perfume* just insist it's not natural."

"Can he follow the scent?"

Wren spoke incredulously to Avatar. "You want me to ask a wolf if it can track a scent?"

He made a curt wave. "Ask him to lead us to the shack."

Wren did so. Avatar didn't need any translation when the wolf started running.

<hr />

Garrick sat huddled in a rear corner of the shack watching the priest build a fire in the hearth. Garrick rubbed his arms to ward off the chill. He ran out of fright when seeing Maddy injured rather than obeying her urging. This was the second time she became hurt trying to help him. Tears of regret filled his eyes. The whole ordeal since Dorgirith deeply troubled him. He kept quiet because he didn't know what to say. He had no words to describe the terror he felt at seeing the creatures or the horrible cold evil of the house. Suddenly everything his father told him about the Dark Way became starkly real, unnerving and sinister. His father thought going to the Fortress was safe. He did experience comfort along with a sense of calmness eating the gingerbread and drinking the tea. He slept peacefully the first night. Not now.

A bang and loud cursing startled Garrick. The priest appeared angry for having injured himself. A small fire now glowed in the hearth, so Garrick thought the priest burned himself. Whatever the reason, he didn't like this priest. He didn't act kind or generous like the Headmaster and others. He behaved vulgar and gruff. He even betrayed them to the Shadow Warriors that hurt Maddy. Maybe that's why the Shadow Warriors left him with the priest, because he wasn't exactly a priest. Besides, what priest would ally with the Dark Way? Weren't they on Jor'el's side in opposing evil?

Malik cussed again. "No water!" He tossed a narrow glare at Garrick. "Can't leave you alone to fetch some, now can I?" He did a quick search of the shack. He swore at not finding what he wanted.

Garrick watched Malik unfasten his belt. Fearful of more violence, he backed into the corner. Malik grabbed him.

"This is to tie you up. Can't have you running off."

Garrick fought Malik. In the midst of wrestling, he landed a kick to the priest's neck. Malik fell sideway gasping for air. Despite the surprise at what he had done, Garrick bolted for the door. He didn't know which direction to flee only that he had a chance to escape. He heard shouts of cursing. The priest came after him.

Glancing back took his eyes off where he headed. He fell down an incline into a small creek. Hands grabbed him. Malik! They fought. A hard slap to the face stunned Garrick. Malik held him tight by pinning his arms against his side.

"I won't suffer death for the likes of a spoiled brat!"

Both heard loud snarling a second before a wolf leapt at Malik's face. Malik released Garrick. The boy fell back into the creek. Stunned, he watched the wolf attack Malik. The priest managed to reach the bank where he grabbed a fallen branch to fend off the wolf. It yelped and retreated. This gave Malik a clear path to Garrick. The boy scrambled up the opposite bank.

The slope slowed Garrick's escape. He felt a tug on his sleeve when Malik tried to snatch him. In moving to avoid being grabbed, Garrick stumbled. He mimicked Malik's earlier action and grabbed a branch to use in defense. The one he picked up easily broke. Garrick crawled backwards to get away. More growling. Two wolves placed themselves between Garrick and Malik. For a moment, Garrick wasn't certain which to be more afraid of, the wolves or the priest? A third wolf joined the two in front of Garrick.

The wolf Malik struck aside lunged at him. He managed to pull his arm away from being bit. "Do something, boy! Don't just sit there. Help me."

When Malik spoke, one of the wolves standing between them moved toward Garrick. He watched in fearful apprehension. The wolf did something Garrick didn't expect. It grew docile, lowered its head, whimpered and licked his boot. The wolf moved to lick his hand, all the while wagging its tail. It then pulled on his sleeve, barked and turned as if to leave. Garrick's uncertain gaze shifted between the wolf next to him, and those surrounding Malik. The wolf repeated the action of pulling on his sleeve, barking and turning to leave. Comprehending what the wolf meant, Garrick quickly followed the animal into the woods.

"Hey! You can't leave me," shouted Malik. When he moved to go after Garrick, the wolf jumped at him. He cried out in pain when jaws clamped down on his left forearm. He collapsed to his one knee where he clouted the wolf on the snout. The wolf released him. Malik made a hasty retreat. He ignored the bleeding pain of injury to escape the wolves.

Malik ran about twenty yards before he tripped over his own feet in a rush to flee. He landed face first on the ground. He became startled at the sight of booted feet inches from his face. His head jerked up to see a large being with bright silver eyes holding a sword. Fear made Malik recoil. Hearing the howling of wolves kept him from moving any further.

"Who are you?" asked Malik.

"Someone Shadow Warriors fear and mortals consider a legend."

"A Guardian?" Malik's brief surprise turned to pleading. "Save me from the wolves!"

Avatar made a brief glance in the direction Malik indicated. "I see no *real* wolves. Only a mortal one pretending to be a priest of Jor'el."

Malik rose to his knees to continue his plea. "No! The Shadow Warriors did it all. I went along to help the boy, free him when I could."

Avatar's silver eyes brightened and his face grew fierce. "You think you can deceive Jor'el with lies?"

"Not deceive, survive!"

Avatar's eyes remained bright and narrow upon Malik. He spoke with severity. "You made your choice with full knowledge of the consequences. Either confess and repent of your sin or accept what fate comes to you."

Anger crept into Malik's mask of contrition. "I thought Guardians protected mortals."

"Those in need, not one who tries to manipulate with falsehood and deceit. Make your choice." Avatar glanced over Malik's head then back to the mortal. "For which is more frightening, facing real wolves or the judgment of your creator?"

Terrorized by the thought, Malik's attention shifted between Avatar and the unknown behind him. In sheer panic, he fled.

Avatar sheathed his sword. He lifted his eyes skyward. "Your will be done, Jor'el." He headed in the opposite direction of Malik.

Garrick didn't know where the wolf headed, only it moved away from Malik. After a few moments, the other wolves joined them. The lead wolf ran in front of Garrick to make him stop. Hesitant, he eyed the wolves.

"What do you want? Are you going to hurt me too?" he asked in a trembling voice.

"They won't hurt you."

Garrick's mouth dropped open at hearing a female voice. A beautiful woman with long auburn hair and bright green eyes appeared. She wore clothes of a forester nature with a crossbow. It took a moment to recognize her. "I know you."

Wren smiled. "We've met several times when you wandered too far into the woods."

"Ay, the forest woman."

She chuckled. "Most refer to me that way." The first wolf licked her hand. She responded by patting his head. "They mean you no harm."

"I—I think they saved me. At least they led me away from him. Why would they do that? I though wolves attacked people."

Wren's green eyes grew bright, yet soft and reassuring upon Garrick. "Wolves are very intelligent and sensitive creatures. They attack prey to survive, much like people hunt to eat. They also attack when threatened, or in defense of a pack member. They do not seek to harm anyone. The same trait of protection is found in a loyal dog. Alger, I think is the name of your favorite dog."

"Ay," said Garrick. A wolf licked his hand while wagging its tail.

"She likes you," said Wren.

Garrick flashed a smile that quick faded, replaced by fear. "Other wolves aren't so friendly."

"Not wolves created by Jor'el. The Dark Way has corrupted nature since the fall of the Guardians. Do not mistake what is touched by evil for that which Jor'el created for good."

For a long moment, Garrick stared at Wren. Her smile placed him at ease.

"Come." She held out her hand. "I'll take you back to Fortress."

"How did you know I came from there?"

She laughed. "It was difficult to miss the procession from Garwood to the Fortress."

"Oh. Ay."

<hr />

Garrick and Wren reached the Fortress at twilight. She took her leave just before the priests at the gate noticed them. Overjoyed to see Garrick, they ushered him to Reagan's office.

202

"Praise be!" said the Headmaster. "Are you hurt? Any discomfort? How did you escape?"

The questions came so fast that Garrick couldn't answer until Reagan finished. "I'm all right. What about Maddy?"

Reagan tried to be tactful. "She sustained some very bad injuries."

"Will she live?" he asked, fearful.

Reagan smiled. "Ay, and you being found safe will aid her recovery."

"Can I see her?"

"Her injuries are not an easy sight."

Garrick squared his shoulder. "I want to see Maddy."

Reagan studied the boy. His demeanor notably altered from when he arrived. "Really? You were not so talkative or sure of mind when you arrived. What changed you?"

"The forest woman helped me escape, along with some wolves. Good wolves, not the Dark Way ones," Garrick added at seeing Reagan's interest. "She said not to mistake such evil for what Jor'el means as good."

Reagan fought a smile. "She is right. Even when others use evil to harm us, Jor'el will use it for our good. I think that is the case with you, wouldn't you agree?"

Garrick shuffled his feet, a bit uncertain and remorseful. "Maybe. All I know is want to see Maddy. I want her to be well again."

Reagan placed a comforting arm about Garrick's shoulders. "She will. In the meantime, you must be strong as she recovers. She has been strong for you."

Garrick nodded in an attempt to gather his emotions. Reagan escorted him to the infirmary. Eldric rose from beside Maddy's cot to greet them at the door. The boy became quizzical of Eldric.

"This is the physician tending to your sister," said Reagan.

"Young master," said Eldric with a partial bow to Garrick.

"Are you a good physician?"

Eldric smiled. His bluish/purple eyes reassuring. "Jor'el has blessed me with the gift of healing. Does that qualify?"

Garrick returned Eldric's smile. "Ay."

"She's asleep, but you can sit with her."

"I don't want to disturb her."

"It will delight her to see you when she wakes." Eldric took Garrick by the arm to escort him to the cot. Garrick drew to a halt upon first sight of Maddy. Eldric steadied Garrick. "Don't let the discoloration frighten you. The injuries will look very ugly as they heal. Eventually her face and head will once again appear normal." He indicated the chair he occupied earlier. "Sit."

Tears swelled as Garrick watched Maddy sleep.

"Remember, be strong for her, like she has been for you," said Reagan.

Garrick took hold of her hand. "I'm here Maddy. I won't run off again, I promise. Just get better, please."

With a sense of caution, Eldric straightened. He spoke in Reagan's ear. "I need to fetch some medicine. I'll be back shortly." He didn't wait for Reagan's reply.

Rather than deal with any of the priests, Eldric spoke the Ancient under his breath. He left the compound without being noticed. A hundred yards from the rear gate, he found Avatar and Wren waiting. She resumed her normal appearance.

"Are you two responsible for Garrick's return?" asked Eldric.

"Ay, but that's not why I summoned you," said Avatar.

Eldric noticed fresh bleeding on Avatar's ankle. "Now you want treatment?"

"No! I have orders from *Captain* Kell," Avatar stoutly replied. "The presence of the children is to remain a secret, even from Dunham."

Surprised, Eldric asked, "Why? He'll be relieved they are safe."

Avatar spoke in a tone unwilling to accept argument. "The plan is at a critical stage. Any news sent may not reach Dunham, and that could place everything in jeopardy."

Eldric nodded with understanding. "I'll make certain Reagan knows the severity of the situation."

"I'm telling *you*," said Avatar with emphasis.

"Reagan knows who I am. He will cooperate without question."

"How does he know? Did you tell him?"

"Of course not! Divine insight. After all he is a Headmaster, the highest of priests next to the Vicar."

Avatar made a curt nod in acceptance of the answer. "Return to the Fortress. We'll report to Kell." He didn't wait for an answer and left.

Wren followed. She spoke after a mile. "We could dimension travel."

Pain and fatigue filtered into Avatar's surly reply. "I've already done three travels with others and two solo."

"So what's one more?" She tried to be humorous only he grunted and kept walking. He favored his injured foot. She snatched his arm in an attempt to stop him. "You're tired, and your ankle needs tending."

Avatar pulled away to continue.

"I'm not Eldric. I don't mock you."

"Oh, like the *boo-boo* you made fun of before we left? The one made worse by avoiding your shot?" he spoke over his shoulder.

Wren quickly moved in front to stop his progress. "My teasing is different than Eldric's mocking, and you know it." At his stubbornness, she changed her tone to sympathetic. "Please, Avatar. This day has been difficult enough. Your wound needs to be bandaged so we can make it back in time, whether on foot or dimension travel."

Her entreaty worked. "Ay. It can use tending."

Chapter 19

TRISTAN, ETHAN AND KARRYN RODE THE REST OF THE DAY TO catch up to Dunham's retinue. Not feeling it safe to switch horses at post-houses, they dismounted every two hours to walk the horses for thirty minutes. It wasn't until well after dark that they steered the tired horses through the evening activity to arrive at Dunham's tent. They too appeared fatigued and somber. Karryn and Ethan dismounted. Stiff from riding and legs unsteady, Karryn held onto Ethan's arm.

Tristan lingered in the saddle. What horrible news they brought. Only six months ago Dunham's wife died. Now he must bear news concerning his children. Before the recent events, Tristan only knew grief in the abstract by what he observed in others. He did experience intense rage upon learning of his grandfather's capture. However, the heartbreak and agony he experienced at seeing Maddy's serve injuries exceeded earlier feelings. Leaving her in such a desperate condition was the most difficult thing he had even done. It also proved Dunham right. When love is discovered, it is surprising how deep the bond goes. Staring at the tent, he realized the pain he felt would be nothing compared to Dunham.

"Tristan," he heard Ethan speak his name and felt a tap on his leg. Ethan watched him with sympathy. Karryn held onto Ethan. Tristan dismounted.

Upon entering, they noticed Dunham just completed his evening repast as told by the plates and cup on the table. He smiled at Ethan and Tristan then became curious. "Karryn? What brings you here?"

"Grave news, I fear," she replied in shaky voice.

Dunham's gaze shifted to Ethan and Tristan. The young man's emotions were very visible. "How so?"

"Hadwin's journey involved Lady Madelyn and Master Garrick," said Ethan somberly.

"And?" pressed Dunham.

"As a result of his and Malik's scheming, I'm afraid Garrick is again captured by Shadow Warriors while Madelyn most gravely injured."

Stunned to the core, Dunham stared at Ethan.

Tristan fought to contain his grief. "We arrived moments too late. Maddy—"

"Is alive and being tended by a very skilled physician," said Ethan.

"I'm sorry, my lord! I didn't know they left the Fortress, or I would have acted to prevent it," said Karryn with discomposure. Silent tears fell. She complied when Ethan encouraged her to sit at the table.

Dunham's stupefied gaze shifted between the young people. "How bad are her injuries?"

"He said it is not unto death. The right side of head and face are broken." Tristan used his hands to indicate the location of the injuries. "Perhaps resulting in permanent damage. It's too soon to say for sure." He closed his eyes trying to stop the tears. His eyes opened at feeling someone embrace him. Dunham. For the first time, Tristan wept.

Dunham ushered Tristan to sit. He sat beside Tristan and opposite Karryn. "Tell me everything."

Ethan began the explanation. "According to Hadwin, he planned the scheme with Malik. The idea was to take them to a cottage while telling you they had fallen back into Magelen's hand. He claimed it was for their safety."

The explanation baffled Dunham. "Why?"

"To thwart the plan. He said duty to you compelled him to act in your best interest."

Dunham's jowls flexed with anger. "And Malik? What did he have to say?"

"We don't know," continued Ethan. "After finding the lady, I immediately hurried in the direction Garrick fled. I spied him and Malik a moment before the Shadow Warriors seized them and—*poof!* They were gone, vanished. I've never seen anything like it before."

"The Dark Way." Dunham swore under his breath. His hand gripped the neck of his tunic.

"Hadwin said it wasn't supposed to happen," added Tristan with a sneer.

"He said Malik approached him shortly after Lady Joan's death. Apparently, they held similar views on politics," said Karryn.

Dunham's brows grew level in trying to understand. "So how did it go wrong? And where did the Shadow Warriors come from?"

"What does it matter? The Dark Way is involved!" a passionate Tristan chided.

"It matters if Hadwin willingly helped the Dark Way or used as a dupe," said Dunham.

"Hadwin is dead," said Ethan coolly. "A result of trying to escape after being told we would bring him to you. He attacked me and tried to use Lady Karryn as a shield for his escape."

Dunham regarded the woodsman-squire. The normal jovial features were hard and unflinching. "You shot him."

Ethan stoutly nodded. "We gave him every opportunity to explain, which is why we can tell you what we have."

Dunham's expression grew harsh in his effort to contain his whirlwind of emotions.

"What now? Do we return to Garwood and search for Garrick?"

In guarded anticipation of the answer to Ethan's question, Tristan watched Dunham. He left Maddy to continue with the plan. Would Dunham falter it now?

It took a moment for Dunham to answer. "No, though my heart is heavy with grief, we must continue."

"My lord, you stand to lose everything."

Dunham slammed his fists on the table and stood to confront Ethan. "If it cost me everything I will not be dictated to by the Dark Way!"

"Others share the same sentiment." Ethan's glance passed to Tristan.

"Master Reagan said my father, and all the Headmasters, have been summoned to Ravendale for the coronation," said Tristan.

The information surprised Dunham. "Coronation?"

"Ram died two days ago. Ramsey is to be crowned before the lords."

"How did Reagan receive word so quickly?"

Tristan flashed an impulsive smile. "*The* captain of the Old Knights informed him."

"Kell." Dunham again touched the neck of his tunic.

"Truly, Jor'el is with us," said Tristan.

"He always has been."

Karryn spoke to Dunham. "My father told me you are the one to whom the sacred medallion has passed. I have not mentioned it before, though I believe I saw it when you confronted Magelen."

Dunham reached under the neck of his tunic to remove the medallion. It was a large oblong eight sided blue stone framed in gold with a golden royal eagle clenching a crown with a sword through the center.

Tristan's eyes lit up with delight. "The Jor'ellian Crest!"

"What?" Ethan asked.

Dunham explained. "Long ago, when Jor'el lived among the mortals, he ordered Rune, the metalsmith of the Guardians, to forge this medallion for the captain of the Palace guards. They were an elite group of mortal soldiers dedicated to the protection of Jor'el's Palace."

"I thought that's why the *Old Knights* were created," said Ethan with discretion in reference to Guardians.

Dunham grinned. "The *Old Knights* served in more ways than simply protecting the Palace. They governed Allon. Many mortals pledged themselves to Jor'el, to his honor and service. Not all became priests. Those who wore this crest on their uniforms were called the Jor'ellian

Guard. Only the most worthy among them was appointed leader of the Jor'ellians and given the medallion."

"Father said the last Jor'ellian Commander fell at the Great Battle while defending the Palace," said Karryn.

"My ancestor," said Dunham. "Since then, my family has carried on his dedicated service to Jor'el and his sacred oath." He placed the medallion back under the tunic.

"Something Magelen now knows," she said with care.

Dunham cocked a wry smile. "Magelen has always known of my opposition. Revealing the medallion, well," he said with careless shrug, "anything to save my children. Same as this venture will help to secure their future—the future of us all." He clapped a hearty hand on Tristan's shoulder.

"The medallion shows there is more than friendship between our fathers," said Tristan.

"Ay. As Vicar, his safety is included in the Jor'ellian oath."

"Is there a way to meet with him beforehand?"

"No, that would require a detour. We are already half a day behind schedule." Dunham spoke to Karryn. "Will you return to aid in Maddy's recovery?"

"No. Although I pray the best for her recovery, my skill is best served elsewhere." She glanced toward Tristan.

Dunham nodded with understanding. "Perhaps, under the circumstances, we should meet with Renfrow before reaching Ravendale."

"He may already be there," she said.

"I'll inform my scouts to learn if he is." Dunham flashed a modest smile. "In the meantime, Ethan, see Karryn is made comfortable in a suitable tent." He waited to speak again when he and Tristan were alone. "You realize if we meet with your father beforehand, there is a possibility the connection will be made between you two?"

"That has always been a possibility. When seen with him in public, what would they dare to do? Kill me?" he groused with flippancy.

"Don't speak so hastily of death!" snapped Dunham.

The rebuke surprised Tristan. "I didn't mean to. I've never known such agony as when I first saw Maddy and thought—Jor'el be praised, I felt a pulse."

"Your father and grandfather have known grief. Will you subject them to more heartache on your behalf? And me?" Dunham side-hugged Tristan about the waist. "I love you like a son, and would rejoice at your wedding to Maddy. Unless, the effect of her injuries have changed your mind," he asked with purpose and watched for Tristan's reaction.

The young man took no offense. He replied with staunch resolution. "No. If anything, I am more determined to destroy the Dark Way!" He then sighed with melancholy. "I don't know if she heard me when I kissed her cheek and promised to return as soon as I could. That's when he said, *Jor'el is with you, Son of Razi*."

"Who did?"

Tristan grinned with confidence. "The physician. Like the soldier in Dorgirith, he is a Guardian in disguise."

Dunham widely smiled. "Another good sign to continue. Your father knows you are accompanying me, let that suffice." He escorted Tristan to the tent flap. "Try to get some rest. Tend me in the morning."

<hr />

Kell and Armus continued to watch Dunham's camp. They paid particular attention to the mortal lord's tent. Their interest became piqued upon sight of Karryn with Tristan and Ethan.

"Do you sense the danger has passed for Karryn to leave the Fortress?" asked Armus.

Kell didn't immediately answer. "I'm not sure," he said at length.

Armus became alert. Kell stopped him from drawing his sword.

"Avatar and Wren," said the captain a moment before they arrived.

"I hope this punishment of diminished power ends soon. Sometimes I can discern the individual, others times I can't," complained Armus.

"Not to mention the draining effects of using simple powers," Avatar groused. He blinked and rubbed his eyes in a gesture of fatigue.

"Is Garrick safe?" asked Kell.

"Ay. He's back at the Fortress with your instructions given to Eldric," said Wren.

"The hounds will once more be picking up my trail," said Avatar.

"How did you manage that? More underwater tactics?" teased Armus.

Avatar matched Armus' humorous tone. "No, though as dramatic. A mortal coming face-to-face with a legend does have a profound effect."

Kell didn't share in the humor. "Did you have permission to make such an appearance?"

"Of course. Jor'el wanted to offer Malik a chance to repent and make the right choice. Alas, he didn't accept the opportunity, so my appearance will become known." Avatar shifted his weight off his right foot. Some blood showed through a new bandage.

"How is your wound?" asked Kell.

"I'm managing."

Wren spoke to Avatar's bravado. "Don't let him fool you. I had to treat his ankle and let him rest before returning. He dimension traveled five times to help me."

Avatar took exception to her intervention. "If I stay off my foot for a night, I'll be fine."

"Do so while we keep watch," said Kell.

Chapter 20

MAGELEN PACED IN HIS STUDY AT RAVENDALE. THE NEWS OF another failure annoyed him. Fortunately, this wasn't of his making or due to Guardian interference, rather mortal ineptness. Still, he didn't want to pass the information to Dagar.

Witter and Altari watched Magelen. "You can't wait. He expects a report," said Witter.

"Do you want to tell him?" chided Magelen. The Warrior commander didn't answer, so Magelen again questioned Altari. "You were specific in your instructions?"

"Ay. For the fifth time: I sent Nari and Roane to Cassius. He relayed your orders. They carried out the instructions with unexpected results."

"There is no accounting for mortal duplicity," said Witter.

Magelen snarled a complaint. "I expected better from Malik. Dunham's man was the unknown factor, but Malik assured me he could be trusted. Nari and Roane should have been there sooner!"

"They acted immediately upon receiving instructions," said Altari.

The water in the basin began to boil.

"You waited too long," said Witter. "He knows when you use power. Remember, your talisman is connected to him."

Magelen straightened his robes in preparation of facing Dagar. "My lord," he said cordially when Dagar's image appeared.

"What news, Magelen?"

"Not good, I'm afraid. Both sets of instructions were followed exactly, but mortal ineptness caused the plans to go wrong, resulting in the death of Sir Dunham's children."

"What?" Dagar eyes flashed to Witter and Altari, who stood behind Magelen.

Altari spoke. "Nari and Roane don't know all the details, as the girl was dead when they arrived. Malik pursued the boy after the demise of his sister. Unfortunately, the boy died from wounds suffered in an attack of wild beasts. Malik said the one called Hadwin killed the girl."

"What about Malik and this Hadwin? They aren't still living, are they?"

"No, my lord. Nari and Roane left no witnesses."

"That is some consolation, I suppose." Dagar asked Magelen, "Does Dunham know?"

"Doubtful. It just happened today and he is on his way to Ravendale. However, by taking them to the Fortress, he disobeyed the king's request to bring his daughter Ravendale."

"Word must be kept from him."

"Why? The plan was to use them to curtail his resistance. Let us proceed as if the plan succeeded and they are both in our custody."

"If word reaches him of their deaths, what then?" challenged Dagar.

Magelen calmly replied, "I claim marriage by force while she was in Dorgirith. Whether she is dead or alive, it makes me his son-in-law, with access to his estates to use in support of the King—*if* he doesn't do so voluntarily. Of course, I will have Ramsey play upon his disobedience to bring Madelyn, which could have prevented her death."

"They are dead, so what purpose would that serve?" Dagar continued his interrogation.

Undeterred, Magelen said, "Being grief-stricken may gain him sympathy and forbearance among the lords. However, if Ramsey or I act, he will be disgraced, thus stripping his esteem and honor in the eyes of his peers. Upon that foundation he has been influential. Take it away and the others will abandon him."

Dagar stroked his goatee in consideration. "There is merit to your argument since mortals rely heavily on personal pride."

Altari involuntarily had a catch in his throat, which drew Dagar's critical eye.

"You have something to add, Commander Altari?"

"No, my lord. Merely agreeing with your observation of mortals."

Dagar slowly returned to his discussion with Magelen. "Utilize your plan if needed; only tread carefully. The sense of change is growing stronger and I don't like it." He demanded of Altari. "What of Avatar? Have you reinforced the effort to destroy him?"

"We don't have the resources to deploy a search and guard Ravendale. If Avatar was sent for a reason involving Dunham, that reason could lie here, since Dunham is on his way."

A throaty growl came from Dagar. His mahogany eyes narrowed on Altari. The Warrior took a cautious step backwards.

"My lord, Altari is right. We don't dare spread our forces too thin. We need more troops," said Witter.

"Both of you fail to see the threat posed by Avatar's presence. His mentor often sent the wretch as a precursor to *his* appearance."

"I do know!" began Altari in rebuff. "Or have *you* forgotten I served as Kell's aide before being usurped by that *wretch*?"

Dagar's fury instantly rose. "*Trobhad!*"

Immediately, Altari disappeared, startling Witter and Magelen.

"What did he go?" asked Magelen.

"Here with me!" Dagar reached down out of view to jerk Altari to his feet. The Warrior appeared in great distress gasping for air, almost on the verge of succumbing.

Witter hurried to speak. "My lord, please! Altari did not mean to dispute you, rather stated facts."

Dagar released Altari, who collapsed out of view. "Let this be the last time you dispute me, Altari."

"Ay, my lord," they heard his raspy voice.

"Destroy Avatar!" Dagar commanded Witter. His image vanished and the water stopped boiling.

"Be quick," Magelen ordered Witter.

In the Nether Cave, Dagar seethed from the discussion. "Dunham is an insignificant mortal nuisance, who could easily be dealt with. The inability to neutralize Avatar is intolerable!"

Altari regained his breath and composure enough to stand at attention. "My lord, there is a way to get at Avatar."

Dagar abruptly turned upon Altari. "You dare to speak?"

"Only to serve to you, my lord. Use Mahon."

Dagar laughed, loud and mocking. "A wonderful suggestion! As if I hadn't tried it before."

"Not in the way I have to suggest."

Dagar scrutinized Altari upon hearing the tone of severity. The Warrior's grey eyes were cold with malice. "Mahon won't cooperate, no matter what is done to him. Griswold nearly ripped the hide off his back and he didn't make a sound."

"Not torture, incentive. The lives of others for the death of Avatar."

Dagar suppressed the inclination to smile. "You hate him so much to use such foul means to destroy him?"

"Same as you hate a certain *captain*."

This time, Dagar smiled. "Wait here." In long, hurried strides he went to the reconditioning chamber. He interrupted Tor speaking to Griswold. "Why are you wasting time when I need troops now?"

"We were just discussing the recruitment of five more," said Tor.

"Not good enough! Avatar is proving troublesome." Dagar looked to Mahon's cell. "I have to bait another trap."

"Mahon won't cooperate."

"Given the right motivation, he will." Dagar caustically grinned.

Griswold cracked his knuckles. "I've been waiting for another chance at him."

"Not him. Cyril, Elgin and Vidar. Three to suffer and die for his failure to cooperate."

Griswold looked crestfallen. "Will you let them live if he succeeds?"

216

"Vidar's turning will be a tremendous personal triumph. The others are negotiable when the time comes." Dagar crossed the chamber with Tor and Griswold accompanying him.

Mahon remained sleeping on top of the jackets with his scarred back exposed. Cyril sat beside him leaning against the stone bed. Cyril moved forward to gently touch Mahon's shoulder. "We have visitors, lad."

The younger warrior's eyes opened. "Who?"

"Me."

Mahon raised his head to see Dagar. "I thought maybe someone important." He put his head down and closed his eyes.

Dagar scoffed a laugh. "You won't be so smug after you hear what I have to say."

Mahon pretended to snore, which made Cyril chuckle.

Irate, Dagar spoke the Ancient. With a flick his right hand, the cell door opened for him to enter. "Your continuing insolence will get others killed. Starting with your cellmate!" He jerked Cyril to his feet, and threw him to Griswold.

Quicker than anticipated in his injured condition, Mahon bolted to his feet. The pain of movement showed in his tightened jowls and narrow eyes.

"Be warned, another show of insolence will include Elgin and Vidar."

"Dagar!" Vidar moved to the bars separating the cells. "What evil are you planning to make such a threat? Griswold nearly beat him to death, isn't that enough?"

"Merely a way to get his undivided attention." Dagar answered Vidar then spoke to Griswold. "Take Cyril."

"No!" Mahon went to intervene when Dagar stepped in front of him.

"He will be held until your full cooperation is assured."

Mahon swallowed back the pain with a snarl. "What do you want?"

A sly grin appeared. Dagar tossed a glance to Vidar and Elgin before replying. "Not here. Come with me."

Mahon fell to his knees in painful distress from the dimension travel bridging the gap between the Nether Cave and the real world. He wore a new Guardian uniform complete with sword. Altari and a Shadow Warrior named Brodrick were with him. Neither showed signs of difficulty.

"On your feet, maggot!" Altari pulled on Mahon's shoulder until he stood.

Mahon looked around. "Where are we?"

"The Region of Sanctuary just north of Lake Joram. The last sensing indicated Avatar heading into the Highlands. There's been no sight or sense since. Kell sent you to find him when he tracked Dagar. The time ending in your capture, remember? Find him again, only this time we'll be watching."

Mahon knew Altari's history with Avatar, so he understood why Dagar chose him. "If Avatar senses *you*, he won't trust me reappearing after so long. He'll know it's a trap. I do this alone or it won't work."

"You don't give the orders, unless you want the others to be destroyed."

Mahon did not back down. "Tell me, Altari, can you find Avatar?"

Altari scowled, fierce and lethal, but didn't answer.

"Oh, that's right, you couldn't. Despite your wonderfully enhanced Dark Way skills—you failed. Which is why you're using me. Stay back at least a mile and a half."

"A mile is the sensing limit," said Brodrick.

Mahon flashed a mocking grin. "Kell and Armus trained Avatar. Dagar couldn't sense him while Altari can't track him. Better make the distance two miles for you."

Brodrick stared to draw his sword when Altari stopped him. Altari rebuffed Mahon. "Mind your tongue, worm! If *you* fail, I will destroy you and make certain Avatar knows it before dispatching him with *your* sword!"

Mahon's brows furrowed, as if distracted. He grew sly in expression. "Avatar's nearby."

"I don't sense anything," said Brodrick in dispute.

"You wouldn't. Now make yourselves scarce while I pursue him." Mahon didn't wait for a response, and took off running in a northerly direction. He ignored the pain movement caused. He had to get away before they realized his bluff.

Despite the pain, Mahon forced himself to continue at a blistering pace. He wouldn't begin tracking Avatar until certain he lost Altari and Brodrick. He knew he risked the lives of Cyril, Elgin and Vidar, but he couldn't think of another way since killing Avatar was out of the question. However, a choice had to be made. If he can successfully contact Avatar, then Kell would be alerted, perhaps saving the others.

By dawn, Mahon crossed into the Highlands where he slowed his pace. He stopped several miles later in a grove of trees on the edge of a glen. Although his energy was nearly exhausted, he closed his eyes to stretch out his senses in search of any nearby essence. Finding none, he sat on a log to rest. He flinched when fresh bleeding made the jacket adhere to his wounds.

"Jor'el, give me strength. Show me that I'm doing right," he prayed while fighting to keep his eyes open from pain and fatigue.

<hr/>

Wren stood watch. Armus and Kell sat in the Guardian meditative position with their legs crossed, swords resting on their laps and hands on the blade. Avatar sat in a more relaxed position with legs stretched out to protect his healing ankle.

Kell woke with a start. He bolted to his feet with sword in hand. "There's a dimensional disturbance." His statement brought Armus and Avatar to stand, the latter able to bear weight on his right ankle.

"I sensed Mahon, and pain," said Avatar with concern.

"Remain with Wren while we investigate," said Kell to Armus, then to Avatar, "The Temple hills." He held onto Avatar's shoulder as they vanished.

Reappearing on the hills overlooking the Temple, neither appeared physically drained.

"If I could stay here, I'd be healed in a day," said Avatar.

Kell ignored the comment to focus on the surrounding area. His eyes narrowed, senses alert. "They're heading for the Highlands."

"Perhaps they sent a rescue party for those Weaklings and aren't looking for me."

"Don't count on it. You're too valuable a prize for Dagar."

"First I'm a decoy, now a prize."

"We split up. You head east, I'll go north."

"There's a glen where I met Valmar after springing the trap. We can meet there."

"I know where it is." Kell headed north.

Fortunately, diminished strength didn't affect running speed. Kell covered the distance to Lake Joram quickly. Although no signs of anyone, he got a strong confirming sense of a presence. He knelt to place a hand on the ground. Mahon, an unknown Warrior and ...

"Altari!" Kell sneered, a hint of pain in on his face.

What would make Mahon work with Altari? He knows the history. Kell could only think of two reasons, either Mahon escaped and Altari is hunting him, or Dagar manipulated Mahon to use against Avatar with Altari and the unknown acting as his handlers. Either way, he had to isolate Mahon to determine the warrior's state of mind. Hopeful he could do so before Avatar found Mahon. That means taking out the unknown Shadow Warrior and Altari without alerting Dagar to *his* presence. If successful, he could spare Mahon and Avatar any unpleasantness.

Again, Kell placed his hand on the ground to determine direction. They split up. Mahon headed north-by-northeast, Altari went east while the other Shadow Warrior went due north. Perhaps he took on a parallel course to Mahon. For a moment, Kell considered whether to follow the unknown Shadow Warrior or Mahon. Altari moved too far off Mahon's course. After brief consideration, he drew his sword to follow the unknown Warrior.

Brodrick lost sight of Mahon almost immediately, but managed to pick up the trail again. Mahon seemed to be moving too fast for effective tracking. Didn't matter. Brodrick had his assignment, make certain Mahon killed Avatar. If not, finish the job by dispatching them. He felt both honored and intimidated to receive the task from Dagar. Even before the Great Battle, Brodrick knew Avatar's reputation as an elite warrior. Anyone who could defeat him would become highly feared. Something he never experienced as a Guardian yet discovered when the mortals trembled at the sight of Shadow Warriors.

Upon reaching the crest of a foothill, Brodrick saw Mahon enter a patch of trees encircling a partially snow-covered glen. He debated how close to get without Mahon sensing him. He judged the glen to be a little over two miles meaning he could risk another half-mile or so. He began to move when a frightening chill ran the length of body. He whirled about and became dumbstruck. Standing there with sword drawn and lethal expression …

"Kell!" he exclaimed in surprise.

Brodrick barely ducked in time to avoid the captain's sword aimed at his head. He drew his sword to parry Kell's second attack. That was all. The captain's sword broke his blade. Before Brodrick could react, he was nearly sliced in two.

Kell scowled in painful anger at the grey light of demise. He recognized Brodrick. Sadly, he became a Shadow Warrior. For that reason, he had to be destroyed. An urgent sense compelled Kell to the glen. He found Mahon collapsed against the log.

"Mahon?"

The younger warrior jerked awake, dazed and confused. "Kell? No! You shouldn't be here. It's too dangerous."

Kell ignored the protests to observe the blood on Mahon's tunic. "What happened to your back?"

Mahon shoved Kell away. "Go, before you are discovered!" He then seized Kell. "Wait! Vidar, Elgin, Cyril. Dagar will kill them on account of me."

"Vidar is alive?"

"Ay. Transported to the Cave during the battle."

"By the heavenlies! Mahon?" Avatar arrived and knelt. "What happened to you?"

"Never mind me. Both of you must leave. I'm not alone!"

"I took care of Brodrick," said Kell. "Was he following because you escaped?"

Mahon bit back the pain from Avatar's examination of his back to speak. "There is no way to escape. Rune altered the locks not to respond to normal commands only a few specific individuals. Somehow the entire Cave is shielded from regular dimension travel."

"Then how did you get here? And why was Brodrick following you?"

Mahon hissed in with painfully annoyance. "What about Altari?"

"I haven't seen him," said Kell.

Hearing the name, made Avatar stop the examination to demand, "Altari did this to you?"

Mahon swallowed back the pain. "No, Griswold, at Dagar's instructions. I never made a sound. I wouldn't give them the satisfaction."

"What does this have to do with Vidar, Elgin and Cyril?" asked Kell.

Avatar looked with surprise at Kell upon hearing *Vidar's* name.

Mahon vigorously shook his head. "No time to explain! If I fail or Altari sees either of you, they will be killed!"

Kell held Mahon's shoulder, insistent upon having an answer. "Fail at what?"

Great distress filled Mahon's face in turning from Kell to Avatar. "Dagar sent me to kill you. If I don't, he will kill them."

Avatar's silver eyes flashed with fury. "Their lives in exchange for mine?"

"There will be no exchange!" declared Kell. He quickly stood. He directed his attention to the southeast part of the glen. "Altari is nearby."

The pronouncement brought Avatar to his feet, sword in hand. "Give me first chance at him," he said to Kell.

Mahon seized Avatar's sleeve. "You both must leave. Help them if you can, but leave me."

"No! You're free, and we're going to keep it that way," said Avatar.

"Better yet," began Kell in a sly, confident tone. "We'll make it appear you succeeded."

"What? No," said Mahon with confused agitation.

Avatar watched Kell in guarded consideration when the captain sat on the log to get Mahon's full attention.

"To convince Altari, you will both put on a good show so that from a distance it will look like you succeeded."

"First a decoy, then prize, now I must fake my own death?" chided Avatar. His temper not abating.

"But when you vanish it'll be white light not grey," argued Mahon.

"That won't matter since you'll have Avatar's blood on your sword." Kell's wily glance went down to Avatar's bloody bandaged boot.

Mahon didn't comprehend the visual exchange. "I won't draw his blood!"

"You don't have to." Avatar sat on the log. He put his sword down to undo bandage around his ankle. He picked open the scab. He grunted while expressing fresh blood onto the cloth.

Mahon watched with concerned curiosity. "How did that happen?"

"Compliments of an earlier encounter with Shadow Weaklings. Give me your sword."

Avatar wiped the blood on both sides of the blade. He returned it Mahon then wrapped his ankle again with the cloth.

Mahon remained skeptical. "If this doesn't work, Dagar will kill them."

Kell took out his dagger. He forced one of the jewels in the hilt to come off then sheathed the blade. Holding the jewel between both hands, he spoke the Ancient. *"Ailleagan agus amhach."* The jewel became a necklace, complete with gold setting and chain. "Put this on. Say it is a lifechain."

"A what?" Mahon followed instructions.

"Lifechain. Given to you by Avatar before you turned on him. With so few of us remaining, it serves as a connection to the heavenlies. If anything happens, say you are destroyed, I will know and will come to avenge you."

Uneasy at this new wrinkle, Avatar voiced his objection. "Kell, there's no such thing as a lifechain."

"Dagar doesn't know that, so hopefully, it will put the fear of heavenly retribution into him. For I *will* come for him when I can. And on that day, every Guardian and mortal who has suffered will be avenged!"

Avatar sat perched on the log, anger in his voice. "To convince Dagar he must return to the Cave!"

"To save you, the others and himself. I said there will be no exchange, I didn't say there wouldn't be risk."

"To trick Altari is one thing, but this is asking too much in his condition! No—"

"I'll do it!" Mahon spoke loudly to interrupt Avatar's vehement protest. "The alternatives are unacceptable."

With urgency, Kell stood. "Hurry! Out in the open."

"You must go." Mahon nudged the captain.

Kell flashed an encouraging smile. "Tell the others to take heart, they are not forgotten. The Temple," he said to Avatar then closed his eyes. He spoke the Ancient to cover his presence before racing back in the direction he came.

Avatar's grumbled under his breath. "Let's get this over with."

Mahon seized his friend. "Avatar—"

"Say nothing! Let's make this look good so all of you will be spared. I'll go first. Follow me, as if striking from behind."

Mahon let Avatar emerge from the trees into the glen. Upon stepping out, Mahon caught a glimpse of Altari. That's when he launched his attack with a shout. Avatar immediately parried. The clanging of blades echoed in the glen.

For added emphasis, Avatar shouted, "Mahon, what are you doing? Are you mad?"

Mahon didn't respond. He couldn't; this was difficult enough. After a few exchanges, he stumbled due to the pain of his uniform being repeatedly torn from his wounds.

Avatar kept his back to Altari's location. "Feign an attack. I'll trip. Then make the final blow," he said privately to Mahon.

With a frown of reluctance, Mahon did as instructed. When Avatar appeared to stumble, Mahon made the most convincing final attack he could. In fact, Avatar barely vanished in time. Physically and emotionally exhausted, Mahon collapsed to his knees laboring for breath. He heard Altari's approach. The way he felt, it wouldn't be hard to sound convincing.

"You didn't finish him!"

"What are you talking about? I landed a lethal blow." Mahon held up the bloody sword. "If not at that instant, he won't survive long." He bent over still trying to catch his breath. The chain dangled from his neck.

"What's this?" Altari reached for the necklace when Mahon caught his hand.

"His lifechain."

"What?" Altari again tried to reach for the necklace only Mahon shoved him away.

"According to Avatar, Jor'el ordered them forged in the heavenlies because of the Great Battle. It senses the life of the Guardian wearing it. Once the Guardian ceases to exist, Kell will know, and come to avenge the demise."

"So why did he give it to you?" said Altari in dispute.

Mahon didn't immediately reply due to pain in standing up. He held the chain, looking at it in sad recollection. "Overjoyed to see me, he didn't want harm come to me again. Little did he know the harm would come to him," he said with a catch in his voice. He tucked the chain under the neck of his uniform.

"We'll see what Dagar has to say about it. Brodrick!" called Altari.

"He won't answer. Remember, I warned him. He got too close. Avatar dispatched him just before we met."

Altari snatched the sword from Mahon, seized him and they disappeared in white light.

In the Nether Cave, Altari held onto Mahon to keep him standing. The return dimension travel aggravated Mahon's wounds. Tor and Dagar stood to one side conversing after hearing the tale. They spoke in low voices though not totally private. Mahon didn't have to strain or use his heavenly senses to hear the discussion.

"Do you believe him about this lifechain?" asked Tor.

Dagar's scowl deepened. "It is a strong possibility. Even without the chain, *he* can sense a Guardian's demise. I can't afford him showing up until our forces are replenished. With Avatar's destruction, he will be extra anxious for revenge."

"Altari said he saw white light not grey when Avatar vanished."

Dagar shook his head in dispute. "The blood on Mahon's sword is substantial, along with his dismay. For all his bravado, Mahon is unpretentious. With Avatar being his mentor and friend, such distress would be hard for him to concoct if it were not true."

"So what do you want to do?"

Dagar chewed on his lower lip in thought. "For now, let him be. If at any time Avatar does reappear, lifechain or not, they die. And I'll take great pleasure in throwing the chain in *his* face when we meet again." He noticed Altari and Mahon. "Get him out of here!"

Altari jerked Mahon's arm to move. Mahon proved unsteady in step both from pain and to keep up the presence of dejection. He was grateful for his weakened condition, which helped him not to smile at hearing

Dagar's assessment of his *unpretentious* nature. When Altari shoved him inside the empty cell, Mahon stumbled to the floor.

Vidar and Elgin waited at the adjoining bars. Dried and fresh blood stained the back of Mahon's uniform. "What did they do to you?" asked Elgin with discomposure.

Before Mahon replied, Griswold arrived with Cyril in tow. The older warrior didn't appear to have suffered new injury. After Griswold left, Cyril examined Mahon.

"At least you're in one piece, lad."

"My back is nothing, but this is something," Mahon said in a quiet voice. He smiled and showed them the chain in prelude to a hushed explanation of his exploits.

<hr/>

At the Temple, Kell impatiently awaited Avatar's arrival. He hated sending Mahon back to the Cave. With the lives of others at stake, he had no choice. All the same, he would rather have secured Mahon and found another way to rescue them. He failed to consider one important factor when formulating the impromptu plan. To maintain the ruse of Mahon destroying him, Avatar needed to return to the heavenlies. Kell originally cringed at Avatar's assignment due to the risk of Dagar venting his spleen in revenge yet glad to have him back. He understood Avatar felt the same about Mahon, thus his protest of the plan. Just like Mahon's willingness to spare the others harm, he knew Avatar would agree. He just didn't like the idea of telling him.

Kell stiffened at the white light, not for fear, rather in anticipation. Upon appearing from the fading light, Avatar staggered sideways. Kell caught him to keep Avatar from falling and helped him sit on the bench. "Your ankle?"

"Left shoulder," Avatar said with discomfort. "Mahon made it look good. Clipped me with the flat of the blade just as I vanished."

"I see blood." Kell examined Avatar's shoulder. "From what you wiped on the blade there is no rip in the sleeve or wound."

Avatar rubbed his shoulder. "A good whack should help convince Altari. If I ever see him again, it won't be pity he'll receive rather the end of sword!"

"Justice will be done. Unfortunately," began Kell with regret, "you can't stay around to see what happens."

"Why not? You are going to fetch them, aren't you? I want to be there when you do!"

"Of course, as soon as *we* can, we shall free them. Right now, if Altari catches a glimpse of you, Mahon and the others—"

Avatar stopped Kell with a firm grip on the captain's arm. "Say no more. They won't be harmed on my account. I hadn't thought of it at the time."

"Neither did I. We made the best plan under the circumstance. To facilitate it, you must return to the heavenlies. Immediately, I'm afraid."

"That soon?" said Avatar with disappointment.

Kell spoke with sober regret. "Being at the Temple, they won't sense the dimensional disturbance. It will also give you the strength needed to bridge the gap."

"Be sure to tell Wren that Vidar is alive. She can use some good news." Avatar stood.

"I will. Till we meet again, my friend." Kell heartily embraced Avatar then Avatar stepped away, took a deep breath and vanished.

A moment later, Kell vanished.

Dawn rose over the horizon. Wren and Armus watched the mortals break camp. Armus placed a supportive hand on her shoulder.

"I know you wish you could have done more, we all do."

"Indeed." Kell emerged from deeper in the forest, which made Wren scowl in annoyance.

"You really need to stop sneaking up on people, Captain! I blindly shot at Avatar. Thankfully he got out of the way in time." She did a quick survey and added, "Where is Avatar?"

"Probably acting as a decoy again," said Armus with a chuckle.

"No, he's back in the heavenlies," said Kell.

Wren paled with horror. "He's fallen?"

"No!" Kell said in haste to her misunderstanding. "Part of an impromptu plan when we found Mahon."

"Then where's Mahon?"

"Back in the Cave."

Armus cocked a brow of dispute. "Kell, you better start from the beginning because Avatar in the heavenlies and Mahon in the Cave doesn't sound like it went well."

"It did, at least I believe it did. I won't know the result of the risk until the day I free Mahon, Elgin, Cyril and *Vidar*," Kell said with a purposeful smile at Wren. "He's alive."

She covered her mouth upon making an outcry of delighted relief. Her gaze passed down to the mortals. They didn't seem to hear and continuing dismantling their camp.

Kell placed a hand on Wren's shoulder to get her attention. "Before he left, Avatar wanted to make sure I told you. He said you needed to hear some good news. I agree, and also greatly relieved about Vidar."

"Did Mahon tell you about him and the others?"

"Ay. He returned to the Cave to protect them."

"How?" Armus inquired.

Kell's features grew harsh. "Dagar threatened their lives if Mahon failed to kill Avatar."

"What?" Wren said flabbergasted.

"Since the Shadow Warriors failed to neutralize him, Dagar tried another way." Kell proceeded to explain the plan and the result.

Still skeptical, Armus folded his arms across his chest. "Let's hope they fall for the lifechain deception."

Kell sheathed the dagger. "Dagar knows I can sense a Guardian's demise, so it will add credibility to the story. Hopefully, it will convince him to spare the others. Avatar returned to the heavenlies because if he stayed and they discovered him, they would know it was a ruse."

"Well, so much for our decoy," quipped Wren.

"Are you volunteering?" asked Armus.

"No, Gresham will serve. He still needs to perfect his stealth from being easily detected." She casually motioned to the trees as Gresham emerged.

"I'm not that bad," he argued.

"You noticed Armus and I didn't flinch when you approached. Unlike Avatar and Kell, who I nearly shot when they snuck up on me."

"With the news I bring I wasn't trying to be stealthy." Gresham turned to Kell and said, "Ram is dead. It is rumored Lord Razi's death isn't far behind."

Kell's brows leveled concern. "Why couldn't I sense that?"

"More than likely the Dark Way masked it. I learned from *stealthily* overhearing mortals discussing it." He emphasized the word for Wren.

Kell ignored the dig to ask, "When?"

"Two days ago."

Kell's studious gaze focused on the mortals leaving. "It will take the four of us to make certain they arrive at Ravendale safely. Armus, Wren, stay on course with Dunham. We'll take the north side, running parallel."

"Dimension or on foot, Captain?" asked Gresham.

"Foot. We won't use our powers unless absolutely necessary. We've kept the ruse so far that Avatar was alone, no need to tip our hand now."

Chapter 21

IN THE STILLNESS OF THE LATE NIGHT, A SINGLE CANDLE LIT A ROOM in the basement of the royal barracks. Carnel paced, nervous and watchful. If his father or Magelen discovered what he was doing, he would end up dead like his grandfather. They said he was an old man of weak mind, but Carnel knew differently.

Unknown to Ramsey and Magelen, Carnel became Ram's secret confident. Whereas the relationship between father and son deteriorated since Ramsey captured Razi, the bond with his grandfather grew stronger. He tried to help when Ram became suspicious of Magelen poisoning him. Ram also expressed deep distress at Razi's capture. However, Carnel couldn't openly voice support for Ram during heated family arguments. With Ram dead, Carnel felt compelled to finish what he started, for his grandfather's sake.

Carnel drew his sword when the door opened. Captain Murdock and Baron Renfrow entered. The latter was a slim man of forty-eight with a countenance making him look continually forlorn even when smiling. His green eyes reflected his moods, which at present appeared cautious. Carnel sheathed his sword.

"Your highness has information to impart that you called us here?" asked Renfrow.

"Concerned that circumstances may alter the plan. The plan my grandfather wanted."

"We'll know for certain when Dunham arrives."

"If it has changed, what then? My life will be forfeit!"

Renfrow kindly grinned. "Be assured, Highness, we made arrangements to secure you."

"How will I know?"

"Dunham's banner will be the signal. If he arrives under the old Dunlap banner, then the plan is halted. If he arrives under a new banner, the plan will continue. Either way, you will be safe. We pledged our honor to that end," Renfrow spoke with reassurance.

Carnel wasn't totally convinced. "The banner could alert Magelen and Ramsey."

Renfrow shook his head. "Dunham made comments about it in reference to Garwood. A new castle deserves a new banner. They will take it as one more sign of his differing views."

"Those differences will be handsomely rewarded if all succeeds."

Renfrow studiously regarded the prince. "Dunham doesn't seek rewards. What he does, he does for principle and deep seated faith."

"I am well aware of the man's integrity, my lord baron. His indomitable spirit concerns my father and makes Magelen quake in fear."

"No one can succeed alone, Highness."

Carnel wryly smiled at hearing the prompting statement, to which he replied, "Are you a doubter when it comes to one who places trust in the *Old Faith*?"

Renfrow returned Carnel's smile. "No, Highness. I was referring to it, not demeaning it."

"Are we in agreement?"

"We are, Highness."

"Then may the Old Faith preserve us."

Renfrow and Murdock bowed in acknowledgement.

"One more thing," said Carnel, delaying their departure. "Convey my best to the Vicar."

"As you wish, Highness," said Renfrow.

Carnel waited several moments after their departure to make his way to the main building. With so much depending upon the planning of others, he wanted reassurance they had not forgotten. The short meeting accomplished that. Preoccupied, he was startled by a voice beside him.

"Rather late to be out, Highness."

Carnel fought to recover his surprise at Magelen's appearance. "Why? Am I not allowed to wander Ravendale when I want?"

"Of course you are. I'm merely concerned. You are so grieved by your grandfather's death, I am watchful that nothing unexpected happens to you in the dark."

Carnel understood Magelen's meaning. While a bit unsettled by it, he could not display fear. He scoffed as a cover. "If it is genuine concern for my welfare, then see I am not disturbed by anyone regardless of the hour, including yourself." He picked up the pace to put distance between them.

Magelen didn't follow, nor did he react when Witter arrived. "He didn't give the appearance of nervousness or discomposure. For all his faults, Carnel is growing up."

"I told you he is more intelligent than you believe," said Witter.

"His intelligence doesn't matter. I hoped to throw a good fear into him, so when I apply pressure he will yield. Tonight, he didn't."

"That concerns you?"

Magelen's eyes narrowed in thought. "I'm not sure. When Ramsey is dead, Carnel will become king. He must have some form of backbone."

"Yet not enough to interfere with your control."

"He must be molded. They all must be. It could just be grief. Ram doted on him. He didn't act too much out of the ordinary."

"What do you plan to do?"

"Watch how he conducts himself this next week. Once Ramsey is crowned, life should return to normal, and Carnel pliable again."

"What about your plans for Dunham's daughter as his intended? That was to be announced at the coronation banquet."

Magelen flashed a calculating grin. "I have a replacement in mind. If I can't undermine Dunham, I will shake his support. See all is made ready for the guests." They parted ways.

Murdock led Renfrow through a tunnel connecting the basement to the corridor of a secret passage called *the ditch*. Once outside the walls, they ran to a grove of trees where Renfrow's horse stood tethered.

"Will you be safe to return?" asked Renfrow.

Murdock wore a cocky grin. "Even if I'm spotted, the men will look the other way. They are ready when the word comes, my lord."

Renfrow cast a cautious glance back to the castle. "Carnel may be sincere, but I don't completely trust him."

"Naturally. Despite embracing our cause, he *is* his father's son. Until we succeed, I'll do my duty with one eye out for betrayal."

Renfrow made a stern rebuff. "For his cooperation we have pledged to keep him safe. Do not compromise our vow."

"I didn't mean to suggest that, my lord. Only will his safety be as a free man or in the comfort of a prison cell? My hope is for the first while watching out for the second."

Renfrow nodded. "Off with you now, I must return."

"My lord, what about *him*? Shall I tell him or wait until the moment of freedom?"

Renfrow stared at Ravendale for a moment of consideration. "Leave him ignorant. What he doesn't know, he can't tell, should they choose to act before we free him."

Murdock frowned to the contrary. "Very well, but Ram shielded him. If I discover his life is threatened—"

"Then you may act, but *only* if the threat is imminent. Now, go."

Murdock clapped his sword hilt, bowed and returned to the ditch.

Renfrow rode to his camp on the road to the North Plains. He arrived two hours before dawn. He discovered Baron Kaleb waiting for him. A peer in age yet decidedly more robust in physique and jovial in character, Kaleb stood taller with a healthy head of black hair and beard. He made himself comfortable, freely drinking of the cider.

"I thought you would be at Ravendale by now," said Renfrow.

"What? Arrive before you and Dunham?" snickered Kaleb.

"Arriving together could cause suspicion." Renfrow took a much-needed drink before sitting and putting his feet up on the table.

"I'll arrive before you. I delayed to speak to you. Have you heard the latest about Ram?"

"He's dead."

Kaleb frowned. "For once I thought I brought you news. I should know better." He drank.

"I just found out from Murdock. Dunham probably knew before either of us. He's always been better informed."

"Not surprising considering his family's connection to the Vicar. So what else did old Murdock say?"

"Actually we met with Carnel."

Kaleb nearly choked on his drink. "What did that popping jay want? We gave our word."

"Reassurance. I told him about the banner."

Stunned, Kaleb sat forward. "Why did you do that? It could put us at risk."

"He doesn't know the extent of those involved. All he believes is a handful of lords will help him be rid of Magelen."

"It's a coup against his father!"

"That fact doesn't trouble him." Renfrow grew considerate. "He made the proper replies when I tested him. He may truly be of the Old Faith."

"You mean Jor'el?"

"Of course. You know the phrase and counter-phrase."

Miffed, Kaleb scowled. "He can still talk."

"Perhaps. Then again, we may have under estimated Carnel because of his father. He even told me to convey his best to the Vicar."

"Why did he ask you to do that?" a new voice entered the conversation.

Both rose at the interruption, ready to draw their swords. They stopped at seeing Dunham dressed in black for night travel. Three others accompanied him, also dressed in black. One wore a hood and hung back. Ethan and Karryn were hoodless.

"Karryn?" said Renfrow in surprise.

"Father." She greeted him with hug and kiss on the cheek.

"I thought you said you left at her home?" asked Kaleb.

"A ruse," said Renfrow with impatience. "Seeing her now isn't what I had in mind. Why did you bring her?" he accosted Dunham.

"There is grave news. May I?" He indicated the cider.

"Of course." Renfrow wiped out an empty cup to pour some cider for Dunham. "Please, sit." He and Kaleb resumed their places. With only a few chairs, Karryn stood beside her father while the hooded individual remained by Dunham.

"Fetch more cups and cider," said Dunham to Ethan, who promptly left. He asked Renfrow again, "What did you say to Carnel about his regards to the Vicar?"

"Nothing. It was merely a parting line when Murdock and I left."

"Good. Carnel is not to be fully trusted whereas Murdock is one of the most ingenious men I've ever met. If not for him, I don't know if Razi would have survived this long."

"He told Carnel about the banner," said Kaleb in complaint about Renfrow.

Dunham chuckled into his cup as he drank.

"What's so funny?"

"With all that can go wrong you worry about a banner."

"It's the signal!" insisted Kaleb.

Ethan returned with a pitcher and cups. He served the cider while the conversation continued with Renfrow speaking.

"I told Kaleb that Carnel doesn't know the full extent of those involved. He only thinks we three are going help him be rid of Magelen."

A low throaty snarl escaped from the one whose hooded head remained bent. Dunham's touched the man's arm while speaking to Kaleb. "Ridding Allon of Magelen and the Dark Way is more personal after what happened. He sought to stop me in the most foul way possible," he voice shook slightly and his countenance grew hard, yet stricken.

The change made Renfrow and Kaleb guardedly curious. "How so?" Renfrow asked.

When Dunham replied, his voice sounded once more in command. "A plot by my own man-at-arms led to my son's capture by Shadow Warriors and left my daughter with possible debilitating injuries."

For a moment, they sat mute with shock. "When was this?" Renfrow managed to say.

"Yesterday," said hooded one in a thick voice. "We tried to reach them in time to stop Hadwin."

"I accompanied Maddy, only given a separate room. I didn't know anything was wrong until too late," said Karryn with great remorse.

"You bear no blame," Dunham said to Karryn then spoke to Renfrow. "Your daughter is very brave. Before this incident, she helped save them from Magelen when Garrick wandered into Dorgirith."

Renfrow clasped Karryn's hand between his own hands. "Listen to Dunham."

Kaleb found his voice, now filled with sympathy. "I'm so sorry."

The hooded one continued in his fierce speech. "Hadwin laid the plan, but a priest betrayed them to the Shadow Warriors. One of my father's own brethren of the faith turned to the Dark Way."

"What?" Kaleb asked with confusion.

"He doesn't need to hide his identity from us," said Renfrow to Dunham.

"You know who he is?" asked Kaleb.

"Why do you think I sent Karryn to help Dunham?"

"A part of the plan has been left unspoken until the last moment," began Dunham to Kaleb. "It is a long held secret I revealed to Renfrow when I sought his aide. Now it is precaution, not mistrust, for which he remains hooded." He stood to continue speaking. "You know of Lord Razi's capture, but not the suffering he endured with the near destruction of his family."

"It is rumored the Vicar is among his family members. Having seen Elias I can understand the rumor," said Kaleb.

"It is no rumor. Vicar Elias is Lord Razi's son."

"That's good to know, though hardly a long held secret."

"Even he figured it out," said Renfrow in jest of Kaleb.

Dunham ignored the dry humor to inquire of Kaleb. "Did you ever wonder why Razi went into hiding for all those years?"

"No, but one could hardly blame him with Ram and Magelen constantly after him."

"For my safety." He removed his hood. "I am Razi's grandson, Tristan. Vicar Elias' last surviving son."

Kaleb stared at Tristan, the strong family resemblance unmistakable. "He looks more like Razi than Elias."

"Which is why I kept him away from court, until now," said Dunham with purpose. "Tristan has been with me for ten years under the pretense of being my squire."

"I think this qualifies as a secret. Considering he is Ramsey's cousin, and his greatest threat," said Renfrow.

Kaleb poured more cider into his cup to take long drink. "One look at him, and they will know. *And* kill him on the spot."

"I won't let my grandfather die," Tristan stoutly declared.

"Don't misunderstand, I agree. However, if you openly attend court as Dunham's squire and are recognized, it will jeopardize the rest of us."

"That has already been considered," began Dunham. "Tristan knows his part is less visible. Ethan will attend me in public." He gestured to Ethan, who bowed. "He's been with Tristan for many years, and also has a personal stake in Lord Razi's safety."

"He took me in when I was orphaned at age eleven. I owe him my life," said Ethan.

"Will you tell us their roles or do they act independent from our plan?" asked Kaleb.

Dunham resumed his seat. "They will act simultaneously but independent. If something goes wrong, Ethan is under orders to get Tristan away."

"Save one heir. That was Razi's intent when he went into hiding," said Renfrow to Kaleb.

"Does the Vicar know? I mean about his part in the plan, not being his son," said Kaleb, much to their amusement.

"Ay," replied Dunham.

Renfrow crossed to his personal chest to fetch a bottle of wine. Back at the table, he poured the remaining cider from his cup back into the pitcher. Kaleb finished his cider. Renfrow distributed the wine. Kaleb stood when Renfrow raised his cup to Tristan.

"We pledge upon the Old Faith that your secret is safe, my lord. Our lives if we break our oath or silence," he said. They all drank.

"How far is your camp?" asked Kaleb of Dunham.

"Six hours east of Ravendale. We rode most of the night to get here. I told Captain Warren we would met him a hour before arrival."

"It'll be daylight soon. You can't return without being seen. Making a major detour will add hours to your journey."

Dunham flashed a smile. "We can manage."

With a sly grin, Renfrow leaned over to Kaleb. "You're forgetting he knows the secrets of the Old Knights."

"You mean the Guardians?"

Renfrow rolled his eyes in annoyance. "Why can't you remember the substitute terms? Old Knights mean Guardians, Old Faith means Jor'el. It's not that hard."

Kaleb shot an arched glance to Renfrow. "So if it's not that hard then anyone can use the phrase and counter-phrases like Carnel did."

"You tested Carnel?" asked Dunham.

"Ay, and he made the appropriate responses," said Renfrow.

"I still don't trust him," groused Kaleb.

"I didn't say I trusted him. Information about the banner won't compromise the plan."

239

"Renfrow's right," said Dunham. "I've made it known about changing things at Garwood. I'm more interested in Murdock. Did he have anything to report?"

"He expressed concern for Razi. He wondered about telling him the plan. I suggested his ignorance would be more believable if we should fail," replied Renfrow.

"My grandfather would never betray me or my father," said Tristan with certainty.

"There is no concern of betrayal rather for Lord Razi's safety. We agreed that if Murdock fears an imminent threat, he is free to act."

"Good," said Dunham. "Now, when do you plan on arriving?"

"I delayed my arrival to see him." Kaleb jerked his thumb at Renfrow. "I could have been there today. I mean, yesterday. Oh, whatever time it is—was."

Dunham chuckled.

"I'll arrive tomorrow afternoon. Only I hoped to be alone." Renfrow motioned to Karryn.

"What do you mean?" she asked.

"I received a note from Ram requesting I bring you. I didn't need to make an excuse for your absence since you went to Garwood. I hope you're being here isn't noticed."

"I spoke to Captains Bartlett and Dwayne to ensure safe passage through the watch."

"Oh, no," Renfrow droned in annoyed vexation.

"Why is that a problem, Father?"

"I received the same request," said Dunham.

"At least your daughter is some place else. Now, I must bring Karryn to Ravendale."

"Why? She can feign illness to remain among the retinue," Ethan asked Renfrow.

"Since she's been seen by my men whole and hearty, I will incur Ramsey's anger for disobeying his father's command. We can't risk any misstep."

240

"I came as I am. I have no gown or courtly dress," she said.

"That is the least of our worries." Renfrow waved it aside. "For Ram to even make such a request there must be a reason, or better yet, a rat behind it."

"You mean Magelen?" asked Kaleb.

"Of course I do! Can't you understand anything?" Anger brought Renfrow to his feet.

"Peace, Father," she tried to soothe him. "I'm not afraid."

He took her hands. "I am." He stroked her cheek then kissed her forehead.

"Your father is right to be concerned. You know what it cost me," said Dunham.

"I won't be alone. You'll be there along with my father, Kaleb and others." Karryn looked to Tristan and Ethan, her gaze lingered on Ethan.

"Cavin, Godfrey, Edison and Lowell," said Kaleb.

Renfrow noticed Karryn interest. "I don't believe she means them."

She blushed then guided her father to resume his seat. She refilled his cup with wine.

"Cavin and Edison should have arrived. Godfrey has the farthest to travel," said Dunham.

"Lowell is joined to the hip with Godfrey," chided Kaleb.

"He left a couple days before I did, so I suspected he'll be there by the time we arrive tomorrow," said Renfrow.

"Oh! Percy, Vaughn, Taggart and Sheldon said to count them in," said Kaleb as an afterthought.

"When were you going to tell me this?" asked Renfrow with mild annoyance.

"I just did."

"That leaves Sedgewick and Walcott unaccounted for."

"Twelve out of fourteen is good, and each in command of a province," said Dunham in consideration. "Since all should be assembled by tomorrow, I shall arrive late tomorrow night."

"When do you plan to sleep?" snickered Kaleb. Dunham's response sounded more serious than expected.

"When my children are avenged, Razi free, Ramsey dethroned and Magelen defeated! Only then can I lay my head peacefully to pillow."

Renfrow held Dunham's arm. "Don't let blind emotion drive you. Lean on us, my friend. You can start by getting a couple of hours of sleep on my cot. I'm not leaving for at least six hours."

Dunham began to object when Tristan said, "Do as the baron suggests. You'll need all your wits and strength."

Dunham looked earnest at Tristan. "I will, if you will."

"Agreed."

"My tent is at your disposal." Renfrow took Karryn's arm. They left with Kaleb.

Outside, Kaleb moved to where his men waited with saddled horses. "I'll see you at Ravendale. Karryn." He smiled while touching his hat in salute.

Renfrow and Karryn moved to a nearby tent. "Captain Bartlett!"

A burly ginger bearded man emerged from the tent. "You called, my lord?"

"Retiring so early, Captain? I thought you had the night watch?"

Bartlett flushed with embarrassed. "A bit of illness, my lord."

Renfrow scowled with disapproval. "Don't you mean too much drink, Captain?"

"No, my lord. Truly, cook's stew didn't set well. That's why I brought Baron Kaleb fresh caught fowl." Even in torchlight, he appeared sickly.

"My daughter and I will make use of your tent since Sir Dunham is occupying mine for the time being. Also, send Atwater to town to fetch some proper clothes along with a courtly gown from a dressmaker for Karryn."

"The lady is going to Ravendale?" asked Bartlett with trepidation.

"We don't have much of a choice now do we, Captain? I know you hold your tongue better than your drink, but can you vouch for Dwayne's silence?"

"Fear of reprisal from you and my sword will keep him silent."

"Too risky at present. Dispatch Atwater immediately."

"I will see to it personally, my lord. She appears to be my daughter's size, and Atwater doesn't have much taste in women's clothes."

"Quick as you can."

"My lord. My lady." Bartlett saluted them.

Inside the tent, Karryn spoke. "I didn't know there was a problem with me being seen or I would have been more discreet in speaking only to Captain Bartlett."

"You had no way of knowing about the letter. That aside, is there something I should know about the woodsman squire?"

Karryn blushed. "I think you guessed already."

Renfrow tugged at his lower lip. "I suspected one of Dunham's squires captured your attention. I hoped for the other, considering his connections." He flashed a teasing smile.

"Please don't mock me!" she chided and sat on the cot.

He sat beside her. "Tease perhaps, never mock." He held her hand. "There is much that can go wrong before this is over. Hearing of Maddy, I can't imagine what I would do if anything happening to you."

"I know you will protect me. So will Ethan."

She spoke with such certainty that he regarded her for a moment. "You lost your heart to a squire. I hope he's worthy."

"I believe he is." She touched his face in a loving gesture. "I will always be your loyal, loving daughter." She hugged him.

Renfrow stopped a sniffle at the sentiment. "Now, I'll leave so you can get some rest." Outside, he spied Ethan a short distance away. The squire appeared to be waiting. "Ethan."

"My lord baron." He bowed. "I hope you are not cross with your daughter on my account."

Renfrow studied Ethan to size up his features and bearing. "How much do you care for Karryn? Do you love her enough to take her from here and keep her hidden from danger?"

Ethan curbed a smile to reply. "Although that would be the normal desire of a man who loves his lady, Karryn would have none of it. We fought beasts of the Dark Way in the bowels of Dorgirith, and share the same oath for this venture. Like my charge, for as long as I have breath and she is in sight of my bow, nothing will touch her. If you doubt my word, you can ask Sir Dunham about my character."

Renfrow did his own curbing of a beginning smile. "I already have. Dunham and I talked extensively when he came seeking help. I know your history along with that of *your charge.*" He paused in leaving to say, "If we survive and things are as all desire, we shall speak again." This time he left.

⁂

Mona, a vassal Guardian from the North Plains, joined Armus and Wren in their observance of Renfrow's camp. Mona had the ability to shape-shift into any mortal when necessary. In her Guardian state, she had long brown hair with bright aquamarine eyes. She wore breeches and tunic. A sheathed dagger hung on her belt.

"I'm not sure which is growing stronger, the sense of change or the Dark Way. The intensity since crossing the border from the North Plains into Midessex is incredible. I don't know if we are enough in number to handle it," she said.

"Numbers don't matter in doing our duty," refuted Armus.

"It was an observation not a denouncement. Has Kell said anything about this change?"

Armus shook his head. "He doesn't know specific details."

"Would he tell us if he did?" she said with an ironic snicker.

"He wouldn't purposely let us go into a situation unprepared!"

Armus' rebuff surprised Mona. "I meant it as a joke about Kell's penchant to parcel out information." She sighed in exasperation at his anger. "Sorry, that didn't sound good either."

Wren intervened. "I think the situation is making us all edgy. I wish Avatar had been allowed to stay. We could use another warrior."

To this, Armus laughed. "I'll remember to tell him you confessed to missing him."

"I'll deny it."

"Then he'll know for certain you said it."

"Armus, I'm truly sorry I offended you. It wasn't my intention, nor did I mean to insult Kell," said Mona.

"Apology accepted. I'm sorry for overreacting. Wren's right about being edgy."

Wren chuckled. "I'll remember to tell Avatar you admitted to overreacting."

"I'll deny it."

They all laughed.

"Dunham and the squires are leaving." Mona pointed toward Renfrow's tent.

"Time for Wren and I to leave. We'll see you at Ravendale," he said to Mona.

Chapter 22

THE NEXT AFTERNOON, RAVENDALE BUZZED WITH ACTIVITY. The lords arrived, and each brought fifty men. Whereas Ravendale could accommodate the nobles, they established individual camps on the grounds surrounding the castle for their troops.

Renfrow delayed his arrival enough for Bartlett to return with suitable clothes for Karryn. After making camp, he received a message from Ramsey.

Karryn watched her father frown as he read. "What does it say?"

"Ramsey ordered a banquet for this evening." Annoyed, Renfrow tossed the letter onto a nearby cot. "I knew there would be a banquet, only I hoped you putting in a brief appearance would satisfy his request and not be paraded before court."

"I told you, I'm not afraid."

"Surely you realize the danger?"

"Of course. Those creatures in Dorgirith were horrid and created to kill. Then Garrick and Maddy." Although tears swelled, her voice and face showed determination. "It must end."

"My lord," called Bartlett just before entering. "Sir Dunham is here."

The announcement surprised Renfrow. "Already? It's not even dusk." He snatched up the letter to briefly consider the contents. "It would have been better if he arrived after the banquet."

"He's not afraid either," said Karryn.

For a long moment, Renfrow held his daughter's gaze. His spirit became bolstered by her confidence. "Then let us finish this, relying on the Old Faith that brings us to this moment."

"Tangiel," said Bartlett.

246

Renfrow stoutly confronted his captain. "If you mean that, then let not a drop of wine or ale cross your lips until this business is done."

"My lord, I haven't taken a drink since we left the North Plains. The stew made me sick."

Renfrow suppressed a grin. "Cook confirmed your story. He tossed the stew after learning about six others. Be ready to escort us to the banquet, Captain."

Bartlett slapped his sword in salute. In crisp military step, he withdrew.

"You're hard on him," said Karryn.

"Bartlett is a good man. Drink can only be a friend for so long when dealing with tragedy. I'm glad to see him come back to his senses after losing his wife."

"You didn't drink when Mother died."

"Each man grieves in his own way. I mourned her passing. But you—" Renfrow held Karryn by the shoulders. "If anything happens to you, I might seek solace at the bottom of a bottle. You are my pride and joy; a gift of the Old Faith when we thought to be childless." He kissed her forehead. "Take what time you need to make ready."

Until the banquet, Ramsey kept away from the hustle and bustle of arriving guests. Instead, he contented himself with planning how to dress for the biggest impact. He stood before a full-length mirror dressed in an elaborate gold suit embroidered with scarlet thread and diamonds. He completed the effect by donning his father's robes of state.

"What do you think? Does this convey the message?" he asked Beryl.

She sat with a sedate expression to watch his fitting. "If you say so."

Her reflection in the mirror showed she barely looked at him. Annoyed by her lack of enthusiasm, Ramsey dismissed the tailor to confront her. "What is wrong? Every time I ask your opinion the answer is the same: *If you say so.*"

"Because it's true. Your words shall reign supreme not my opinion." She spoke with a nervous stutter, still unable to look at him.

"You lackluster behavior of late is growing tiresome." When she became upset and turned away, he grabbed her shoulder to make her face him. "This should be a happy time. I shall be king and you queen."

Beryl fought to maintain her composure by biting her lower lip.

"Speak, woman! Don't continue to bore me with your tedious melancholy."

She sat up straight in the chair to comply. "Do you care for me?"

He huffed a grunt. "What kind of question is that? We've been married for thirty-five years."

"A fair one I should think, considering you are asking me to prostitute myself!"

"So that's it," he chided. "I thought you understood what is at stake."

"I do, but do you know what you ask of me?" Her voice rose with emotion.

"As my wife, and soon to be crowned queen, I ask you to help secure my throne!"

Beryl attempted to calm down by clenching her trembling hands together. "Don't you see the risk? It took me four years to conceive Carnel, and we have no other children." At his silent consideration, she pressed her case. "You agreed to give me to Dagar! What if I don't conceive, what will happen to us?"

"I'll find another way." He waved with impatience.

"Another?" she fearfully repeated. "You mean a new queen? You would cast me aside?"

"I didn't say that."

"You said the agreement is a child of the king's wife. What other meaning is there?"

"Two wives," he flippantly said, then thought. "Ay. Two wives," he said convinced.

"Two is against Jor'el's—" she shut her mouth at his sharp glance.

"You dare speak that name in my presence?"

Beryl paled with alarm as she scrambled for an answer. "I didn't mean *him* exactly. It's just not done in Allon; having multiple wives."

"And if I, the King, chose to make it so, who are you to argue?" He pressed her when she didn't immediately answer. "Well?"

"Your wife of thirty-five years. The mother of your son and heir. What would become of Carnel's claim if you marry again? You think she will be content to simply be a whore of Dagar or will she want to bear the King more children? No, it would place Carnel's life in danger. See what Magelen did to Razi's family!" she boldly countered despite her fear.

Ramsey's ire ignited. "Razi is a threat! So are his offspring! Including the Vicar."

"Elias? You believe he is Razi's son?" she asked with surprise.

"Don't play naïve, woman! It is obvious who his father is."

To avoid further inciting Ramsey on the subject of faith, Beryl reverted to the original discussion. "Then you will expose Carnel to Magelen's spleen by taking another queen?"

"I didn't say for certain I would marry again, just the possibility *if* you don't conceive." His tone changed to cheerful in hopes of ending the conversation. "Now we're getting ahead of ourselves. This is a time of enjoyment."

"When must I—?" she asked, her bravado wavering.

Ramsey shrugged. "I suppose it's up to Dagar to decide after the coronation."

Beryl seized his arm, her voice filled with pleading urgency. "Will you at least promise me to speak to Magelen about alternatives should I not be able to bear a child?"

With an agreeable expression, he said, "That I can do."

"Thank you." She wiped a few anxious tears from her eyes.

He took her hand. "In answer to your first question, how can I not have feelings for the woman who's been my companion for so long, and the mother of my heir?" He kissed her hand.

Beryl's gaze turned woeful. "You've changed, Ramsey. These last few years you've grown distant, even hostile. I just needed to know you still cared for me."

"Then know this, I want to secure the throne for us and for Carnel. As for my changing, I'll have to think on that another time, when all is more settled." Ramsey smiled and stepped back to spread his arms. "So what do you think? Do I look like a king?"

"For tonight. However, that old style belonged to your father. If you will allow me to help the tailor, I can design one more fitting for you."

Ramsey heartily laughed. "That's my Beryl." He hugged her.

Being held against his chest, he couldn't see her smile fade into a painful frown.

The Great Hall of Ravendale was resplendent in decoration. Aromas of every imaginable delicacy filled the air. Nobles wore their finest and most expensive attire. Karryn's grip on her father's arm tightened when they entered the hall. Bartlett's taste in clothes showed in her splendid burgundy, white and gold gown. He even bought a wonderful gold studded jewel headpiece to match the gown. This far exceeded those she wore at home or Garwood on a daily basis. Renfrow chose a complimentary suit of white with gold and wine accents. Bartlett made certain his formal uniform was spotless and the boots highly polished.

They just received instruction on the seating arrangement when Dunham arrived. Ethan and Captain Warren escorted him. Warren was a genteel man in his mid-thirties and every inch a polished professional soldier. Dunham spared no expense in his brown and gold suit or that of Ethan's attire, save Ethan didn't carry his bow. They joined Renfrow and Karryn.

"My lady," said Dunham with a smile of greeting.

"My lord." Karryn returned the greeting with a curtsey.

A measure of admiration filled Ethan's eyes upon sight of Karryn. A blush rose to her cheeks and smile on her lips. At the exchange, Renfrow loudly cleared his throat. Karryn assumed a modest posture while Ethan donned a formal expression.

"It appears everyone has arrived." Dunham observed those assembled in the hall.

"Indeed, my lord Dunham." Elias wore the official robes of his high priestly office. An assistant accompanied him.

"My lord Vicar!" Dunham fought to hide his surprise. "I didn't expect to see you until tomorrow."

Ethan's visible shock matched Dunham's verbal speech. He quickly regained his facial composure when nudged by Warren.

"I am no exception to a royal summons." Elias' gaze passed from Dunham to Ethan. "Although it is good to see some are exempt."

"Through hard reasoning," said Dunham.

Elias chuckled. He smiled at Karryn. "My dear, you have grown into a beautiful lady."

"My lord Vicar, you look the picture of health."

Elias laughed. "You are very kind, but I thought your father taught you not to tell fibs."

She sweetly smiled. "No fib. You truly do look well."

He took her hand; his features conflicted. "We all must do what is necessary."

"We will," she replied with unwavering confidence.

Elias squeezed Karryn's hand. "You should be proud, Renfrow. Such courage wrapped up in so pretty a woman as to fill an old man with hope by her few words."

Ethan coughed aside an impulsive chuckle.

"Where there are some who speak too often when they shouldn't say anything," said Dunham.

Ethan's smile vanished. He bowed at the rebuke.

"It is obvious why, even to these aging eyes." Elias' voice grew lower as he continued. "Guard your hearts this night and trust Jor'el."

"Tangiel, Vicar," said Renfrow under his breath.

Elias and his assistant moved to mingle with the other guests.

Dunham leaned closer to Renfrow. "It begins. Courage and faith to you, my friend."

"And to you." Renfrow escorted Karryn to their seats.

Dunham, Ethan and Warren made their way to a table directly across the hall from Renfrow, Karryn and Bartlett. While the nobles sat, Ethan, Warren and Bartlett stood behind the respective chairs. Elias sat at the far end of table with Dunham.

A loud pounding echoed in the hall, followed by trumpets announcing the royal arrival. The steward declared, "His Most Royal Highness, Prince Ramsey and Her Royal Highness Princess Beryl. His Highness Prince Carnel."

Everyone rose. Men bowed and women curtsied, as the royal family made their way to high table. Magelen followed Carnel. He appeared unusually pleased, confident and deadly this evening. In fact, he paid particular attention to Dunham then flashed cold blue eyes at Karryn.

She stiffened at the attention. Did he recognize her? Surely she appeared different enough from Dorgirith not to capture his scrutiny. Magelen wasn't the only one casting eyes at her. Carnel did also, yet with worry bordering on sympathy. In shying from Carnel, Karryn caught Ethan's studious gaze. She knew his keen observation missed nothing.

Once at high table, Ramsey spoke. "My lords and ladies, enjoy the feast. Tomorrow begins a new reign in Allon."

The slight of not asking Vicar Elias to bless the meal drew curious glances along with a few murmurs from the crowd. No one voiced any loud protest. Soon the noise of conversation, music and laughter filled the hall. Some enjoyed the festivities, as told by boisterous humor or raised voices in merry discussion.

Elias, Renfrow, Dunham, Kaleb, and Karryn displayed the proper amount of decorum to satisfy most observers. A few times Karryn caught Ethan's regard. Once he managed to raise a cup in salute when serving Dunham. A word from Dunham sent him back to his place.

While the feast took place in the Great Hall, Tristan waited for Murdock outside Ravendale. He again wore black clothes along with a black wig and beard. He donned the disguise before splitting off from Dunham's main group to make his way to a prearranged hiding place. If one were to make a close inspection the disguise was obvious, yet passable in the dark.

Tristan scrutinized every inch of the castle in view. Ravens, and other unnerving creatures, decorated the facade. Being here for the first time filled him with fury. His hand clenched the hilt of his sword. From these walls came the orders to kill his family. Somewhere in the bowels of that sinister castle, his grandfather sat rotting while his father, Dunham and Ethan walked into the enemy's lair.

"Jor'el, you appointed the hour for this bold venture. Aid us, as we seek to bring justice and the honor of your name back to Allon. Protect my father, grandfather, Ethan, Dunham and the others. Maddy—" he swallowed back his emotions for determination. "If it be your will, please heal her. Yet if I survive, whatever her condition—" he stopped at hearing the signal. He made the counter-signal. A man appeared.

"Captain Murdock?"

Murdock held up his right hand to show a signet ring with a wolf and eagle. "At your service, my lord. Same as the house to which you were born. Minus the bad disguise."

"Hopefully no one will get close enough to know."

"That's the plan. Now, we must hurry. The banquet is underway."

Tristan followed Murdock on the same route inside as with Renfrow when they met Carnel. Murdock stopped in the compound to let the night watch pass. Once clear, they darted from shadow to shadow until they reached the dungeon.

"Pull the hood up to obscure the disguise from the torchlight." Murdock waited for Tristan to do so before they moved down a long hall. They paused at stairs leading down. "Blackburn! Scully!" he called.

A lean man of middle years came scrambling up a flight of stairs. "Ay, Captain?"

Tristan hung back to remain in the shadows.

"Blackburn. Where is Scully?"

"Right behind me."

Heavy boots on the steps told of Scully's compliance. Hardly what Tristan expected of a guard. The large older man appeared winded when he reached the top of the steps.

"You wanted to see us, Captain?"

"Scully, your duty is the front door, not downstairs! What were you doing? Playing dice?"

Their abashed expression showed Murdock guessed correctly. The captain held out his hand. "I think you'd rather give up the winnings than being flogged and losing a month's pay."

"Ay, Captain." Scully gave a pouch filled with coins to Murdock.

"Captain, who is he?" Blackburn asked concerning Tristan, which made Tristan shrink further back into the shadows.

"None of your concern. Scully, return to your post. Blackburn, has the prisoner been fed?"

"Er ... not yet, Captain."

"Then I suggest you fetch his food."

"Ay, Captain, but if Scully and I aren't down there, who—"

"Now!"

The guards saluted before exiting the front door.

"How?" Tristan asked, motioning in the directions the guards left.

Murdock explained as he led Tristan downstairs. "I made certain they were on guard tonight. Scully is old, fat and lazy. Blackburn is a schemer I know a few facts about. One fact is being the lover of a married kitchen wench. He steals away to see her every chance he can when on duty and she away from her husband. He won't be returning anytime soon."

At the bottom hallway, Murdock made a quick visual search. No one else joined the dice game. Removing the keys from under his belt, he unlocked the door to Razi's cell.

"My lord, you have a visitor."

"What now, Ramsey? Come to bring me some celebration cake with poisoned icing?" asked Razi with mocking acidity. He rose from the cot when Murdock and another entered. "Who are you?" He wasn't prepared for being engulfed in a hug. "Here now—"

"Grandpapi." Tristan pushed back the hood and pulled off the wig.

Razi blinked in shock. "Tristan? What are you doing here? Foolish boy! Murdock, get him out of here!"

"No! Murdock helped me get in—to rescue you. Everything is ready. The others are in place. We just need you to lead."

"What are you talking about?"

"Didn't Murdock tell you?"

"The less he knows, the less he can tell if it fails," said Murdock.

"I'm here. The plan hasn't failed!" rebuffed Tristan.

"What plan?" asked Razi.

"Dunham, Renfrow, Kaleb and nine others, are ready to topple Ramsey. Each has a prearranged assignment. Mine is to secure you beforehand to present you as king when all is finished. That's what I'm doing." Tristan spoke in rapid response.

Razi tried to comprehend the explanation. "I suspected something might happen after Ram died. Twelve out of fourteen agreed so quickly?"

"Not quick, although those who agreed are leaders of a province." Tristan grabbed Razi by the hand. "Now, come, we must leave."

Razi balked. "I don't have the strength to run or fight."

"You must! We depend upon you."

Razi resisted, as he stared at Tristan. "You, not me, must lead them."

The shocking statement made Tristan stutter in response. "I'm just a boy to some of them. You were born to be king."

Razi's old blue eyes grew misty. "My time is near. *You* are the fulfillment of Jor'el's promise to be my heir—to be king."

Pricked by the refusal, Tristan said, "I'm not leaving without you."

Hearing voices, Murdock stepped out of the cell "Someone's coming!" He swore. "Blackburn. The wench must not be there. My lords, hide at the end hall. I'll take care of him."

"No, take Tristan and go!"

"Grandpapi—"

Murdock heeded Razi and shoved Tristan out the cell. He locked the door. "Disguise," he hissed in warning at hearing footsteps on the stairs.

Tristan did a bad job of putting on the wig so that it barely covered his blond hair. The hood held it in place. He bent his head when Blackburn arrived.

"Ramsey is in a generous mood. He ordered a special meal prepared," said Blackburn unaware of anything amiss.

"Did you taste it to make certain there is no poison?"

Blackburn hesitated. "No."

"Do so!" said Tristan in a raspy, disguised voice.

Blackburn became curious of Tristan, so Murdock took the tray to get the guard's attention. "Take a bite of everything."

Blackburn first hesitated. Murdock's prompting made him comply. He smiled after each bite when nothing happened. "It's safe, Captain."

Murdock gave Blackburn the tray. "Carry on." He and Tristan climbed the steps from the dungeon.

Blackburn moved to the cell where put down the tray to unlock the door. Before he could put the key in the lock—it happened. Blackburn gagged; horror on his face. He sunk to his knees then to fell to the floor in convulsions. Razi peeked out the cell door to witness the final throngs of Blackburn's fit before the guard became still. He waited a moment, but no one came.

"Jor'el, please protect him!"

Chapter 23

BEFORE THE DANCING BEGAN, MAGELEN SIGNALED TO THE steward. The man pounded the large golden staff on the floor to get attention. The background music stopped and everyone directed their gaze to high table.

Magelen rose to start his address. "Noble lords and ladies, His Royal Highness, soon to be King Ramsey, has a favor to bestow this night. Give heed to your King." He spoke with deliberate yet delighted purpose. Even his smile held a hint of pleasure in resuming his seat.

"Thank you, Grand Master. Although the passing of my father is a deeply grievous event, a new day is a cause for celebration. One celebration my father looked forward, but shall sadly miss, is the marriage of his grandson and future heir, Prince Carnel."

Carnel maintained a subdued manner when Ramsey gave him a passing indication.

"This night, royal favor is bestowed with the choice of bride from among the most fair and noble of ladies of this court." Ramsey's eyes scanned the room then came to rest on Dunham. "What say you to such a favor, Sir Dunham?"

Dunham curbed his reaction at being singled out to reply. "Who am I to speak, Highness, since I know not the favored bride?"

"The unfortunate news regarding your daughter has reached us. She was among those considered for the favor."

Dunham clenched his fists in an effort to contain his emotions. He simply nodded.

"Along with daughters of Sir Percy, Count Sheldon and Lord Godfrey." Ramsey looked at each of the lords when named. They received the news with the same stoic expression as Dunham.

"Gracious ladies all, Highness," said Magelen, much too generous to be sincere. He then added, "Do you not agree, my lord Dunham?"

"Indeed," he said in compelled reply.

"In the end, the favor has been won by a lady whose quiet manner and discretion is most appealing." Ramsey turned his gaze to Renfrow and Karryn.

Karryn paled in fear, which prompted Renfrow to say, "Highness, please—"

"I am pleased to bestow the favor upon Lady Karryn, Baron."

A whimper of distress escaped Karryn's tightly pressed lips.

"Highness," began Elias loud enough to draw attention. "Has the Prince agreed to this choice?"

"Naturally, Vicar. He has been involved since the beginning."

To this statement, Carnel shifted in his chair in obvious display of dispute. Beryl made a gesture of caution to her son. He kept silent.

Ramsey ignored them. "The first dance shall belong to the happy couple. After which Lady Karryn will be escorted to a guest chamber where she shall be prepared for the wedding. The ceremony will immediately follow the coronation."

Overcome, Karryn fell back against the chair. Renfrow caught her for support The scraping of another chair happened when Dunham bolted up to restrain Ethan.

"Is there an objection, Sir Dunham?" asked Ramsey.

"No, Highness. News my squire just told me concerning an update on my daughter's condition."

Ethan's hostile expression placed the ruse in jeopardy. He flinched in pain when Dunham gave him a hard nudge toward Warren. The captain seized Ethan.

"Condition? We heard she was killed in an accident," said Ramsey in firm dispute.

Dunham made a quick recovery to the miscue. "Due to the severity of her injuries some may have made that assumption, Highness. Sadly, she took a turn for the worse, which is what my squire told me." He sent a harsh glare to Ethan. "Tell the physician to do what is necessary to ensure her recovery." He motioned for Warren to take charge of Ethan.

Warren struggled to maintain hold of Ethan, whose fury almost defied reason. By the time they reached the courtyard, Warren became fed up. He shoved Ethan into the shadowy alcove where he slammed him against the wall of the building.

"Will you ruin everything? Think, man!"

Ethan didn't respond. His livid sneer told his thoughts.

"Act without a plan or on impulse and she dies! So will others, whose lives are at stake if one false move is made."

To this argument, Ethan spoke in a tight voice. "I don't want that."

"Neither does Sir Dunham, or Baron Renfrow." Warren maintained his hold to press Ethan. "Your word of honor not to act tonight."

Ethan boldly met Warren's gaze. "My word of honor. I will not act tonight, but given the chance I will secure her."

"Return to camp and *wait!*" Warren shoved Ethan out of the alcove.

Ethan left Ravendale without looking back. He knew Warren was right. Any unplanned attempt to interfere, and Magelen would kill Karryn. "Jor'el, keep her safe and untouched this night."

Inside, Karryn's tacit nature helped to mask her inner heart and mind over Ethan's reaction. The look on his face showed that if he had his bow—oh, she was grateful Dunham intervened! She took the time during the distraction to regain her composure. Not Renfrow.

"This is unheard of! Have I no consent in my daughter's future?"

Ramsey bolted to his feet, his face flush with insult. "You are lucky to be father-in-law to a future king! Be content with that. Carnel!" He waved his son from the table.

Karryn tugged on Renfrow's arm to make him sit. "Father, don't make him angry," she said, low and urgent.

"We'll find a way out this, I promise," he said in hurried reply. Renfrow stood when Carnel stopped in front the table.

"My lord baron, I seek the honor of the first dance, and all dances hereafter with your daughter." Carnel spoke with formality yet his eyes conveyed some personal distress.

Karryn squeezed Renfrow's arm, which prompted him to respond.

"The honor is yours, Highness." Renfrow helped Karryn come around the table.

Karryn took Carnel's hand to be escorted to the floor. The music started when they assumed positions for the dance. She averted her gaze anytime he tried to catch her eye. He wasn't an unappealing man, who obviously wanted to get her attention. She had to maintain an aloof attitude to keep her composure.

After the dance, several ladies-in-waiting came for Karryn. Carnel spoke. "Allow me to escort my future bride to her chamber."

Uncertain, the women looked to Ramsey. This made Carnel add, "It will give us a few private moments to discuss our future."

Ramsey didn't immediately reply, rather studiously regarded his son.

Beryl spoke. "You did the same in speaking to me after told of your father's choice."

"So I did." Ramsey cocked a grin and nodded to Carnel. "Return when you are finished."

Carnel offered his arm to Karryn. She resisted the urge to look at her father when leaving the hall. Two royal guards fell into step behind them. She took notice of them.

"For your protection," said Carnel.

"Do I need protection from you, Highness?" she spoke in thinly disguised anger.

"No."

They said nothing more on trek to the guest chamber.

"Allow me." Carnel opened the door for Karryn to enter. "Wait out here," he commanded the guards before following her inside.

Karryn heard Carnel enter but kept her back turned. Her left hand touched the sleeve over her right forearm, her right hand cocked as if ready to punch out in defense. Whatever happened, she would not yield tamely.

"My dear, Kar—" Carnel touched her shoulder. She whirled about. His speech halted when a dagger pressed against his chest. Surprised horror filled his face. "How did you bring that unnoticed into the hall?"

Karryn didn't answer. She held the blade steady against him. Her features stark and direct.

Carnel flinched at her expression. "Are you going to kill me?"

"Only if you touch me again."

"I wanted you to turn so we can speak face-to-face, not to accost you in any manner."

She kept the dagger against his chest.

Carnel stared back at her. "I can take it from you."

Karryn's intense glare told him not to even try.

He held up his hands in a gesture of yielding, and stepped back. "Your tenacious silence is a very appealing quality."

She didn't move or speak, simply held the dagger ready.

He grew serious, his voice low and pressing. "Put it away! It won't do for someone to enter and find you armed. By the *Old Faith*, I mean you no harm. Your father trusts me."

Neither his use of the cryptic statement nor invoking her father surprised Karryn. She lowered the blade, yet kept it ready.

He huffed at her partial compliance. "Less threatening is better, I suppose. Please, can we sit to speak?" He indicated a sofa.

"If you tarry too long your father will grow suspicious."

A hint of disdain crept into Carnel's voice. "His *talk* with my mother wasn't done with words. She didn't have a dagger, otherwise he wouldn't have succeeded."

The statement made her stop short of the sofa. "And you ask me to trust you?"

"I am not my father's son when it comes to women!"

She saw the truth reflected in his disapproving sneer and glowering eyes. "Perhaps not."

Carnel softened his tone to cajoling. "Put away the dagger. You, your father and the squire have nothing to fear from me."

Karryn paused in putting the dagger away at hearing a reference to Ethan. "What made you include the squire?" she asked with discretion.

Carnel laughed. "Don't play coy. He wasn't speaking to Dunham. By the look on his face, everyone now knows he is your lover."

"No! We haven't—I mean not until—"

"You can get flustered like other women," he teased.

Karryn didn't take it well. Again, she held the dagger ready. "This discussion is over. Leave!"

Carnel became insistent at the dismissal. "I want to help you!"

She stood her ground. "My help will come from elsewhere."

The sting of rejection made him flush with anger. "Pray it comes before the wedding!" He slammed the door behind him.

Overcome by the emotions she held in check, Karryn sank to her knees. The dagger dropped, as she buried her face in her hands and wept.

After midnight, Dunham and Renfrow returned to Dunham's camp. Inside the main tent, they discovered Tristan dozing at the table with Ethan working on his bow. Ethan slapped Tristan's arm to wake him.

"I'm not surprised to see you," said Dunham to Ethan, "but I am you," he said to Tristan.

"He wouldn't come! He said his time is short and I am the future." Tristan shook his head with bewilderment. "How could he refuse after we risked everything to come for him?"

Ethan vacated the chair for Dunham to sit. "He is a very wise, devout and intelligent man. He has his reasons. He will not abandon you. Think of all he has done to protect you."

"What do we do now?"

"Continue with the plan. His absence changes nothing."

"And Karryn?" asked Ethan in a harsh tone.

Renfrow spoke. "Despite what I feared coming to pass, she knows what is at stake. It is not a sacrifice any of us want. Our success is what will ultimately help Karryn and Allon."

"We depend upon you to keep your head clear, your eye sharp and your aim true," added Dunham in stout comment to Ethan.

"My bow has never been more ready than it is now."

Dunham gazed intently at Ethan. The woodsman squire stood rigid in posture and fix in feature. "Take Tristan, and both of you get some sleep or you will be no good to any of us."

"Are you staying here tonight?"

"No, I'm returning to the castle. It's too risky to refuse royal hospitality."

"Then I shall accompany you."

"No."

Ethan stiffened with ire. "I kept my word to Captain Warren and awaited your return."

Dunham rose to confront Ethan. "Can you keep your head in regards to Karryn if you are inside the castle?"

Ethan's jowls flexed with conflicting emotions at the challenge.

Tristan intervened. "He'll stay with me tonight." He tugged hard on Ethan's arm to leave.

"I know Karryn lost her heart. By his reaction, the feelings are mutual," said Renfrow.

Dunham grinned. "You'll find Ethan's tenacity equal to Karryn, though he is much more talkative. A keener and more lethal shot, I have never seen. I wonder if any of the Old Knights could best him."

"It is high praise to compare a mortal to *legends*."

"Not really, his skill is unmatched. As for the *legends*, I pray they are nearby. We can use their help."

Doubt filled Renfrow's gaze. "Do you believe they still exist?"

Dunham took no offense at the inquiry. Instead, he smiled. "It wasn't just Ethan's bow or Tristan and Karryn's bravery that saved my children in Dorgirith. An unknown man dressed in *my* livery—but not among those who accompanied me—delivered them from Magelen's clutches."

Renfrow listened with curiosity. "You saw him?"

"Tristan, Maddy and Garrick did. His actions answered my prayer for divine protection."

"Then but not later."

"Cursed Shadow Warriors!" Dunham swore.

Renfrow gripped Dunham's shoulder in a gesture of warning. "We have talked more than is prudent. We must be careful to avoid to discovery."

With steady confidence, Dunham said, "If we are discovered, we will not survive the night. If we see the light of day, take solace in the Old Faith and legends. Now, let's return to the castle."

"I'm not as comfortable about it as you," Renfrow confessed.

"Fois agus bi furasda, Freiceadans nèamh thairis sinn." Dunham spoke the Ancient for encouragement.

Renfrow grinned at the sentiment. "Ay. We need the watchful eyes of *legends* this night."

They became alarmed when the tent flap opened in an abrupt manner. A cloaked, hooded man entered.

"Be at ease, my lords!" He tossed back the hood.

"Murdock? What are you doing here?" demanded Dunham.

"To tell you that an attempt has been made on Lord Razi's life."

"Tristan said nothing about it."

"Lord Razi is whole. It happened after we left. I made Blackburn taste the food Ramsey ordered specially prepared. Nothing immediately happened, so it must have been a slow acting poison. When I returned after seeing Tristan safe, I found Blackburn on floor just outside the cell door. I disposed of the body in hopes of preventing discovery."

"Why have you left Razi alone?" chided Renfrow.

"He is safe, my lord. I have the only key. The men are ready."

"How many soldiers have agreed to help?" asked Dunham

"All save Ramsey's personal company of bodyguards. Captain Galton is loyal to a fault. He will be providing security at the gate and in the Great Hall."

"We can deal with a single company." Dunham cocked a pleased smile. "Let us pray divine blessing continues to a successful end." He steered Murdock to the tent entrance. "Time to return to royal hospitality."

"I'll see you both safely to your quarters," said Murdock.

Chapter 24

O N A KNOLL TWO MILES FROM RAVENDALE, MONA, ARMUS AND Wren watched and waited. His fingers showed nervous energy in clenching and unclenching the hilt of his sheathed sword. When Kell arrived, Armus gave voice to his frustration.

"I'm surprised Magelen hasn't sent out patrols."

"If he believes Avatar is neutralized, and no other Guardians a threat, he won't waste Witter or Altari on a scouting mission," said Kell.

"Seems wrong to be lax with such a gathering of mortals."

"We've managed this long to keep our presence unknown," said Mona.

"With the plan about to unfold, we're about to take more drastic measures to make sure the coup succeeds," chided Armus.

Mona turned from Armus to Kell to ask, "You have a plan?"

"Hopefully it doesn't involve blood and a lifechain," groused Wren.

Kell's expression told his disapproval of her dig. "For Armus, Valmar, Jedrek, Barnum and me to assume mortal form in our reduced capacity *is* a great risk to our lifeforce."

Wren clamped her mouth shut, however reluctant.

"I thought only I could shape-shift," said Mona with some confusion.

Kell shook his head. "Becoming a specific mortal is your specialty. You know we can take on the appearance of *being* mortal. You, Wren, Gresham and Zinna will serve as backup."

"Where are Gresham and Zinna?" Mona didn't see them.

"Zinna is watching the northern route to Ravendale. Gresham guards the eastern road. You will take the west while Wren stays here."

"What about Chase and Priscilla?"

"Water and wind aren't really helpful on land," Wren continued in her put out manner.

"Enough!" snapped Kell.

"I'm sorry. This situation has me more on edge than is normal."

Wren's apology sounded far from sincere, and Kell let her know it. "I understand this is personal, which is why I have tolerated your ill humor—until *now*. If you can't hold your tongue and follow orders, you will be immediately reassigned."

Shocked, Wren balked. "Captain! I would never shirk my duty."

Kell scrutinizing gaze held her attention. Her disturbance went deep. She never failed to protect a charge before. However, her dedication to duty went without question, thus he softened his tone. "I summoned Eldric. He will be here shortly to wait with you, in case any of us should need his services."

"What about Maddy?"

"He will give us a report when he arrives."

Wren took the pouch off her belt. She held it out to Kell. "I ask the same promise from you I did from Avatar—use it sparingly."

Kell suppressed a grin to repeat Avatar's reply. "With Jor'el's help, they'll be in need, not me." He said Armus, "Time to join the others."

To conserve energy, Kell and Armus proceeded on foot. They made a wide arc around Ravendale. Sometimes they hid to avoid mortals. Mostly they ran at great speed to reach the abandoned outpost of Redford Crossing twenty miles away. Barnum, Valmar and Jedrek waited. Jedrek was the youngest of the warriors at twelve hundred years old. His blond hair and amber eyes signified his special power of fire. Among the others, he appeared lithesome and agile.

"Glad to see everyone made it unscathed," said Kell.

"For the time being. Five against an unknown number of Shadow Warriors doesn't bode well for remaining unscathed," said Valmar.

"That's why we're going in disguise."

"With reduced strength, maintaining our cover and fighting will be difficult," said Barnum.

"Ay, being in pairs would be better. Yet since we're only five, which one of us will go solo?" asked Jedrek.

"Six," said a new voice.

All drew their swords when he stepped from around the corner of a building.

Kell's brows level in angry confusion. "Avatar? What are you doing here? I told you to return."

"According to Jor'el, my assignment isn't finished. Not as a decoy, rather my role in the High Trio. Jedrek is right, it's best to be in pairs for this business."

Kell sheathed his sword though he remained unconvinced. "You're being here is risky after your little adventure in fooling Altari. If you lose your cover due to injury, the rest of us may be exposed. Not to mention the danger to Mahon and the others."

Avatar flashed a casual smile. "Then I won't lose it."

"I should have let Wren shoot you when she asked," quipped Armus.

"A wasted arrow. His hide is as thick as his head," said Barnum in return humor.

Kell glanced to Avatar's right ankle. "Are you healed?"

Avatar stomped his foot. "Totally." Kell's consideration made him ask, "Are you going to send me back after being dispatched again?"

"No. To ensure everyone's safety, you're with me disguised as members of Dunham's group. Armus and Jedrek with Renfrow. Valmar and Barnum with Kaleb."

"What exactly are we doing?" asked Jedrek.

"Making sure Tristan survives! He is Jor'el's promised heir for Razi. Our future restoration is linked to him. Personally, I hope to secure Razi to fulfill my pledge. Other than that, we are not to interfere."

"What if Dunham or others are at risk of being killed? If the plan is in danger of failing? Are we are to stand by and watch?" Anger found its way in Armus' voice.

Pain reflected in Kell's face. "If acting requires using your power, you must refrain. If you can do so without revealing your identity, then act.

Remember, we are legends. Any premature revealing of our presence will jeopardize the lives of our imprisoned comrades and risk our future return. In this case, acting can cause more harm than inaction."

A moment of deep bitter silence followed. This was not what warriors wanted to hear.

Kell broke the profound quiet. "When we are within three miles of Ravendale, we change into a mortal persona to join our respective groups." He led them back the way he and Armus came. At the three-mile mark, he stopped.

"Jor'el be with all of us." Kell brought his hands together, bent his head and spoke the Ancient. Although becoming a specific mortal was reserved for shape-shifting Guardians, warriors taking on the appearance of mortals retained their familiar features. Kell had black hair and hazel eyes. He stood six and half-feet tall, considerably shorter in height and smaller in physical stature though still strong. His uniform transformed into the livery of Dunham.

The others mimicked Kell's transformation. Avatar retained his goatee with steel blue eyes replacing his usual silver. He stood the same height as Kell. Armus remained brown haired with brown-eyes, leaner in bulk for a Guardian yet muscular for a mortal. Barnum still appeared larger than Armus even in mortal form. Valmar's bright violet eyes turned to a nice mortal blue while Jedrek's eyes became a dull light brown. He was shorter than the others by a couple of inches.

"To your assignments." Kell waited for the others to leave before speaking to Avatar. "True, I could have sent you with Armus, but not the others."

"Why? All are fine warriors."

"You said it, we are the High Trio; we act together."

Avatar snorted a contrary sarcastic laugh. "Right. So next time you'll be the decoy and I'll be captain. Kell, your motive is obvious. Only this time, you shamed me in front of more than just Armus and Wren."

"No shame was meant. If you fault me for anything, it is to keep you and others alive."

Avatar's gaze focused in the direction the others left. His jowls clenched and the goatee quivered in a familiar expression of suppressing anger. "That's not what Altari thinks."

"You know I do the same for Armus. How I wanted to spare Mahon and the rest from Dagar. As captain, I feel everything that happens to each Guardian, including Altari! Try bearing such a burden for a single day then fault me for my actions." Kell took several deep breaths to calm his temper. When next he spoke, it was with lament. "I pray Jor'el blesses this venture, for I don't know how many more friends and comrades I can stand to lose."

Avatar sent a partial glance to Kell. "If Altari didn't fall for your lifechain ploy, Mahon *is* lost. When I get my hands on him, I'll know."

"We're here to help the mortals, not for personal revenge. Altari will be dealt with in time," Kell chided.

"Not revenge, justice. Or at the very least, gain intelligence from him."

"Altari said the same about justice before forfeiting his position by disobedience."

Roused to new offense, Avatar faced Kell. "I have never disobeyed your orders, so why do you continue to remind me of Altari's actions?"

"I didn't bring up Altari, *you* did!" Kell pointedly reminded Avatar.

Avatar scowled at the counterpoint. "Running from him hasn't been easy, then Mahon! I'd rather stand and fight."

"How do you think Armus and I have felt these past hundred and fifty years? We're not just hiding from Altari, but also Dagar—which has allowed the Dark Way to rule!"

All of Avatar's combativeness subsided at the stern rebuttal.

Kell held Avatar by the shoulder. "Don't let Altari's present actions cause *you* to act reckless. I need you to keep your wits, not only as my Trio Mate, but more important, as my friend."

Avatar's glance at Kell became skewed. "Altari hates me while Dagar wants to take me apart due to my friendship with *you*. Maybe it would have been safer to go with one of the others."

Kell laughed, breaking the tension.

Avatar's usual wry grin appeared. "Despite my selfish spasm, I was sent to help bolster *your* efforts—twice. So, I will."

"Your spasm and my tantrum. Now, let's join Dunham without further delay."

Ethan sat on a stool outside the tent where Tristan slept. Working on his bow provided a means to keep active. His mind prevented him from resting. Being of nobility, he knew Karryn would marry someone equal in station. For that reason, he dared not hope for returned affection. The situation changed upon discovering her shared feelings. His heart soared when she agreed to marry him.

Alas, his elation became dashed by a most foul, unexpected turn of events. He watched her bravely withstand the shock then fought to control his thoughts of what she must be enduring since he left. Ethan paused in his work when Tristan emerged.

"Something wrong?" he asked.

With a huff in dejection, Tristan sat on a stool beside Ethan. "I can't sleep. I keep hearing his words of refusal."

"Maybe I should lace an arrow with something to make you see reason."

Tristan averted his eyes. The avoidance ended when Ethan grabbed his arm.

"Talk to me. What troubles you?"

"I don't know if I have the courage to do this alone."

Ethan grabbed an arrow to hold in front of Tristan's face. "I'm going to stick you because you are not alone. Not as long I live."

Tristan pushed the arrow aside to lean closer. He spoke in a low, hushed voice. "He told me *I am* the fulfillment of Jor'el's promise as his heir. I always knew I was the last surviving son, the one to carry on the family, but not the heir of a divine promise!"

"He meant it to be kept from you for as long as possible. He didn't want to overburden you with such knowledge."

The statement stymied Tristan. "How long have you known?"

"Since the day we left to join Dunham."

"Ten years?"

"He swore me to secrecy, along with your protection." Ethan raised the arrow again. "Why do think Dunham and rest are doing this? For him and *you*. So take heart, and get some rest."

"What about you? I suspect you can't sleep because of Karryn."

Ethan's jowls tightened. He began to examine the straightness of each arrow then sighed. "I keep seeing her face the moment it happened, and fight against worrying about her safety. If any lay a hand on her— may my arrow find its mark."

"I try praying and telling myself to trust Jor'el, but it so difficult."

"Why?" asked a new voice.

Ethan bolted to his feet with bow in hand. Tristan also stood. They watched a figure emerge from the shadows into the torchlight by which Ethan worked. He equaled Tristan's height of six and a half feet, with a goatee, friendly features and dressed in Dunham's uniform.

He continued to Tristan, "Do you trust your friend and his bow?"

"Ay."

"Then if you can place trust in a weapon made of wood and a man of flesh, why is it so difficult to trust the eternal one who created and controls all things?"

Tristan stared at the man. "Do I know you?"

"You can both sleep easy this night." His gaze lingered a moment on each before he motioned to the tent.

Ethan picked up his quiver to escort Tristan inside.

Tristan jolted, as if waking up. "The man from Dorgirith!" He rushed to look outside the tent flap. Gone. Ethan moved to shoulder, so Tristan pushed him back from the tent opening. "It was him; the Old Knight— the Guardian from Dorgirith!"

"Are you certain?"

"Ay!" Tristan grinned from ear to ear. "He's right, we can rest. Karryn and Grandpapi will be safe tonight."

"He's out here, they are inside."

"Doubting so soon? Did you not feel reassurance?"

"No, I speak logistically. And, I did feel a sense of reassurance when he looked at me."

"He may well be inside right now." Tristan went to his cot to retire for the night. He looked up and said, "Thank you, Jor'el."

Concealed in the shadows between two larger tents, Kell waited, now joined by Armus. Avatar arrived. He kept glancing at the tent.

"Something of interest?" asked Kell.

"Tristan resembles Razi more than I first realized. Although he appeared familiar at Dorgirith, I didn't pay attention. His heritage and task is weighing on him this night."

"He is the reason we are here," said Kell.

"I thought it was Wren's job to state the obvious?" snickered Avatar.

"I still regret not letting her shoot you," chuckled Armus.

Avatar smirked. "What are you doing here? And where is Jedrek?"

"Still at Renfrow's camp. I came to pass along some news. Ramsey chose Karryn for Carnel's bride. She remains at Ravendale since the wedding is immediately after the coronation."

"This adds a complication to the plan," said Kell.

"For Ethan also," said Avatar. "I heard him and Tristan discussing how difficult it is for him to keep his wits due to concern for her safety."

Displeased, Kell said, "We don't need his attention being divided."

"Ethan won't risk Tristan's life. It would violate the oath he swore to Razi," said Armus.

"We can't take that chance." Kell instructed Avatar, "When things start happening tomorrow, I want you to find Karryn and either keep her safe or get her to safety. Ethan is needed elsewhere." He stared in the direction of Ravendale, his lips pressed together in thought. After a moment, he dismissed Armus. "Return, and stay close to Renfrow tomorrow."

Shortly after Armus departed, they became alert for action. Eldric arrived in his Guardian form, which made him six inches taller than them. Avatar let his sword fall back into the scabbard. Kell was more demonstrative in slamming the blade into the sheath.

"Cover your essence!" scolded Kell.

"I did, until now, to let you know I'm here."

"Even that small use of power may alert them. And why are you not in mortal form?"

"I couldn't get here as quick." Eldric bowed his head while bringing his hands together.

"Not here! Join Wren at the knoll and then change."

"Wait. How is Maddy?" Avatar asked Eldric.

"Remarkably well considering her injuries. Jor'el is being gracious in allowing my treatments to be effective without using my power."

"That's good to hear. Make sure Wren knows," said Kell.

"I will." Eldric left.

Chapter 25

IN THE GUEST CHAMBER, KARRYN SAT NEAR A WINDOW FACING toward the west. She remained awake all night, not daring to fall asleep. Her eyes appeared tired and red-rimmed. She hoped for the rising sunlight to reveal her father's camp. She didn't know if it would be visible from the room, but waited for a chance to catch a glimpse. Her mind argued, reasoned and prayed for what the day would bring. With the plan about to unfold, she became a pawn rather than a participant. Any action she took to be free or an attempt by her father, or Ethan, could jeopardize everything! Whatever happened, she had to be prepared.

There came a brief knock on the door followed by someone entering. The large Shadow Warrior with the cold grey eyes approached. Karryn gripped the arms of the chair to steady her nerves. He wasn't alone. Several of Princess Beryl's attendants accompanied him. One lady carried a gown, the others various accessories. Karryn didn't pay much attention to them, as she braced herself to deal with the Warrior.

"Lady Daylen and the women will prepare you for the ceremony. Don't give them any trouble," said Altari.

Karryn rose when Daylen stepped forward. Daylen flashed a friendly smiled at Karryn. She then spoke to Altari in a tone intolerant of noncompliance.

"Wait in the hall as we carry out the *Queen's* instructions," she emphasized the title.

Despite a glare of displeasure at the command, Altari withdrew.

Daylen softened her tone toward Karryn. "Relax while we prepare your bath." She coaxed Karryn back into the chair. In doing so, she placed a small folded piece of paper in Karryn's hand. She held Karryn's gaze for a moment then ushered the maids into the antechamber.

Karryn waited until they were gone before moving to the window with her back to the room. She carefully unfolded the paper to read: *Remember my promise to help. C.* Carnel? He made a pledge, only she didn't place much stock in his words. She knew her father didn't completely trust the Prince. Still, he took a risk sending such a note. It must not be found in her possession.

After a quick glance to the door, Karryn crossed to the hearth. She shoved the note under the few remaining embers from last night's fire. She blew on the coals to create enough heat to reduce the note to a burnt lump. Hearing voices grow louder, she returned to the chair and assumed an impassive attitude.

Daylen appeared. "The bath should be ready shortly. Have you inspected the dress?" She gently beckoned Karryn to the bed when the dress lay.

The white gown shimmered with gold diamond accents. It was everything a wedding gown should be. Overcome by sudden fear, Karryn seized the bedpost to catch her balance.

Daylen whispered, "The Queen adds her support to her son's pledge."

Uncertain of what to say or do, Karryn remained silent.

"Lady Daylen, the bath is ready," said a maid from the threshold.

She waved an acknowledgement. Daylen spoke to Karryn with soft reassurance. "Trust in the *Old Faith*. There are more involved here than you know."

Bolstered, Karryn released the post and headed to the other room.

Meanwhile, in the royal apartment, Ramsey stood before the couch where several suits were arranged for his inspection. He smiled with great satisfaction. "The gold and purple for the coronation. The white and maroon for the wedding and reception." He gave Magelen a friendly slap on the arm. "Tailor outdid himself. See he is handsomely rewarded."

Magelen flashed a toothy grin, more to cover his annoyance than pain from the physical contact. "Ay, Sire. Is there anything else? Orders concerning Lord Razi perhaps?"

Ramsey's jovial mood soured. "Why spoil my moment of triumph with trivialities? Besides, we already discussed the arrangements."

"The special diet didn't work."

The news made Ramey's frown deepen. "He didn't even become sick?"

"He never received the food," said Magelen with emphasis. "I learned from Scully that Murdock discovered Blackburn dead in front of the cell door with the tray beside him. It is believed he tasted everything beforehand. Murdock tried to conceal the incident by having Scully dispose of the food while he dealt with Blackburn's body."

Red-faced with rage, Ramsey bellowed, "Send for Murdock!"

"He is waiting in the hall." Magelen fetched Murdock.

The rugged captain showed no anxiety or fear to royal scrutiny.

"Grand Master Magelen told me a rather disturbing incident occurred last night involving my uncle."

"Indeed, Highness."

The casual response infuriated Ramsey. "Well? Why didn't you report it immediately?"

Murdock continued in an unfazed manner. "I did not wish to disturb the festivities, Highness. I hoped to conclude my investigation and indentify the person responsible for attempting to poison Lord Razi. Any mention of the incident before then might cause unrest among the guests." He made a nodding bow of his head. "My apologies if I acted wrong, Highness, my intent is to maintain your good name among the lords."

"You are aware of the serious nature of this incident, Captain?" demanded Magelen.

"Of course, my lord. That is why I chose to keep the situation quiet for the moment. To act prematurely would warn the perpetrator, thus reduce the chance of capture. I'm certain His Royal Highness would agree that given the tenuous situation with the lords, it is best to begin his reign without incident."

Insulted by Murdock's brashness, Magelen gripped his medallion. This action made Murdock shift his attention to Ramsey.

"Your Highness, I'm only seek to serve you as faithfully as I did your father in shielding you from enemies who would harm you. If after your coronation, you wish to discharge me, I will happily go into retirement. For now, allow me to continue my service until the day is done."

Magelen jerked Murdock's arm. "You are a bold one!"

"He's also right." Carnel entered unnoticed. "The kitchen steward came to me upset. He feared speaking to you and causing unwanted upset today," he said to Ramsey. "Apparently one of the maids was found dead earlier this morning. He said she fixed some special food for Lord Razi last night."

"The food never reached him. One of the guards tasted it and died," Murdock said to Carnel. He then spoke to Ramsey. "Highness, this confirms that whoever is behind this means more trouble."

Ramsey shot a quick, piercing gaze to Magelen. The Grand Master gripped the talisman until his knuckles turned white. "I think we best proceed with caution."

"Ay, Your Highness," Magelen replied in calmer voice than his posture showed.

"Return to your duty," Ramsey instructed Murdock then to Magelen, "Carnel will help with my fitting."

Angry, Magelen went to his chamber. He snapped orders to any servant he met along the way. Finding Witter and Altari's waiting intensified his foul mood.

"What are you two doing here? Make certain Razi is secure."

"He is. We came to report a disturbance that indicates a presence," said Witter.

"Avatar?" asked Magelen.

Altari shook his head. "Unlikely since I witnessed his battle with Mahon. However, Mahon claimed Avatar gave him his lifechain, a medallion forged after the Great Battle to help keep track of the few remaining Guardians. If the lifechain is removed or the Guardian destroyed, Kell would know. And Kell would be eager to avenge the destruction of his protégé."

Magelen became red with anger. "Why didn't you tell me about this lifechain?"

Despite the mortal's anger, Altari calmly replied. "I told Dagar. It is doubtful Kell would mask his arrival, which means it is probably Armus. We searched for his essence but turned up nothing past the initial sense."

"I posted Nari in the Great Hall and Roane at the main gate," said Witter.

Neither reply pleased Magelen. "Is there any way to unmask Armus?"

"*If* Armus is here, he will not be easy to find," began Altari. "Next to Kell, he is the most powerful Guardian. Also, with our reduced strength we, dare not risk going beyond our abilities to search for him rather be ready for confrontation."

The water in the basin began to boil. From out of the steam, Dagar called for Magelen.

"Say nothing to Dagar about your suspicions!" Magelen snapped at the Warriors then prepared to face the powerful Master of the Dark Way. "My lord, good morning," he said when Dagar's image appeared.

"Magelen. How goes it this fine day?" Dagar flashed a predatory grin.

"Well, my lord. Carnel's bride is chosen. She will await your pleasure by this evening."

"Not Beryl?"

"She is past the age of childbearing, lord. Lady Karryn is young, thus sure to be fertile, insuring an heir to my position. I confess to feeling the years weighing on me."

"Weakness? On our day of triumph?"

"No, a general weariness. I will succeed in fulfilling your plan."

"Good. Bring the lady here for me to view this evening."

"As you wish." Magelen made a bow of acknowledgement. "Anything else, my lord?"

"Contact me when Razi is dead!" Dagar waved both hands. Immediately his image vanished and the steam dissipated.

Altari appeared relieved. "He doesn't know about the essence. The disturbance was not enough to breech the transverse."

"It doesn't change what must be done!" chided Magelen.

"And it shall be." Altari slapped his sword and left with Witter.

At dawn, Dunham arrived back at camp for the formal processional. This was not on the royal schedule, rather a private agreement among the lords with Dunham leading the way. He stared in the direction of Ravendale. The large, dark foreboding form of the castle took shape in the growing light of day.

"Like the rays of the sun bring illumination to the day and chase away the night may our venture return your light to Allon and stem the darkness, most holy one," he prayed.

"Tangiel," agreed Tristan and Ethan.

Ethan made certain everything about his best uniform was perfect and his bow ready. He held the reins of two finely saddled horses. Tristan wore the same disguise he did when sneaking into the dungeon with Murdock.

"I hope you both slept," said Dunham.

"We did, after our divine encounter," said Tristan with a large, delighted smile.

This piqued Dunham's interest. "How so?"

Tristan's smile never wavered. "The Old Knight. The same one from Dorgirith."

Pleased, Dunham patted Tristan's shoulder. "Still, we must be careful."

"What shall I do? Return to the dungeon?"

"No. More than likely Ramsey will use him today, if not at the coronation then later. Mingle with the crowd, and be ready to act on a moment's notice. The rest of us will continue as planned."

"What about Karryn?" Ethan asked.

"To free her before we are ready may prove hazardous."

280

"If she marries—"

Dunham put up a hand to stop Ethan's objection. "Renfrow doesn't want that either." He softened his tone. "Fret not. Action will be taken before any vows are made. Murdock assured us the army is ready. We only have to deal with Galton's company of royal bodyguards. Until then, keep your wits sharp and your bow ready." He said to Tristan, "Join the crowd as soon as you're ready. Ethan."

Dunham took the reins from the woodsman and mounted. Ethan did the same on the second horse. He and Ethan rode to the front of the procession.

The respective captains, squires, wives and small military escort accompanied each lord. Kell and Avatar stood among the soldiers escorting Dunham. Armus and Jedrek did the same with Renfrow's men; Barnum and Valmar joined the soldiers escorting Kaleb.

Warren arrived and saluted Dunham. "All is in place, my lord."

"Excellent. On your way."

Warren saluted and rode toward Ravendale.

Dunham looked back to those following and waved his hand. The procession headed toward the castle. Upon approach, Dunham caught sight of the disguised Tristan among the crowd. He quickly looked away, not wanting to draw attention to the young man.

Captain Galton waited at the gate. He was a large, muscular man with a weather-beaten face. Warren dismounted to speak to him. Galton ignored Warren to raise both arms and step in front of Dunham.

"Halt! No one is to come armed into Ravendale this day," he said in reference to Ethan.

"The King requested a demonstration of my squire's renowned skills. You should have been told he is an exception," Dunham chided.

"I was about to inform him of the arrangement, my lord. I suggest you check the guest list, Captain." Warren motioned to a scribe seated at a table just inside the gate. Six assistants flanked the scribe. Roane stood beside the table and warily eyed Dunham's group.

Galton didn't move so Dunham added his stern desire. "Check the list, Captain Galton."

"Dismount and follow me, as I do so."

"I will not dismount! Tend to duty immediately, or risk displeasing the King."

Galton gripped the hilt of his sword at the command. Warren stepped between him and Dunham. Galton marched to the table. He exchanged a few gruff words with the scribe. He grew impatient while the man shuffled through the pages.

"Well?"

"Ay. There is mention of an archer. Right here—"

Galton snatched the paper to read for himself. Growling, he flung the paper back at the scribe before returning to Dunham. "You may pass," he said with disgruntled unwillingness.

Dunham kept his eyes straight ahead to ignore Roane. The Shadow Warrior watched Dunham's men entering the courtyard. Roane didn't react when Kell and Avatar walked past him. The scribe and his associates began counting those with Dunham. An associate told the number of soldiers to the scribe—ten.

"Wait!" called the scribe. "Your escort is to number eight, not ten."

At the dispute, Kell directed his gaze to the soldier standing between Roane and the table. Reacting as if sensing something, Roane stepped forward, only to be diverted when the soldier began coughing as if trying to breathe. He grabbed Roane in support. Despite the violence of the cough, Roane shoved the soldier aside, which knocked him into the table. This spilled the jar of ink all over the pages of names. The scribe bolted to his feet to avoid being splattered by ink. During the distraction, Kell and Avatar slipped away from the escort.

"Clumsy oaf! Now look what you did!"

Dunham dismounted once inside the courtyard. He suppressed a smile. "You were saying about a problem with the number?"

Irate, yet thwarted, the scribed bowed. "Your pardon, my lord." He focused his attention on rescuing the papers.

282

"Wait!" Roane snatched Dunham's arm. "Why is there a discrepancy?"

Ethan and Warren came to stand beside Dunham, ready to defend him if necessary.

Dunham boldly met the Shadow Warrior's eyes. "All my men are accounted for. If there is a discrepancy it lies with those responsible for making the list." He jerked away from Roane.

Warren remained steadfast in his place while Ethan escorted Dunham from the table. When Roane didn't move, Warren left.

In the shadow of a building across from the table, Kell exhaled. He shook his head and rubbed his eyes from the effort.

"You tell us not to use our power, but do so the moment we arrive," said Avatar wryly.

"To avoid immediate discovery."

"When Roane focused his attention on Dunham, did you repel him also?"

"No, I just made the soldier sick. Dunham is a fully trained Jor'ellian. Roane may have mistakenly identified him as the source of trouble. Now, find Karryn. I'll locate Razi."

"What about Ethan? He is armed."

"Securing Karryn will take away his motive to abandon his post."

"If you're not with Dunham, I won't know if Ethan leaves."

Kell paused in brief moment of thought. "I'll give you until the trumpet calls for the coronation. If I've not heard from you securing Karryn, I'll fetch Razi. After the ceremony will be too late to act."

"Either way, I will let you know." Avatar made a quick scan of the area. "I'll start with the closest building. Unless, of course, you make Roane turn a blind eye so I can cross the compound." He received a jabbing elbow in his side for Kell's answer. The moment the door opened, Avatar dashed from their concealment to slip inside before it closed.

Having Roane turn a blind eye wasn't a bad idea for Kell to rejoin Dunham's group unnoticed. Seeing Renfrow arrive, he decided to watch and wait. Armus and Jedrek marched past Roane. Good. The mortal façade masked their essence. Next came Kaleb with Barnum and Valmar

283

among the soldiers. Again, the disguised Guardians made it past Roane without the Shadow Warrior taking a second glance. Kell prayed the divine blessing would continue.

Once the courtyard filled with enough bodies to use as screens from prying eyes, Kell mingled to rejoin Dunham's group. Fortunately, Roane focused on another arriving party. In the jostling crowd, someone ran into him. Kell jumped, ready to act. He came face-to-face with Dunham.

"My lord," said Kell with an apologetic nod. He relaxed and released the hilt of his sword. Dunham said nothing rather stared at him. From most mortals a Guardian could mask their appearance. With some, it proved more difficult. Dunham fit into the category due to his dedication to Jor'el and knightly training.

Dunham grinned. He spoke the Ancient in a private tone. "I'm glad to see the numbers were wrong for a reason, *Captain of the Old Knights.*"

By the statement, Kell realized divine insight had been granted Dunham. They never met. Even from the faithful remnant, the Guardians took great care in concealing their activities. Kell allowed a small smile to accompany a silent nod of acknowledgement.

Renfrow and Kaleb arrived. Kaleb's wife accompanied them.

"Gentlemen, it is time we make our appearance," said Dunham.

"Are you ready?" asked Renfrow.

Dunham sent a confident glance to Kell before replying to Renfrow. "Ay." He moved toward the Great Hall.

Kaleb didn't notice the brief look, but Renfrow did. Kell flashed a friendly smile at the baron to say, "After you, my lord." Renfrow complied in following the others.

Since last night, servants transformed the Great Hall from a banquet room into one suited for a grand coronation. Attendees would remain standing with thrones for the King and Queen. Kell watched the nobility mill about. They spoke in muted voices. The reason for such caution became obvious upon spying Shadow Warriors posted around the perimeter. Kell's interest became diverted from his observation by Renfrow's question to Dunham.

"How will we deal with *them* when it is time to act?" Renfrow made a discrete motion toward the Shadow Warriors.

"I think they will be taken care of without any help from us," replied Dunham.

The answer first stupefied Renfrow, who then asked, "You mean the *Old Knights*?"

At Dunham's private smile, Renfrow cast a careful glance to Kell.

For Renfrow to be given such privilege as to single Kell out from the conversation also had to be of divine allowance. Although the baron was also among the faithful, Kell didn't want to draw too much attention. Their exchange was brief, with just enough brightness in Kell's gold eyes to bolster Renfrow's confidence. It sufficed. The baron faced forward.

Renfrow spoke out the side of his mouth to Dunham. "May they protect Karryn also this day."

While Kell appreciated Dunham's confidence and Renfrow's prayer, he returned his focus to the Shadow Warriors: Nari, Bern, Indigo and Cletus. Roane entered. He spoke a word to Nari before taking up a sentry position. Considering the circumstances, Kell was surprised with only five stationed in the Great Hall. More Shadow Warriors could be somewhere lurking around the castle. He hoped not, but a possibility. They just had to take the situation as it unfolded.

Kell took careful note of his fellow Guardians. Armus and Jedrek waited close by with Renfrow's men. Valmar and Barnum remained near the main entrance. Even in disguise, their collective presence in one place could alert the Shadow Warriors. The fact that it hadn't, meant divine shielding went beyond the normal safety of disguise.

Kell stopped his survey of the room when Altari entered with Magelen. Kell clenched the hilt of his sword to stem the rising anger. Even after a hundred and fifty years, betrayal by his former aide still stung deep. He felt eyes upon him and carefully turned. Armus. By the stony expression, Armus also noticed Altari.

After escorting Magelen to the platform, Altari left the Hall in hurried steps. Not good! Had he sensed something? Avatar perhaps? He was originally sent as a decoy.

Are you using him again as a distraction, Jor'el? Please, no. It's too dangerous for him and the others, Kell silently prayed. He noticed Armus mirrored his concern. Their second visual exchange became interrupted by the sound of pounding.

The herald instructed people to remain in their places, as the coronation would be being shortly.

Avatar ventured further into the castle by making educated guesses in which way to take to the guest quarters. Normally he employed his heavenly senses to determine Karryn's exact location. In the heart of enemy's lair, that would be unwise.

"Hey! What are you doing here?"

Avatar stopped when accosted by two royal guards. He had to be convincing. "My lord sent me to find suitable clothes when his became soiled by a clumsy servant spilling wine on him. However, he failed to tell me which room is his. Can you point me to the guest quarters?"

The soldier paused in answering upon hearing the sound of nearby trumpets. "The coronation will be starting soon. You better return to your lord." The soldiers grabbed Avatar to turn him.

Avatar resisted. "Not without fresh clothes. I'll report you for deterring me from my duty, and Sir Dunham will tell the King when asked why he came in soiled clothes!" he loudly protested.

"Dunham?" repeated one soldier. He turned Avatar around to more closely survey his livery. "Down the hall then up two flights of stairs. His room is the first on the left."

"What are you doing letting him go?" asked the other.

He leaned closer to his companion to say, "Captain Murdock's orders, remember?"

"Oh, ay!" He waved at Avatar. "On your way, and be quick."

Avatar hurried his steps in the direction indicated. Obviously this Captain Murdock held great sway over the soldiers for them to yield to his feeble excuse. At the top of the stairs, Avatar ducked into a dim alcove to consider the situation. The wedding was scheduled to take place immediately following the coronation, which was about to begin! In order to find Karryn in time, he had to use his senses. If done carefully, it shouldn't present a problem.

With guests gathered for the coronation, he reckoned the Shadow Warriors were concentrated in the Great Hall. In such a large compound, he hoped he travelled far enough from the hall to avoid detection. He took a deep breath, and ever so slightly, stretched out his senses. He first tried to perceive any Shadow Warriors nearby. None. Good. He pushed a bit further to find Karryn. He stopped at touching a presence, close, at the end of the hall.

"Oh, I hope that's her and not trouble," he muttered to himself.

Avatar glanced out of the alcove. He quickly drew back upon spying—*Altari!* In a brief moment of confusion, Avatar tried to discern what he sensed. It felt more like a mortal than a Guardian. Nor did he sense Altari nearby. That concerned him. Had he been sensed? He carefully peeked around the corner. Altari stood before the door of the last room on the hall; the room Avatar believed Karryn to be staying. Altari showed no sign of being alerted. Instead, he concentrated on getting attention of those in the room. A woman appeared in the threshold.

"The King commands the lady to the Great Hall," said Altari.

"Is the coronation complete?"

"It will be shortly. Now bring her."

When Altari turned from the door, Avatar ducked back into the alcove. *Please, Jor'el, not now! I don't need to confront him now.* His lips moved in forming the words his mind prayed. A feeling of calm settled over him. He dared another glance down the hall. No sign of Altari. Women emerged from the room with one dressed in an elaborate wedding gown complete with veil. Avatar momentarily lifted his eyes to the ceiling. "Thank you," he whispered.

Avatar followed, determined to get Karryn away from the women with as little commotion as possible. Unfortunately, Altari didn't go far. He waited at the top of the stairs. Yet, Altari appeared to be distracted between being watchful down the stairs and waiting for the women. This forced Avatar to duck into the open doorway of a nearby room.

"What took so long?" Altari demanded of Daylen.

"Only a few moments. Why the rush? The wedding isn't until after the coronation."

"Grand Master's orders." Altari grabbed Karryn's arm. She made a short outcry of pain and fear.

Daylen intervened. "Will you hurt your future queen?"

Altari released his grip, which allowed Daylen to ease Karryn away from him. "Go! I'll be right behind." He motioned down the stairs.

Wonderful! Altari would not yield Karryn to a mere soldier. Avatar couldn't use his power to distract Altari, or become another decoy without causing harm to others. The only option was to hope for an opportunity to act before reaching the hall. All this had to be done without Altari's knowledge.

The majority of those assembled in the great hall watched in grim silence. The file of priests stopped near the raised platform. Ramsey and Beryl sat on their thrones, though they had not yet received their crowns. Magelen waited on the steps in front of them. Carnel stood to the right of his father's throne. The Prince's attempt to mask his discomfort proved dismal. No one dared make a comment.

Among the crowd at the rear of the hall, a disguised Tristan arrived. With everyone's attention turned to the front of the hall, he had no problem gaining entry. He caught sight of Ethan. Despite the initial frown upon seeing him, Ethan made no further reaction.

Ethan wasn't the only one to spy Tristan, so did Kell. Being at camp, he knew the disguise Tristan wore; only he didn't think the mortal was supposed to be here.

Magelen's raised voice echoed in the Hall. "Vicar Elias will now come to perform the coronation." He motioned to his left.

Two royal guards and Nari flanked the Vicar to escort him from a side room to the platform. Elias displayed no emotion.

A cunning smile appeared on Ramsey' face. He spoke to Magelen. "Aren't you forgetting someone, Grand Master?"

"Forgive me, Highness." Magelen's taunting tone matched Ramsey's. "The most honored guest." He waved toward the back of the hall.

Guided by Witter's hand on his shoulder, Razi moved from the back of hall to the platform. His appearance caused a variety of reactions from those in attendance. Elias fought to keep his face from betraying any emotion. Dunham, Renfrow and Kaleb showed varying degrees of surprise, disbelief and anger.

Now Kell understood why Tristan showed up. He had been unable to reach Razi in time. Tristan couldn't mask his shock as told by his puffing chest and clenched fist. Not good. Kell saw Armus and Jedrek move carefully through the crowd. Tristan flinched to make defense when Armus grabbed his shoulder.

"Act natural or all is lost," Armus hastily whispered.

For a moment Tristan couldn't look away from the chestnut eyes so bright and commanding. He made a brief nod. Armus released him.

After Armus' intervention, Kell returned his attention forward. His jowls tightened in concern for Razi.

Ramsey's sarcastic smile widened. "Well, look who is here? Lord Razi. Come to swear allegiance to your new King?"

"I see no king rather a usurping *nephew!*" Razi loudly emphasized the relationship.

A great murmur arose from the crowd with statements of, "So, it's true! He is King Ram's brother!"

"Silence!" Ramsey shouted. A reluctant hush fell over the crowd. "Uncle or not, *I am* the son of King Ram. I will be crowned! And *your* son, the Vicar," he motioned to Elias, "will perform the coronation or die in front of your very eyes!"

"No, stop—" Tristan's raised voice suddenly became still when Armus seized him by covering his mouth. Barnum and Jedrek stepped in front to shield the action from being seen.

Elias and Razi exchanged glances of concern at the outcry.

"Who spoke?" demanded Ramsey. No one answered. "Who spoke?" he repeated.

"I will learn who, Sire." His hand on the talisman, Magelen approached Elias. "You recognized the voice."

Elias didn't reply.

"Tell me!" Magelen shoved the talisman in Elias' face.

"You don't scare me, creature of darkness," said Elias, calmly.

"*Anail bi air falbh!*" declared Magelen in the Ancient.

Elias began to choke. His eyes grew wide with distress. He desperately gasped for air.

"No!" Razi cried in protest. Nari stopped his advance.

Tristan struggled against Armus' persistent hold. He bit Armus' hand to break free. Then it happened—fast!

"*Cridhe sguir!*" Magelen clenched his hand into a fist. Elias collapsed to the floor, dead by the look of the eyes rolled back in his head.

"Long live, Lord Razi! For Allon, for Jor'el!" shouted Dunham.

"For Allon, for Jor'el!" echoed Renfrow, Kaleb and many others.

The Hall erupted with hostility at the rallying cry. Men from the various provinces attacked the royal guards with weapons they concealed to gain entry.

Using the sword hidden under his cloak, Tristan fought his way closer to the front of the hall.

Altari and the women just arrived when the mêlée broke out. Karryn removed her veil for a better view. The other women took refuge behind the thrones to escape the chaos.

"Shadow Warriors! Restore order," shouted Magelen.

Kell drew his sword when he felt a jostling on his arm. Avatar.

"I couldn't get Karryn away, and I can't act as decoy any longer!" Avatar spoke with frustrated urgency.

Kell drew Avatar behind a pillar. Taking a deep breath, Kell closed his eyes. Slowly, he allowed his essence to escape. He didn't allow enough out for identification, just to be sensed.

"Guardians! In the compound," Altari shouted. "Warriors, find the enemy!" They raced from the Hall.

"Get Armus to act as decoy and keep them away from here!" ordered Kell.

Avatar hurried to comply. He barely exchanged a few words with Armus before they left.

"Keep alert for their return," Kell told Valmar, Barnum and Jedrek.

"Magelen?" asked Barnum.

"I'll deal with him if needed. We must protect Razi and Tristan!"

"Come, Renfrow and Kaleb need help," said Valmar to Barnum. They went their separate ways to continue in their undercover assignment.

With the Shadow Warriors gone from the Great Hall, the forces under command of the lords started gaining the advantage. Kell, Barnum, Jedrek and Valmar added their blades to the conflict. They used enough strength to be considered mortal yet victorious in every encounter.

Ethan's bow proved lethal in the close confines of the Hall. At one point, he noticed Karryn near the platform trying to avoid the battle. Dressed in the wedding gown she appeared stunning. More important, she was unarmed. Ethan dodged behind a pillar to escape the swinging blade of a soldier. Unfortunately, the soldier reacted quicker than Ethan anticipated. The soldier's dagger plunged hilt deep into Ethan's chest just under the sternum. The impact knocked the air from his lunges. He staggered backward when the soldier ripped out the dagger. Ethan fell hard to his knees then against the pillar. He struggled to breathe due to the deep wound. The soldier moved on.

From the platform, Ramsey watched the clash in angry disgust. "We need more soldiers!" At that moment, Murdock rushed in with more troops. "Murdock! Restore order."

"No, Murdock, do as you agreed!" Carnel countered.

"Ay, Highness," Murdock acknowledged Carnel then commanded his men, "Seize any soldier or civilian who resist the coup!"

Stunned, Ramsey bellowed, "I am betrayed?"

"You betrayed your father! How does it feel to have the same done to you?" Carnel didn't wait for an answer. He aided his mother from the Hall.

Rage propelled Ramsey to pursue Carnel. However, this brought him face-to-face with Razi.

"Going somewhere, *nephew?*"

Magelen confronted Razi. "You know the power I command!"

"Not greater than the power invading this place." Razi allowed a smile to appear.

"*Luths—*" Magelen's speech was cut off by a vicious backhand from Razi.

Despite his very advanced age, Razi put all his strength into the blow. Magelen fell down the platform steps to the Hall floor.

Ramsey seized Razi. A struggle ensured. Though Razi managed to strike Magelen, Ramsey was younger and stronger. Soon he landed a few punches that overpowered Razi. Ramsey tackled him on the platform.

Seeing his grandfather in danger, Tristan hurried to help. A soldier impeded his advance by slamming him into a pillar where he struck his head and became dazed. The solider also landed a blow with the flat of his blade that injured Tristan's right hand and knocked the sword away. Fighting light-headedness, Tristan launched at the soldier. He used his larger size to drive the soldier into the wall. The stunning impact made the soldier drop to his knees. Tristan swayed with dizziness upon turning. Magelen approached his trapped grandfather. With deadly focus, Magelen spoke the Ancient. Despite the dizziness, Tristan had to act fast.

292

"Jor'el, give me strength!" he pleaded in prayer.

Tristan pushed past the disguised Kell in an unsteady rush to the platform. He snatched the first weapon he found, a dagger. "For Jor'el and Allon!" He cried in a loud voice and leapt at Magelen from behind. His momentum drove the dagger hilt deep into the base of Magelen's neck.

The Grand Master never made a sound. The sheer shock of death registered on his face. He hit the floor with a hard thud. Tristan ended up on his knees, breathing hard from exertion and injury.

Kell pulled up in his effort to reach the platform to see Tristan strike down Magelen. He wasn't the only one who noticed the Grand Master's end. All activity in the Great Hall ceased.

Dumbfounded, Ramsey staggered back from Razi. He gaped at Tristan. "Who are you?"

Tristan rose to remove his disguise and reveal his family features. "I am Tristan, the Vicar's son!"

"*My* grandson! The rightful heir to the throne," Razi declared.

The implication frightened Ramsey. He anxiously looked for an escape. Dunham blocked the nearest exit. Panicked, Ramsey jumped from the platform. Those in the Hall avoided him. He tried to grab anyone he could to use as shield. Finally he managed to seize Renfrow by the arm. Being five inches shorter than Ramsey didn't stop Renfrow from putting up a struggle. Ramsey kneed Renfrow in the abdomen then sent him to the floor with a clout from behind. He took Renfrow's sword.

"Father!" Karryn stepped forward intent on helping.

Ramsey seized her. He held her against him with the blade to her throat. "Let me out or she dies!" he demanded of Dunham.

"Karryn, down!" came a shout.

She heard and stomped on Ramsey's foot. The painful reaction made him remove the sword. She ducked out of reach. An arrow struck Ramsey square in the chest and sent him backwards to the floor.

Karryn looked in the direction the arrow came. A seriously wounded Ethan swayed. The bow fell from his hand before he collapsed. She ran to him. A cry of fear escaped at seeing his bloody doublet.

"No! Ethan!" She seized his face in an effort to rouse him. He didn't respond. A man in Dunham's livery knelt opposite her. "He can't die," she pleaded with tears on her cheeks.

Tristan fell to his knees beside Karryn. "Is he—?"

"No, he's still alive," answered Kell. The bright gold/hazel eyes seemed to glow with encouragement. "I'll take him to the infirmary where he will get the best of care."

"Go with him. I'll be along shortly," Tristan told Karryn, though she didn't need any prompting.

Tristan returned to the front of the hall where Razi knelt beside Elias' body. Dunham knelt opposite Razi. Tristan dropped to his knees. Tears swelled, as he looked upon his father.

"Ethan?" asked Razi in a choked whisper.

"Alive." The word barely spoken before Tristan wept. Razi comforted him.

With great sympathy, Dunham said, "We'll see that all is secure."

Razi simply gave a nod acknowledgement.

Dodging into alcoves throughout the castle, Armus eluded the Shadow Warriors' attempts to find him. He retained his mortal persona, only giving off a small sense of his essence to distract them. A few times he spied Avatar, keeping an eye on him. By the time Armus ended up leading the Warriors back to main courtyard, they were totally frustrated.

"This is getting ridiculous! Is it Armus or isn't it?" complained Nari.

"It feels like more than one Guardian," insisted Roane.

"He's toying with us, giving off multiple senses to keep us away—" Altari grew stiff with alarm, which swiftly changed to concern. "Oh, no." He touched the talisman he wore. "Magelen is dead," he said at sounds of cheering coming from the Great Hall.

"I think a strategic withdrawal to the Cave," said Witter.

294

"Why?" Roane asked.

"The remnant succeeded. With Armus here, Kell won't be far behind! Are you ready to face your ultimate end?" challenged Altari.

Nari placed a hand on Roane's shoulder. "No, we aren't."

"*Siuthad!*" the others spoke in unison and vanished.

Altari didn't journey to the Cave. Instead, he reappeared at the edge of a forest two miles from Ravendale. His hand held the talisman, as he focused on the castle in the near distance. He wasn't alone for long. Witter arrived.

"I didn't think you would leave," said Witter.

"We have to secure the other talisman before Armus does."

Witter nodded. "After dark, once things have calmed down."

Chapter 26

THE EXCITEMENT IN THE GREAT HALL CEASED HOURS AGO. BY Razi's order, Magelen's body was taken to the lowest part of the dungeon. There was no ceremony in preparation, rather laid on the floor in a room with no windows. The bars were double locked and chained. Such precautions didn't stop Altari for arriving inside the room. He dimmed his appearance. The lack of interior light didn't deter him.

Altari just took the talisman off Magelen when he bolted upright. Light from his disappearance became overlapped by the light of another's arrival. Hurriedly, Armus approached Magelen. *Gone!* He didn't need to use his senses to detect a familiar presence. Frustrated, he vanished in dimension travel.

Reappearing on the knoll, Armus took a breath of recovery from two successive travels.

"Well?" asked Kell. He, Avatar and the others gathered on the knoll.

By Armus' expression and shake of the head, it wasn't good news. "Altari arrived just a moment before I did!"

"Blast!" Kell chided. "I should have acted immediately to secure it."

"You were helping to keep Ethan alive," said Barnum.

Kell took a deep breath and slowly exhaled. "I know. I hoped sending Armus soon after to retrieve it would level the playing field."

"Even if Armus succeeded, Dagar would use the secrets of the Cave to find other ways of unleashing his power," said Gresham grimly.

With a none-too-pleased expression, Kell replied in rebuke. "And we will find other ways to help the mortals. For now, I must return to Ravendale."

"Altari may sense you, which is why you sent Armus," said Wren in protest.

"In disguise," Kell countered. "*This* mission isn't complete."

Those who remained loyal to the former king were rounded up and held in the upper dungeon by Murdock. They numbered forty, mostly servants or extended family members.

Carnel and Beryl were confined to the royal apartment under the watchful eye of Captain Warren. Not until well after supper did Dunham arrive to speak to them. Renfrow and Kaleb accompanied him. Beryl's eyes were puffy red from weeping. Undoubtedly, this had been a very trying day for her.

"Madam, my condolences. We hoped to spare him," said Dunham.

"We both know that was an unlikely outcome," she said in quiet voice of lament.

"If not for Magelen's influence, it could have been possible."

Beryl sniffled. "You're being kind, my lord."

Carnel placed a comforting hand on his mother's shoulder. He inquired of Dunham, "What will become of us? Will the pledge be kept?"

"Of course, providing you renounce your claim to the throne as agreed." Dunham motioned to Kaleb, who came forth holding a document. "The terms require your signature and seal."

Carnel took the scroll to read it. A long moment of profound silence passed before he spoke. "Well, these are very thorough terms."

"We tried to include as many contingencies as possible, to protect both sides," Dunham added when Carnel looked dubiously at him.

"Is there something wrong?" Beryl asked her son.

"Not wrong, restrictive."

"Under the circumstance, a believed necessity," said Dunham.

Beryl took hold of Carnel's arm. "Then we will be spared?"

He softly smiled with reassurance. "Ay, once I sign and seal it."

Beryl covered her mouth to stop a sob, though a whimper escaped.

"Madam, we gave our pledge for your safety," assured Kaleb.

She shook her head while attempting to bring her emotions under control. "You mistake my relief for fear. The prospect of living a quiet, solitary life is most welcomed."

"So you shall, Madam," said Dunham kindly.

"May I inquire as to where we will live out our days?"

"A very tranquil place off the East Coast called Glendower."

"Your own private island, Madam, where no one shall trouble you," added Kaleb with a smile of compassion.

Despite his tone, the statement concerned her. "Sounds more like exile."

"A harsh word, Madam," began Dunham. "Retirement may be better suited, as you will both be well provided for with little interference."

Carnel wryly snickered. "I suppose a bride is out of the question."

Renfrow shot the Prince a harsh, narrow glare, not accepting of the ill-timed humor. He remained a silent observer.

Carnel recanted. "I didn't think so. Bachelorhood is a small price to pay for one's life, I suppose."

"Your signature and seal," insisted Dunham, the agreeability now gone from his posture and voice.

Carnel crossed to a desk. Dunham, Renfrow and Kaleb watched him sign then use sealing wax into which he stamped his signet ring.

"Your terms, gentlemen." Carnel handed the scroll back to Dunham.

"At dawn, an escort will take to your new home." Dunham bowed to Carnel and Beryl. Kaleb and Renfrow mimicked him in paying respect.

Ethan lay on a cot in the castle's infirmary. He remained unconscious. Razi sat in a chair beside the cot. After being assured by Elias' assistant, Jarrod, about care for the Elias' burial preparations, Razi went to the infirmary. He gnawed on his lower lip. It had been heart wrenching to witness his last son's murder at the hands of the Dark Way. Yet with the pain came a seed of hope. Magelen was finally defeated, and Tristan survived.

Razi gazed across the room with a bittersweet smile on his lips. Tristan dozed in a chair beside the cot where Karryn lay sleeping. He was glad Tristan finally convinced Karryn to rest. So great was her concern, she wouldn't listen to her father's advice when Renfrow came by earlier to inquire after Ethan.

Razi returned his attention to Ethan. With such a serious wound, the bleeding took a long time to slow. The blade went deep. It would have been better if it passed through Ethan's entire body, at least then the fear of internal bleeding would be less with two holes for draining.

He laid a hand on Ethan's shoulder and prayed, "Please, spare him, Jor'el. There is so much he needs to know." His voice became choked and wiped the tears from his eyes.

Razi turned at hearing soft footsteps to see the arrival of the man who carried Ethan to the infirmary. He bent over Tristan and Karryn. In a low voice, he spoke what sounded like a foreign language. He then approached Razi.

"My lord." As he smiled, the hazel eyes turned to gold.

"Kell. I thought I recognized you earlier. What did you say to them?"

"Only to remain asleep so we can speak. First, I want to apologize for not being able to keep my promise to you until now. Many times I wanted to help. Alas, circumstances prevented me from aiding you, even in disguise." He motioned to his uniform.

"I understand. Although there were times your presence would have been of great help. Then again, how can a legend help?" said Razi in an attempt at levity.

"Allon has not been abandoned. Twelve of us remain in a limited role." Kell tried to sound encouraging.

Razi cracked a partial grin. "So, who helped Tristan in Dorgirith?"

"Avatar."

Razi chuckled. "I'm certain Dagar didn't like that." His humor was short-lived, as his anxiety returned. "What now, Kell? How many more will I lose before my own death?" His voice broke with emotion.

Kell gripped Razi's shoulder and softly smiled. "None. Ethan will live, and Maddy make a complete recovery."

Razi looked across to Tristan. "I'm glad I didn't die before I could tell him of his heritage and destiny. Elias would have told him if I couldn't—he didn't finish his task." He swallowed back a new wave of grief. "The task you said Jor'el appointed him to complete."

"Oh, he did," said Kell with certainty. "The copies of Verse and Prophecy are safely locked in his personal vault at the Temple." Kell also regarded the sleeping Tristan and quoted:

> "For a time of peace shall come and he shall rule with truth, honor and the blessing of Jor'el, to restore that which was lost."

"Then it is over? Dagar's reign is finished?" asked Razi, hopeful.

"Alas, no. This is not the time for our return or Dagar's final judgment. This is merely a reprieve in the midst of darkness. A time to refresh and awaken what was nearly lost."

The answer deflated Razi. The disappointment translated to his voice. "For how long?"

Kell shrugged. "For Tristan's reign most certainly. After that, I don't know."

Razi stared at his grandson. "I wondered if I would ever know peace now that my days are almost done."

"You shall live long enough to experience rest and enjoy your family."

Razi covered his mouth to silence an impulsive reaction of relieved joy. "Thank you."

"Don't thank me, I'm only the messenger." Kell grinned. He nodded to Ethan. "It is time to speak to another's heritage." He stepped back when Ethan stirred.

Razi touched the young man's shoulders. "Ethan."

Ethan's eyes blinked before opening. He appeared confused. "Razi?"

"Ay, my boy. How are you feeling?"

"Like a skewered pig with a headache."

Razi merrily laughed, and loud enough to wake Tristan and Karryn.

"Grandpapi?"

"Ethan's awake and a made a joke."

Tristan scrambled from the chair and Karryn hastened to the bed to kneel beside Ethan.

She smiled through teary eyes. "Thank Jor'el you're alive!"

Ethan grinned, a bit shaky in regard of Karryn. "They didn't *harm* you, did they?"

She smiled and stroked his hair. "No. Jor'el protected me."

Ethan closed his eyes with a sob of relief. His eyes opened when she kissed his cheek. "What happened after I shot?"

"It's a long story. Just know, the plan succeeded," said Tristan with a wide smile.

"The Dark Way is finished?" asked Ethan in almost breathless disbelief.

"Ay. It died with Magelen."

It took a moment for Ethan to digest the news. "How long have I been asleep?"

"Almost the whole day."

"You had us worried that you wouldn't wake." Karryn caressed Ethan's cheek.

He smiled at her. "I'll live. I now have a reason past watching out for his ornery hide," he said concerning Tristan.

"More reason than you realize, with what I have to tell you," said Razi.

"Ah, he finally wakes," said Renfrow, happily. "I came to inquire about his condition before retiring. And to learn if you have gotten any rest." He spoke the last sentence to Karryn.

"I can sleep now that I know Ethan will recover."

"He needs lots of rest to recover." Eldric arrived. He carried a cup in one hand. "The medicine is for pain, and will make him sleepy. It is time for all of you to leave." He moved past Razi to take a seat on the bed to give Ethan the medicine.

"Lord Razi will speak to him now," said Kell, much to Eldric's chagrin.

Ethan stayed the cup from his lips. "Is it something important?"

"Nothing that can't wait until *after* you drink the medicine," insisted Eldric. "It will take a few moments to work. Time enough for a *short* conversation," he added at Kell's frown.

Ethan gagged when he finished. "I hope the foul taste is worth it."

Eldric spoke to Razi. "Please keep it short, my lord. He really does need to rest." Kell escorted Eldric from the infirmary.

Curious, Ethan asked Razi, "What is it you want to tell me?"

"There are facts about your family I dare not tell you until safe to do so. I instructed Elias to tell you if I couldn't." Razi grew melancholy. "It is a sad state to live each day while your children die and you are powerless to stop it."

Tristan comforted Razi. He tightly held his grandson's hand in an effort to fight back his grief to proceed.

"Not all is lost. I have pride in a grandson, and *another*, whom I could not freely tell until now." Razi looked directly at Ethan.

"What do you mean?"

"After the Great Battle and Ram became king, the danger was too great. Janel and I did the only thing we could to save those we loved by severing all ties to her family. It grieved her until her death, and something I sorely regretted. They took me into their home without reservation after we wed in secret. But we had to protect them." Razi smiled in fond remembrance. "Before Janel died, she made me promise that if I ever learned of a survivor to look after them. Janel's youngest brother was Toby."

"My grandfather," said Ethan in wonderment.

Razi took hold of Ethan's hand. "Ay. His youngest son, your father, married one of my granddaughters, which is how I learned of you. Happily, I kept that promise to Janel. I am your uncle by marriage but great-grandfather by blood. Tristan is your cousin by blood and marriage."

302

Ethan's face screwed up.

"Are you in pain?" asked Karryn with concern.

Ethan shook his head. Tears fell from the corner of his eyes "No! All these years I thought I was alone. That I had no family left in the world."

"You've been like a brother to me since we met," said Tristan.

"Blood relation is different than friendship, even a deep friendship."

"You are now free to claim both." Razi widely smiled. "Along with the hand of a lady since you are of royal lineage and not a common woodsman."

"A common woodsman won my heart," said Karryn.

"Along with my approval before this revelation," said Renfrow to Karryn and then to Ethan, "I prayed for your survival. Words cannot express my gratitude for saving Karryn."

Ethan weakly smiled, for it appeared the medicine made him drowsy.

"Rest now. I'll come back in the morning." Karryn kissed his forehead.

The Guardians waited on the knoll overlooking Ravendale. Kell had yet to return. Avatar and Armus became alert a second before the captain arrived in his Guardian form.

"How is Ethan?" asked Valmar.

Kell smiled. "He'll recover. Razi told him about his family."

"Which is?" asked Avatar.

"Oh, good, your ignorance returned also," teased Wren.

"She told me she missed you," Armus said to Avatar.

Wren flushed at the counter humor, making Avatar laugh. "That was worth returning to hear; only it doesn't answer my question."

"Ethan is Razi's great-grandson by way of Toby, Janel's youngest brother," said Kell.

"Do you remember Toby? Or did your memory get lost in frequent travels between dimensions?" asked Wren.

Avatar spoke in wry reply. "Now I understand why you confessed to missing me, you lost your aim and needed target practice."

When the others laughed, Wren smirked at Avatar.

"On a more serious note, what happens now that the coup succeeded?" Jedrek asked Kell.

"I don't know yet. I'll return again tomorrow in disguise—*alone*," he said to Avatar and Wren in an attempt to stave off any retort. Neither spoke or reacted, so he continued. "How the mortals proceed may determine what we do next. Until then, we enjoy this victory."

Chapter 27

THE FOLLOWING MORNING, RAZI SUMMONED THE LORDS AND priests to the Great Hall. Before beginning the session, Razi spoke to a disguised Kell.

Tristan stood off to one side, curious. Finally, he mounted the platform. "I'm sorry to interrupt, but I know you are not attached to Dunham, despite how you appear," he said to Kell. "You're one of the *Old Knights*, aren't you? Not the same as the ones I met in Dorgirith or at the Fortress of Garwood."

Kell smiled. "You are correct, my lord."

Razi spoke privately to Tristan. "This is Kell."

Tristan's eyes grew wide. He barely kept from repeating the name. Rather Razi's warning glare made him speak in quiet awe. "Captain."

Kell snatched Tristan's arm. "Do not bow to me, my lord. It is I, who am here to serve you." He noticed men arriving so he said to Tristan, "Be of good courage, for like your grandfather, you are highly favored. My lords." Kell stepped down from the platform to take up position beside the door and witness the proceedings.

Razi smiled widely at Tristan. "Now, to complete what was started yesterday." He called for attention from those assembled. Once everyone grew quiet, he spoke.

"A great victory has been won for Jor'el. Allon faces a new beginning. Through tragedy and turmoil, by Jor'el's grace and mercy, I survived. Now I stand before you with humble thanks for the loyalty and sacrifice many of you made to bring about this day." Razi glanced to each lord, ending on Dunham, where his gaze lingered a moment before proceeding. "I realize all of you expect me to accept the crown.

However, I'm very old. My remaining days are numbered. Therefore, it is to my grandson, Tristan, that I pass the crown."

Disgruntled murmuring began among the lords, forcing Razi to put up his hands and call for order. "Hear me! I deeply regret that my announcement causes disappointment, perhaps even concern. I have been personally assured in my spirit by Jor'el that I will live long enough to aid Tristan in cleansing the kingdom of any Dark Way remnants, along with reestablishing the worship of the Almighty."

"He's just a boy," said Sedgewick.

"I realize that, my lord," began Tristan. "It is not a responsibility I wanted at this time, and share your disappointment that my grandfather will not accept the crown. Yet, I pledge, I will endeavor to learn what I can from him for as long as Jor'el allows him to remain."

"He is the son of promise," said Jarrod, the chief assistant priest. "Even his father knew it." He held a large book. "Vicar Elias completed his work, and we are diligently making copies to distribute to the provinces. For now, hear the words of Prophecy regarding Lord Razi's grandson." Jarrod opened the book to read.

> *"For a time of peace shall come and he shall rule with truth, honor and the blessing of Jor'el, to restore that which was lost."*

At the conclusion, a deep hush fell over those in the room. Tristan glanced with uncertainty to his grandfather.

Razi spoke encouragement. "It is your destiny. Do not fear what is appointed you. Jor'el is with you. So am I." He then addressed the others. "Gentlemen, you have heard the will of Jor'el. In two weeks, we shall assemble at The Temple for the coronation to begin the steps of rebuilding."

"What about Ravendale?" Dunham asked.

Razi's face turned harsh. "It will be destroyed, first by fire to cleanse its evil, then whatever remains, taken down and cast into the depths of the sea."

"Some spoils from this place would be recompense for all we suffered," said Vaughn.

"It would be unwise to remove anything from here, for all is polluted by the Dark Way," warned Razi.

Vaughn continued in dispute. "Then we leave empty-handed? We came to free you and crown you king, not a boy."

Dunham took exception to Vaughn's dispute. "You heard the prophecy. What more do you seek then to be rid of the Dark Way and have peace restored?"

When Vaughn stirred with insult, Razi stepped down from the platform to ease the tension. "Gentlemen! Let us not quarrel at this critical hour. At the coronation, announcements and recognition shall be given to the satisfaction of all. You have my word." With sincerity, he focused on Vaughn.

It took a long moment before Vaughn responded. "So be it."

"What about Magelen? Where should he be buried?" Renfrow asked.

"He won't," began Razi stoutly. "He will perish in the fire that consumes this place."

Renfrow nodded in satisfaction of the answer.

Razi's gaze swept over those assembled. "My lords, I look forward to the gathering in two weeks. Jor'el be with you all until then." He took Tristan by the shoulder to steer him to a private room off the Great Hall.

"I don't know if I'll be ready in two weeks," said Tristan.

Razi chuckled. "My boy, you are more ready than you think. In fact, you are two years older than Ram when he became king."

"How does that make me ready? I've spent my life in hiding or under the guise of a squire, not being groomed to become king."

Razi made Tristan face him. "What brought you to Ravendale? That made you act against Magelen in a time of crisis?"

"To destroy the Dark Way."

He held Tristan's shoulder to continue the probing. "Look deeper inside for what compelled you when everything stood against you."

Tristan's frustration turned into understanding at the challenge. "Faith and trust in Jor'el."

"Exactly! Faith and trust have sustained me throughout my entire life. Despite all the tragedies and years of imprisonment, Jor'el kept his promise." His smile turned poignant yet hopeful. "And *that* same trust and faith is what will help *you* rule."

Tristan shyly looked at the ground. He wiped away a sniffle.

"Does that thought frighten you?"

Tristan shook his head. "I wish my father—"

Razi embraced Tristan when he wept. "Elias was proud of you."

Tristan wiped his eyes. "Some things were never spoken between us."

"Because they couldn't be said openly, not because they weren't true. I know his pride and joy because I was there the day he wrote the prophecy concerning you."

Puzzled, Tristan asked, "How?"

Razi motioned for Tristan to sit on a bench along the wall. "I felt compelled to visit Elias, so I left the cottage and went to the Temple. Needless to say, he was vexed with me," he chuckled. "He chided me for being so bold as to visit him."

"He did the same to me when I visited him in secret."

Razi grinned. "You and I are much alike, except for the outcome of our daring ventures. You returned to Garwood. I was captured by Ramsey when leaving; rather, betrayed." His face turned harsh in recollection.

Tristan stirred with anger. "Betrayed by whom?"

"I don't know." Razi shrugged. "A slip of the tongue by one of Ram's soldiers alerted me to the act of betrayal. Apparently, they waited nearby for my departure, thus being preplanned and not happenstance. Ramsey acted quickly to dispel such a notion, but it didn't work. "

Tristan's brows drew level with annoyance. "When word reached us, I wondered how you were captured."

"The *how* really doesn't matter—"

"Of course, it matters! The injustice—"

"No," said Razi with loud interruption. "Jor'el is in control of all things. If I weren't captured, the plan would never have been conceived; you would still be at Garwood under the guise of the squire; Ramsey king, Magelen more powerful and the Dark Way unchecked."

Tristan blinked, as the ramifications took a moment to sink in.

Razi gave Tristan that moment before proceeding. "You see, my boy, it all truly works together for good. The totality of a situation is what you must learn to consider as king, not just the narrow scope of what you can see before you."

Tristan frowned with discouragement. "I have a lot to learn."

Razi chuckled. "It all starts by seeking Jor'el for his wisdom." He patted Tristan's shoulder. "For now, let's *learn* how Ethan is doing this morning. Other lessons will come in time."

***

Two weeks later, a festive atmosphere greeted everyone arriving at The Temple for the coronation of a new king. Razi and Tristan waited in the room off the main part of sanctuary. Both wore fine royal attire. Beaming with joy, Razi appeared younger than one hundred and sixty-eight years. Tristan paced, nervous.

Ethan entered. Instead of the brown and gold livery of Sir Dunham, he wore a handsome blue and silver suit. As always, he was armed, only now with a beautiful bow of rosewood with silver fittings and magnificently crafted leather and silver quiver.

"Everyone is assembled," he said.

"You seem a bit pale. Are you feeling well enough to stand with Tristan?" asked Razi.

"I'm better than he is. He looks like he's going to faint," quipped Ethan.

"I'm about to crowned king! I've never felt this nervous."

Ethan wore a large grin. "Just wait till your wedding day."

"That's not funny!" Tristan waved a finger in Ethan's face. "I haven't heard about Maddy's condition since leaving Ravendale."

"Because such a report is best given in person." Dunham entered along with …

"Maddy!" said Tristan with astonishment. She appeared whole and hearty with no bruising or scarring, nothing to tell of her serious injury.

"Tristan," she said with tearful smile.

"You can speak?"

"Speak, walk, everything!"

"A divine healing," said Dunham.

Unable to keep from weeping, Tristan embraced Maddy and held her close. He then took her face in his hands. "I told your father that it didn't matter how you recovered, I would marry you whether whole or not."

"Jor'el had other plans for both of you," said Dunham.

"Perhaps a wedding along with a coronation?" asked Ethan with a smile and wink at Tristan.

"It is best after the coronation," said Razi. He amended his speech after receiving a withering glare from Tristan. "Not long, but after. Let the lords grow accustomed to you as king before taking a queen."

"A couple of months," said Dunham to bolster Razi's efforts. It did little to curb Tristan's annoyance.

"Queen?" Maddy flashed an uncertain smile. "I never thought that."

"I never thought to be king," Tristan encouraged her then spoke to Razi and Dunham. "In two months we marry, no longer."

Both simply smiled in agreement.

A priest entered. "Lord Razi, Vicar Jarrod is ready."

"Maddy and I will take our places beside Garrick. He is also here, and in his right mind," Dunham merrily said.

Shortly after they left, trumpets sounded.

"That's our cue," said Razi. "Ethan, lead the way."

Ethan hesitated a moment to speak to Tristan. "If we purpose to do anything …"

"It's because we were meant to do it," Tristan finished the quote.

"Then purpose to do your best as king since you were born to be crowned."

Tristan's gaze turned suspicious. "You knew that also, didn't you?"

Ethan roguishly smiled. "There was more to my pledge than I told you."

The trumpet sounded again.

"Ethan. The lead." Razi nudge him with a chuckle.

Unknown among the crowd, twelve Guardians mingled in disguise. Like at Ravendale, they moved in smaller groups. Not only did this serve for security in watching for any unexpected appearance of Shadow Warriors, it also gave them a chance to enjoy the celebration.

Kell and Wren ended up near the front to the right of the high altar. Avatar and Armus stood across from them. Any moment, the event they clandestinely helped to bring about would happen.

The trumpets continued as Ethan led Razi and Tristan down the aisle to the high altar where Vicar Jarrod waited. Jarrod received unanimous vote from the priests to take Elias' place as Vicar of Jor'el. When they stopped, the trumpets ceased.

Using the new book of Verse, Jarrod read passages to conduct the coronation ceremony. Tristan made the proper responses. He then knelt and bowed his head to receive the crown. The crowd applauded when Jarrod presented Allon's new king.

Tristan sat in the chair placed on the platform for his use. He raised his hands for silence. Those gathered complied. "As promised by my grandfather, Lord Razi, I will make my first official proclamation of recognition to those whom such is due." He held out his hand for Ethan to come forward with a scroll. "What is written is based upon the order which once ruled Allon. Order established by Jor'el's Guardians when they governed." He flashed a glance to Kell before he opened the scroll.

"From each province a lord shall be appointed to govern and comprise the Council of Twelve, with the lords directly answerable to the King. The Council shall be called upon in times of crisis for counsel and guidance, as well as for establishing laws and enforcing those laws. Whereas the word of the King is final, the will of the Council shall be given due consideration. The members are as follows: Lord Godfrey of the Highlands, Lord Edison of the Northern Forest, Sir Dunham of the Southern Forest, Lord Sheldon of the East Coast, Baron Quinn of the West Coast, Lord Taggart of the Delta, Baron Kaleb of the South Plains, Baron Renfrow of the North Plains, Sir Percy from the Lowlands, Lord Cavin of Midessex, Sir Lowell of the Meadowlands and Vicar Jarrod of the Region of Sanctuary."

Tristan looked form the scroll to the crowd. "My lords, I will depend upon your wise counsel and support, as we seek to restore the kingdom."

"Ay, my liege! Sire," the lords acknowledged.

Tristan returned to reading. "The Fortress of Jor'el shall be rebuilt and therein reconstitute the unit formerly known as the Jor'ellian Knights." He smiled in looking up from reading. "My lord Dunham, do you accept the task to carry on the duty your ancestor faithfully fulfilled?"

"Sire! It would be an honor."

"Then no longer hide the medallion of the First Jor'ellian you've worn for so long."

Dunham reached under the neck of his doublet to display the sacred medallion.

"Baron Vaughn."

"Ay, Sire?"

"Being a renowned architect, are you up to the challenge of overseeing the rebuilding of the Fortress of Jor'el?"

"Ay, Sire!" said Vaughn with a large, pleased smile.

"Sir Sedgewick and Lord Wilcott, be so good as to lend your expertise to Lord Sheldon and Baron Quinn in assembling and commanding the royal navy."

In unison, they acknowledged the assignment.

Tristan held out the document. Ethan began to take it only Tristan wouldn't yield. Instead, he flashed a wry smile. "How now, cousin, would serve your King?"

Ethan grew suspicious. "In whatever manner you say, Sire."

"Then kneel." Ethan did so. Tristan rose to draw his sword. "For years of faithful service, and with gratitude I cannot adequately express, I hereby knight you, *Sir* Ethan, and given the title King's Champion to continue your duty of protecting me."

The action rendered Ethan speechless, which made Tristan chuckle.

"Rise, Sir Ethan." Tristan tugged on Ethan's shoulder. He turned Ethan to face the audience. "Baron Renfrow, what say you now of the woodsman squire? A worthy suitor for your daughter's hand in marriage?"

"Indeed, Sire."

"Then let us be off to the feast, to celebrate Jor'el's victory and toast the happy couple!"

Rather than partaking in the feast, the Guardians left The Temple to make their way to a predetermined rendezvous in the surrounding hills. Among the massive crowd, Armus and Avatar lost sight of the others. Even a good distance from the multitude, they didn't see their fellow Guardians. That didn't matter. With great satisfaction they witnessed the coronation.

"A happy ending to my return," Avatar spoke in a light teasing voice. "It would be nice if it means regaining our full strength. Dimension travel is draining, while maintaining this façade is exhausting,"

"Once we're under cover, we'll shed our disguise."

When they reached the tree line ..."Armus!"

By the time Armus heard the distress, Avatar collapsed to his hands and knees. He also reverted to his original Guardian state. *"Atharraich!"* Armus immediately returned to his Guardian self and rushed to Avatar's aid. "Are you wounded?"

With great fatigue and disappointment, Avatar replied, "No. Nor did I lose my cover by choice. It is finished. Tell Kell—farewell." Avatar disappeared.

Armus heard someone call to him, but ignored it, stunned by the abruptness of Avatar's departure. The others arrived, all in their natural state. Kell knelt while the rest formed a circle around Armus. He still didn't react until Kell took hold of his shoulder and asked;

"Are you all right?"

Befuddled, Armus answered, "Avatar disappeared!"

"We saw no light, white or grey," said Jedrek.

Armus spoke with confusion. "There wasn't any *light*. He simply disappeared. Yet not before saying to tell you, *it is finished* and *farewell,*" he said to Kell. "What did he mean?" he asked in a voice strained with vexation.

"Let's get further under cover and I'll explain." Kell lead them deep into the safety of the trees.

Agitated, Armus repeated his question. "What did Avatar mean by *finished* and *farewell?*"

"With his mission complete, Jor'el recalled him, that's what he meant. In reference to his *mission*, not his lifeforce." Kell spoke with reassurance in an attempt to soothe Armus.

"Just like that?" Armus snapped his finger, his temper slow to cool.

"He left the way he came, sudden and without warning."

"Why? The plan succeeded. Magelen is defeated."

"Dagar won't remain quiet for long."

"Ay, he'll find a way to regroup and make it difficult for Tristan," said Valmar.

"And we will act accordingly when needed," said Kell.

"With Avatar returned to heavenlies, Mahon back in the cave and we remain as legends," groused Armus. His arms folded over his chest.

"Under the circumstances, it may be better Avatar didn't stay," said Barnum.

Kell grinned. "He would hardly agree with that. However, it is more than likely we will not see Avatar or anyone else until our restoration."

"Until then Vidar and rest continue to suffer," chided Wren, very upset.

"The moment my full strength return, I will appear, and Dagar will curse the day he chose to rebel!" Kell declared. "For now, all we can do

314

is hope and pray Jor'el gives them strength to survive until Prophecy is fulfilled."

"What good was this coup if there is more to wait for?" Wren continued in her argument.

For her sake, Kell tempered his response. "Today is a turning point for Allon." He took her by the shoulder and escorted her to the edge of the trees to observe the festivities. He quoted Prophecy when the others joined them.

> *"From his line shall come forth a son to restore his father's throne; and a daughter from Allon to bring back the glory of Jor'el. Those after his own heart shall he seek and find.*
>
> *From the fowls of the air, to the beasts of prey and the faithful shall he gather to himself the hope of Allon.*
>
> *Among them shall be one whose birth shall be linked to his by a season. Whose soul shall mirror his own and the twain shall become one in desire and purpose. And by her shall the path be made straight for the strength of Jor'el's host to return.*
>
> *And he shall give the Guardians charge over Allon."*

"When the son of Tristan and a daughter of Allon are joined, we shall be restored. Today's coronation showed the time is closer than before."

"Still doesn't answer the question of how long," argued Wren.

"When the wind blows hot and fierce, you can sense a storm's approach. You don't know the exact time it will start, only certain that it will come," said Priscilla.

"Thus, we are certain Jor'el will act, for this shows us reality." Jedrek used his hand in sweeping motion of the festivities taking place around the Temple.

Valmar nudged Jedrek to say in teasing concerning Wren, "She might have enjoyed it more if Avatar had stayed."

"Hah!" Wren smirked.

Kell laughed. "Until our full restoration, let us enjoy this time of reprieve."

Explore the Kingdom of Allon

www.allonbooks.com

Featuring:

- Read excerpts of Allon books
- News and Events
- Photos and Videos
- Links to:
  - Facebook - The Kingdom of Allon Page
  - Newsletter
  - Contact Shawn Lamb

Made in the USA
Charleston, SC
26 June 2016